SUBTLE AND ELEGANT—AND ONLY THE BEGINNING

Marquardt called us.

"We have a mur_____leon job. Joseph Rosenc_____

"We'll be rig_____

I drove. It w_____alley, in foothills that w_____basaltic extrusions.

The house was an impressive mansion, as I'd seen from the nav, but that didn't do it justice. It was part Tudor, part Classic American, and all Modern Ostentatious.

I pulled into the apron, then had to park on lava gravel. Silver hopped out, I followed.

Marquardt was in the foyer, awaiting us.

"Gos Gold, Ms. Wickell. You'll pardon me if I'm not glad to see you," he said.

"Likewise," I offered, while looking around.

Marquardt led the way left into a large front room with bay windows, and pointed.

"A classic clubbing with a blunt instrument. It doesn't appear the victim saw anything. It would be someone familiar or invisible. He was well-liked by his staff. I have no reason to doubt that they just found him like this, after hearing a thump."

"Likely," I agreed.

The body slumped in a chair at a desk, head over the table and slightly misshapen. Next to the head was a blood-greased candleholder. On the desk were old-fashioned books, two reading tablets, a partially eaten sandwich of what smelled like roast beef on pumpernickel, a bowl of plums, and a jar of Curry's Cracked Kernel Mustard.

"Actually rather subtle and elegant," I said.

Baen Books
by Michael Z. Williamson

❊ ❊ ❊ ❊

Freehold
The Weapon
Contact with Chaos
Better to Beg Forgiveness . . .
Do Unto Others . . .
Rogue
When Diplomacy Fails . . . (forthcoming)

The Hero (with John Ringo)

To purchase these and all Baen Book titles in e-book format,
please go to www.baenebooks.com.

ROGUE

MICHAEL Z. WILLIAMSON

ROGUE

This is a work of fiction. All the characters and events portrayed in this book are fictional, and any resemblance to real people or incidents is purely coincidental.

Copyright © 2011 by Michael Z. Williamson

All rights reserved, including the right to reproduce this book or portions thereof in any form.

A Baen Book

Baen Publishing Enterprises
P.O. Box 1403
Riverdale, NY 10471
www.baen.com

ISBN: 978-1-4516-3787-8

Cover art by Kurt Miller

First Baen paperback printing, July 2012

Distributed by Simon & Schuster
1230 Avenue of the Americas
New York, NY 10020

Library of Congress Cataloging-in-Publication Data: 2010022797

Printed in the United States of America

10 9 8 7 6 5 4 3 2 1

❀ ❀ ❀

For anyone
who has left a piece of their soul
in a foreign land.

❀ ❀ ❀

◎ INTRODUCTION ◎

IT ISN'T EVERYDAY a one-and-a-half-year-old walks in and orders lunch.

I mean one-and-a-half Crainne planetary years, of course. That's two-and-a-half for those of you using Earth standard. Still, it was a surprise.

This curly blonde little munchkin streaked in at a run, heaved herself into an empty booth and sat up straight. She clasped her hands on the table, looked at me from five meters away and clearly said, "Peetzaz."

She was too adorably cute to refuse. Figuring an adult would be along in a few seconds, I asked, "What kind, lady?"

"Cheez."

So I dished her a slice of cheez peetza. She accepted it with a huge smile when I brought it over, and said, "Tinks, man." Mannerly little thing.

I didn't see an adult. She sat happily, munching it upside down, and making very little mess. She was clean, neatly dressed, obviously no hungrier than any other kid,

1

and had a bottle and towel with her. She finished, put the plate in the trash, came back and scrubbed the table top and seat with a napkin, threw it in the trash, and headed out. She stopped at the door, turned, and loudly said, "Bye-bye!" to one and all.

Startling. It was then I realized she hadn't paid. Ah, well. She was cute.

She was back the next day. This time she clutched a one cred chit in her hands. She passed it over with a coy smile when I brought her pizza out. She was packing away adult-sized lunch slices, but she wasn't particulary small, as I said. She had all her teeth, clean. She had clear skin, a bright smile, and was obviously well-cared for except for lunchtime. Very odd.

She paid almost every day, and sometimes appeared midafternoon as well, waving her bottle and saying, "Drink." I'd ask her if lemonade was okay, and she'd nod her head once firmly and say, "Yes." Then she discovered "roobeer" and would have nothing else.

Finally, one afternoon, I saw her grab a hand as she ran outside. There was a bag over the arm, typical for dealing with kids. I hurried from behind the counter, but she and her parent were gone by the time I got outside. I wanted to find out what the story was. She was obviously loved, but left alone here and there.

That may mean something else to you than it does me. In the Freehold, it's not uncommon for kids to run around unsupervised. It used to be perfectly safe, since our crime rate was almost nonexistent. This assumes the kid is old enough to avoid all the nonautomated traffic, which I was sure she was not. After the war, we did have some theft and robbery, and some organized crime, though. Professional childcare is expensive. Friends and neighbors, however, are free. Why did she not have an adult, or older child, or someone?

She began showing up with her bag, too. It was almost as big as she, and even with its low mass, it was cumbersome. She didn't seem to mind. She brought money every day now, rather than just usually, and one day brought a ten with a note attached that said, "For past meals. Thanks." Clearly her guardian knew what she was doing. Well enough. She took to hanging out longer, and I began feeding her free again. She would lurk with a pile of napkins, and whenever someone spilled or dropped something, she'd announce, "Uh oh!" and dive on it with napkins, scrubbing the spill and throwing out trash. She also cleared the occasional table and wiped them down. I usually had to redo it, but the effort was worth rewarding. She was too darn cute, and patrons began tipping her. She was obviously the deciding factor between my place and others for some customers.

One day shortly after that I got a surprise. She came running from the dining room to the office, stood in front of me and said, "Shainj!" To illustrate she unpeeled her diaper, and handed me her bag. Well, it wouldn't hurt me to do it once. "Tinks, man," she said when I was done, and raced out to wash her hands and wipe more tables.

She was doing okay on tips, too. Her clothes, plain and clean and only about four outfits, began to get nicer and more varied, but not extravagant. I wondered if she did her own shopping, too. Not likely, although if she found the right salesclerk . . .

That afternoon I finally saw her parent. Father, specifically. She ran out, shouting "Bye-bye!" and grabbed his hand. He drew her up into a big hug, and walked off happily talking to her. I recognized him. He was one of the local escorts.

Another note, since your society may be different. Prostitution is not only legal here, it's a recognized business and highly respected. This, however, was shortly after the war with Earth. The economy was a shambles, and there were far too many volunteers for it to pay well. The restaurant business was good, with traffic recovering and lots of out-systemers, but the sex business was downright saturated. Also, during the war, all the diseases we'd eliminated came back by the shipload. I hoped he was being safe. Especially since most non-Freeholders still regard escorts as trash.

I was getting the picture. He was alone with her. Her mother had probably died during the War. He couldn't find another job (if he'd ever done anything else—he wasn't that old), had a local room in the business district near the port, and no neighbors to look after her. He sent her in here, out of the weather and safe and occupied, while he took care of business for whatever few creds he could get. Time was before the War that one couldn't get an escort for less than Cr250, and that wouldn't include sex. After the War, twenty-five creds would get anything you wanted some places, and maybe a disease or two as bonuses.

Now, I don't know how things work in your society, but here, that created a problem. Morally, I should be helping him, since he was working for the best of reasons—his kid.

Morally, someone that proud and determined would be insulted if I offered charity. I scrawled out a note, "I need wait staff," and sent it with her. The reply was, "Thanks, but I'm self-employed." I got that picture, too. He'd ask for help if and only if she was in danger of starving. She clearly wasn't. I've never met a better behaved, prettier, more cheerful little kid. And she technically was a street-urchin, too.

So I began to boost her tips a bit, here and there. She learned how to sweep floors, once I cut a broom handle off short enough for her. She was too small to steer a sweeper. She would stack boxes and trays, and showed an amazing aptitude for simple tasks. I had music in to liven things up, and she demanded, "Lowd!" so I raised the volume. She nodded and clapped and danced while she worked, seemingly channeling energy straight from some hidden reactor, and customers threw more money at her. Her idea of dancing involved a huge grin, a waving mop of hair, and jumps straight up and down while waving her arms. She seemed tireless. I had to explain again and again that she wasn't a relative of mine. She even climbed onto a table at one point and danced until it almost fell over. I insisted she stop, and she looked at me with huge, sad, baby blue eyes and said, "Alright."

I had to meet this kid's father. I mean, she was too young to say her own name, too young to be toilet trained, and was more polite and better raised than most local eight-year-olds. I had to meet the man who was raising her. I gave her a note that read, "Come by when you can. We need to settle the bill."

Her father showed up with her that night about nine,

which is one div before local midnight, ten divs of 2.7 hours each to our day. He was who I thought he was. About fifteen local years, or twenty-two Earth. Good looking, healthy, well-muscled even for our gravity, and dressed professionally. She ran straight in, yelled, "Hi!" and grabbed her cleaning tools.

"I'm Dan," he said.

"Dan, I'm Andre," I nodded. "I'm afraid I've never caught your daughter's name."

"Chelsea," he said, using the old spelling.

"She's an incredible kid. You must be very proud," I said. There was no need to ask. It showed in his face and body language.

"Yes I am," he admitted. "I just wish her mother was here to see her."

"During the War?" I asked.

"Yes," he agreed.

"May I ask?"

"No," he said. That was the end of that, then. Considering the nukes, kinetic strikes, vicious nano and bio vectors, random gunfire, gang rapes and assorted mayhem the Earthies inflicted on us in order to "civilize" us, I could make several guesses, none of them pretty. Thank the God and Goddess we kicked them the hell out. Eventually.

"So what do I owe you?" he asked. "In addition to my heartfelt thanks," he added. "I'm trying to find someone to watch her while I work, but there aren't many people who live in this area, and I have no transport."

"Actually, Dan, I owe you. Or her, rather," I said.

"Thanks, but—"

I rode over his protests, "Dan, you see that?" I pointed to where she was sweeping the corner booth. "She's putting in two or three divs a week doing grunt labor I don't want to do. She's good for business, and pizza and pasta really don't cost much at my end. I figure I owe her for a month at a half div a day. That's fifty days times six creds a div. So here's her one-fifty. I'll pay her weekly from now on. My daughter is available to sit when I'm not open, and she charges three a div. Just make sure Chelsea's bag is full, and give me some notice, and we'll take care of things. That's how it is," I finished, making sure he couldn't object.

Not only was it a fair deal to me, it was good karma to take care of those who needed it. We had a lot of rebuilding still to do after the pounding we took, and we wouldn't do it by being selfish bastards. Besides, this man had to have the biggest balls of anyone I've ever met to be surviving here and raising a kid that well. Maybe some of the local help, including my second cook, would learn something from it.

Chelsea, now that I had her name, came running back. "Finisd," she said.

"Thanks, Chelsea," I said. "Want some cookies and milk?"

"Yes," she said, nodding once in her no-hesitation fashion. Dan sat quietly, unable to reply, while I dished up a plate of warm cookies and glasses of cold milk.

When I came back, she was on his lap, babbling away in near-English, and he was talking back to her. Not babytalk, just plain conversation, technical terms replaced with basic words. She clearly understood what he was saying. Well, he was no moron, and her mother had obviously been bright, too. I predicted a good future for her.

I caught sight of him the next day as I was cleaning tables outside. He wandered along the street, taking food samples from each vendor he passed. He stopped at Charlie's and paid for a hotdog, then loaded it with peppers, relish, sauerkraut, mustard and olives. Got it. Ten samples and a cheap sandwich was nutritious if not filling, and as long as he rotated, no one would complain. Certainly not when he had Chelsea grinning in his arms.

Soon after that, he stopped doing alley business and started doing high-end business calls. That paid better, and was far safer. The rate was still low, and the overhead higher—nice clothes cost, especially after the war. Chelsea took easily to evenings, and even occasionally slept in the farthest back booth until he was done.

It turned out he was renting a closet from someone, not quite a flophouse. I can see why he wouldn't leave a child there. She was much safer on Commercial Boulevard. He pinched money and scraped.

He had a plan. A few weeks later, he had enough to rent a small space, about eight meters square, and stuck a cot and a broken coordinate mill into it, doing most of the installation by shoving and cursing, with me blocking it as needed to help it walk right. The place was diagonally across the street in a corner of a near abandoned warehouse that someone apparently still owned. We were recovering from the war, but it was slow. There are some things that a small, solvent government does better. Borrowing money to build infrastructure isn't one of them. We knew that when we started, but we stuck to our principles. The Freehold never spent more than it had from Residence fees, and there were a lot fewer people declaring Residency after the War. It was bad for a time.

But, he had this space he could sleep in, and a broken mill, which within a month was a working mill. He made a replacement hinge for one of my ovens and refused to let me pay. He found ways to fabricate things people thought impossible, or that the major shops couldn't do cheaply enough. He leased a little more space and installed a bathroom—he'd been using a half-functional one at the rear of the warehouse, across a rubble-strewn floor—and ran a solar power system to keep his costs down.

It was odd, though. He would not get certification for ship parts for the port, and he would not run an ad on the nodes. He was word of mouth and listing only. He did okay with all the out Port businesses, but he wouldn't make the jump to the big money inside.

One day Chelsea came through the door with a grin a meter wide. She was carrying, right shoulder arms, a Little Weasel. That's a Little Weasel four-millimeter rimfire single-shot rifle. They're scaled down for kid's use as a training weapon. She still wore shooting glasses, and looked disgustingly cute. Of course, she *always* looked disgustingly cute.

She held out her left hand, waving a target at me. "Andre! Look!" she shouted. I took the paper, glanced at it, then again. It had perhaps ten holes in it. It was hard to tell precisely, because they all were in a tight cluster, dead center. I whistled. "*Nice* shooting, Chel!"

"Thank you!" she said, taking it back and running to show others.

Dan had a Merrill Targetmaster rifle over his shoulder. I figure he'd been teaching her. Impressive. Not many kids that age have that kind of hand-eye coordination, and not many adults can be patient enough to help them over the bumps. He was a good man, and I was proud of his friendship, even if we never spoke much.

Lots of kids helped with the family business, and she was sort of family after a few weeks, effectively family by the time she was seven. Even though Dan had his shop running well, and was usually there, she would typically stop by after school, do some quick chores like trash and cooler inventory, disappear for homework and dinner, then come back for a bit more.

She was there after school one day, mucking out a pile left by the older kids. They spent well and ate well and left trash accordingly. It was in the cans, but there was a lot of it.

Right then, a woman in a scarf and robe came in. I couldn't understand her, but she was frantic and needed help. She pantomimed a child and repeated something about "yardim." The poor woman was jabbering away in some language I didn't even recognize. She was distraught, obviously. Tears and ragged breathing and clear pleading for any kind of help made her point that something was wrong. I had no ideas except to call City Safety. She nodded and gestured as I raised the phone, and I got the definite impression that she was saying, "Please hurry!" in whatever language she was speaking.

Chelsea came running in from the back room, said something that sounded like, *"Beer süre beklayin,"* and ran

for the door. The operator answered and I said,
"Unknown emergency, translator needed." I gave the
address as a doublecheck, as they obviously had it on
screen already.

Seconds later, Dan arrived at a sprint. He said something back in the same language, and the woman turned
to him, sighing in relief.

They spoke for a few seconds, swapping gestures, and
it was obvious he was completely comfortable with the
language. He never hesitated over a word.

"Her son is missing," he said. "She last saw him near
the old warehouse next to the East Gate, and now she
can't find him." Damn. That was a diagonal block over,
but there wasn't much open between here and there.

Chelsea said, "He probly found the slide."

"Slide?" he asked.

"There's a slide into the cellar. We play there," she
explained.

"And I told you not to," he said, then turned to the two
arriving Safety officers. "Lost child, four years old, male,
brown curly hair, brown eyes, green shirt and yellow
denim, speaks Mtali-Turkish, last seen near the East Gate
at the old warehouse, may be playing in the lower level.
Spread out from there, I'll check inside." He turned and
scooped Chelsea up with one long arm. "Where?" he
asked her as he strode out. Over his shoulder he called
something and gestured with one hand for the woman to
wait.

I got her a lemonade and a seat, and pondered. He was
military. Had to be. There'd been no hesitation in him
taking command, no dispute from the Safety officers, his

description was detailed, complete, and brief, and he spoke Mtali dialectic Turkish without trouble. That was an old conflict. He must have been a young enlistee and gone straight there. He was older than he looked.

In less than ten segs, everyone was back, with a crying little lost boy in tow. He was unharmed, and threw himself on his weeping mother. Dan translated as a report was made, and kept reassuring her and refusing her offer of a reward. I was surprised to see Chelsea throw in a few words. That's right, I recalled, she'd recognized the language and run for a translator.

Ordinarily, the better you know someone, the easier it is to figure him or her out. With Chelsea and even more with Dan, the more I knew, the more confusing they were. Kids are talkative and boastful. Not her. Not a word about her personal life ever. I thought I was close to the family, close enough to know there wasn't anyone else. And I knew almost nothing.

Chelsea developed much like any normal adolescent. She pulled a few dumb stunts from rebellious hormonal exuberance. She came by with the usual boyfriends and occasional girlfriends until she decided she preferred boys. She worked hard, occasionally begging a schedule change for a concert or to go dancing—she still loved dancing.

Now, it wasn't common before the War, or now, but we had occasional violence during the aftermath. That had all ended after only a couple of years, however, so I was stunned one day when four kids came traipsing in the door, pulled out guns and demanded money and jewelry. It's just not done here, and I was in shock. I was also unarmed. I mean, I usually go to the bank armed, but daytime? In my own restaurant?

What I'm about to relay burned itself into my memory. It was unforgettable and staggering. And if anyone doubts it, there are witnesses to corroborate, and lots of them. Here's what happened:

Chelsea was near one of the punks, and moved like a leopard. She bent his gun wrist back on itself, kicked his ankle while leaning into him, and stepped forward. Her left foot ground his left arm into the floor, and her right was behind his head. His right elbow was braced against her thigh and she still held his wrist. He must have had a fantastic view right up her skirt, and an equally fantastic view down the barrel of his gun, now in her left hand. It was about two centimeters from his right eyeball.

She was fast, but Dan . . . Dan was a striking snake. It simply isn't possible to move that fast, only he did. By the time I turned to see what he was doing, the robber nearest him had Dan's instep behind his head and the other toe in his guts. Dan was horizontal, turned in midair, and drove his heel straight back into the guy's head. I could hear the neck snap.

He landed on his hands, rolled behind a table, jumped forward into an arch, and snagged the fallen gun with his right hand. His left fingertips barely brushed the doorsill, and he was rolling, onto knuckles, wrist, elbow, shoulder, and back. His right foot was almost at his buttocks, and he landed flat on it, sprang upright onto his left and fired twice at the two remaining kids, now running down the street. He fired twice more as he flipped over a car and landed in a crouch next to a van. The gun waved in a motion that seemed to cover the entire sphere of space around him, then he teleported back inside in a hop. He landed on his right shoulder, and the gun panned from near left to far right corners as he rose, then down in a smooth arc to the left and toward Chelsea's captive. It might have been five seconds. His jacket had an abrasion through it and some burned skin showed, but he wasn't even breathing hard.

Then he burst into sweats and shakes and flushed red. His breath panted and his eyes dilated. I thought it was some kind of seizure. He laid the gun carefully on the counter, dropped down, and began doing pushups. Chelsea shook her head at me as I started to move, then spoke to him. "Are you alright, Dad?"

"Yes," he grunted in between pushups.

"CNS reaction?"

"Yes," he agreed.

She remained standing, and I figured if they knew what was happening, I should just stay out of it.

City Safety was there seconds later. The kids' guns were outsystem trash, unsuppressed, and the loud roars had brought a lot of response.

Chelsea told her story, I told mine. They bundled up the surviving punk to hold him for trial and one of the officers looked down at Dan. He squinted slightly, nodded, and looked at Chelsea.

"Combat NeuroStimulant?" he asked her.

"Yes, it is," she confirmed.

"What unit?"

"I don't know," she replied.

The Safety Officer knelt down next to Dan and began speaking. They mumbled back and forth for several segs, while Dan probably passed the two-hundred mark on pushups. I was beginning to understand.

I'd seen documentaries. Some of the Special Warfare soldiers have an implant for use in combat. It releases endorphins, sugars, oxygenating molecules, and synthetic adrenaline. The end result is a trained soldier with half the response time and twice the speed and strength of anyone else. That explained his speed. But if one stopped operating before the compound burned out, it created tremendous stress on the body. That explained the pushups. He was burning off enough energy for six normal people. And if I'd known for certain he was a vet eight years before, Chelsea would have had free room and board for the duration of her juvenile life without question.

The Safety Officer was getting louder. "Sir, I don't really care about that. I have orders to report this person's location if he is ever spotted. I need to know if that's you."

Dan dragged his legs under him, drank in seconds a full glass of water Chelsea handed him, and sighed. "Yes, I am," he admitted. He looked sad, angry, dejected and disgusted all at once.

The SO stood up. "And that's all I needed, sir. If you are okay, and the witnesses agree, then we'll have the bodies removed and that's it. Please call if you need anything, Captain." He saluted as he left.

Special Warfare. Most of them died during the War. In the process, a few hundred of them took tens of thousands of enemy troops and six billion Earthies with them. Dan was one of the best trained killers in the galaxy. Yet he was the gentlest man I know.

Except that he'd just killed three men in five seconds with no hesitation.

He was upright now, and looked calmer if still sweaty. We stared at each other at length, and he finally spoke. "Boost takes a lot out of me."

"Is that the minimum dosage?" I asked. His breathing was almost normal now.

"It's a one-shot mechanism, and it's not intended for surprise response," he said. I looked puzzled and he explained. "Boost is used primarily as an offensive enhancement. Upon preparing to initiate hostilities, it adds an additional force factor, and is especially of psychological use, since it creates an overwhelming relative power factor against an opponent. It doesn't work quickly. There's about a five-second lag."

Got it. He'd triggered it as the fight started, and it was over by the time he reached full speed. Then I did a double take—he'd been *unenhanced* during the fight. Just how fast was this guy when enhanced? How fast had he been during the War when younger, in regular training, and "Boosted"? No wonder there were almost mythical stories about our Special Warfare people.

"Is it time to talk yet?" I asked.

He nodded. "I organized and trained the Earth mission troops," he said. "I used every resource I could get, and stole what I couldn't. Those were the best troops ever trained, no exceptions. We did what we had to do, because the choice was to let our society be destroyed. Some people seem to think that makes it easier."

"At least you were face-to-face," I said. "Didn't that help? I understand the bombardment controllers—"

I should have kept my mouth shut and listened. He came out of his chair. "Bombardment zeros!" he snapped. "They pushed buttons and saw flashes. *I* had to look at people as I went in, knowing they were about to die. I had to look at them as I left. I had to watch the local news for confirmatory intelligence as they tore each other to pieces over scraps of food, torched their own homes, ran screaming in terror knowing no one locally could save them, and we weren't going to. I watched children—" his hand waved in the general direction of Chelsea, who was sipping tea a couple of meters away. This seemed familiar to her "—scream and die. Then I had to document it." He was silent. So was I.

He mumbled, almost into space, "Somewhere in the docs is a picture of a little girl, who looks just about like Chelsea did right after I came home. It was all over the news loads. I remember the kid; I saw her as I blew a water-pumping station in Minneapolis. There she was, dead from smoke inhalation, because there was no water available. It was a job, I had to do it, so I did.

"Then I had to come home and look at *my* daughter, and wonder if her parents, if they survived, hated me as much as I hated the bastards who killed Deni."

I wanted to ask if he felt any different because his actions were technically justifiable, but I'll admit I was afraid. He saw it, too.

"Can't talk to me now that I'm a killer, can you, Andre?" He had a disgusted, knowing grin on his face.

"Once I get used to it," I said, as firmly as I could. "The

resistance people I sheltered had their own share of grief, but I knew about theirs ten years ago."

He nodded. "Fair enough. I've done enough talking for now. I have things to do." He stood and turned to leave.

"Hey, Captain," I said. He stopped.

"Dan," he corrected me, without turning.

"Dan, then," I said. He faced me half over his shoulder. "You and Chelsea saved my life, and my customers. Thanks."

He nodded and left.

❈ CHAPTER 1 ❈

THE NEXT MORNING, there were two men waiting when I opened. They were clean cut, well-dressed, and didn't register as a threat.

"Gentlemen," I nodded.

One replied, "Hello. You are Andre?"

"I am."

He brought out ID and I choked.

Naumann, Alan D., Marshal, Freehold Military Forces. Image. Code.

I looked up, and he said, "I'm discreetly trying to locate a certain veteran, going by the name of Dan, who was here yesterday."

I took a deep breath.

"Well, sir," I said, "with respect to you, that's not something I'm at liberty to discuss."

I waited for a nuke.

Instead, he said, "Fair enough. May we purchase food, and wait?"

"By all means," I said, completely blindsided.

Okay, so the number one man in our military, who was responsible for us surviving and winning the war, wanted to talk to a friend of mine, who apparently was the reason half of Earth blew up, who had then disappeared for a decade. For some reason, I didn't want to be in the middle of this meeting.

Naumann and the man I presumed was his bodyguard sat down in a booth where they could see the door but not be seen easily, selected easy-to-prepare stuff—a grilled salami sandwich and an anchovy focaccia—and sat. They ate slowly and seemed completely at ease.

They talked little. They were there when the lunch crowd started filling the place, and requested juice shakes after a while.

I clicked my phone on, and I know they saw me do it, but they didn't seem disposed to any kind of action. Dan answered on the second buzz.

"Dan's Machine and Tool."

"This is Andre. There's someone waiting here to meet you."

". . . yes?"

"The Marshal."

I heard him sigh, before he said, "Thanks." He disconnected before I could say anything.

I was pretty sure he didn't want to make this meeting.

I really didn't want to make that meeting.

It had been a decade since I came home, as much home as any place could be, and I wanted nothing to do with the military at all. Especially not with that rat-faced dogfucker who'd used me as a lead pipe.

But, my good deed of yesterday, if it could be called that, had left three dumb bastards dead, and my cover fragmented into orbit.

It was my fault. If Chelsea hadn't been there, I'd probably have sat back and ignored it. Andre has insurance, and it's not as if they'd have made it far anyway. But when that gun swept my daughter, I went into combat mode.

Still, there wasn't much else to do, except go face Naumann and tell him what I thought. It's not as if he could actually do anything to me.

I'd be damned if I was going to dress up, though. I did the courtesy of washing the assorted coolant, solvent and grease off my hands, and headed across the street in work pants and a shirt. I did check my gun first. Not that I thought it would do me any good.

Traffic control in this area is supposed to be managed by the city's system. They've set it to stop-and-go traffic, to improve stop-by business, so the theory goes. No one really wants to stop in an industrial area near the port, unless they already have business. But it meant I was across the street fast, just under some clown who decided to go airborne in lieu of waiting for a signal.

I hadn't formulated any kind of response before I was walking into Andre's place. The usual lunch crowd was there. A couple of them nodded to me, and I nodded back, perfectly relaxed on the outside. Acting is part of my job. Was.

I stepped over and slid into the booth. Yes, it was Naumann. A little older, but remarkably well kept. Killing billions of people didn't really bother someone like him.

"You wanted to see me," I said.

"I'd prefer to discuss business in private."

Well, that was direct.

"Follow me," I said.

I stood, faced them and started talking about nothing. I turned, indicated the door, and walked ahead. Outside, we spread slightly, and they followed me across traffic. I glanced about for any obvious tails, and noticed they did the same.

Then I gritted my teeth. It was frightening how automatic that training was. I kept situational awareness for myself, certainly, but here I was falling back into team mentality, for someone I despised beyond loathing.

The door recognized me and opened, and the sign blinked from "LUNCH" to "OPERATING." I left it like that, not that I expected a lot of traffic on a Berday afternoon.

I knew the bastard wanted something military. If he wanted my remaining contract time he could get pronged. I didn't think he'd make a public issue of it, for security reasons. If he wanted debriefed, I'd done that via post, and had nothing more to add. Whatever he was here for, I wanted to get it over with. That part of my life wasn't one I cared for.

His guard was just far enough back to give an indication of téte a téte, but with a hint of thug if anything happened. Not that I planned on anything, but I assessed him. He was like me a decade ago. I could probably take him if I had to, but I couldn't take both. Unless I was suicidal.

He probably shouldn't test that, so I confirmed mentally that this was a peaceful meeting, and leaned against a stock rack.

"So what do you want, Naumann?" I deliberately didn't use his rank.

He looked a little dazed as he spoke.

"I need you to track down Kimbo Randall, your man from the Earth mission."

Uh? "He's dead. They all died."

He shook his head. "No, he's alive. So are twenty-two others."

For some reason I didn't find that to be good news.

"How?"

"The same way you did, only most of them IDed themselves when they came back."

Damn. I felt . . . mixed. Twenty-three alive. But one hundred seventy-six dead. Our system saved with only a few million casualties. Earth destroyed as a power with six billion dead. All the anguish and soul searching came back and I had to fight it. I'd done it. My plan, my orders, my implementation. I'd killed more people than any monster in history.

The HQ got attacked while I was out doing recon, though . . . or at least I call it recon. I was out going insane and trying to force myself to come to terms with it, when the UN forces attacked and killed my element . . .

I said, "I saw corpses come out, but didn't know which were which."

He nodded. "Randall survived. So did others. Most of them retired quietly when offered the choice. A couple served out their terms. Randall reported in, debriefed, took his back pay and disappeared."

He looked uncomfortable as he continued, "He's been conducting assassinations. We only knew it was one of ours, not who, until we got a tiny scrape of DNA. I should say we stole it. Novaja Rossia doesn't know."

"He's been killing people for ten years?"

"About eight, and he's picked up the pace. About one a month. You trained him, you can stop him. I don't know that anyone else can."

I didn't want to have this conversation.

"I trained him to wipe out cities. Assassination is your problem."

"I need you," he said. He wasn't pleading, he was stating a fact.

"To fix another mess for you."

He shrugged. "If you want to look at it that way, I don't mind."

I remembered this. He was the fucking sociopath. He could blithely demand a city be wiped out and not be bothered by it. He manipulated people, used people, and he got away with it because he used them effectively and sparingly. Completely, coldheartedly logical, without any compassion in him. He rewarded people not because he cared, but because it created the mindset he wanted in them.

I'd mulled all this over years before. Why me?

Because I'm a nice guy. I don't even step on spiders. He groomed me and polished me to be his tool. You don't send a sociopath to kill, because he will enjoy it. You don't send one to infiltrate, because you won't have any hold over him if he goes native, and he just might, if he thinks he can get ahead better. Earth had the oldest, most corrupt government in humanity. A sociopath could have gotten along with bribes and threats, and might either have not followed through, or followed through too gleefully and blown it all.

So he sent a nice guy, knowing and accepting it would ruin me when I finally stopped thinking about it as a project and considered the human beings behind it.

That, and he knew I'd have that focus, because I have narcissistic tendencies. I like being that good, and I don't really think about other people. I took pity on them, because I thought I was better. Hell, I am better, but why does that matter? It's entirely subjective.

At least, I had been narcissistic. I thought about them a lot more now I had to interact with them, and I always cared, when I bothered to think.

I can think of better strategies than what we used. They might have involved more casualties for us. They would definitely have meant fewer casualties for Earth.

But he *wanted* casualties. He and I had tried that on Mtali and I hated myself, and then I'd fallen right back into the same self-absorption and done it a second time.

This dogfucker could scale up mentally and emotionlessly to an entire fucking planet. He wanted them all to hate us, and fear us, and he'd gotten that. I despised him for that, and I hated myself for falling for it.

It took me a second to remember all that and burn over it again, then I said, "Why me?"

"Because you're the best we've got. Hell, we've been looking for a decade and didn't find you, right here in the Capital. You stayed hid, calm, solid."

"So? There are others who can do that."

I was forcing him to be honest and open, and he hated it.

"You, because, it's got to be utterly silent. He certainly has friends back here, so anything we plan will be compromised. You can do it with cash and never be seen. No one knows you exist."

"You really know how to fuck a guy." Once again, I was the only tool who could do the job, and it was my duty, etc.

"I wouldn't ask if I didn't need it. He killed one tracker already."

"Really. Anyone I know? Anyone I should care about?"

This wasn't going how he wanted it to. I'd changed, and he had no hold on me anymore. He actually said, "Please—"

I cut him off. "Resources?"

"Cash. The rest I don't want to know about."

I leaned back and casually said, "So, I can nuke a city to get him?

"You know better than that." He actually grinned. I was so furious I wanted to kill him right there.

"You better spell it out."

"Yes, I want you to kill him. Be certain he's dead. Minimize casualties."

"Not bring him in alive?"

"Do you think you can?"

"Not if he doesn't want to, no."

"We can't trust his word, he has to be an object lesson."

"Yeah, you're fond of those. Have you noticed yet that they're not working? Not Mtali. Earth just hates us and is still arguing to incorporate us. Think this'll stop anyone who really wants to freelance?"

My voice was getting loud.

There wasn't much he could say, so he didn't. He was right this time, though. I hoped.

I asked, "No support at all?"

"What do you have in mind?"

"I need Special Projects support—ID, devices, et cetera."

"I can't spare a team. It would be too obvious to pull one."

I shook my head. "I want one person only. Preferably female so we look like a nondescript couple." Why did that disturb me? "Must be good at ID, weapons, electronics. Very good. If I'm doing this alone, I'll need lots of gear fast."

"I'll see what I can do."

"I haven't agreed to do it yet." It made sense. But *he* was involved. That made me leery.

"We need you. This guy has killed thirty-seven people on a bunch of planets, and sooner or later his background will come out. That risks our other troops."

Yeah, that was the assessment I had. Eventually, we'd all get slimed.

"You knew that would get me. Asshole."

"Yes, I am. But I need it done and you're the only one who can handle it."

My tactical brain already knew how to run it. I wanted to make him reconsider, though. Both agenda overlapped.

"I want five mil in cash up front."

"Done," he said with a nod.

Asshole. So I ended the interview.

"Then get out of here and don't come back."

He placed a card down on my desk, turned and left. He was really serious about needing me.

As he reached the door, I called, "Naumann."

He turned.

I knew the answer, but I had to ask. "Did Deni . . . ?"

He did sound gentle when he said, "I'm very sorry. No, she did not survive the attack on your safehouse."

I'd known that was the case, but I still winced. I wondered how long he'd practiced for that, too.

"I'll have her personal effects delivered."

He gave me a moment to refuse, and I didn't. He turned and left.

In the decade since the War, I'd tried hard not to think about it. Now it all came back in a cascading storm of emotion and pain.

Most of my friends were dead. Lots of innocent Earthies were dead. So were a few guilty ones. I'd watched entire cities burn, first from my instigation, then from the frightened animal instincts of the residents. They lost power, communication, supply, the things that kept industrial creatures human. Then they beat, raped, burned, killed, trashed their own cities.

When I was young, I could convince myself I was "better." But that all depends on context. I was faster, stronger, much better at problem solving, but when it comes down to it, my contribution to my species is my daughter. My contribution to my society is its continued existence, and a good many millions of other troops and civilians did as much, in their own way.

I'd reread my journal once. I noticed it had little mention of other troops. Part of that was because I didn't want to dwell on dead friends, but part was also because I was an asocial little fuck. Then I'd been forced to watch the repercussions of my actions, and realized I deserved to die. Even if the attack was justified, and I could argue that both ways, for me to survive wasn't moral. I was too dangerous to be allowed to live, and the burning hatred I feel when I remember is more than anyone should stand. If I'd been tried as a war criminal, I'd have demanded they kill me, to be merciful.

I don't want to remember any of it, but I don't have a choice. Even if I didn't have a near eidetic memory, it was the kind of thing one never forgets.

The reason I was alive? My daughter. An accident borne and born of a huge error on my part. I was still alive because she was innocent and needed the best protection possible. As she got older, the old self-hatred got to me more and more.

That's why I'd changed my name, I realized. Ken Chinran never came back from Earth. He died with the rest.

Now he had to be reborn.

Perhaps he could end with an honorable death.

❁ CHAPTER 2 ❁

THE NEXT MORNING, I forced myself awake. I'd slept a tortured sleep, with undefined bad dreams and twitches at every sound. Some things mark you for life. I'm marked enough by Earth that I have to have city noise to be comfortable, and my hindbrain panics when it stops. Of course, some noises sound like threats.

I ate a couple bites of cheese, didn't bother showering as I was going to be getting filthy in dust. Hard work with the machines makes me feel good, and I had enough contracts.

Andre always wondered about my low profile. I lived simply, owned the building through a combination of scavenged military funds left from Earth, savings and lots of long days. I didn't need a lot of income, and didn't need to expand. That kept me out of sight and safe. I lived upstairs, worked downstairs, and kept everything Spartan and simple.

I walked quietly downstairs, though Chel had long since left for school. It was habit. I'm only noisy when I decide to be, and was very soft footed even before training.

31

Naumann's card was still on the desk. It read "Alan David" with no last name, and had a contact code. I sent him a brief note with a fake name and appointment time for thirty segs. I wanted him to have to rush.

Out in the shop, I powered up a pantographic coordinate mill and gave it a pattern to work from. I watched it cut and twist and shave, following whatever pattern its AI found to cover the entire surface of the model as efficiently as possible.

While I meditated to crumbling chips and peeling shreds, a woman walked in. Decent looking in the angular style, dressed in business casual—white tights and sleeveless turquoise tunic with a coat draped. She had dark collar-length hair with a chestnut tinge restrained with a band, sharp shoulders and oval hips. She was lighter-skinned than typical, faintly olive rather than tanned or dark. Pert. Cute. Small. She might mass sixty-five kilos and wasn't over one hundred sixty-five centimeters. She had a bearing that told me at once who she was. That and a doccase.

"I'm Dan Lockhart. Can I help you?" I asked.

"I'm Cynthia Charles. I'm looking for a Kenneth Puvalis," she said, giving the name I'd provided. Yes, she was my assistant. I should have been happy. I wasn't. Naumann had set me up with a woman who was no doubt competent, would blend in most places, and was very pretty. It was that last part that made me suspicious. Why pretty? Luck of the draw, or did he have plans to hold her over me? And even after all these years, I wasn't keen on attractive woman as assistants. Call it a psychological issue.

Actually, that's exactly what it was. She had poise, exuded confidence and competence, and that was why she was here. My own nerves were the problem, not anything or anyone else. Still, I coded the door for "OPERATING" and turned back to her.

"That's me," I admitted. "And you are?"

"Sergeant Instructor Silver McLaren. I suppose I'm reporting for duty." She handed over the case. I didn't waste time checking it. It would have the cash I asked for.

"Good," I said. "I never want to hear that name or rank again. Did our employer brief you?"

"Painfully," she admitted. "It doesn't sound like a fun gig." She looked me over. I could tell she wasn't very enthusiastic, and my terseness wasn't helping her. That wasn't my problem right now.

"It never is," I said. "Did you volunteer? Or were you persuaded?"

She thought about that for a moment. "I did volunteer, but I suppose he was persuasive. Good for career, interesting experience, all that."

"So decide right now if you're a real volunteer. There's no turning back." Oh, shit, I hated this. It was dèjá vu of forming Team Seven. Come with me, kid, it'll be a hoot! Trust me. Big rewards if you survive.

"Oh, I'll do it," she said. "That's why I enl . . . signed up. This is just different from what I expected."

"Fair enough," I said. "Get used to strange things quickly. Did he tell you I'm not real keen on the mission?"

"He sort of intimated that, yes. And told me of your background," she added.

"Yes?" I prompted. There was a question hanging.

"Nothing," she said.

"You want to know what it's like to kill billions of people and why I'm still sane afterwards," I told her. "If we're going to work together, we need mutual honesty. What you like to eat, how you feel, what type underwear you wear, everything."

"Okay," she said. "So what was it like?"

"It was terrifying and revolting beyond words. And I haven't yet decided if I am sane. What type underwear?"

She looked startled, smiled faintly and said, "Blue Wicklon thong today. Is that a hint as to how personal such questions are?"

"Score one," I said. "I'm deranged, prone to nightmares and violence, resentful, morose and old inside if not outside. We're going to track down one of my friends and kill him for the sin of competence in the free market, for killing people who most likely deserved to die. If he finds us first, we die.

If we get caught, we get nailed under whatever local laws we have. That could be Mtali or Earth. Mtali would be disgustingly unpleasant for you; they don't like women. Earth would be lethal; they don't like Freeholders or our type specifically." I didn't say "Special Warfare." "If you can handle all that, we have a job. If not, say so now." My face was in a slight snarl from stress, and I left it there. I needed to see how she reacted.

"It's a job," she said, though I heard the last word as "mission." She was handling cover fairly well. "I can handle it."

"Right," I said, taking that as intent. I wanted proof, though. And I needed to know how she'd hold up. We could get departure orders tomorrow. Or right now. "Tell me your training and experience." I still hadn't asked her to sit down. We were standing between two of the mills, not visible from the door. She let herself stand with her back to the door, though. Not a good sign.

She took a slight breath and said, "I started in Field Improvised Electronics, which I maxed. From there, I took supplementals in Mechanical, Explosives and Demolition, and Cover and Intelligence Assets. I got eighty-five percent on the test for E and D. The rest I maxed. I was teaching Mechanical until I got detached for this. I've been to the Operative Support Course and Blazer Field Support Course."

"Service time? Duty stations?" I prompted.

"Five years, three months. I did a detached tour at the Lab on Gealach, a tour with Second Special Warfare Regiment and a Temp at the Hirohito Embassy." Her presentation was confident and smooth.

I waited as she matched my stare. The seconds stretched out. She twitched first, that tiny signal that says confidence has cracked.

"And what else?" I asked.

"That's my career, sir," she said.

There was just a hint of defensiveness in there, and I went at it with my attitude as a pick-axe.

"So, a bunch of nothing," I said, sounding disgusted. It wasn't as bad as that, but she was a bit cocky about a career that included no combat. I had to hit that right now.

"I wouldn't call it 'nothing,' sir," she said.

"I would," I said. "Labs, training exercises and diplocrap.

Very good prep for undercover stalking. This isn't a dinner or a clever little gig building a recording device to fit in a corsage." She started to protest and I continued, "Skip that, let's see your work. You teach mechanical?"

"Yes, sir."

"So build me a pistol. Ten millimeter Alesis caliber. Here's the tools," I said with a spread-armed wave around the shop.

She looked around, fixed me with her eyes and asked, "Is this a test?"

"Yes," I said. "My ass depends on how well you do your job."

"Hmmph," she said, but turned to the machines. That tunic was cut low, showing off a lot of nicely toned back. "Will standard polymer and metal suffice, or do you want ceramic?"

"Easiest and quickest job you can do that is reliable."

"All my work is reliable," she said frostily.

"I'm sure it is," I said. "It's not the technical issues that really concern me."

She was facing my primary prototyping mill, now, nodding in familiarity. She brought up power and started asking it questions. "So what is your concern?" she asked, head turning only slightly over her shoulder and voice raised over the hum of the machine. "You think I'm going to freeze up?"

"Well, you've never been shot at before, have you?" I asked.

"Sure, in live-fire exercises," she said. She sounded proud of it. "I've heard a few cracks."

"Right, but no offensive fire," I said.

"No. But I'm sure I can deal with it." I could see the indulgent smirk even with her back to me. It was a nice back, too. Dammit, she didn't look like Deni, why was she reminding me of her? And she was too cocky, but it was all façade. Damned youngster.

"Well, that's the test, isn't it?" I said. She was still facing away from me. I crouched about twenty centimeters to get a good angle, then drew and fired. I still had one of those punk's guns from that mixup that had started all this. I'd been carrying it as a curiosity.

BANG! BANG! BANG! BANG! BANG! Five shots, unsuppressed, echoing in sharp cracks and tinny pings from all the metal surfaces in the shop. The first was about ten centimeters above her head. The second went past her right ear. After that, I kept them wide in case she dodged. They tore chips out of the upper wall above the stock rack.

Arms flailing, she came up on her toes, caught herself on the horizontal motor arm and staggered back. She whirled, eyes meter wide in horror. "ARE YOU FUCKING INSANE?" she shouted.

Well, she recovered quickly from shock. Good.

"We've already established that," I answered her, hand low, pistol pointing at the ground. "That's not the issue. Now you've been shot at. Next time, instead of jumping, take cover. Then consider doing something about it. That's today's lesson."

Panting hard, she leaned back on the worktable, hands gripping the edge. "You are off the fucking edge!" she said, sounding terrified. "You are a major space case!"

"You're welcome," I said. I kept a flat expression. This was the first test of many.

"I cannot work with you like this," she snapped. Her face was hard, mean. "You are seriously out of it."

"And how crazy would I be if I wasn't fucked up after what I've done?" I asked rhetorically. There was an embarrassed silence for long seconds. "Go," I said with a shake of my head. "If you can't handle me, you can't handle our target, and you can't handle the environment we're going to be in."

"What?" she said, sounding as if she hadn't understood me.

"Go," I repeated. "I'll have him send me someone else."

Raising her voice in anger—or was it from temporary hearing loss?—she said, "I am assigned to this task, I will do it."

"I thought you'd decided I'm a loon?" I asked.

"You are," she said. "You are totally round the bend. But the job's got to be done. I will not quit."

"Want to bet on that?" I asked. "I don't. It's my ass, and I'm not trusting it to a quitter."

She took a deep breath to steady the heaves she'd been having. "I may talk about quitting, but I never do," she said. "I was last ass in my company the entire way through Basic, but I made it. I didn't know how to swim and damned near drowned, but I did it. I had to go through survival training twice because I flubbed the orienteering test. I wet my pants and cried in the Black Ops support course, but I stuck it out. We had a blowout my first day on Gealach and three people died, but I stayed there. I rant and bitch, but *I don't fucking quit* and you can't make me." There was palpable defiance and aggression there. If

I wanted her to leave, I'd have to pick her up and throw her out physically. And she knew I could do it and didn't care.

I couldn't help myself. I grinned. I had the real core of her here, and it was an honest soldier. Everyone gets scared. Being scared isn't the problem. Letting the fear take control is the problem. "*That*'s what I wanted to hear. Now get that gun made."

She looked confused for a moment, then acceptance ran across her face. She shook her head and sighed and got to work, but she kept her gaze angled so she could watch me, and shifted as I did so I was never out of sight.

She really did learn fast.

The pistol she finished a div and a half later was ugly, but certainly functional. I'd given her a task I could do myself, so I could grade it. Combat worthy it was. Without proper tempering and finish it might not last five hundred rounds before failures became a problem, but that was plenty for a field expedient.

"Good start," I said. "I need to plan some stuff. Come back at three divs and we'll pick up then."

"Yes, sir," she agreed.

I left her hanging until she grabbed her wrap and pouch and headed out.

Yeah, she'd probably do. Now I had to get in the mindset of her being an expendable asset. I hadn't had to do that for years.

Shit.

She left, probably to get lunch and a drink or a hit of something to unwind from being shot at by deadly lunatic, one each. I checked on the job the CM was handling, watched it feed a piece automatically, caught the one it had just finished, inspected it and left the machine to run.

Then I drew up plans. Training us, easy in concept, it would just take practice and effort. Locating Randall, that would take intel and patience and thinking. Building an initial kit of ID, weapons, accessories for our pursuit, with a lot of holes because of unknowns, that was her job under my direction. Tentative plans for escape and evasion after killing him, largely blank. Well, I had to start somewhere.

So much for zen and machine tools. My brain was heavily involved in tactical calculus. I enjoyed it. That angered me.

I was only too glad when she returned.

"I need a pair of climbing gaffs, low enough profile they look like dress sandals."

"That's a new one," she said. "Very creative." Her moué was almost a smile.

I deliberately turned and left her to it.

I watched from the far side of the shop as I messed about with the optical etcher. She was sure and comfortable with the machines, even for a new concept.

When she was well occupied, I turned smoothly, drew and fired again. I put the first round low over the machine because my own guns are a lot better than the crap those punks had. Quieter, too.

She dropped, drew and shot back. I made a surprised but instant dive behind the laser flatcutter.

Let me be specific. She dropped, rolled, disappeared behind the mill and poked back around just enough for her left eye and the weapon. The weapon was a Benelli

Model YYZ eleven-millimeter compact. She was wearing form-fitting tights and a low-back, sleeveless tunic that came just below her hips. Where in the hell had she stashed that cannon? I hadn't seen *any* kind of holster on her.

Her aim was pretty accurate, too. One shot dinged the floor to my right, then she held her fire. "You can come out now!" she shouted, sounded smug and cheerful, muttering an added, "Asshole," that I wasn't supposed to hear and pretended not to.

"Better," I admitted. Better, hell. She'd been fast enough I only got off two shots, and one had been nowhere near her. That was pretty damned effective.

"I told you I could handle it," she said, panting. There was a scrape on her right elbow and her tights were gray down the side from her dive for cover. Neither was bothering her. Good. She started reholstering the pistol in a small of the back rig under her tunic. It's not the safest carry, if you get knocked down on your spine, but it's not bad and it can be very discreet.

"Fine," I said. "Come into my office for a moment." I turned, she followed. "Door," I said as I entered.

She really wasn't going to like this, but it was another test of attitude. As she closed it, I grabbed her.

I'm not as spry as I used to be, but I am still strong, know how to use leverage, and don't hesitate. I gripped her wrist, pulled and twisted. That left me standing in T-stance for balance, with her backwards over my left knee. I batted her left arm aside as she yelped, and relieved her of the pistol. It went on my desk. A bit of clutching that wasn't sexual found nothing stashed near her groin. She had a good Branch Shepherd Knives ten-centimeter folder clipped down her right sock, and another smaller one hooked on her bra between her breasts. She had a collar tab knife, the type that are very popular among wannabes and not much good, but can still cut, in the neck of the tunic.

"Tell me if I missed any or I'll go probing," I said.

"Ouch! That's it!" she said. "Spare magazine in the holster."

I twisted her back to her feet, a process that confused her. She'd been swept over, held immobile by her own mass across my knee, now was back on her feet and disarmed and intimately if professionally felt up. It had taken me seven seconds. I said, "Yeah, that was pretty good shooting. Right up to the point where you got captured." She could be proud of what she did, but she wasn't going to get cocky or I'd slam her down.

She calmly looked at me and said, "I think I understand now."

"You have a start," I said. "I believe I can rely on you."

"Good to know," she said, and fixed me with a stare. "When do I get to know I can rely on you?"

That surprised me.

"That's a good question. I don't have an answer, but we'll work on that."

Yeah, sure I was over being an introspective narcissist. I'd completely missed this being a two-way matter.

"You've driven home that this is going to be truly succulent," she said, sounding very much like a sergeant.

"It always sucks to be us. Learn that now. Tonight you start sleeping with me."

It was her turn for that completely shocked look again. "Excuse me?"

"If we're going to be a couple for cover purposes, you start looking like my lover. I didn't say 'sex' I said 'sleep.' But we stay close."

"That makes sense."

"I snore."

"I guess I'll manage."

Chel came home from school about then, through the back door. She took in a quick glance, nodded almost imperceptibly as she came to a reasonable but wrong conclusion about either business or pleasure in progress, and started to head past with just a "Hey Dad," and a nod.

"Wait, Chel," I said. She stopped and turned. "Silver's here on business. Military business."

With a cautious twitch of an eyebrow that's going to rip some guy's heart out soon, she extended her hands to shake and threw in a couple of centimeters of bow. "I'm Chelsea Lockhart. Pleased to meet you," she said.

"Silver McLaren." Silver gave her just as much grip and bow. Not many people do that for adolescents.

As Chel queried us with a glance, I said, "I've got something to take care of in a few days. Silver will be assisting me."

"Offplanet?" Chel asked. Dammit, why did I have a smart daughter? Then she, the only one who knew me well enough to read my cold face, said, "Outsystem." It sounded like a dirge the way she said it.

"'Fraid so," I said. "But Silver's going to be here. Undercover. As far as anyone is concerned, she's a fling with me, okay?"

Her eyes widened slightly and she said, "Okay, Dad. Am I supposed to like her or hate her guts?" She smiled slightly. Silver chuckled.

"Might be best if you hated her. It'll account for any stress around here."

"Okay," she agreed. "I suppose you'll tell me what I need to know, and I shouldn't ask questions or spy on you?"

"Who are you and what have you done with my daughter?" I replied. It wasn't much of a joke. Chel has been a snoop her entire life. A pretty good one, too. She improves as I whack her when I catch her.

She grinned. I hugged her, and the warmth calmed me down. She really is the only thing that keeps me sane, and alive. She has a good grip, too.

"You can eat at Andre's or the Access tonight. I need to go out with Silver."

"Okay, Dad," she agreed. "Thanks. Don't do anything I wouldn't do."

"Yeah, that's funny when I tell it," I said.

Thanks, kid. Not that I was planning on anything, but that would have been a dousing with ice water.

She tripped out, through the stair door and up to our residence. When I started, I was afraid living in an industrial area would be tough on her, but there are other kids in the area, a park, and while her school handles a lot of transients, there are a few locals. She did okay.

Idly, I realized I could now cash in the two unlimited tickets I'd kept on hand in case I needed to escape in a hurry. Nor did I need to live next to the port anymore. It was relaxing and uplifting in a way.

After, of course, I killed one of my friends.

I never wanted a normal life, but there must be a moderate middle somewhere.

I turned to Silver/Cynthia, and said, "Let's go shopping. Got a list?"

"I've been working on one," she agreed. "Cash cards for Earth, mixed currency and cards for Novaja Rossia, Caledonia. Cash and bullion for Mtali. Two hundred K each. ATF Outfitters should be delivering Stash Luggage brand bags this afternoon, if your daughter will sign for them."

"She will," I agreed. Yeah, she's a good kid.

As we walked to my shop van, she said, "I have clothing for me. Athletic, casual, business casual for here, Earth and generic colonies. I can't do a non-English speaker's accent worth a damn. I have a couple of formal gowns and a tux. All the shoes are built for use and looks. Expensive."

"So we go shopping. I want disposable handguns, reliable but cheap. Taurus or similar. I want a take-down riot gun. Get the Merrill. Collapsible hunting rifle I can use for sniping. Probably the Chandler. I'll take care of that one. Any electronics you might need, and something to stash them in, obviously. Whatever you need for an ID kit, and some cracking tools."

"That and hand tools, and some surgical gear for manipulation, and I'll stock up on makeup. How many phones do you want?"

"I want six sets each of ID, phones and comms. Make us a married couple, a dating couple and a business couple."

"I'll get local ID from a bank, too."

"Good," I agreed. I wasn't sure Cr5 Million would be enough by the time we were done.

Something hit me.

"What's your status for this? Orders? Temp duty? Discharged?"

"We discussed that, the . . . boss and I," she said. "Seemed safest to say nothing. My unit was told orders will follow later. Captain Hull was told to forget about it, so was the first shirt. I guess they're hoping this is short enough it doesn't matter much."

"Unlikely," I said. "Seventeen days between planets, and we might need to hit five or more planets. This is a long temp."

"We'll do what we can."

"Yeah. I just remember all the compromises last time. They didn't help."

My shop van is unmarked, a bit older, completely nondescript. When I meet clients and want to put on a better image, I have a basic high-traction small truck, like everyone else around here uses. I'm invisible.

We were silent a few moments as I pulled into traffic, then she spoke.

"Dan," she said. I made eye contact. "The Earth Insertion is testable material at the schools now. It didn't go perfectly, but you're regarded as brilliant for how you pulled it off. Entire courses changed to incorporate your doctrine."

I suppose she thought that would make me feel better.

What I heard was, "We're raising an entire generation of elite troops to be programmable killing machines who think of wiping out planets as a job, for which they expect reviews and promotions based on their body counts."

I guess my complete lack of an expression clued her in. We traveled in silence.

I wasn't angry with her. She couldn't know, it was impossible for her to know, and I hoped she never did. She was also genuinely trying to open up to me as a person. It might be an attempt at friendship, it might only be so we could operate better as a team, but it was honest either way.

I was going to have to find a way to connect with her. At the same time, I was pathologically afraid to do so, because she was expendable for this mission.

I understood the reasons Randall had to be eliminated, even if I didn't like them. Sooner or later, his actions would come back on us. That would endanger everyone in the Forces. So it was critical that I stop him.

Logically, if she could distract him long enough for me to get a shot off, I had to do it. The end result of that would probably mean she died.

I wasn't going to let that be personal. She was a tool, and had to stay that way.

I didn't want to be sociopathic.

I drove, we'd go into stores, split up and buy supplies. I haggled enough where I could to either be in character for those who knew me, or not appear blatantly desperate to those who didn't. At the chain outlets, I just offered basic pleasantries, paid cash and left.

Within a div, we had a respectable haul of mostly

nondescript hardware in the van. Any home hobbyist would have been busy for weeks. We'd have days at most, to convert it all into easily and discreetly transportable components. Some of the electronics, especially, would result in criminal charges on Earth or places like Mtali.

As Silver climbed in with an armful of packages from Universal Fasteners, I said, "Dinner."

"Thanks," she said.

"You'll have to pretend to like me."

"Will this involve you shooting at me?" Her tone was sarcastic and unamused.

"Not during dinner," I replied.

She didn't reply. Not verbally.

There was a Timmons Meat nearby. The elk steak was adequate. The vegetables were crisp. The beer was commercial but respectable. We looked enough like a working domestic couple to pass. I probably wasn't known here, but there was always a chance, and a good cover benefited from practice.

Back at the shop, we unloaded it all into the dock area, stripped what packaging we easily could, and finished around midnight. It was a productive enough day.

"I'm going to get cleaned up," I said.

"Go ahead. I'll finish checking some of these boards first."

"Got it."

My side of the residence is a great room with a kitchen and bathroom at the south end. Bed in the corner, office along one side with comm, chairs toward the middle and empty space on the west for exercise or whatever. Chelsea has a smaller suite across the hall. I have two spare rooms for guests, which I've never had, or storage. I don't have much to store, though.

I stepped through to the bathroom, tossed my clothes at the automatic washer, a great invention that, and got clean. Finished, I pulled on shorts and T-shirt, came out and hit the comm to clear out leads and messages. I'd have to come up with a reason for shutting down for several weeks that was believable. I'd divert some business to a couple of competitors I respected. Existing jobs would have to be completed, though.

She came up while I worked, and headed into the bathroom. I noted it without any comment, and took care of two inquiries, a request for quote and some random comments on social trees. I don't do much with them. Dan is a loner.

A few segs later she came out clean, damp and naked. We're not a psychopathically modest culture, and we were both soldiers. Or she was and I used to be. Nudity isn't really an issue.

Or it shouldn't be. I found myself very disturbed. Not aroused—that might have been expected. Just disturbed and wrong feeling. In fact, I felt worse for not being aroused, because her body was perfect for her. Everyone comes in their own shape, and hers suited her. Olive skin and dark hair, smooth, slightly angular lines, that tone of youth. If I'd have seen her in a club when I needed some comfort, I'd have zeroed in on her at once.

I went about getting undressed myself, mostly. I sleep in a T-shirt and briefs because I chill easily. I was about done when she said, "Okay, goodnight." She slid under the covers, rolled her back to me and went to sleep.

I didn't. I wasn't comfortable.

Oh, I had a field-supported mattress that would flex for contours and not transfer any vibrations from the other side. The room wasn't soundproof, because I like sensory input of my environment to feel safe, and I'm used to city noises, or woods noises, desert, ship, whatever. That wasn't the problem.

Sexual tension. There it was now. Out in the open. At last. I'd slept alongside women soldiers before, but usually in sleeping bags or curled up in cloaks. I tried to recall a mission where I'd done this, and couldn't. I'd had a couple of short relationships when Chelsea was younger, but nothing recently except the occasional friendly fling or professional escort, who left at once. Occasional sensory environment fantasies with friends on the nets who knew me only by a nickname were not the same. The last woman I'd really shared a bed with I'd been involved with socially and professionally, and was the mother of my daughter and now dead. Hell, long dead. Ten Grainne years, fifteen Earth.

Next to me was a highly toned young woman, with an attitude and look I liked, near naked and within arm's reach. I couldn't touch her for all the obvious reasons. And the purpose of this exercise was so people would think we *were* sexual. That, and it created a better bond for the masquerade psychologically. It had all the advantages of a real relationship, without the sex. That was exactly the problem.

I lay there for most of a div, 2.7 hours, sweating slightly and not sleeping. No, I could not "accidentally" grope her. I couldn't snuggle. I couldn't do anything that would give my body a hint that anything was going to happen. It was strictly a cover. My body didn't believe it. Then I realized my brain didn't, either.

Eventually, I got up and headed through to take a long, hot, soaking, mind-numbing shower. It almost worked. Eventually, it did. Then I came back and slept, exhausted, as far away from her as I could get and still be in the same bed.

◉ CHAPTER 3 ◉

THE ALARM WENT OFF at two divs. That's about five a.m., allowing for our longer day and different clock. The warble sounded and the lights came on. I was on my feet at once, because if I hesitate, I fall back asleep.

"Good morning!" I said, doing my best impression of the type of morning person I despise. "Time for our morning workout!" I added.

"Right. Okay," she croaked, eyes squinted and face pinched. She didn't look bad in the morning, but she certainly wasn't pretty. She rolled out and clutched at clothes.

I was dressed in seconds, pulled on my running shoes and snugged them down. I hopped into the kitchen and grabbed the kits I'd prepared the night before—two of the detachable assault packs from the SW's large rucks, filled with water, some sundry items and food bars for warmup. I came back through, dropped them on the bed and hit the bathroom. She was running a brush through her hair to get rid of the crinkles. She wore tight shorts, running shoes and a ziptop, and looked disgustingly trim. When I came out, she had hold of one of the packs.

"Why these?" she asked.

"Practice," I said. "We might need to carry gear, and if we can run with it, we can run without it. We'll work up to boots in a few days, too. Grab your weapon and let's hit it." I pointed at the pile as I leaned in and grabbed a pack and my holster.

We slipped out quietly. Chel was still asleep and wouldn't be up until 2.5 for school. No need to wake her. Then we were down the stairs and into the shop, quickly through the machines and out the back personnel door. Silver apparently thought it was fun. It wasn't likely she'd done anything like this. Heck, she was only six years—less than nine Earth years—older than my daughter. That was almost scary.

We walked the first couple of hundred meters, stretching out our pace to let muscles warm up. Then we moved into a loping jog.

I wanted to start easily. As I'd told her, the purpose was to get used to gear. We were both in good shape.

I was still in decent shape.

I wasn't in bad shape.

I'd thought I was in shape.

Yes, I practice military hand-to-hand regularly. Yes, I have a fairly active lifestyle, walk regularly and carry large loads around the shop. I found out then there's a huge difference between an active lifestyle for a civilian and a top-trained soldier.

The pack fit okay, pulling at my shoulders only a little.

My holster wasn't bad, though it bounced a bit against my hip. The weather was a nice twenty-three with a slight breeze coming from the northeast—sea breeze; we were about twenty-five kilometers inland. It was still dark. I headed straight for Perimeter Road so we could parallel the fence around the starport for a bit.

I was sweating and ragged by the time we got there. I got worse as we ran along it, heading west toward the mountains. Breath was burning my throat, my guts were hard and lumpy in pain, and I was bulling my way through from sheer bloody-minded determination. At least I still had that. I didn't have my wind anymore.

I turned us around after three kilometers and headed back, against the sea breeze. It was past dawn now, Iota rising and the wind freshening against us. That was good because it was cool against the clammy sweatiness of my body, bad because it was more resistance.

I was only too glad to be back at the shop, my lungs screaming, muscles spasming and sweat pouring out of me. She was still fresh. Obnoxious little bitch. Then I saw her indulgent smile. She was trying to politely mask it, but not well enough.

Another lesson had to be delivered. "Pushups," I said, and dropped, still wearing the pack.

She actually tried to keep pace with me.

First of all, men have far more upper-body muscle than women. This is why women carry their rucks on their hips, men on their shoulders. Second, I might not be fifteen anymore, but I still carried heavy loads often, and Special Warfare Candidate School had taught me about pushups. You get very good at them when they're handed out like candy. I recalled several days when I'd had to deliver 1500 or more for some minor infraction.

She stayed with me up to seventy. Not bad. In fact, I was impressed. But I pushed through to one hundred fifty. She was impressed. I counted them as I went, nose down to the cast floor of the shop, inhaling the tang of metals, plastics, ceramics, solvents and oils, then up. I focused on a tiny chip in front of me, barely deep enough for a fingernail, and pumped up and down.

Then I sat back against the number two mill.

"Well, I've got to work on my running," I admitted. There was no point in pretending.

"You'll be fine in no time," she replied. She had that hint of bother that said she was afraid of saying more lest she annoy me or embarrass herself. She zipped her top open, the stretchy fabric bouncing free from her chest. "Damn, that feels better," she said with a smile. She was admitting she wasn't as tough as she'd made herself out to be. So, she'd been pushing, too. That was a good sign. I respect determination.

Oh, damn me, that was a perfect pair of breasts. If I'd walked by in the park and seen them, I'd have stared discreetly and politely. Now I had them intimately close and off limits.

They say Lawrence of Arabia was a masochist who only got off on pain and suffering. Was I that way, too?

I wasn't sure I wanted to learn all these things about myself. I just wanted to raise my daughter in peace. After that . . .

Yes, I had seriously considered checking out after she reached adulthood. I could arrange an honorable accident, leave no note as to my past, and no one would ever know.

Except, of course, Naumann knew now, Silver did, Chelsea did, Andre could guess . . . if I killed myself now, no one would believe an accident, and if I didn't leave a note, they'd suspect foul play.

I couldn't even die in peace.

I don't know if a god, the god, some god and goddess or some committee exists. If they do, though, when I get to the afterlife, someone is getting an ass kicking, and if they think their being omnipotent will stop me, they've never met a pissed off Operative.

I cleaned up and went to the shop, because I did have actual work lined up. One of the warehouses needed new bearing rollers for their loadout system. Silver went to her "job." I actually don't know where she disappeared two divs a day. I should probably learn that, though I assumed it involved talking to Naumann about me, hopefully through mail drops. I couldn't imagine he'd risk another face-to-face, but I should find out.

I worked until lunch, and was able to stop thinking. The rollers were straight tube, with pressed in bearing surfaces on each end. I did that part by hand, once I had them cut, because there were only fifty of them and it was easier to hold the piece and crank the press than to set up the Brett Loader to do it. I hate having the mechanical monstrosity walk around the shop anyway. It feels too much like a person I can't stop.

I grabbed a calzone from Andre at lunch time. It felt as if everyone was watching me, and probably a few were. The story of the robbers was out, and a few knew I'd been the agent who dealt with them. Probably quite a few knew I was a vet, and it was statistically certain the story had blown out of proportion. I wasn't exactly discreet at this point.

Had Naumann chosen me because he knew I could be manipulated? Was this even more dangerous than he'd hinted and he expected me to be taken out in the process?

Well, bring it on, dogfucker. I'd welcome it.

Andre handed over my usual and smiled.

Maybe I was reading too much into things.

I finished the steaming pastry, finished setting the bearings, and delivered the crate of goods. McMillan are honest business people, so I was happy to let them accept an invoice with net fifty.

Silver's runabout was parked near the shop when I got back. I glanced at the time and yes, that's how late it was. The bay door was open so I slipped in quietly and looked around.

I heard her voice. She was in the reception room that led to the stairs and lift. I'm a natural spy and a trained one as well. I eased into a slouch next to the engine lathe and listened. Chelsea was there, too.

"So what's your dad like? How do you handle him?"

Chelsea said, "He can be very intense. Unforgiving, some ways. He has no patience for quitting."

"Yeah, I found that out," Silver said, a slight rueful tone in her voice.

"But he's very generous and compassionate. He lets me be my own person, even if he's strict. I love him a lot."

"Sounds as if he's a good dad."

"I suppose. I know I feel luckier than most of my

friends. Though I'm not sure how to handle this new past of his. He'd told me he'd been a soldier, and done some rescue work. He said he'd been in some ugly combat and didn't want to talk about it. But now . . ." she paused, ". . . I dug into the records about his career and unit. They're . . . disturbing. I never realized how much abuse he took, even before the war. Even before Mtali. He's spent sixteen years dealing with death and pain." She sounded hurt.

Yeah, I'd wanted to save her from that. That, and there's just no way to explain it. Nor could I trust anyone with that information. No priest, no therapist. The only counselor I had was me.

I'd never thought about that, either. I'm probably a shit counselor.

"Yes," Silver agreed. "I've seen the stuff you probably couldn't find. It's a sad story. The military uses its resources, and he's just another resource to them. One that can cause a devastating amount of damage. Yet he's a totally different person from Marshal Naumann, who's done about the same. I think Naumann handles it better."

"Oh?"

"Yes. But he doesn't have a family, and he's . . . colder. Probably sociopathic to some degree. Your dad's really too nice to have done what he has. And he's still nice after taking it all. He's a very strong man."

"It doesn't sound like a job you put a nice person into," Chelsea said.

"Would you want a cruel one doing it?" Silver asked.

Right. A cruel one like Naumann who could sentence people to die and not feel compassion. The right person at the strategic level. At the tactical level, he would be war crimes waiting to happen. Instead, send a nice kid. You'll fuck his brain, but his guilt will stop him before he randomly kills people in compensation for the stress. A few may even kill themselves. Another may even start killing others, but rationalize it as moral because he's being paid.

I'd avoided going mad by not thinking about this. I'd flushed a large part of my past from memory. Now I was recalling it, and recalling why I'd flushed it.

I made a little noise and entered. Chel was upstairs by the time I reached the shop room, and Silver was near one of the machines.

"This arrived for you," she said, and pointed.

It was a meter-long, narrow box. It didn't match anything I remembered ordering. I pulled out my knife and grabbed it, and stopped.

Return ID was Alan David. That was Naumann's name.

Deni's personal effects.

Deni had a family. There was no ill will that I'd ever heard of, but she, or he, had saved this for me. If she, I was even more touched, hurt, raw. It meant we'd both known we were lovers and been unable, and afraid to admit it.

If Naumann was behind it, I couldn't know if it was an honest gesture, or manipulation. I suppose that depended in part on whether or not he'd seen the contents.

I slit the binder tape and it snapped back. I took a breath, opened the box . . .

Her sword, which I'd suspected. Combat fittings at one end, dress fittings on the blade inside the crushed linen wrap. An Eaves custom wakizashi, of the style we favored in the unit.

There were a couple of printed pictures of her, which I flipped over quickly. A last generation memory zip, which I'd have to get decoded and run through my system to read. Some souvenirs, a few of which I recognized, from various planets, including a prisoner receipt from a drunken brawl in which we'd gotten arrested, some coins and notes, a grenade pin and some small gems and carved wooden talismans.

I found the note. It was basic paper from a desk pad.

"I'm sorry this isn't on nicer material. I don't plan ahead that well. That's why you're the officer.

"As I write this, you're across the op room from me, finishing boarding plans for the mission. We're both pretending not to notice the other, not to need each other.

"You're reading this, so I'm glad one of us made it. If we both make it, I'll show you this, and make a ritual of burning it. Then we'll formalize things. Then we'll be in bed about a week.

"I love you. Beat you to it.

"Deni."

Well, at least I knew Naumann hadn't seen it. He'd never have let me have it if he had.

Yes, I loved her. She loved me. We knew that and could never admit it, because we served in and out of the same unit, and supported each other, and at the end I was her commander. And I knew it when a stressed-out mission and a weird schedule found us alone for an hour, and our daughter was conceived.

And I loved my daughter, but part of me hated that bitch Deni for sticking me with her, because it meant I'd had to stay alive, facing what I'd done, and now I had to go back there.

This stuff would mean more to me later. For now, it could go in a closet.

McLaren was good at reading people. She was on the far side of the shop studying my on-hand material inventory. I was as alone as feasible.

I carefully closed the box and carried it upstairs, where I could wrap it and hide it, even from me, until I was up to dealing with it.

I gradually shipped incoming jobs to other shops around the port, and even over to the harbor area. I completed the ones I had, and kept the machines running on stuff I came up with, just for the hell of it, so when anyone came in I was busy as hell and could claim overbooking as a reason not to take jobs. That also justified my publicly expressed desire to take a vacation. My standard line was, "In a few days."

The worst part was playing the love-smitten single father. In public, Silver got felt up and caressed every little while, and we threw a few kisses in there now and then. Damn, but that woman could kiss. She accepted the role as camouflage and ran with it. Little gifts, occasional comm messages. Then soft, chewable lips brushing mine, with hands on my chest and shoulders.

I made it a point not to go to bed until I'd gotten some

kind of release from somewhere. Otherwise, I couldn't have slept, with her next to me.

But I wanted the human contact. When I'd been working sex for quick startup cash, that was the one part that I really enjoyed. I knew the clients needed and wanted that contact, and I could accept that as valid human touch, even if I hated myself too much to have any emotional involvement. Their need filled mine.

There was no way I'd emotionally involve with a subordinate I might have to order to die. Not again. Not ever again. But I wanted that body. I couldn't have it.

I'd found a situation where a smart, sexy woman made things tremendously worse and more depressing than I'd started with.

I didn't want to consider that I could reach lower emotional depths.

Silver did good work. Her qualifications were honest. She arranged multiple usable IDs for several systems, faked up plenty more that were decorative only, converted cash into various other exchange media, built concealed weapons, tools and scanners for us. She could rip circuitry and code and rebuild faster than anyone I'd ever seen. That's always been my weak point. I'd been machining a decade, largely self-taught, but I did it full time. She could keep up with me. I wasn't worried about explosives. If she couldn't swing that, I could.

I hit the banks, and so did she. We needed multiple IDs of pre-paid, collateraled cards, because I didn't intend to make payments. We'd use them until they were depleted, or until we had to scrap IDs. So each ID had three to five cards with a limit of ten grand each.

Each day she went to work for a couple of divs. Each afternoon she came back with more resources, and an intel report. For all I know, she showed up on base in uniform and had a cover of being out on local assignment, which would technically be true.

I really wanted to take a week and do a bare bones insertion, starting in the mountains and walking/hitching back, and break into my own perimeter, and possibly on base as well. But, the latter posed a serious operational security leak, and the former part would take time we just couldn't spare, with me about to abandon my business for as long as it took.

At least we had intel. She brought us DNA scans, a list of previous victims with bios and backgrounds, lengthy lists of connections.

One afternoon she came in, looking very serious, and said, "We believe he's in Caledonia."

"Right now?"

"Yes. We have tickets for tomorrow at two-seventy."

"Won't those be a bit obvious and pricey?" I asked.

"No, we've had open tickets on retainer. Typical for business these days."

"Really. I should know things like this. Except I've not been off planet since I got back." I was paranoid enough not to mention I had a similar setup. I should have made the connection, too.

"Well, can we do it?" She looked hesitant, about the mission or about me, I wasn't sure.

"Yes." I was nervous, too. I felt that gutfall that I recalled from last time. Kiss everything goodbye and hope you'll see it again.

"I'll pack personal stuff."

I nodded. "I need a div alone with my daughter."

"Absolutely," she agreed, and was out as fast as the door moved.

It was time for a discussion with Chel, that I'd never wanted to have, and would rather avoid. I had to, though, for all the reasons you can guess.

I cooked up a lamb curry, with her favorite vegetables, and got out the good rootbeer and a bottle of Silver Birch Special Reserve.

It didn't fool her, of course.

She came in from school, smelled the food, saw the bottles, and said, "You're leaving tomorrow."

"I am," I said.

I got tackle-hugged. This was going to be hard on me, too. I'd never been away from her. Not since she was three days old.

We ate, and it was somber. I'm not a vid person, so there was nothing to distract us, though it might have helped. She had one shot of the liquor, and two of her root beers, and picked at her curry. I wasn't that hungry myself, but I knew I needed food.

I cleared the table, and said, "So, we need to cover some things."

She tried to smile. "Don't burn the place down. If the thought of something makes me giggle I shouldn't do it. I don't need to set any records . . ."

"Yes, all the usual stuff. But this is more important, and new."

She nodded and came over.

"Now, I told you you can't come. This is a military mission and the people involved are dangerous pros. In addition, don't talk to anybody. Nothing. Not even Andre. I'm so ass over heels I took my new girlfriend and went on a trip and left you behind. You hate the fossil-hunting bitch. Whatever. But not a hint that it's duty related. Your life depends on it. And stay armed. It won't do you any good, but there's no reason not to."

"They don't like us armed at school, Dad. You know that," she said.

Playing me off against the school, of all places. I could only assume it was adolescent rebellion on her part. "I don't care what they like," I said, exasperated. "It's your right, and I pay a lot of money for you to go there, so they can get stuffed. Carry a fucking gun."

"Yes, sir," she said. That told me she believed that I believed what I was telling her.

"Good," I said. "Don't be nice, either. If someone makes a move on you, shoot. Don't give them first-aid if wounded, just keep shooting until you get the head. Then get it again. You've got court legal cause to be afraid. This type of asshole is especially dangerous if wounded."

"Ripper?" she asked.

"About that mean," I nodded. "A ripper is slightly faster. Slightly. But this guy and his cohorts are much smarter and much trickier."

She said, "So you're going to kill someone?" She looked really bothered and trembly.

I sighed. Dammit.

"Yes. I am. I can't tell you why and you need to forget it, but a lot of people's lives are riding on it and I have some specific skills, so does Silver. I shouldn't even say this much, and you're at risk if you ever mention it. Remember what I said we were doing?"

She's a decent actress. She clouded up and said, "You're taking that hatchet-faced slut on a vacation and didn't invite me. I guess I'm glad you're dating, but you could have some class. Maybe getting over it will let you find someone worthwhile."

"Good," I agreed. It was good. The way she delivered it, I not only believed it, I felt contempt for this asshole father of hers.

"Now, let me tell you a few more things," I said. She nodded. "First, hit me. Full contact punch."

She studied me for a moment, then tossed a creditable sunfist.

I wasn't there. "Again," I said. She punched once more with a parallel kick. I slipped past the punch, and instead of deflecting her leg aside, I got my hand underneath and followed the motion through and up, taking her foot with it and up past two meters. She went down, slapped the ground to break her fall—good form, I was proud of her—and tried to sit up.

Her eyes were very wide when she saw the Merrill growing out of my fist. The muzzle was against her nose. That got her attention, and I panned it down, following her throat then to center of mass, just under her breastbone. "I'm not Boosted," I told her. "You've never seen me all out. Until last week. Now, imagine me Boosted. Imagine me just this fast, from behind. You're dead." Helping her to her feet I said, "You did well. Have a seat.

"You're young, flexible, smart, well-trained and a very

good girl," I told her. She smiled just slightly and I said, "And that means shit in a fight. Fights go to the mean ones who don't stop. That's me and my target. Fights go to those who expect to get hurt and don't care. Who have years of experience killing people. Who are tired and cynical and lumber through like a stumblebeast, not like a leopard or ripper. You're graceful and strong and any normal attacker is going to find you more than he wants to screw with. But he or I could kill you and barely notice."

She was looking put upon. "So why'd you train me?" she asked.

"Same reason I keep weapons, fire extinguishers, insurance, first-aid kits and tools. You can't fix everything. You can't stop everything. But you're better off with a chance. And your chance with this guy means shoot first, shoot second, reload and shoot some more. Distance is your friend, and remember he may dodge when closing. Kung Fu is great, batons are great, and none of it will matter if a vicious guy who can press your mass with one hand gets hold of you. The gun might not even matter. But it's better than anything else, because it only takes the strength of one finger, and can be done from underneath in a clinch. So says the old guy with five unarmed kills and several hundred deadly shots."

She was really looking scared now, as I'd never discussed my past with her in any detail. "You really mean it," she said.

"I do," I nodded. "And the alarms will be active, as will the traps. So let your boyfriend in through the front and don't sneak him through the window."

She flushed red at that. "How'd you know?" she asked. "I thought we were quiet?"

I tried not to smile. I really did. It was a weak, sickly smile, because this was my little girl and I'm psychopathically protective. Maybe too much Earth "morality" soaked in. I knew she took sex training in school. I knew every boy and girl she'd dated because I'm a paranoid asshole. She had a sex life, but I wanted to pretend it didn't exist. Stupid, I know. "No one is that quiet in the throes of passion. And I'm not stupid, and footprints on the deck are easy to decipher. So bring him through the front."

She nodded, swallowed, and said, "I thought you didn't like him?"

"Not really," I said. "He's a punk. But you won't stop seeing him if I tell you to, you're old enough to make that mistake on your own and learn from it, and frankly, he's irrelevant to the real problems I'm facing"

"You'll sleep in my room," I said, "because it's harder to get into from outside. That won't stop them, but it might slow them down. And I bought that fifteen-millimeter Armtech riot gun. Keep it by the bed, and take it with you when driving." As her face reacted I said, "Yes, I'm leaving you the van. And Andre will be watching, so no stupid stuff. You can get spread in the back if you really want to, but it's not as comfortable as a bed."

"I know," she said, smiling. She said it just to throw me off guard. Not an image I wanted. But hey, I'd taken the conversation there.

"Will you screen messages?" she asked.

I winced. "Probably not." She looked confused and upset and once again she was my little girl. "Outsystem calls are monitored most places. And there's few enough of them relatively that they're easy to trace. Very basic traffic analysis will narrow it down to only calls to the Iota Persei system, and any suspicions will be proven with my pic. So I won't. Sorry. Andre's here if you need any help, and here," I said. I handed over the flashcard. "That's Marshal Naumann's ten-div-a-day emergency number. It's wired into his skull. Don't call if you don't have to, but do if you have *any* confirmable fears. 'Is that bad enough to call about?' is a confirmable fear.

"So call if you need to, but not if you don't, but don't hesitate and don't abuse it," I said with a grin. "Because one hundred seconds after you call that number, there will be a Black Ops counterterror squad and three battalions of Blazers and Mob surrounding the building. Memorize it and keep the card. He'll stop by with other information, including a bailout plan, in a couple of days. Now let's look at the Armtech."

She followed me through to my room. I keep the weapons on a rack in the closet, where I can get to them in a hurry. I have the basic five everyone should have, plus three—now four—more for her. I have my Merrill pistol, a last generation M-5 rifle I bought surplus, subcaliber rimfire practice versions of each and a twenty-millimeter Pendleton riot gun, police spec. To her Little Weasel I'd added an Alesis carbine, not as massive as the M-5 but decent for a military engagement (and we were invaded by Earth not ten years ago, so don't give me that "it can't happen here" crap. Arm your adolescents. We may need them again.) and she had a little Merrill that would do the job and fit inside her clothes without bulking up. Now she had a fifteen-millimeter Armtech.

I slipped it off the rack, inspected the already open

chamber and handed it over. She took it, inspected the chamber and dropped the bolt. It was a bit large for her, but manageable. "It's a double-roller blowback with a gas piston shock absorber," I told her. "But it will still kick. Take it to school tomorrow and go practice afterwards. Do a test range with it this weekend." I handed her two boxes of ammo to supplement the ten rounds in it and the two magazines clipped to the butt and receiver. It was a bulky weapon, but the best thing for her to have at any range practical. "And the ammo in your pistol is at least six months old," I told her. "Shoot it out after you buy some fresh."

"Yes, Dad," she agreed. She felt a bit reassured with the riot gun in hand. I'd really scared her.

I hoped I'd done so for nothing.

⦿ CHAPTER 4 ⦿

WE BOARDED THE SHUTTLE without trouble, because there is never any trouble on a Grainne launch. We had tickets; they let us aboard.

I actually felt a little nervous. It had been ten long years since I did this, and that was leaving a desolated Earth. Before that, it had been my trip to Earth. None of that was conducive to pleasant memories.

I'm not claustrophobic, but I felt confined. I actually appreciated Silver's presence.

That seemed to be the other part. I was back in "military" mode and operating without orders, support of a chain, or with any backup besides her. So the two of us were our element. Everyone else was an outsider.

I guess my brain shut off. We talked about something, I zoned out staring at couchbacks, then we docked at Vista Station.

We had regular luggage, and some well-concealed gadgets that no Customs flunky should be able to identify.

We had several shipments going to mail drops, and to our embassies, which would take some wiggling to get hold of. We had our wits for making more, and a lot of cash.

I elected to do Customs at this end, because I figured they'd be less suspicious of someone asking to be inspected.

It was straightforward enough, but there was an element of nerves. We were officially in Caledonian space by electing to do this, and any discrepancies would end our trip right now.

The inspector was Indian in ancestry, with slicked black hair. Fit enough generally, dour and bored. He spent some time scrutinizing our ID and passports, which were from FreeBank. I made sure to look relaxed and keep a hand around Silver's shoulder.

"You seem a little nervous," he said to her.

"First time out," she muttered weakly.

"Ah. Well, there's nothing to worry about." He smiled and waved us through.

He didn't check the bags. He accepted our medical and immunization declaration, which was valid but under fake names. That meant Randall could have done the same.

Once in our small stateroom aboard the *Princess Caroline*—double bed that folded down from the wall, workdesk likewise, closet recessed around lavatory, commode and shower stalls—she untensed and sighed.

I met her eyes and said, "Yeah, you have to be less nervous when we arrive, and for future trips. Especially arrivals."

"I know," she said. "I wasn't really afraid of being detained, but of blowing the mission."

She unfolded the bed and sat down with another exhaled sigh.

"That's fine," I said. "Everyone takes a bit to get used to it. Remember this is the easy part. The worst that happens is a Caledonian jail, and we get bailed out. They're nice enough people, and civilized. More likely, there's some kind of meeting, we look clueless, bumbling and apologetic, and off we go, to acquire more hardware later.

"When and if we get to other systems, it's a case of bribes working, or invoking threats to higher ups. But we're the offense here. We don't apologize and we don't shrink back, unless it's a deliberate act."

"Got it," she nodded. Then she smiled. "I think I'll be fine after the first round."

We were in that cabin for most of seven days out and six days in to Caledonia. She couldn't find any vid she liked. There were some I might watch, but I couldn't concentrate. We didn't want to do too much interaction with other passengers, so meals were about the only time we left. It was cleaned daily, neat, smelled faintly of flowers and with a touch of ozone for clarity. The staff really did try, but it wasn't enough.

I'm a loner, didn't have any privacy, and I couldn't think of a diplomatic way of saying, "Can you leave for a half-div while I stroke off?" A shipboard shower stall is neither romantic nor comfortable. Her flipping channels got on my nerves. Me fuming in silence got on hers. She had an annoying habit of taking forever in the shower, when I needed to get clean, get off and get to sleep.

Which is all part of traveling with someone, especially

other troops, and something you learn to cope with. I just hadn't had to in a long time.

I did find it soothing to have a warm back against mine at night. Human companionship was something I always lacked.

The meals managed to be adequate without being either too institutional or flashy. I was impressed. Ships are usually one or the other. The housekeepers were agreeable to our request to come at dinner time, when we had everything secured. I didn't want them wandering in otherwise.

I also had to put in long divs researching. Randall was in the Caledonia system. Great. Who was the target? We had nothing concrete.

I made a list starting with the Queen and other Royals and working down.

I ruled out the Royals. The only group that would target them was the decades old, increasingly pathetic Common People's Action Group. They didn't have the money, and they'd never hire an "elitist" to do their killing. That, and my team had slaughtered them in a previous engagement. There were others who didn't like the monarchy, but they all realized it was politically and promotionally bad to target them, because the Caledonians overwhelmingly loved their Royals. That was the basis of their colony, now nation, after their parent Earth culture got rid of its royalty in one of the UN treaties.

I supposed it was possible that someone with enough money hired him to settle some petty score against an underling, but there were too many tens of thousands of possibilities to consider that.

In between were a few hundred notable business and political people who might be significant enough. I gridded them and managed to eliminate a few who were either too old, too meaningless or too noncontentious to matter.

That took most of a week. I'd have to spend the next week doing the heavy thinking on the rest. Also, there were some in from outsystem. I had to cut the ones who were definitely short notice, or strictly transient, or had made plans after the DNA intel date. Again, targets of opportunity were possible, but I had to stick to predictable strategic targets.

Right before we hit jump point, I did screen a message to Chel.

"Hey, kid. I'm about to leave system, but I am going to say goodbye. I'll have updates relayed to you, and I'll get back as soon as I can. Miss you. A lot. Be good. Love you."

I just had a lingering fear that this would be the last she saw of me. So I had to send something.

Silver and I reached a détente the second week. She watched vid in the passenger lounge and turned down occasional passes. In the stateroom, I gave her a half div to send coded posts to a repeater back insystem that updated her social pages and noted she was doing a remote training course in the Hinterlands and would be out of contact for a while. She kept the screen turned away and used earbuds while she cruised and hopped whatever nodes she wasted time on. I spent that time staring at the ceiling above the bed trying to parse the chart I'd printed and had lying on my chest. Or, I went into the shower and pretended to be alone. Then she took her ridiculously long showers (okay, but she started it) and I did my nightly random node hop for mental relaxation.

Then we went to bed and I pretended I was only pretending to be interested in this woman in such a way people would think I really was, with her warm back against mine. I hadn't had a bed partner in years, and that had been my then-little girl. The last adult partner was even more years.

During the days, I took a few more potentials off the list here and there. Some were definitely not targets. Either removing them would put someone more potentially dangerous in place, or destabilize something. While I was sure Randall could do multiple hits, his MO was one, then move. Rushing to get multiples would be risky. Of course, he might elect to start doing that. He hadn't so far, though. Some I deleted on gut feeling. They were potent and had enemies, but had enough friends that killing them would generate support for them and ill will for any competitor trying to benefit after the fact.

By three days out I narrowed it down to one hundred twenty-six people who might be worth killing for enough money, and who might have enemies with that kind of money.

I leaned back, sighed and rubbed my eyes.

"Dan," she said.

I stretched and looked over. We were traveling as Dan and Cynthia Charles.

"Can I offer some advice?"

"Please," I said.

"You've been alone for a decade. It shows. You're

instantly edgy around anyone else, and can't share. You also can't express yourself."

"Probably," I agreed. I'd been expecting commentary on my list. Not on that.

"This is a nice ship, and it's culturally Freehold, not just a flag of convenience."

"Right. And?"

"Go spread someone," she said.

I blinked.

"You need company, and you need to unwind. Go to the spa, take a div, and get your head back on a bit straighter."

I almost blushed. Not because I was embarrassed. I was embarrassed not to have thought of it. Also, that I was so obviously having trouble with people.

"Keep the advice coming," I said.

Yeah, that was a good idea. I got away from her, which was good for all kinds of reasons, and I got some physical sensations and synaptic rushes that really did help.

The spa had real leafy plants, wood veneers and scented air with attractive people in tasteful form-fitting clothes and elegant accessories. It offered everything from plunge to massage to fairly exotic sex. All I needed was human companionship, and that was easy enough.

I feel guilty about one thing. Bjirka, as she was known professionally, seemed to have a pretty good time herself. I wasn't sure if it was real or an act; either was possible. However, I kicked in Boost and three segs later I knew it wasn't an act. Every muscle in her body cramped and spasmed and her grin was still a meter wide when I left. They'd counted our doses on active duty, so we never got to try that. Physically, I got a bit more thrill from it. Psychologically, it was very satisfying. As they say in show business, always leave them wanting more. She was pretty much annihilated.

The part I felt guilty about was that I'd picked her because she looked a bit like Silver. It was a grudge fuck by proxy.

I felt even more guilty when I got back to find Silver had ruled out three more possible targets.

However, I was able to sleep better, and I was more relaxed. Actual human contact is necessary to mental well-being.

The jump between systems was as disorienting as I remembered, and I was out of practice. My reflexes and coordination were shot, and I had trouble even standing. A nap straightened me out, but it was annoying. Silver had no significant problems.

A few potential targets left system during our transfer. We crossed those off. One other came home. One made a large charitable contribution, which didn't take him off the list, but did make him someone to consider separately. A generous martyr taken out of the way could be used for a pity option for further fundraising. That had been done politically in one very high-profile case a couple of centuries earlier. I expect it had been done more than once.

I availed myself of the spa once more before we reached orbit. Once down I'd have no such options. Silver and I were a married couple, and we needed to be a boring, unremarkable married couple. Visiting brothels, no matter how classy, would stand out in the oddly conservative culture of Caledonia. They're modern and casual about sex in general, but marriage is very important. There wouldn't be any stigma, being offworlders, but it would still be commented on. Discretion was great cover.

We transferred to their insystem shuttle. Very nice. The couches were comfortable, padded for extra support, and the services were all voice or touch controlled. It was a brand new Lola Aerospace AtmoSurf 5, in pale blue and white. There was no skywhip, which is part of why they use the Surfers. We went down in a series of graceful, dipping glides, a couple of sharp skilike turns, and a long, screaming approach. It was slower, but more interesting than a skywhip insertion.

Rollout was the same, and with the new port expansion we didn't have to wait for docking. We unsnapped, shimmied out of those amazing couches, laughing softly at how awkward that was, stretched, and joined the debarkation line.

Surface gravity is 1.05, slightly lower than ours. The air was thicker even than Earth's, but with comparable O_2. It's quite a nice planet, and I'd enjoyed my stint here with the embassy a lot. I knew a bit of my way around the general map of the capital. The adjusted twenty-three-hour Earth day was short for me, but we'd be on an odd schedule as mission dictated anyway.

Once out, we grabbed bags, caught a "limo" that was an oversized van, ground only, and checked in at the New Raffles. A bellman in uniform took our bags and buzzed the door faster than we could get out.

"Good morning, Mr. and Mrs. Charles. How was your trip?"

"Long," I replied. "Is there a package for us?"

"Yes, a bag arrived for you. I'll have it sent up."

"Thank you."

The elevator was fast, the luggage awaited, the view was good and offered a clear field of fire across the city center.

I slipped the bellman enough bill to make him happy without being flamboyant, and he closed the door on his way out.

I felt better already. I had more space, a spare bed if I didn't like sharing, and the bag was from the embassy, and should contain some weapons. It wasn't marked from the embassy, of course. It was marked from a safehouse used for the purpose.

I popped it open, rooted through the packing, and found a nice concealable pistol and some supplemental tools.

Silver already had a secure link up, and was pulling an encoded intel update.

"He's still here, as far as we know," she said. "Faint DNA traces, and I have a map."

"Excellent. Those will hopefully include stalk sights and recon OPs he's using. We can narrow this down."

We ordered food in. Their version of Chinese is not bad, though unlike anything on Earth or Grainne. I scanned maps while shoveling food.

The geography of Randall's positions put him definitely near and in the capital. There were no concrete scans elsewhere, and the probability on those there was low. They were also unpatterned. So he was in the capital for now. He'd been here close to twenty days or more.

Based on his existing MO, I expected him to target someone within fifteen days.

That radius and timeframe, even with some leeway on both for coverage, put us down to seventeen possible targets.

There were two of us.

It was time to earn our pay.

☸ CHAPTER 5 ☸

I SHORTLY HAD A QUANDARY on our targets.

Ten of them were going to be attending a major industry forum at the Parliament Hall. There'd be security all over the place, government, private, everything.

Now, it was possible that the forum was a useful distraction for him while he went after a target elsewhere. However, it was also possible he planned to wade right in for a target at the forum, and use the intermeshing security as a cover, and rely on them to get mixed up for additional distraction.

The good news was the ten at the conference were much easier to track, and for some matters could be considered one target. So we were down to eight.

Silver reported, "Masterson is going out to the mountains for a week."

"He was never a strong chance anyway," I said. "But we can pull him off the list for the week and add him back in if we need to."

Seven.

Three of the six individuals had solid, consistent patterns and whereabouts at present. That was a bad idea from a security point of view, but indicated they didn't feel threatened. A secondary input, but worthwhile. It also meant I could rule them out. None of the traces we found were anywhere near their routes.

So, three individuals, one group.

I was betting on the group.

For one thing, the odds did favor it being one of them, from a straight statistical analysis. There was no strategic calculus I could use at this point; it was not a military matter.

It fit, though, with the training and mindset I'd used. I'd taught him everything he knew to that point, and there was little he could pick up elsewhere that would be comparable. My plans, training and doctrine colored his.

Hell, mine were what everyone in the galaxy was going to use until something even more brutal came along. I should be proud of my legacy.

If it were me, I'd hit the conference. Lots of distractions. So much muscle in one location would make people lazy. They'd worry about protesters, press and commercial spies. They wouldn't be looking for an assassin. It would send an object lesson to others, that nowhere was safe. It would allow peers to witness the matter, which would have psychological impact for any future threats, offers or other negotiations.

Lastly, it took serious balls and was a way to show off. That was something we knew about his personality before we deployed. He had to fight hard to keep subordinate and invisible, even when we were building our personae on Earth.

He was going to hit the conference. He was going to be very methodical and high tech, and he was going to laugh at them while he did so.

Silver had been working with me all along, with the scans, the mapping and other details. Now I needed her expertise on gear to determine how this would go down.

"So, if he's going into the conference, where is he going to hit them and what is he going to use?"

She stared for a moment, made a gesture for "wait," and turned to her system.

I sat patiently. She pulled up maps, blueprints, floor plans, seating charts, ran them in different pans and layouts. I'd let her have the desk. I had the bed. I liked being able to sprawl, though it was hard on the shoulders, eventually.

At last, she said, "It comes down to three probable methods. Please check me."

"Go ahead," I said.

"He can hit them on arrival or departure, but there will be a lot of crowding. He can hit them while they're seated in the auditorium, but that increases the likelihood of either collateral damage, or a miss because of a collateral in the way. Or he can hit them during their presentation at the podium."

"That's when he'll do it," I agreed. "It's the easiest and most dramatic. Everything he wants. A separate, visible target and easy to exfil after the fact. So let's figure out how."

She said, "You tell me, how hard would it be to get a rifle in there?"

By "rifle" she meant any weapon to conduct a shot with. I'd probably use a long-sight radius pistol myself.

"I expect they're going to have scanners dialed up. Whole weapons, components, anything questionable. In this case, the security are professionals and will be harder to fool."

"What else might you use?"

"Explosive. Again, easy to detect most of them by vapor."

"And he's never had a collateral, nor used explosive in close quarters." His MO was gadgets.

"Chameleon suit," she said, pointing at the screen.

I looked over. A previous victim had been killed in semipublic, smashed into a tree and the ground, and no one had seen anything.

"Are modern suits that good?" I asked.

"I can't find you a node because they're still heavily classified, but yes."

"Damn. What do I need to know?"

She stretched back in the real leather chair, showing nice lines, and said, "Well, the current ones are spectrally near perfect. They're also thermally near perfect if you're willing to seal one up. Of course, there's limited wear time in that case. If he has a small oxy bottle, he can probably manage twenty segs or so. Call it half-an-hour in Earth or adjusted Caledonian time."

That was disturbing.

I said, "Okay, let's look at this. He gets in early when security is lax, finds a cubby hole, waits them out. He could even have press or maintenance ID, and have access to some areas, including restrooms and food. When it's time, he throws on the suit, walks across the stage, shoots or nails someone up close, then sprints in the confusion."

"They'll see distortion at that point," she said.

"Yes. I wouldn't do it. I'd go for a shot. I'm a better marksman, though."

"He's not up to standard?"

"He was one of my backfills. Never had the full pipeline of training. I just focused them on the espionage aspects, not the combat."

"Ah."

I flipped the file in my mind. "He shot low Master. I shot perfect every year."

"Perfect?" She looked stunned.

"Yeah, it's one of the things I'm good at."

"I'm impressed. Is that common?"

"No, not even among our unit. We were expected to make Expert, and they preferred Master."

She shrugged. "Marksman will have to do me."

"That's better than most, and better than almost any other military."

"Thank you," she said.

"Am I right, though?" I asked, ignoring the compliment exchange. "I don't want to plan for something and be wrong."

"We're guessing," she admitted. "It's a good guess, though. Scents point to location. MO points to method."

"Right, so let's assume we're wrong and plan a backup." Of course, that backup would have to assume this was the right place. We couldn't cover two at once.

I wished I had an entire platoon now. Of course, an

entire platoon, even of Operatives, left a deployment signature that could be traced. For this, it had to be me.

"Poison?" she suggested. "Tagged binary neural toxins, one before, one on location."

"Do you know how to do that?"

"No. I'm theorizing."

"Research it."

"Looking." She used hands and mic and queried quickly. I wondered how traceable these searches were to the Caledonian Intelligence Service, and if there were moles in there. I was paranoid, but was I paranoid enough?

"Possible," she said. "Expensive. Would take a professional lab, nothing you could do in a home shop. It would definitely make people wonder."

"Not that, then. He likes to do things himself." Or at least he did a decade before. "Okay," I decided, "we assume the chameleon. If he goes for a shot, I chase him down. If he tries anything else, I chase him down. It doesn't matter if they arrest me after I shatter his spine. As long as I maim him, we're good."

"That makes sense," she said. She looked disturbed.

"Yeah, we're going to kill him, and it's not going to be a fair fight."

"I know," she agreed soberly. "It's not just that it's unfair. He's a hero, really."

"A broken one," I agreed. "Think of him as an abused pet turned vicious."

"I'd rather think of how to deal with a chameleon," she said. "The best method would be sonar or laser detection. I assume they'd notice that and neutralize us instead. So we use mics to determine he's moving, then blow dust through the ventilation system, or scatter something on the ground. He'll leave footprints or a swept area. Ionized dust will stick and degrade the screens. After that, anything directed at him—dust, pellets, that will bounce or shadow him."

"I like the dust. We have two local days to prepare it and sneak it into that ventilation system, hide it so they can't see it, exfiltrate, fake some kind of ID to get us back inside, and get near the podium."

"You don't want much." She looked a bit put upon.

"I trust you to do the job." I did.

"Thanks . . . sir."

"Can we triangulate with mics?"

"Easily. But you can't see the sound."

"Can we put directional indicators in a pair of glasses and hook it to earbuds? There's enough press around no one should notice the gear."

"I could. I can't do that in the allotted time."

I nodded. "And I want them to see him, too. That hinders his escape. Hopefully."

"Will do," she agreed as she grabbed shoes and a touristy backpack. She was out the door with a wad of cash in seconds, leaving me to figure infil, exfil and cover.

Eight hours later, we both looked dreadful. Greasy hair, dust, grime, general dirt. We were at the back gate to the convention center across from the Parliament Annex, with a backpack full of nastiness. It was early autumn and quite comfortable in the temperate coastal zone. Humans do try to pick comfortable environments when possible.

My earlier recon had revealed what I thought I could use. The gates were designed to stop traffic. Patrols and fences were to stop pedestrians. There were gaps we could get through. I surmised they relied on regular patrols to keep homeless out, but we weren't going to be homeless. Silver had fabricated us two generic ID badges. Staff often appeared in the back of technical photos or candid shots, and the blowups were good enough for placement of bar code and picture. No one ever actually looks at an ID up close anyway. Not the kind on menials.

Getting into the grounds wasn't hard. We lurked near a pedestrian gate with nicotine inhalers charged with scented water only, and made a point of waiting in shadows out of view of the entrance. It wasn't long before someone else came out. He was another menial of some kind, and he already had inhaler in hand as he reached the gate.

I said, ". . . but I guess we need to get back to work. We've been out too long."

"Okay," she said.

I nodded at him and grabbed the open gate as he nodded back, and waved my ID in the general direction of the scanner, but not close enough to actually trigger it yea or nay.

I nudged her, we grabbed two rolling grease dumpsters and headed toward the refuse dock. I whipped out a trash bag from a pocket, she slid the backpack in and it went into the slimy filth in the tub.

At the door, I spent five minutes running the fake ID over the scanner, wiping it off, scanning it, bending it, scanning it again. I kept a dopy expression on my face. She managed to do the same, but I could feel the tremors of nerves through the air. She still needed practice in this.

Eventually, someone walked by inside, saw the

movement and opened the door. I looked stupid, and in a slow monotone said, "It's no workin'."

"Do you know where to get it replaced?" He was security of the generic type. Older, probably retired. Merely a uniform, badge and scanner to provide official color.

"No," I said, keeping to my cover.

"Pass and ID office is in the front foyer on the mezzanine half, left side, through the glass doors. They open at eight a.m."

I stared blankly, then nodded slowly.

The man sighed and moved on, muttering about "'tards."

We started to park the dumpster and he called back, "Hey!"

"Whu?" I said, hoping it was nothing serious.

"Why'n't you use her card next time?"

"Oh."

He sighed and kept walking.

Once he was out of sight, Silver pulled the pack from the protective plastic. It was still mostly clean. I led the way, having memorized the map.

We went upstairs on padded feet. I shimmed a mainte-nance door; she picked a secured padlock in ninety seconds flat with a rake, tension wrench and magnetic coder, then we were in the far upper mezzanine where the ventilation systems were. I checked by eye and number. That one there.

Silver trembled after crossing the catwalk. Heights were definitely not her thing. She didn't hesitate, though. Good troop.

We pulled a cover quickly, used a foam block to stop it slamming, then fastened the dust dispenser to the inside wall, up out of reach. Rather, she did that, showing long, sinuous curves through the filthy coverall. The device was a drum with a radio-triggered servo. The drum looked like an antiseptic dispenser. It had fake wires that led to an area near one of the outside boxes, where she cut them and jammed them into the insulation so they'd look deliberate. A drop of cement to hold them, and we closed up carefully to avoid any loud noises. The dust was mildly antiseptic and harmless, so even if it was discovered, there was a good chance it would be left alone. Its purpose wouldn't be apparent to anyone.

We skinned out of the coveralls to regular clothes, a bit sweaty, and wiped the fake grease from our hair, until it turned back into styling gel. A flip of her comb and a wipe of our faces and we were normal staff. The badges went on our pockets. The pack and coveralls went into a fresh trash receptacle for some real menial to dispose of after a few liters of real trash found their way atop. Silver kept a handful of tools in an apron and pockets, and we went about hiding a spare transmitter, in case we couldn't get our main one in.

Then we slipped out the back, faking punching out on the time scanner en route, and wove back out onto the street. It was cooler by then, but not bad.

She grabbed another small pack from a deep shadow under a bush. A quick trip into a chippy for a laborer's snack and the bathrooms, where we put on clean shirts more appropriate to our tourist status, and took a ricktaxi back to the hotel, munching fish and chips as we went.

Their local whiting is so-so. It probably has to do with both the environment in general, and the lower and different brine concentration of their oceans, than Earth's.

I cleaned up and went to bed, running through mental practice for the upcoming face-to-face. I was interrupted a few segs later by cool, damp, firm breasts against my spine.

"Uh . . ." I mumbled and woke up.

"Sorry. I'm very unnerved. I need to hold something to calm down."

I had suggestions on what she could hold, and dammit, I was not going there.

I gave her five segs. I could feel her heart pounding, slowing, reaching normal, and her warmth against me. When she seemed better and I couldn't take any more, I gently detached, rolled out, climbed into the other bed, and said, "I need to sleep alone or I won't be rested."

It was literally and figuratively true.

Tomorrow I might kill a friend.

◈ CHAPTER 6 ◈

THE TECHNICAL OFFICE, at the Freehold embassy accepted Silver's request. Of course, it's not actually called the technical office. It's not called anything and doesn't exist. But, to her request, additional ID was produced, and we assumed identities as university analysts.

"They're not happy," she said.

"Oh?"

"They had a couple of people tagged for this. My mission code bumped them. They were going to be doing bona fide espionage."

"Well, I understand that. Did you apologize?"

"As much as I could through code groups," she said.

Appropriately dressed in local suits complete to a tie for me and a ruff for her, with a camera case and well-maintained and well-worn gear she'd picked up for it, we showed our ID thrice, were scanned and inspected and allowed in to the convention auditorium with several thousand of our closest friends. The security was definitely above average. The inspections were reasonably complete given the time frame. Of course, Randall could have been inside for days already, with a rifle. We were betting on the up-close touch though.

We were early, and found seats only three rows back from the rope. The rope was over a stun barricade, and was twenty meters from the platform. The platform had a stunstrip along the edge. Capital Police patrolled both edges. I wondered if they had tanglers in the gap in between. Possibly not. It was sculpted and colored carpet with the summit and sponser logos. Behind us, the seats curved back and up in blocks with broad flat aisles for access.

I settled back. Silver wandered away with portable gear, shooting shots and pretending to cover the event and attendees. That wasn't really what our passes were for, but no one mentioned anything. Once in the hall, we were assumed clean. This would also apply to Randall, if he'd found some way to spoof any finance-sector ID, which wouldn't be too hard.

It was probably going to be a very long day. The ten targets would all be in this hall, all on that stage, sometime in an eight-hour span starting in two hours. They'd be other places, too, but crowded hallways were unlikely. He might target them out of their vehicles, but that meant either a long-range shot, or risking being seen up close. I might do that. He wouldn't.

It was the typical convention. Shuffling in seats led to expectant silence led to presenter with leading joke, introduction of the man who needs no introduction, who stepped up and made leading joke, commented on important issues of the day facing the finance information sector, followed by introduction of the first speaker.

Ms. Cape took the podium, waved over her display, and brought up charts. She was a very good speaker, and I would have been fascinated if I could have followed more of it. I got the parts about M1 through M4 money sources. I understood inflation, deflation, purchase and sale of debt. After that, she was speaking Ancient Mesopotamian.

She talked for an hour. I'm sure it was all fascinating, but I had to pretend to be attentive, run my recorder, occasionally pan the crowd, while keeping an eye out for a threat that might not be there and could be invisible if it was.

So I played it as a journalist. I tagged the high points of her speech, summarized on a pad, noted the audience attention and response. That let me get into intel mode and study it by traffic analysis, cryptologic assessment, and such.

She concluded, there was a brief break, and I clicked my phone.

"Spell me at breaks," I said.

"Observing now," she replied. Good.

Breaks were good times for him to maneuver, with all the confusion. He'd have to avoid crowds, but the noise and movement would cover him, and if he wasn't in the chameleon, it would handily fit in a large doccase.

I let my brain reboot, hurried to the restroom with a legion of others, bought a hit of oxygen from a kiosk, then hurried back. I resumed my position, called Silver and said, "Back."

"My turn," she said.

The schedule was well-planned. Most were back in seats, or at tables, or up in el-boxes when the second presenter came up. I watched more intently. Mr. Rothman was one of my more likely targets.

He was also dry as stale toast.

He read in a monotone, flashing graphs with a remote, with little liveliness or presence. He could almost have been a hologram. He might be one of the most brilliant bankers in space, but he was not good at public presentation.

He was certainly important, though. All eyes were on him, and all kinds of notes and murmurs ran through the crowd. They stayed quiet, but never stopped. Whatever he had to say kept their attention. So I watched the curtained wings, the arching, scaffolded overhead, the gallery above and behind where more recorders and the lesser media loitered. It was a sleekly modern facility when seen from this side, though the working bowels were somewhat less impressive.

I was almost busted when the man next to me asked, "What do you think about that notion on logarithmic easing at inverse interest?"

"I'm just trying to get it all down at the moment, so I can follow up later," I said.

He was bursting with excitement and wanted to talk further, but I shushed him with a gesture, made a quizzical face, scrawled a note, and checked my gear. He took the hint.

It was a tiring task, pretending to be fascinated by something I couldn't parse, while trying to be a spy not looking like a spy.

Was that a faint shimmer on the stage? It might be. It might also just be airflow across the curtain. It was hard to tell at this distance. Nor did the video tanks show anything. They were zoomed in on Rothman.

I could get a little closer. I'd have to judge the time on this, because I'd have to go through his own guards to pull it off. There really wasn't any way of keeping discreet after this. Direct intervention meant the masks were off.

I considered again waiting until the exfiltration phase, but that meant the bait would be dead, and his own security milling about. If I pursued at that point, I'd lose lead, still risk public visibility. No advantage.

But I didn't know if Randall definitely intended to do this. Once I committed, I'd lose the lead.

This was the problem with aging. I knew the odds and didn't like them. At fifteen, they'd been a challenge. At twenty-eight, they were chains.

That shimmer was definitely closer, definitely not airflow, and this was a good time. I hit the button and nothing happened.

Of course he would have a damping field set up. I couldn't trigger it from here. Or hell, it could be a security protocol in the hall.

All I could do was try to slip in and wrestle with a ghost.

Silver was very good. She realized I was moving, deduced why, and keyed something manually into her pad.

The air turned hazy with powder, and there was most definitely an outline there. Definite to me. Everyone else looked up at the vents. Every one of Rothman's security detail. They were unreactive for over a second and I took marks off.

The shift turned into an outline swishing through the dust. He was slowed because he had to carefully maneuver around gawking people who couldn't see him.

The security detail reacted at last, closing in on the minister and shuffling quickly offstage, as masks came out. This clearly hadn't been in Randall's plan, and he hesitated. By then I was near the stage.

The press were in a mob to get photos of the spewing dust and the choreographed movement. I bounced on a chair, onto a cop's shoulder and then to the stage. Lacking time for pleasantries, I jumped again and tried to hit Randall with a flying kick.

Tried to. By then, he was paying attention and dodged. As I passed by, he struck me in the calf, a blow that paralyzed the muscle but not the nerves. Jagged jolts of pain ripped through it. Between that and the swirling white dust, I was at a huge disadvantage.

The security detail turned to me, still not seeing him, and the press shouted and pointed because their cameras could see the distortion. There was obvious hesitation and trepidation about the crazy man fighting the ghost, but momentarily, the guards figured out what was going on. Half rushed the minister out. The other half came at me and Randall. Having no idea who was on the dance card, I was sure they meant to take us both.

But in the meantime, I was busy trying to stay alive and get the upper hand.

I had him right where he wanted me. If he couldn't take this target, he could take me instead. That would be an object lesson right back the other way—the best Naumann had had failed. Why don't you just leave me alone?

I was the better martial artist. He was near invisible. I'd trained for a lot of contingencies, but not that.

Then a blade came out of a rip in the open air, right in front of me.

I figured where the arm was, caught it and the mimetic material protested in spectral waves along his forearm. He tried to wiggle the blade toward my wrist, but I had the elbow, heaved, jabbed, and his own hand and knife cut the suit and caught something underneath. He grunted, and now there were two small apertures in clear air. I felt heat rush from them, and could smell the body inside. It was him.

He managed to kick me off, literally, with a heavy boot to the ribs. I never saw it, nor felt the wind up. Good kick, the bastard. I curled up with lances of pain reaching from my side to my balls and my head, my kidneys, and cramping down my thigh. He did the smart thing and ran.

I collapsed around my ribs, wheezing in agony. That hadn't worked. I'd saved Rothman's life, but that was less important than stopping Randall.

The guards then swarmed me.

Of course, they had no idea what had happened, other than I'd tangled up with someone in a chameleon. They were wisely not going to assume I was a good Samaritan, or that it was anything other than the two of us brawling. Their principal was safe and surrounded, I was down, the other fleeing and being pursued.

Silver did the right thing and stayed far away from me.

I made no move to resist when they stretched me and cuffed me, but I did utter some strange noises as my ribs grated. I was saved by a paramedic.

"Uncuff him, you bloody idiots. His ribs are broken."

They uncuffed me, but kept muzzles pointed at my face. They seemed reasonably well-trained, so I relaxed and did nothing to disturb them. The medic started working.

"Sir, where were you hit?"

"Kicked, toe, roundhouse, between fifth and sixth ribs, left line. I can feel them grinding."

"I need to put you on a backboard," he said.

"I understand," I agreed. There were three other medics now, and cameras all over the place despite the security barriers. Some were remote flyers, others just raised at high angles. I threw my right arm over my face, which was fine until they wanted to strap it down. I couldn't really protest without giving away that I had an identity to hide, which most certainly wouldn't fit with heroic intentions. I settled for eyes closed and slack jaw to look as little like the regular me as possible. The cervical support and forehead strap helped cover parts of my face.

I felt the splint inflate under and around me and set in place, then I was on a gurney, being wheeled out, and into an ambulance.

Okay, *this* was going to take work.

I really didn't want to be interviewed. Randall might have sources in the government, and I certainly couldn't have press getting clear photos of me. I was strapped to a backboard on a gurney, however, being wheeled into an ambulance.

It was crowded in the ambulance. The pneumatic splint plus gurney with all the monitors, plus the paramedic, plus a police officer cradling his stun baton just in case, made for no room.

I could conceivably escape the restraints. I could conceivably Boost enough to overcome the pain and disable these two, and the driver. It might result in a punctured lung, but that was manageable. The problem was, that would create a huge scene and make me a target.

The only thing to do was relax and wait. Once at a hospital, I'd have some resources and cause less of a scene, assuming I wasn't restrained to a bed. Would they consider me a flight risk? Probably. I would.

We twisted through streets easily. They had the advantage of remote control of traffic signals and lane clearance. The trip was comfortable enough apart from the knives being stirred and twisted in my side. With focus, I dulled the pain down to mere trauma rather than a sword on a jackhammer. It was an impressive kick I'd make the dogfucker pay for that.

The officer said, "Sir, I am directed to ask you for information on your activities."

I said nothing. I didn't think he'd try force in a moving ambulance with a medic at hand, but I was morally prepared for it if he did.

Nothing happened.

They rolled me into a hospital, and then into a secluded area. At least, being in a nicer area of the city, they didn't have an actual detention ward.

I didn't wait long, whether due to triage or police interest. They had the ID I'd been carrying, and it would read as valid without offering anything useful. I feigned disorientation and unconsciousness. I hoped that would work with all the monitors on me. To make it work, I focused on the throb to exclusion. It might limit my alphas.

I alerted slightly as I was rolled into an exam room. A doctor was waiting, southern Asian in ancestry, middle aged, good shape.

The doctor barely looked at me. "Ribs, no obvious sign of pneumothorax. Administer a neural block. We need to take care of that other case. Sir," he finally looked in my general direction, "there are accident victims we must treat ASAP. We'll be a little while getting to you, but you are in no danger."

I said, "I understand. Thank you." The cooperative angle would be my best defense at this point, and if I was in no immediate danger, I wanted them gone so I could depart.

I was still restrained, though, and there was a policeman in the chair next to me.

I couldn't think of an easy way to distract him, nor to wiggle out without alerting him. So I waited. Something would present itself shortly. I studied him with peripheral glances. Constable patrolman. Decent shape. Young. Quivers of eagerness. This was a low-skill tasking, but for an important suspect. He hoped for some small fallout for his career.

He didn't ask anything, likely because they wanted to have gear, professionals, and me in prime shape so nothing I said could be excluded. They were losing time, though. Perhaps they had traces on Randall? If so, we'd need to get that information, too.

The something I needed presented itself in about twenty minutes.

Silver walked into the room, in a suit.

She strode in, flipped open an ID folder, and said, "Jeanette Ash, Home Office. I need to interview this detainee, please."

She used just enough sergeant poise to make it work.

The young constable stiffened and I could see his perturbed expression as he stood.

"Uh, madam, I was—"

"It's fine," she said with a smile. "He's restrained, and injured. I just need a few minutes. I'd suggest tea and a sandwich. You'll be here for a while after I'm done."

That was hilarious. Indeed he would.

"Yes, thank you, madam," he said, as he hesitated, grabbed his coat, and left in a polite hurry.

As soon as he cleared the door, she hit buttons to secure it and opaque the screen.

She flipped open her doccase, tossed a suit coat and a lab coat on the bed with two other IDs, slapped a patch on my neck and started pulling restraints.

I gingerly turned and stood with some pain. Whatever she gave me worked fast. I reached for the coat and almost passed out.

She had to pull it up my left arm and help me shrug into it, then repeated that with the lab coat. She snapped the ID badge onto my pocket, and slipped another over her neck. According to those, she was an executive, I was a care nurse.

We slipped out the door, toward the rear of the building, and looked to make a clean escape. My leg wasn't as bad as my chest, but I had to force myself not to limp. We took an elevator down, then turned through another corridor. Everything was signed of course, and we could have asked for a guide light, but she seemed to have familiarized herself with the map.

It was quiet back here, with only occasional activity in side rooms, but a good cover never hurts. I played my role.

"I am concerned about the patient, though," I said. I took station on her right, because it was easier for me to face left, and she could protect my injured side.

"The family knows their options, and they are visiting regularly," she said.

"Yes, and good for them," I agreed.

Right then, we passed a section door.

"Pardon me, sir," someone said behind me. Male. Probably from that doorway to the left. Hopefully, I could bull my way through.

"Yes?" I said as I turned.

It was a security guard.

"Are you new? I don't seem to have you in my scanner," he said.

"Yes, I just started today."

"Not a problem. I just need to scan you into the system and ungh—" he went down as Silver whacked him at the base of the skull, hard and followed it with a patch of something else.

"Let's go," she muttered.

We were just in the chute to the dock doorway when the intercom said, "Emergency. Please remain calm. The doors will seal for quarantine. The contaminated area is—"

We maintained pace, walked out as the latches flashed red, and the doors locked behind us. We were out in a light drizzle.

She even had a car waiting, a very plain gray Leyland Econ, and parked with a special marker well inside the official zone. She popped it manually, we climbed in, me lowering myself gingerly with my left arm in an awkward position, and we disappeared into traffic.

Shortly, we were at a different, less visible and more popular hotel, where a nondescript couple wouldn't be remarked upon. She doffed her coat, pulled a small knife from somewhere and slashed mine since I couldn't easily move. She unbuckled me and helped me shed the coat. That done, we were two people in pants and shirts going into a hotel.

I moved very deliberately and slipped to the back left of the elevator. She stood right ahead of me, protecting my side. There were three others already in, coming from the pool and spa in the sublevels. Typically, no one spoke, so we reached our floor and grinned and talked about sightseeing for the cameras as we walked.

Once in the room she sighed, the bravado went out of her, and she burst into shivery sweats.

"I think I broke my hand," she said, wincing and tearing up. "I'm sorry. It's minor compared—"

"Get it fixed," I cut her off. "Find a clinic, burn the ID if you must, pay cash, get it fixed. Find me some reconstructor nanos, and we'll go back to it. Do we still have sandwiches?"

"I can make one."

"I'll be fine for a couple of hours. Fix you, then fix me."

"Right," she agreed. She wiped off her face, took a couple of breaths, and steadied up. She slapped meat and bread and a smear of mustard together and I took it with my good hand. She turned and walked out, shoulders up and face clear.

I made sure the door was latched and coded, then limped to the bathroom. I generally hate drugs, but I was beat up badly. I took two industrial painkillers and a muscle relaxant with a full glass of water. I eased down on the bed, feeling the bones grate, propped my arm carefully on a pillow as nerves flared, and passed out.

"Dan," I heard, and twitched awake, and almost threw up from the pain. I never sleep that deeply. Unless drugged, of course. The sandwich was uneaten on the bed, except for one bite I'd taken and dropped unchewed. I'd been out that fast.

I grunted. She held up a tube. I nodded. She poured it into me. Ugh, it was nasty. It also had some kind of narcotic in it. I was back out at once.

I woke again, to daylight and a mouth that tasted like a stagnant ditch. I shifted and it only hurt a bit.

She was already awake.

"I'm sorry about last night," she said. "I shouldn't have lost it."

"You held it together long enough to fake ID, get in, get me out, evade ID and get me treated. You did nothing wrong. I'm impressed with how fast it went."

She smiled.

"Don't be," she said. "I made up a folder full of ID. I have police, medical, military, all built on their standard formats. Most of them can even be encoded to be real, long enough to get through a perimeter once. If anyone ever tries."

"They rarely do. They trust the system. That's to our

advantage. If the ID doesn't work, they'll assume it's defective."

"I'm starting to accept that," she said. "I knew it intellectually."

"Yeah, it's different in practice." I sat up.

Shit, that hurt.

"I think my ribs are still messed up."

"Probably," she said. "We need to get you to a clinic."

"It has to wait. Here and now that's an identifying feature of the suspect. Wait a few days and we go somewhere else. I'll get by on painkillers."

"That's not smart," she said.

"This is combat," I replied.

She looked worried, but nodded. I could tell she didn't agree.

"I was able to get on stage during the confusion," she said.

"Yes?"

"You did cut him. I have a blood sample. One little drop they didn't see at once."

"You are increasingly trif at this," I said. She smiled again. I added, "Don't get cocky, though. That's a fast way down."

"Understood," she said. "I've acquired enough tracking gear so we can do a better trace, but we'll need to drive around."

"Then let's drive. Remember they'll be doing the same."

She nodded, and changed outfits. Mercifully, I was doped and getting used to it.

"I do need the ribs fixed," I admitted.

"I know you do," she said. "I'll find a distant clinic."

"We don't have time."

"If you die, the mission's a scrub."

She was right about that.

I collapsed into the car—a Ford this time—and she drove. I managed to stay with it, but it hurt like nothing had before. He'd caught something there.

I said, "These multiple phones are a hassle. I wish my implant transceiver still worked."

She said, "I could have come up with something for that before we left."

"I thought they'd been dumped due to leakage." Great. That thing still worked?

"Dumped due to compromise of frequency and limited power. Tech has changed. I could run a modern phone into it. If I'd known."

"Well, crap. Sorry." I wish I'd known.

She said, "The new implants are better. Lower profile and improved scramble."

"Also secret enough I wasn't aware."

"With respect, I suggested to the boss we use someone younger and more up to date."

"There'd be advantages to that," I said. "I'm not sure they're enough."

We were quiet for a bit.

At least this wasn't Earth. We left the metroplex and it got dark and quiet fast. The surface changed from highway to road. An hour later we pulled into a smaller town, and on the south edge was an all hours clinic.

We walked in through the lit entrance, and she pulled out more ID. "I have your wallet, honey," she said. I didn't have to feign the pain and appreciation.

"What happened?" the duty nurse asked.

"We were backpacking and he fell onto a stump this morning. Showered and changed and the twit tried to get through it with painkillers and OTC."

I found it easy to look sheepish and hurt.

They put me in a chair, and in twenty minutes I was ultrasounded, X-rayed, taped, tapped and full of painkillers that let my brain mostly engage. I had a slight piercing and pneumothorax from a rib. He'd hit me good.

There was no bill. We'd paid an insurance charge with our entry visa. I couldn't recall if that ID had been covered, or if they'd do the books later and get a null. This ID was going away in ten minutes, though.

"Go easy for a couple of days, Mr. Carn, and make sure to follow up with your own practitioner. You will need additional treatment to make sure it heals straight."

"Yes, ma'am. Thank you." I looked at Silver and said, "I guess we'll have to take the floater ride instead of hiking up the hill."

We made it to the car, and I did feel significantly better with a valve in my side and the ribs straightened. I would take it easy for a couple of days anyway. I had to track Randall to wherever he was.

I felt guilty about resting, but I had to. Pain, fatigue, medication and age conspired to drop me comatose where I reclined as Silver drove. I woke enough to be nauseated and groggy as I walked in a haze to a room, then collapsed carefully on the bed to curl up on my good side.

I was so out of it, I remember waking up to see Silver stripped nude, toning her skin. I closed my eyes and when

I woke again it was hours later. I realized I'd missed the show. Not that it would have done me any good.

I heard Silver say, "So that stuff destroys your short-term memory."

"Oh?"

"Yeah, you told me the story of how you got kicked three times, though the tellings were consistent enough to make you a credible eye witness if you ever get called."

I wondered what else I might have muttered upon seeing those delicious curves, but she didn't seem bothered and didn't mention, so I didn't ask. Casualties say all kinds of odd things anyway. It's one of those intimacies of combat.

"That's good to know," I said. I checked the time. I'd been out five hours. I felt better, but I was still groggy as hell. Age was catching up on me. At some point, I'd need to work on a schedule that allowed for actual sleep.

I stood up, head a bit dizzy from medication, fatigue and aftereffects of the nanos, but with pain greatly diminished. I'd need some more work later, but this would get me along for the time being.

"We need to get back to it," I said.

"I managed some punches," she said.

"Oh?"

She waved at the two comms networked and sequenced.

"I set them to find police protocols, and draw reports. He's been busy."

"How so?"

"Well, they have DNA, too. So we have to expect them

to come looking for you as well. They are pursuing him, though."

"I hoped they wouldn't do that."

"I gather you expect it to be ugly?"

"If they corner him? Hell, yes. They really don't want to do that. You have leads, though? Can we get ahead of them?" I felt awake now, surging with mental challenge.

"Possibly, if you know what we're looking for."

"Well, they're looking for both of you. He is identified as prime suspect, mixed-race Caucasian-Pacific-African, forty local years, thirty-five Earth years, male, armed and very dangerous, no image available. You are described as Caucasian with some Asian, accurate height and mass estimates, forty-five local, false ID, dangerous, possibly armed, a flight risk and a 'person of interest.'"

"This was supposed to be low key. That aside then, where do we go?"

"Much of the interest is on the east side of the city, in these three burbs."

"Let's go. You drive."

I felt so-so for the drive. No severe pain, but I still had trouble concentrating through the haze. I've always been able to sleep easily. I had to learn to fight it on duty. After all this time, I'd have to relearn.

I was feeling better, though. Modern medical care was something I always appreciated.

She asked, "Are you alright?" She did look a bit worried.

"No, but better than I should be."

"Good. I managed some additional supplies, and I brought the pistol."

"Well done. May I?"

She reached under the seat, shifted something, and handed me the pistol.

It was even in reasonable condition. I checked it over again. CanTech brand, which I'd heard of and seen in manuals but never fired, ten-millimeter Alesis, not very concealable, but not overly large. Standard shape frame, typical controls, fifteen rounds in it. I could do a lot worse.

I said, "This is one of the easiest systems to get weapons in, laws aside. There are too many people in the outerland, too many businesspeople wanting self-defense, and a few criminals willing to cash in."

"Are you complaining?"

"No, just amused. This is a decent piece, just like last time I did an exercise here."

"Do you have a plan?" she asked, with a faint look of exasperation.

"Not really," I said. "We find his whereabouts, I go try to kick him up, if I manage, I shoot him, at once, in the back, very ungentlemanly. Then either I E-and-E and we depart, call the embassy, or I get arrested and Naumann makes some discreet calls. I'm agreeable to more of a plan once I know what we're dealing with."

She had earbuds in, and it occurred to me I should, too. I grabbed for my bag, stuck them in, and let her program the channels.

She said, "They found the car from yesterday. So they'll have DNA on us eventually, though there's bound to be several others in there. I did give it a spritz with solvent."

"I assume that stuff's still illegal here," I said.

"Yes. We'll dispose of it before we leave planet."

"We'll need to change deodorant and shampoo regularly to help spoof chemical trackers."

"Got several," she said. Good. Very good at her job.

She paid attention to the road, and I watched for tails, anything interesting, and the scenery. There wasn't much. We were heading into the outskirts. As with most settled worlds, expansion followed coasts and river courses due to ease of cheap transport. Progress inland went slower. This wasn't far from the coast, but was rather quiet. Nonindustrial firms were based here, and a greenbelt, then wealthy estates, but there were also some hotels, eateries and shopping centers. Visitors needed recreation, and it was common to bring the family as one of the perks.

The chatter I heard was largely about traffic control and a couple of accidents causing diversions. If they started channeling traffic here, we'd need to evade. I wished I could drive. She was good enough, but not a trained combat driver.

A bit later she said, "They think they've found a bolt hole, as they call it. Industrial space in one of the parks."

"We need to check it out, then. Much as I want to keep out of sight, we need whatever intel we can get. That also is very much something he'd look for. We spent a lot of the Earth mission using industrial space. I'm not sure he went anywhere else." I wasn't sure I remembered the details. That bothered me. He'd stayed at our facilities. Deni and I had reconned and set the safe houses. I think.

"I want a scrap of chameleon," she said. "I've narrowed it down to three. Knowing who he acquired that from will help a lot."

"Which three?"

"Ours are licensed from Chersonessus. It could be ours or theirs, or Novaja Rossia."

"Interesting. Yes, that would narrow things a lot."

Right then I heard a warning. "Be advised of traffic diversion around Parke West. Civilians should be dissuaded from the area by traffic warnings and zone management. Local traffic may proceed. Report, investigate, and be prepared to detain any subject evading zone restrictions if instructed."

That was interesting. Whatever they were doing, they planned to move in a bit, and wanted to do so quietly. Useful intel for me, and of course, for him if he were listening, which he should be. So I needed to watch for him exfiltrating in case I could get a shot, and then for any intel.

"Any way to narrow down the location?" I asked.

She said, "It's in Parke West. I've got locations on the response units and can estimate an area."

"Drop me, find a place to lurk, come back when I call. I may need emergency exfil."

"Be careful," she said.

"Will do. Turn fast at that intersection, cruise behind the market. Drop me, park in front, shop for a bit, then go elsewhere. I'll walk it."

She turned fast enough to seem she'd forgotten an errand, but not fast enough to be remarkable. The access behind the shop was rutted and worn, with a portable chiller trailer, dumpster and waste tanks. The side was fenced against a broad expanse that looked like it might be a golf course or trotting field.

Silver slowed over the ruts and potholes, and I popped

the door, hopped out and flipped it closed again. I felt decent enough, except for the stench of garbage. She powered gently forward and around, and I was alone.

◎ **CHAPTER 7** ◎

IT WAS A BIT CHILL, but I found it rather refreshing, actually, and the evening damp was pleasant rather than the type that sucks the heat out of you. I turned and walked the other way, across the inlet she'd taken. There was no sidewalk, but there was a well-worn path through the grass along the verge that occasionally dipped onto that lot, which was the rear of some commercial campus. That was good. Pedestrians weren't unexpected here.

Just past there was the business park. I needed to get into his space before the cops did, accomplish either his execution or an intel sweep, and get out. For the former, exfil was less critical.

My phone had unit numbers on screen. Those were probable locations.

Dressed as I was in a pullover shirt and slacks in gray, I wouldn't be out of place. Still, I was exposed and would have limited time before I did get questioned, and at least asked to depart the area.

This was an active evasion scenario. I could most likely get questioned safely, but once I did, I was done with the recon. So I'd be skulking around while pretending I wasn't.

I could see two police cars from here, so they might be able to locate me if they had multispectra imaging. There was a rising fog from the well-watered growth, and some evergreens and local flat-leafed bushes that would disperse my image somewhat. I kept walking, and angled across the "park" aspect of the facility toward hard cover—other buildings.

Shortly, I slipped into visual shadow, then into real shadow, with building and treeline to mask my presence. I took a glance at the phone on its dimmest level. Silver had eliminated one building, leaving four, and changed two. The new one was the one closest to me. I bet it wasn't the right one, but of course I would check it. I walked over the lumpy ground to it, then onto the pavement alongside.

This one was officially vacant, which made it a worthwhile hide. There was a rear emergency exit. I gave good odds to it not being alarmed, and possibly not even locked. I was half-right. The door moved slightly at a pull, and I slipped a flexitool in to shim the catch. It opened and nothing happened.

Inside was dark, creepy and had some odd shadows from the windows, trees and distant lights. Some few bits of litter decorated the tiles, and it took seconds to determine it was well-vacant. I slid back out the way I'd come in.

My choices were across the street or three doors down. Down was also vacant. Across was a recent rental for a packaging company. That fit his MO better, but the vacant was easier to check. Cops were closing in as fast as Silver and I, and I had to get results, not be safe. I decided to cross.

A few buildings farther down still had lights and vehicles. Some of them likely ran three shifts. This back end, though, was largely vacant, less modern and cheaper. Perfect for needs such as ours, but harder to be invisible in at the moment. I crossed at an angle away from my current position, and oblique to the next target. There was a car at each end of the street, and if they were paying attention at all they could see me even through the rising fog, but neither made a response. Either they didn't consider me worthwhile, or they had me under surveillance and were watching.

I strode between two other buildings, the southern of which was occupied, and disappeared from their view again. I glanced for an update.

Patrols on foot, it said. Yeah, there was that, and the risk of boobytraps if he wanted to protect something critical. That wouldn't be logical, since it would definitely trigger a response. However, he was plenty willing to kill, and depending on what he had hidden, he might.

I'd just have to watch for triggers. To that end, I pulled on my own spectral glasses and looked for anything out of place. I started back north behind the building, toward the fence that separated me from the target. I'd have to clear that somehow.

I paused frequently, in short halts that let me check around for police, under the guise of sorting messages on my phone. Tension built, but I felt calm and secure enough. The fence wouldn't be a problem. I could see a hole from here. Apparently, other travelers came through here, whether laborers or inquisitive youths I couldn't tell. The tear was big enough for me to climb through, and the mesh crushed down enough to act as a step about a half-meter up. That indicated regular traffic. The mesh they used for fences here was tough stuff.

I looked around and through and down before I stepped. This would be a good place for a trap. Clear. I tested it with my foot, rose, over and down.

That put me in the lot proper, and I could see a police car cruising slowly along, lights off, just a wraithlike outline in the street. They were very close, very cautious, and this was now a race.

I sprinted across a drive and into the car's visual shadow, though there was little real shadow here. A light post stood between this and the next unit, throwing lengthy dark shapes. I hugged the building and stepped foot over foot along the wall. I dropped down below the frame of a window, and reached up to check it as I went past. Latched.

Then I was past, and into the alcove of the emergency exit. It had a code pad, a scanner, a handle and a key box for admittance.

That suggested an approach. I held my breath and listened. Car engine, a faint hum over the delicate rumble of traffic a kilometer away, which brought back memories of the distant sound of destroyed Minneapolis as I'd departed it on Earth, after inflicting ten million casualties. A flush ran through my brain and guts, and I shook it off. The now mattered. The past was gone.

I tapped a message to Silver. *Need emergency response override code for building.* If she could get me that, I'd be inside with much better chance of silence. Randall wouldn't want alarm bells any more than I would, though I'd expect it would instantly light on a board. But, would the police be told at once, or would the fire team be sent first? I should have a few minutes. He might have alarms of his own, or boobytraps, but those would be silent, hopefully.

I'd set the buzzer and felt it tingle. Silver had replied, and yes, she had a code. I reached up, tapped it into the pad except for the last letter, then stood as far back as I could. I was almost out of the alcove, stretched out a finger and tapped, and swung around to the outside fast.

There was a puff, and I saw and smelled a bare whiff of gas. I held my breath and counted ten, leaned far along the wall for a deep draft of fresh, damp air, then swung back around and through the haze, pulled the door and slipped inside. I had seconds to clear this building before the police came in.

Inside the entryway was clear. Doors ahead on each side were open. Beyond them the space opened into the main bay, with offices far up front. I saw no indication of sonar sensors, nor of any frequency of laser, nor of IR. A passive thermal sensor was possible, but awkward. With hyperaware senses I heard and felt nothing, so I stepped forward while drawing weapons and leaned into the left side room, left arm presented ready to block with knife, pistol refused in the right.

Sleeping pad, blankets on the floor. Small box of clothes. Dark curtains pinned in place. It was vacant of people and tools, so I ducked, twirled and went for the other room.

Tools. Boxes. Clothing. Printer for ID. Pocket coordinate machine on a table. Cut scraps of several materials in a box in one corner. No Randall. I swept and cleared and checked under a cabinet to be sure, then pocketed the pistol and went for evidence. No comm, no coder, no high-tech tools, but I did grab a handful of scraps and pocket them, along with a sheet that might be an invoice, though he should have burned that if so. It was worth checking.

A buzz of message tingled me. I took a quick glance. It read, *Incoming.*

That's when I heard the front door being worked.

I assumed front and rear entrance, coordinated.

I made it back across to the sleeping room, quickly determined nothing was of note, and leaned to glance behind the curtain. I couldn't see anyone holding an over-watch, so they had men front and rear but I could clear the window.

I Boosted.

They yanked the outer door and jumped through. I had a long, leisurely second to reach through the curtain, pop the latch, place my fingers on the window lip, and snap my arm. The pressure tossed it open a good fifteen centimeters, I flicked it with the other hand, stepped up, out and down, pulled to reclose it, turned and ran as I heard them rustle and shift into the room I'd just vacated. I cleared the drive, hopped the hole in the fence, and moved for more shadow.

The area was quickly filling with a lot of cops, and someone would question me at length if they saw me now. I had what I hoped was good intel, figured he would be leaving system, and had to plan ahead for that. He wouldn't rush. He'd arrange three routes if he could, switch between at least two of them and possibly improv another.

I slipped out through bushes and was behind this entire row of buildings, on the broad verge to a main road. I kept the growth as visual blocks. I shifted around and zigged back north, slipped aside, then again. It was something I'd learned early in my training, and it was fun as well as useful, the tension adding spice. I dropped down, duck-walked around one, and kept easing back, watching the arc in front and periodically behind.

In a couple of minutes I was free, crouching through a shallow drain cut on the east side, just a landscaping feature, not really a ditch. Once on the sidewalk I stood and walked as if I belonged. I clicked my phone and called Silver.

"East side, bushes, heading north on walk. Come get me."

"Rog."

Pedestrians weren't common in this area, but I was dressed like a laborer returning from work, and believable in context. Ordinarily, no one would have given me a glance. With the heightened security, though, I got tagged.

I saw the lights shift in the mist, knew it was a car, and clicked the phone again.

"Yes?"

"Hey, lovey, I'm on my way home now. It was a long night, eh? Lots of customers." I kept an eye on the lights' approach, and knew the car was stopping.

She said, "How long are you going to be? Any stops?"

"No, I should be home on the bus." I heard the door, turned slowly enough to not be any kind of threat, and said, "Oh, wait, there's a connie needs to talk about summin'. Lemme call back, okay, lovey?"

"Okay," she said, and we cut.

That should give her enough lead to come bail me.

The cop kept fair distance. While he wasn't handling his stunner, he looked very ready.

He said, "Good evenin', sir. May I see your ID, please?"

"Surely," I agreed, and slid it out of my pocket. "Is summin' up?"

"Nothin' serious," he lied, "I just need to verify people in the area due to an investigation."

"Oh, right, then," I agreed. My accent wasn't perfect, so I kept my answers short.

Of course the card was fake, and made so it scanned FAULT. The question was, would he accept that? Laborer with a work pack, not the suspect. I shouldn't look a lot like the me they wanted, given what they had. I didn't fit Randall's assumed description.

Then he said, "Sir, I'm reading a fault on this ID. You are also in an investigation area, and it's quite late. Where are you coming from?"

"Work," I said.

"Work where?"

I hadn't had time to develop a cover, of course, so I had to bluff. "Garden Estates. I just hired on in the kitchen."

Of course he pinged that, queried the employee list, and found no one matching both my name and description.

"Sir, please step over and place your hands on the hood of my car."

I could take him easily, but it would be more discreet to go along. Their lockup couldn't be that bad, and it would hide my motives behind something less obvious, perhaps petty theft.

I placed my hands on the roof of the vehicle, and let him pat me down. I didn't immobilize him. I wouldn't have been able to. My hands cramped slightly as a neural field gripped them in place. I knew how to break from that, but that would be tantamount to violently resisting arrest, and this scene would not get smaller.

I did say, "Phone in the right front pocket, folding knife in left."

He replied, "Thank you, sir." He carefully relieved me of those.

Another vehicle rolled up, and two more constables got out. They were all rather polite, a bit aloof, and reasonably professional, other than the fact they didn't treat me as a dangerous threat. Maybe I'm paranoid, or maybe it's my experience. I was being courteous, so they were decent back to me. Well enough.

They went through my jacket and the pack, found technical tools and the pistol. That got their attention in a big way. They focused on it, rather than the intel cracking stuff, which should have been far more interesting under the circumstances. Or maybe they wanted to deal with easy charges first.

"So what is your purpose in being here with a pistol, sir?" he asked as he drew my arms down and cuffed them behind me.

"I should probably wait for an attorney to discuss that, sir," I replied.

"Are you sure? That means a ride to Processin'."

"I'm sure."

"Very well. Sit down carefully on the curb here, please."

I did so. It was chill, slightly damp and a bit gritty.

Nothing happened for several minutes, and I presumed Silver had gotten well clear. They chattered on comm, without mentioning her, or pursuit, or anything in the area. It was just me. So she could continue pursuit primarily, and work on release for me second.

Eventually, a van came. It was an unremarkable egg without insignia. It pulled up right in front of where I sat. The officer lifted me to my feet by one elbow and faced me against the back of the van. I kept spatial awareness up for threats, but didn't try to glance around. As long as it was peaceful, I'd play by the rules.

The driver was my height, male, light brown hair. He slapped a pair of binders above the existing pair. The arresting constable thumbed his pair off.

The driver asked, "No statement?"

"None. Possessions here."

"Understood." He then patted me down himself. I approved. That was pretty good procedure.

He thumbed the door, it opened, and he assisted me up into one side of the rear.

"Watch your head on the roof," he said.

Inside was a featureless metal block, with howling air conditioning and bright lights. A claustrophobe would turn into a gibbering nut in about ten seconds. The driver took an interminable time, and I couldn't track direction or distance enough to matter. Believing that hands behind the back is a dangerous position should there be an accident or "accident," I maneuvered my hands in front of me, by dint of athletic flexibility. I rolled, arched, got them past my buttocks and stepped through.

It's a good thing I didn't need to relieve myself. The vehicle looked designed to be sluiced out, but there was nothing one could use for facilities.

In the Freehold, if you actually commit an infraction worthy of response, City Safety will arrive with lots of weapons and escort you peacefully to Citizens' Court. Put up a fight and you're likely to be dead. They transport you in the back of a car, and very few people resist. The Citizen sorts things out and schedules hearing dates, etc., and you're released. If you are really brained out or vicious, you could be detained with a shock collar. I'd studied detention on various planets and nations, so I found this entire industry of specially made vehicles, restraints, doc programs, all fascinating.

Twice we stopped, sat for several minutes, and then someone was shoved in alongside. One man in his fifties, then one in his twenties. We didn't talk. I presumed there were others in the other half of the vehicle.

Believe it or not, one of the big things for me was trusting the driver. I'd frequently traveled in ships, aircraft, boats, locked in and having to rely on someone else for my life. It was always either by contracted choice or with a fellow soldier I had commonality of background in and could trust. This was merely a ground vehicle, but manual only and subject to collision. The odds were remote, but they bothered me.

When we arrived downtown, we were marched out into a stark, lit bay. I expected to be hassled about the cuffs, now in front of me, but no mention was made. So why the insistence that cuffs be behind your back? An elderly lady, presented as detained for domestic violence, was not cuffed due to her age, yet she obviously had been accused of violence, so why wasn't she?

What a bizarre proceeding was to follow. These constables and officers were theoretically part of the same organization, but seemed to follow some strange, Kafkaesque plan detached from reality.

We were slowly processed in, thoroughly and not uncomfortably searched, and stuffed into a holding tank. The only toilet was in clear view of everyone, male, female, prisoner, employee, whatever. My experience made this no issue, but I'm sure for many it would be demeaning and embarrassing. I couldn't decide if that was its purpose, or if it was just lack of concern.

After being biometrically IDed, we were led to another holding cell. I asked about contact and was told, "You won't see a phone for the next four to six hours."

That was interesting. They had mine, and complete control of me. It still didn't seem repressive or dangerous, but what harm is there in allowing someone to communicate? Presumably the idea is to process them into either detention or release, allow the legal process to commence. All this takes time and money, and I can't figure out how further communication is bad for that.

This was an experience few tourists get. I kept notes. No, I don't recommend it.

My guess is the toilets in the holding cell have never

been cleaned. I doubt they can be—when is the cell empty? There was no furniture, just concrete and block walls and shelves. It was crowded at 2300; it was elbow to nose by 0600. It was cold. It stank.

Leftover food sacks littered the place. This was good, as the brown paper could be used as insulation to stop one from freezing to the floor. Ones with sandwiches still in and mashed flat could be used as pillows. The leftover sandwich bags made handy cups to get drinking water from the sinks over the toilets, centimeters thick in gray slime mold. I recalled tricks from my military survival training, which I never thought I'd use domestically. If you pull your arms inside your shirt, you maintain body heat. Sleep as much as possible. Save small things like toilet paper for later use. Talk little, and try to help others. I gave some of my hoarded brown paper to a man with no shirt who had to be suffering from hypothermia on that floor.

No one seemed disposed to trouble. In fact, everyone in the cell was very polite. Those who had to sit on top of the wall over the toilets because of lack of space would courteously look away while you used them. I could handle that, but I imagine most of the locals would not find it at all pleasant, being more body shy than Freeholders, and no one likes to be watched eliminating. It's instinctive. One is rather helpless at that moment.

At 0600 local, they brought us breakfast. The guards handed it out personally to ensure that every prisoner had a meal. This must be procedure, as they clearly didn't care. Breakfast was fake ham on soggy bread with stale cheese, and a cut up apple, with a bag of sterilized, sour-tasting milk. To drink the milk, you had to chew off the corner of the bag. I saw one poor derelict, filthy and hungry, eating leftover food that had fallen around the toilets. Clearly, this man needed a hospital, not a cell. Some few had sketchy bandages from fights. One man who kept demanding his medication had apparently been there for eight hours already. He was obnoxious, either from desperation, or from needing help. Still, if he had medication, he should have been taken elsewhere. He wasn't exactly built like a boxer.

I was finally taken upstairs to the regular cellblock. It had steel bunks, and we each took a thin but functional mattress with us. I actually had no idea what time it was. There were no clocks anywhere and the guards literally would not give us the time of day.

No sooner had we got in there, however, when a curse-screaming, obnoxious woman guard told us she was turning the phones off until we cleaned up the mess left by the last occupants, of whom only three were still present. I resented being held incommunicado, I resented not being asked first, before being given an ultimatum—I'd be glad to clean it for the sake of cleaning it, and to have anything to do for a little while. Most of the rest of my cellmates felt the same way, the sole exception being a screaming, cursing twenty-two-year-old admitted drug dealer.

We picked up the trash and swept and mopped in short order, and I recognized other military veterans from their cleaning style. The drug dealer spent the time calling the guard every unimaginative name in the book, while boasting of his prowess in acquiring stolen property. In response, the guard shouted that she was leaving the phone off to teach us a lesson. What lesson? That this punk was an idiot? We all knew that. Was she hoping we'd attack him so she could gas a few of us? We offered no hassle or resistance at any point. She initiated hostilities.

We all took care of the man with the prosthetic leg. Everyone was careful of the toilets and toilet paper, as we all knew we'd have to use them eventually. Leftover food was shared with new arrivals. The prisoners, with perhaps two exceptions of sixty, were polite, courteous, and addressed all guards as "Sir" and "Ma'am."

The guards ignored every request, either without comment, with "I'll see," or with, "That's not my job." Taking care of prisoners? Not their job. Just signing papers. We were all there for a reason, right?

At noon, they brought lunch. Fake ham on soggy bread with corn chips and nasty chocolate chip cookies. Some analog of fruit punch in a bag, chew off the corner to drink, just like last time. That's two sandwiches, an apple, fifty grams of corn chips and a third of a liter of liquid in twelve hours. Barely enough to keep someone from curling up with pangs, especially in the cold. One experienced inmate offered to swap his sandwich for another drink. He got no takers. The sandwiches were that bad. I choked it down in small nibbles and made it last. This was literally a low-grade version of the capture training I'd had, and would have bordered on war crimes if done against POWs.

At 1330, there was a court call. My name was called, last on the list, while I was using the toilet. I finished, ran to get my mattress (it has to leave the cell with you) while my cellmates yelled at the guard, "Sir, there's one more bloke coming, please wait a moment."

He slammed the gate in my face.

I said, "Sir, I'm your last person."

"I'll come back for you," he said, back to me. He didn't even have the guts to look me in the face while lying to me. He lied to me, in uniform, wearing a badge that he'd taken an oath for. As a veteran, I downgraded this guy to "scum" in my rating.

Every time the guard came back for someone, I'd politely ask him, "Sir, I missed my thirteen-thirty call. When is the next one?"

The responses varied from totally ignoring me, to telling me "Soon," to telling me, "I don't have a file on you." Clearly, he did. He'd called my name. He was continually lying to me. A professional, he was not.

I finally called Silver around 1600, with a hefty five-pound charge to her phone. I told her I'd likely be there another day, and she said, "The Department says court runs until twenty-one." I wasn't hopeful. It might run until 2100, but the regulars were sure no one got called after 1600.

More prisoners came in, and there were no more mattresses. Another exchange took place, and in perfect Pythonesque fashion, the departing prisoners were required to remove the mattresses from the cell, even though there were those inside who had none. Repeated requests of, "Sir, we need some mattresses," were met with the standard, "Soon," but no mattresses. They were left outside the bars as a taunt. I couldn't have set it up better myself as a means to psychologically break people. Except they weren't interrogating anyone for intel, had laws against it, and was from sheer idiocy rather than intent. It amused and disgusted me. It didn't intimidate me.

After shift change, we had two other guards, one young man, and a slender elderly lady with curly hair. These two people deserve thanks, promotions, and praise from the city, because they acted and treated us like human beings. They were genuinely embarrassed by the petty bullies around them, kept apologizing for them, and did their best to help us.

Let me reiterate: they did their jobs as required. That was unusual and worthy of note.

On missed court calls, they took names and made inquiries. They got no answers, but they did ask. The man who needed his medication, who had previously been told that the medics were "gone for the day," was scheduled for sick call. They gave us the time. They explained procedures. They got us mattresses. They were treated exactly as they treated us—politely, and every request was complied with without hassle.

Eventually I was called for interrogation.

"Scholl! Is Scholl here?"

"That's me," I called loudly, and stood from my rack.

"Follow me."

I was prepared for a lot of shouting, some shoving, threats, food deprivation, low-key harassment, which was illegal but probably SOP.

I was pleasantly surprised.

The guard led me through a dingy corridor, locking us through gates via the control center, to a room, directed me in and closed the door. I could see one camera, deduced where the others must be, and assumed they were recording already. Two floods lit the seats enough for visibility without being excessive. This seemed to be legit. I took the one facing the door. It was hard but adequately shaped, and fixed to the floor.

A few moments later, a man in his Caledonian thirties walked in and sat down. He wore a badge on his shirt.

"Good evening, sir. I'm Investigator Mead. May I have your name, please?"

"Andrew Scholl," I said, making us both liars. He already had that ID, of course.

A sealed, transparent evidence box appeared in a window on one wall, illuminated and secure.

"So where'd you get this gun?" he asked.

I gave the only reply I could. "I brought it in my luggage."

"The number says it was stolen here."

I shrugged. "I brought it in my luggage."

He sighed and looked annoyed.

"I'm trying to help you," he said. "I know you're a Freeholder. Have you military ID? If you do, we can clear any weapon charges and just return it to the owner."

. Technically, that was illegal. They did do favors for military, though. He was lying about the latter. They'd chop it up for "analysis."

"No," I said.

He looked me up and down. He knew I was military, and was probably starting to figure I was clandestine. That could be problematic.

"Sir . . . "

I stayed uncommunicative. "Sorry."

A beep on his phone caught his attention.

"It seems bail's been posted." He sighed again. "You'll be given a sheet with reporting instructions and bonding rules. You must obey them, and may not leave the system in the meantime. We'll see you in court."

"Very well, sir. Good day," I said. I waited until he indicated I should stand and leave.

I wasn't released, though. I was shoved back into the cage. I figured out afterward it was just bureaucratic idiocy. At the time, it seemed like a clumsy interrogation technique.

At 1800, we were brought dinner. You guessed it—fake ham and soggy bread with stale cheese and corn chips and nasty cookies and orange juice. The man trying to exchange his sandwich for a drink had no luck again.

I stayed with my form. I ate leftover chips to keep up my strength, poured a bag of water to keep myself hydrated. Nodded to conversation but said nothing. Stayed with my bunk so my mattress wouldn't be stolen, though no one seemed disposed to fight.

About twenty-two hours, some fool who had smuggled marijuana and matches in past their search lit up. The guards made no attempt to find out who had done so, they simply shut off the phone again. People who had been brought in at the same time I had, just now getting up to the cell after twenty-two hours, came in and had no way to call.

They still had no way to call when I left at midnight.

Someone called my name again, on a list, and I was first at the bars, having moved my mattress to a front bunk during an earlier lull. I lied and said I didn't have a mattress, so someone else would have the use of it.

We were marched downstairs, lined up, processed out in ten minutes. I was never actually told that my charges were dropped. We weren't actually told we were being processed out until another prisoner asked and was answered. They scanned me again, loaded a bag with my possessions minus the gun, the glasses, invoice and the coding tools, but I did have the pocket knife, phone and pieces I'd picked up. A bored overweight woman handed me the bag through a grille and said, "Don't open that until you're outside."

They opened the locked steel door, told me to go up to the first floor and through the door. I did so, and was in the lobby of the police department. No warning, no nothing. Through that door and out of our hair, you. To be fair, the guards on this last leg were fairly decent, probably because they knew we were being released.

Even though I'd known I was safe, seeing Silver was a great relief. I was pretty fatigued, too. There wasn't much time for that, though.

Once we were outside and in the car, I fished the sliver out of the bag.

"Chameleon," I said.

"Novaja Rossia," she said, that fast.

"Good. Does that help?"

"It will. Right now we need to follow up. I think they've cordoned him."

"Oh? Do tell."

She shrugged. "Activity, radio traffic, some media presence."

"Ah, hell, we don't need a circus."

I was emotionally beat and physically wiped out, but we had a job to do.

❀ CHAPTER 8 ❀

WE HIT THE ROOM, I showered and cleaned up, washing several cubic meters of grit and grime away, dressed in business combat wear—suit and shoes designed for maneuvers and wrestling—and went out on the hunt.

They'd tightened communication protocols and Silver couldn't bust their signal in time. We blocked the city on map and drove, using traffic analysis. Lots of signals came from the north central. I tracked the news to rule out other incidents. We found signals only to have them fade, then found tantalizing taunts that went nowhere. We located other incidents including a vehicle crash that made the news about the time we arrived. Then there was a report of a police cordon on the RumorNet node. It did not show up on any official press. That was promising.

Randall apparently really wanted his target. There must be a time limit, which was useful information and bore more research. We finally had enough data to zero in on a cheap apartment block. About 1100 local, we identified which unit. It was the one with all the cops outside.

That suggested to me that he wasn't here, and this was a setup. If I knew I was being tracked, I'd have left a lot of false trails. One very clear trail was a trap. They didn't know who they were dealing with, and they were between me and him.

I gestured. Silver was already parking as I did so. I climbed out, put on my public spook façade and checked for the right ID. I sought the largest gathering of uniforms, blocking the walkways from the adjoining park.

I strode up quickly, pushed politely through the gawkers and slowed as I approached, stepped over the official tape, picked one sergeant out by eye and said, "I need to talk to the scene commander."

"That's nice. Just move outside the cordon, please, and—"

Cops really piss me off. They need to stick to serving and protecting and not trying to be epic heroes.

I interrupted him by grabbing his arm and shoved an ID in his face. I deliberately didn't raise my voice, just spoke clearly. "I am Captain Anders. I have pursued that suspect from outsystem, and I have important information about him. I need to speak to the scene commander."

"Okay, sir. Please come with me." He pointed at the two approaching officers and then at the cordon. "Jasta, Lanning, take over here." They looked surprised, but diverted from slamming me to cordon control. The sergeant seemed very embarrassed, but realized his best bet was to bump me up higher. Good enough.

We walked over to the commander at a near trot.

Others had seen our interaction, and followed me suspiciously. I eyed him as we approached. Gray, slightly overweight but with good tone. He seemed competent and not too standoffish or grandstandish, if that's a word.

As I approached, he said, "Chief Malcolm. District Seven. You are?"

"Captain Anders. Appointed by the Freehold Council."

He looked at my ID at length. It was good. Silver had copied it with a real diplomatic blank. Officially, the military doesn't get those, for this exact reason—accusations of espionage. In actuality, Operatives steal them, use them for patterns, and destroy them.

He said, "Interesting. I didn't know they did that."

"Not often, no. This merits it, though."

"Very well. So who is he?"

"He's one of our Blazer troops, or used to be. He's had some mental trouble. Aftereffects of the War. He's very dangerous, but I can talk to him. We served together. I can get him out without violence to anyone, if I can see him. If you go in, it's going to be messy and there are going to be multiple casualties."

Actually, I was going to fucking kill him and make any excuse, or not make any excuse, as needed. I liked having the dialog, though. This could work.

Malcolm gave me this squint that foreshadowed a negative. Dammit.

First, he wanted to believe he could control this situation. Second, he didn't like intruders, and I don't blame him. Third, there was the political issue of him letting an outsider resolve it. Fourth, he didn't know me, or what my actual credentials were. Fifth, I just *might* be a distraction or accomplice.

"Then you can remain here, and talk to him after we bring him out."

There was absolutely no argument I could offer under the circumstances, and fighting him wouldn't help. Well, I could probably distract them enough to keep them alive, but then Randall would escape, and we'd start over.

I just nodded, because I wasn't going to try to speak.

"We'll be fine," he assured me in a deep, confident voice. "My team has the latest training and equipment. One traumatized veteran is no problem."

I stood back, and hoped for an opening where I could inject some reason and wisdom. The problem is, a lot of these units like to kick in doors. Everyone wants to do their job, but these are people who have a bit of an ego trip. Sometimes, a lot of one.

They had a murderer, an assassin, so they were going to wade in and bring him out, hold him up as an object lesson.

I, of course, have developed a theory about object lessons . . .

The team looked competent and fit. I had no doubt under any normal circumstances they'd do a vidworthy job, from the flash bang to the hauling of the subdued perp.

That's the second problem. They come in en masse, with lots of noise and firepower, and maintain the upper hand. That's great on whacked-out druggies, middle-age money handlers, disturbed abusers and ganger kids. They were up against a professional, trained to do the same thing they were about to attempt, and do it better. If I could actually tell them who I was, as I'd led a raid to rescue their Princess, now Queen, some years before . . . But there was no time, and the lives of a few cops wasn't important in the big picture. I had to keep my cover.

Part of me screamed to do something. This was a legitimate raid, well-intentioned, and these fifteen men and three women were going to die. Their families were going to suffer massive anguish. I knew exactly what was going to happen, what it was going to look like, how dreadful it would be to them. Heck, I'd done it myself once, while carrying a baby.

Malcolm said, "Proceed," and they swarmed the building.

I did not find an opening in which to suggest further caution. I forced myself to remain still.

The tac team got placed last. They were quiet, efficient and enthusiastic. I looked at their placement and dispersal and cringed. It was literally textbook, as I'd done it twelve years before. They'd learned from the best. Us.

Then the explosions started. A flashbang, some cutting charges. Some shots. Malcolm looked very pleased and comfortable.

Then the shooting continued, interspersed with shrieking screams of agony, gouts of smoke, and more explosions, including one that ripped the side off a floor above. It rained down onto the ground in drumming thumps of debris.

Malcolm gave me a sideways glance, angry and tense, then headed in himself.

I couldn't fault his courage.

Four very worried officers with carbines followed him.

I brought up the rear, not asking, just acting as if I belonged. They didn't question me, but I think they didn't notice me.

Power and lights were out in the building. Once that was determined, I followed them up the stairs. Four floors, each of them seeming farther away and with thinner air. I was having emotional flashbacks, traumatic stress pummeling me. Dammit.

We got to the fourth floor, two cops with carbines went first, then the chief and I, then the last two brought up the rear and skipped through between us.

Then they stopped.

There was some illumination here from their weapon lights, and some through a destroyed door. Tendrils of smoke floated lazily past. They didn't add much to the scene, because it was so outré nothing could add to it.

The squad outside the door still smoked, doused in gelled petroleum, probably diesel or paraffin. Some oxygenating compound had been released, and the glop had burned right through their faces to bone and brain tissue. Guts still sizzled, and the corridor smelled like scorched bologna with the metallic sauce of blood and the tang of fuel, with a hint of ozone. Chief Malcolm turned and spewed, trying to avoid contaminating the crime scene, and splattering his hands and the wall. It wasn't going to matter much. It did add slightly to the smell.

They'd shattered the door on entry. Textbook. Except Randall had planned for them to do that, and used that as a trigger. Three other bodies were well-bruised sacks of blood from a concussion wave, which had also peeled the wall sheathing. I gingerly moved to the doorway, wary of triggers. There could be more. Malcolm let me take point. Pity he hadn't believed me earlier.

The room was full of rubble and bodies and lingering eddies of dust. I looked at the traps and could tell which page of which manual they came from.

The two that entered through the door had run onto a hard floor covered in ball bearings. Even their grippy shoes hadn't helped with that. One had a broken neck. The other had a muzzle burn against his temple, just under the helmet brim.

Two came through the window and caught on a transparent mesh. The first was prone on a bed of caltrops, and he hadn't died quickly. They were only a few centimeters each. His buddy had landed on him, though, which had probably driven some into his face and throat, judging from the crimson pool starting to skim over. They were probably laced with some neural toxin, since those would be crippling but not lethal wounds. Then I saw some of the window shards sticking out of him.

His buddy had intercepted a spike. It was above the reinforcement on her armor, right through her lower jaw and spine. That had to hurt, too. Her face was in a rictus, and there was a stain under her. The spike had probably been driven in by hand, as she moved in free flight.

The ones who came through the wall had fared no better. Sticky aerogel doesn't show on sonar scans. They blew a hole, dove in and got gooed, then were exterminated with pistol rounds through the atlas. Randall undoubtedly had garments with a keyed enzyme to counter that specific adhesive. The foam around them looked like soap suds tinged pink.

I heard a faint noise, and very carefully eased through the door, looking for any kind of sensor or trigger.

The one who'd come through the ceiling had carefully selected his spot to place him in a corner, facing into the room, with clear crossfire with his buddies. We have the same manual. The expression on his face could almost be sexual, until you deduced it was pain. He'd hit a bed of long, very slender, almost molecular spikes. A quick leap had pulled his feet free, but then he'd landed ass first on much longer ones back in the corner. He was impaled, right through the pelvic girdle and assorted nether regions, possibly as deep as his diaphragm. He might still be alive, and he might be salvageable, given that the puddle of slime under him was mostly gut contents and only a liter or so of blood. Every tiny twitch caused excruciating agony, though, which caused him to twitch more. He was in so much pain he couldn't even scream, which probably reduced those twitches a bit. His breathing was very shallow but apneic. He'd been there ten minutes with his brain undoubtedly cauterized by the hormones, convulsions and neural torture. He'd need to be doped to the teeth, then extracted carefully to avoid bleeding out—some of those needles were possibly through his kidneys and inferior vena cava—reconstructed with nanos, all under massive amounts of drugs, then he'd need physical and psychological therapy.

I trod lightly so as not to shake the poor bastard. I looked above him.

The team intended to follow him had never made it. As they blew that hole down, Randall's explosives had blown up. I guessed the frag as razor blades and molecular wire debris. Through the entry hole, I could see two of them tossed and dead. The bottom third of those men was ground meat.

The whole place smelled as if someone had cut loose with explosives in a slaughterhouse which, in effect, he had.

Malcolm looked stunned and traumatized just by the emotional overload.

I said, "You figure you know how to handle one old troop gone bad, eh?"

He gasped for breath and words, finally strangled out, "How did you know?"

"Because it's what I would have done."

I walked off in disgust.

I realized then that I'd leaned well into the room. Luckily, that moaning, impaled thing had not been intended as bait for more. Apparently, Randall lacked the real killer instinct some of us have. Either that, or he'd been pressed for time.

I was downstairs and outside before Malcolm caught up.

He shouted, "Wait, you! You don't just get to walk out of here after my constables died."

I said, "I wanted to talk to him, and take the risk myself, of deescalating. Now I have to chase him."

"The bloody hell you will on my planet."

My only excuse is that I'd shifted into combat mode. Randall was nearby, and could easily kill more. If he saw me, he'd be smart to shoot me at once. I had nerves like naked wires a meter out from my skin, feeling for any hint of danger . . . and Malcolm grabbed my arm.

I disentangled, pulled, pushed and he staggered and sprawled.

At that point, things got much worse, because I didn't want to fight his nervous, trigger-on-finger constables; running would create visibility and a scene; and standing still meant I could get shot by Randall.

I decided I was safest surrounded by arresting officers. Within a local hour, I was back in the hoosegow, charged with assault, battery, resisting arrest, hindering an investigation, conspiracy and probably obscene acts with kittens. Luckily, Silver was observing and had bail ready, in cash, before they even processed me.

It would have helped, if there hadn't been a stop order on my release, from far up the food chain.

Another hour, as Randall fled and was probably unfindable at this point, I was escorted by plain uniformed men, all almost exactly one hundred ninety centimeters tall, with firm builds. The only uniform was plain blue coats with clipped-on badges and no other marks. I thought I knew what that meant.

It didn't seem possible, and was either very good or very bad. We entered a van with no windows. I wasn't restrained. I saw no reason to evade in the midst of traffic, though, with these men around me.

I was invited out of the vehicle. That put us in a bay that led to a corridor with lovely lighting and fine carpets, then inside a cozy, wood-paneled office with a carved desk. The woman behind it wore a plain, elegant suit to match her elegant hair and features.

"What exactly is your rank at this point, Operative Chinran?" she asked.

I did the only thing I could. I bowed enough to be polite, and said, "Thank you for seeing me, Your Majesty."

The House Guards left, except for one in the corner. He barely betrayed nervousness at my presence.

Annette had been Crown Princess the three times we'd met, first at a dinner followed by a diplomatic intel téte a téte, later after she was taken hostage and I and some of my goons blew up everything around her and barely chipped one of her teeth, in the process of killing the kidnappers. Her mother had died five years ago, now.

"Please sit," she said, polite even when angry.

"Thank you, ma'am," I said. I really didn't want to be here, but it might be useful, and I had to be diplomatic. I went with the program.

"You're stalking one of your own, loose on my planet, and I don't even get a courtesy note from your ambassador?" she asked, sounding miffed but reasonable, for now.

"The ambassador doesn't know, ma'am, and we'd much prefer to keep it that way."

That raised her eyebrows.

"I see," she said, and leaned back while taking a sip of tea. She waved a hand in offer, and I nodded and poured myself a cup. No servants for this matter, and I wouldn't insult her bodyguard by expecting him to. I'd be disgusted if he agreed.

"Ma'am, I can't tell you much more than you already know. Someone is loose. Very dangerous. I have to stop them. No one can know. Any leaks will only hurt my efforts, not them."

"I suppose that makes sense, and I'll help you with that

matter. You do realize this is an international, intersystem incident, of course."

"Yes, ma'am, and we'd like to limit it to one."

"Should I order the ports closed?" she asked, reaching for a phone.

"Please don't. Anything that indicates anything out of the ordinary will make it worse."

"Very well," she agreed. "I hope something can be done for the families of eighteen Tactical Response personnel."

"I'm sure something can, ma'am, and it most certainly should be, but that's something the ambassador will take care of, after orders from the Marshal. Unfortunately, I have to resolve this first."

"So what do you need from me?"

"Ma'am, you are most gracious under the circumstances. I need as little attention on me as possible, and to be able to move freely."

"Will a Royal Warrant and appropriate ID assist in that? And access to any reports from investigations?"

"Very much."

"I'll have them issued at once. I want you to understand, though, that this is because I owe you my life, I believe you are honest, and most importantly, it seems the fastest way to resolve this. I advise you not to make things worse by abusing the privilege I'm about to grant you." Her expression was not challenging, but it was not friendly.

"Ma'am, that's exactly how I take it, and I am very thankful. My goal is to resolve this quickly."

"This will be text and scannable," she said. "I advise discretion in showing it. The media will ask questions. I'll have to publicly deny anything. I dislike that." She frowned slightly.

I knew that. She knew that. I really had her worried. She'd seen us work up close, and now knew what could happen one on one, as well as the activities during the War. She wanted him and me out of her system as fast as possible.

Then the phone chimed. She clicked it on. "Yes?"

Someone said, "Your Majesty, Mister Rothman has just been killed by a rocket fired through his window."

She closed her eyes, sighed and turned back.

"That is most unfortunate. Please express Our condolences to his family. We are discussing responses right now, but we cannot furnish details."

"Yes, ma'am."

She looked back at me.

"So, should I close the ports now?" She leaned on her hand and stared through her fingers. Very unroyal. I deduced that meant I rated fairly highly on her list.

"Ma'am, he could easily lie low here for months. Or, he'll just falsify identity and walk through."

"We have a DNA trace."

"There are ways to fake that, even in a star port. He hasn't so far because it's been useful to him."

"You're sure? We both used it to locate him."

"He wanted to be found. If I find him, the worst is that I die. If you find him . . ."

"Yes, though I'd rather end this sooner, even at some loss." She sat up and sighed.

"He'll be leaving. I'll get him shortly."

"See that you do. This code," she passed over a

laminated card, "will contact my immediate staff, should you need support."

The audience was clearly over. I took a polite gulp of the tea, placed the delicate cup carefully down, stood, bowed, and said, "Thank you for Your gracious help, Your Majesty. I'll finish this as quickly as I can, and only call if I need to."

"Good day to you, Ken," she said, stood and offered her hand briefly.

As I left, I realized she was one of a bare handful who knew my real last name and rating.

At least the House Guards were a little more open on the return.

"Where are we to take you, sir?" one of them asked.

Ten minutes later I was at a train station three squares from the hotel, and ten minutes after that I was back in the room. I had all my possessions in hand, including the "stolen" gun. Interesting.

At some point, I'd have to tell Her Majesty what contemptible scum existed in Her prison system. For now, I had more pressing matters.

❀ CHAPTER 9 ❀

I DEBRIEFED SILVER, and not in the way I'd like to debrief her of those very nice briefs she wore when not wearing a thong. Yes, frustration was getting to me again.

"He's either heading offplanet now, or will find a hole somewhere. The latter is cheaper and more efficient. Don't move if you don't have to. The former is safer with me following him."

"It also gives him a chance to travel and spend money," she offered. "Also to acquire more gear. There's a finite amount and type of resources in any given system."

"Good thought," I agreed. I didn't know if he was the recreational type. I'd never known if he was, and he had changed. He probably hadn't been then, seeing as he'd been fighting the system to try to reenlist when I recruited him for the unit.

"How do we track the starports?" I asked.

"I have software," she said. "The more we refine the

parameters, the better. But, the more we refine them, the greater risk of a disguise working."

"We'll need several searches, then."

"I'll need both our comms and try to borrow or buy another."

Caledonia had four starports. It was quite the cosmopolitan system, in one sense of the word. Silver actually was able to create a patch through a coded police channel to the Caledonian National Police and into their line to the security cameras at the ports. She was sure it was secure, and I believed her. It would have been nice to jack right in through the CNP's line, and HM Annette would allow it, but I had to assume he could track exception codes, or that someone would note it and, permissions aside, make a scene, hoping for promotion.

That wasn't the problem. Nor was the volume of people a problem. A few thousand a day left the system. However, tens of thousands only left the planet, and went through the same ports. They used different lines, but he could easily change from one to another at one of the orbitals.

Silver's training was impressive. A good Special Projects troop is a better grade of spy than most actual agents because of their training. We never had enough of either them, or Operatives or even Blazers, because there just weren't enough people with the combination of high intellect—top .5 percentile—psychology and fitness.

She helped me set up search parameters around his photo; with enough slack we started getting hits at once. We tightened it slightly, and left it to run. I scanned through the faces it had captured, and we set up five more patterns, hoping for gait, physical proportions, ID types and unusual itineraries.

I was most concerned about appearance. ID was probably a waste of time, as was itinerary, and gait and proportions were very unreliable without recent video to work from.

I had a face every few minutes; the estimate was several hundred for the day. This could continue for some time, and I had to rest in there. To my advantage was that once I knew where he was, I could call for backup at the far end. In theory.

Silver worked backward toward my encounter with him. There was no guarantee he'd fired the rocket. It could have been a remote system set days before, or he could have consulted for someone else. I hoped to find out which, but didn't know at present.

I worked in realtime, and she occasionally pinged one to me to double check. We got nothing all day.

We took shifts for showers, restroom, food runs, kept the "Do Not Disturb" sign lit, reinforced with an occasional step outside to nod and greet the housekeepers, and offer occasional tips. We took turns doing calisthenics, and she went to the hotel gym every day for a brief run. I prefer calisthenics. That is to say, I prefer me doing calisthenics. She'd take breaks for pushups and crunches to keep awake and burn off nervous energy. When she did I got to listen to her "Uh!" and "Urh!" once she passed forty. It sounded deliciously sexual, and I could only compensate with louder music and trying very hard not to look at her.

I'd look at the images that registered, and the ones she

forwarded. Some were close. Some I had to squint to define. None were he, that I could tell. I saved a few for further review, and overlaid the two images. Some things are very hard to change, even with surgery—eye spacing, forehead height, cheekbones. Most people won't go through that kind of surgery, even in our field. None were quite right, but some were close enough to make me second guess myself.

It was tedious, tiring, intel work. With ten operators, it would be easy. We had two. My eyes got gritty, hers got red. My ass got sore, so I stood, then my feet got sore. I was utterly revolted by more tasteless sandwiches, better than the prison's but reminiscent of them. I took sleep in combat naps once a day, with a two-div rest at night. Then I found I was off the local clock and running on Freehold time again, a much longer day cycle than theirs.

On top of that, we had to track the news, intel reports from the embassy, and attempt to run periodic DNA scans.

We got lucky. It was only three days before he left. When the image came up, I jerked in my seat. Yes, that was definitely him, a decade later. I ran an overlay to be sure, and it was perfect. He was aboard a shuttle, and if I had someone on the receiving end I could stop him. I contemplated that contact code, and decided I owed Her Majesty Queen Annette the courtesy of a warning.

We were on the road in less than three minutes, me driving while Silver rammed through seats for us on the soonest shuttle we could conceivably make. I violated many traffic laws, and had the Royal Warrant handy in case anyone saw me. I lucked out.

Tickets arranged, I hit voice, called the code, and got a very neutral response.

"Palace Reception, may I help you?" a man asked.

"My name is Kenneth Chinran."

"Please stand by, I will transfer you. It might take several minutes."

"It needs to take a lot less, sir. Whatever code you have for me needs to be raised a level."

"Sir, you are already at the highest code possible. Please stand by. Connecting."

The Queen's voice said, "What do you have, Ken?"

"He's leaving. You can possibly stop him at the orbital. My assistant has the information."

She fairly shouted, "Chief Watson, get online now. Go ahead."

Silver spoke. "Caledonian Elegance *Firebird Aurora.* Boarding at Sapphire Station at one four two nine Capital Time."

I added, "We are in pursuit."

She asked, "Do you need to make the apprehension?"

That was a very diplomatic way of asking, "Dead or alive?" If I needed to make the kill, they'd hold him for me.

"However you can best apprehend him is fine, ma'am."

"Understood. You will be waved through security."

"Roger. Chinran out."

Silver asked, "Ken Chinran?"

"Me."

She looked confused.

She said, "You know, I don't think I was ever told your real name."

"Not even regarding Earth?"

She shook her head. "Nope. Black Ops Seven, but no names. Still secret."

Shit. But it made sense. Why tell anyone? There hadn't been any, wasn't any, reason to. And our IDs as Operatives were always secret.

"Yeah, that was my real name once."

She looked at me a bit oddly. She thought she knew me after all this time together, but which parts of me were real? Which were cause, effect, or just cover?

Did I know, anymore? I felt much more "Dan" than "Ken."

We parked the car in the drop-off zone, and I flashed the warrant at the constable on duty, and handed him the keys. He raised his eyebrows, but nodded. We strode quickly through the door, found another duty officer, showed him the warrant.

"Sir, we need to board as quickly as possible. This is an emergency."

He nodded, walked us right to the front of the line, and we checked in. There were a few mutters but more inquisitive sounds. A powered cart awaited us, and we rolled through the crowd and right to the flashing security cordon. A flash and a scan of the warrant and we were through, and then aboard.

I contemplated ordering the pilot to lift early, but that would mess with astrogation, and there was nothing I could do at this end. Docking issues would take time.

The crew ran through the launch procedures. Decades ago, I'm told, all craft were similar and one could ignore the briefings. These days, with vertical launch, air launch, catapult, skywhip and other methods of getting to orbit, one does have to pay attention. This was an air launch, from high-efficiency compression jet to nuclear-chemical rocket. We rose and kept rising, the sky changing color out the ports to cloud, bright sky blue, brilliant deep blue, then to violet, and then black with a misty pale blue layer far below us. In an hour, we were in low orbit and approaching Sapphire Station.

Docking was straightforward and smooth. Good pilot, even with massive AI power in the loop. I got ready to debark. We were docked at right angles and under centrifugal G.

"Ladies and gentlemen, there's a security issue in the gate area that necessitates a short wait. Please remain seated, and we'll keep you informed."

Oh, shit.

I looked at Silver, she at me. She nodded, I unbuckled and we moved forward fast, bumping between couches.

The purser said, "Sir, madam, I need—"

I cut her off with both the Royal Warrant and my "Citizen's Council" ID.

"Ma'am, that security issue pertains to us. We have to debark right now. Please contact whoever you need to."

She twisted her mouth, nodded, and called the captain via a hush screen. There was some negotiation, she showed our IDs, and then there was an interminable pause, while passengers stared and commented some more. Eventually, she turned and said, "There's someone waiting to meet you on the other side of the lock."

"Thank you very much," I said.

The lock opened, and we were in the dead space

between hatches. There was minor leakage. I could hear a faint hiss. If we were in here too long there'd be a problem. There was an emergency O_2 supply mounted on the forward bulkhead. I watched it with one eye and the hatch with the other.

The hatch ahead swung open, and we crossed into the station. We still had the inner door ahead. Silver hit the bar, closed the outer door, and then we waited for whoever manned the inner door to open it.

It swung, and we were face to muzzle with an entire squad of troops, fingers on trigger. They were agitated and sweating in full armor.

I raised hands, said, "I have Royal and Freehold ID."

"Slowly," a uniformed captain said.

"Yes, sir," I agreed, and carefully drew the documents again. I could smell residue and blood nearby. There had been some ugliness.

He'd apparently already called down planetside and confirmed. He waved us in and the weapons lowered.

I said, "May I ask for an update? We've heard nothing since lifting."

His expression was both disgusted and annoyed.

"Apparently, he smuggled weapons through, or already had them stashed aboard. We tried to cordon him off and lock him, but he saw that coming. So we tried a public standoff, betting on our marksmen versus him. We were under the impression he didn't like collateral casualties."

"I had hoped he wouldn't," I said. Oh, damn, what had he done?

"Apparently, he doesn't. He was quite willing to bet

we didn't either, and he had the offensive position. His shooting was quite good, and even his misses didn't hit any civilians. I had six troops go down, the crowd scattered and hindered us, then he blew his way through a bulkhead. We locked the station down for departures, but we can't do that for long."

"I can eyeball every passenger, if that will help," I said. "You'll have to check cargo, et cetera, and search in detail. Cynthia, advise them on search procedures, please."

"I do know how to conduct a reconnaissance, sir," he said, sounding put upon.

"I'm sure you do. We know how to conduct one for our people."

"Understood," he said. He gestured and several of his troops came over. Silver took control comfortably and directed them.

I asked, "Where do you need me?"

"We have a ship waiting to leave now. Can you check that one first?"

"I can. Depressurize the hold and the cargo compartment, then cycle back. Manually inspect anything larger than a personal bag. Where are the passengers?"

"Through here." He indicated a gate lock to the side. Number X-1.

I followed him through, and stood back at a gesture from him. His troops slipped past me as I stood aside, and filed around the area. It had crosshatched windows on one half, to reassure the human mind that it wasn't a drop off into space. The other half had murals on the bulkhead. Nice facility.

He spoke clearly and loudly, "Pay attention!"

The passengers stared at us, a combination of annoyed, eager, and wanting any distraction from the tedium of waiting. There's only so much most people can do with the nodes and vid while waiting for a flight.

"We will be able to board you in a moment. We are conducting a search of all bags, and all persons. I need you to form a queue here, regardless of your flight zone or class."

Someone, of course, objected. I can't blame the man. I like encountering people who don't think like sheep.

"Do you have a warrant for this search?" he asked. I didn't recognize his accent, and while I might approve of his attitude, it would hinder us.

The captain pulled out a chit and said, "I have a Royal Warrant and a Royal Commission. If you wish not to have your luggage searched, you may make other arrangements to transport it. If you wish not to let me compare your face to your passport, you may elect to remain in the station until you do."

Fortunately, the man looked amused.

"I guess that's reasonable enough," he said. "I should be less irritable next time."

"Thank you, sir."

"I'll go first then," he said, and made his way to the front of the line.

I looked him over. He was nothing like Randall in build, color, shape or mannerism. I nodded faintly and continued.

I walked down the line and scanned the passengers. It took seventy seconds at most.

"They're fine," I said.

"That fast? Are you positive?"

"He's not female, not a child, doesn't fit certain body types, has visible racial markers. He's not in here."

The captain leaned in and said, "Sir, you can't mention profiles here. Someone will sue."

"You asked. I told you. He can't be female, a child, a scrawny Caucasian, a fat Asian, or several others. No one on this flight is remotely close."

"Very well, then." He looked at his phone. "The ship's been evacuated and purged as you asked, and the cargo has been pulled. They're repacking it now, and they'll check the luggage." He led us to a tram station.

I said, "Before repacking, get hands on ID and two people to vouch for every cargo handler, then lock that area off if you can."

"Noted. Thank you."

There were thousands of people awaiting transit. We rode trams in broad arcs between gates and I looked at them and saw nothing. They were grateful to be released, but I knew they'd be aggravated again at the cargo search and related delays.

More troops arrived on station from their moon Ness and from planetside.

"You'll need to do an EVA for him in case he's suited. I'd start evacuating any compartments not in use. Check on manifests for anything that requires life support. He'd hide in a kennel to get down."

"Seriously?" the captain asked me. "You'd really do all this to exfiltrate?"

"I shouldn't be sharing this much with you, but yes."

"There's no bloody way we can search every craft and

every station to this level after every arrival or departure. It's an impossible level of security."

"Welcome to my game," I said.

We, and they, searched cargo, evacuated containers, checked passengers, manifests, contractors and restaurants, engineering spaces, station crew, station lodging. We weren't going to find him, but I had to go through the motions and we might get lucky. Meantime, we might find a trace elsewhere.

The only positive in all this was that Her Majesty's intel apparatus were going to be looking for him as well. He could still retire rich, but he had two systems that were harder to operate in, and a slowly closing net. It was in his best interest to sneak off quietly, but I didn't think he would.

I'd wanted to be in pursuit and out of the system. Instead, I was stuck in low orbit doing searches I knew wouldn't yield anything.

I told Silver, "My guess is he'll board back down to the surface and will leave via another route. Or has already."

"Does that mean we scan another half-million passengers?"

"No, because it's irrelevant. We need to figure where he's going."

"What about the DNA traces?"

"They're going to be on every shuttle. Bet me."

"No bet," she said with a shake. "This is tough."

I half-chuckled.

"This is just warming up."

She didn't look happy with that prospect.

They found us what passed as a stationside stateroom.

I'm not complaining. It was barely big enough for one, but it had a real bed and a small shower, just big enough to stand in. We took turns cleaning up. I didn't want to rest, but needed to, so I lay down to the sighing of the vent. I was fully dressed, next to the wall with the emergency masks. Just in case.

I must have been tired. I wasn't aware I went to sleep until the captain buzzed me.

I grabbed the phone and activated the earbud.

"Yes."

"Sir, we're done. He's away."

"How?" I asked as I jerked awake, nervous electric tingles running through my legs.

"One of my troops was found trussed in a locker room. We had to mix patrols, which I warned against from an operational perspective."

"So, he rode down in uniform, unquestioned, with both elements assuming he was with the other."

"So it seems."

"How long ago?"

"Twelve hours."

"Long enough he lifted back on the next shuttle and is now headed out. Or, he found a nice hole groundside. Or, he wants us to think he did, and is already on a flight out. The latter most likely. Can you check each ship as it reaches jump point?"

"We can try. I'll have to run that up the chain, of course. Is it worth it?"

Was it worth it? Would he sneak aboard a station, a military craft, the base on Ness, a research vessel, a cargo craft, a tramp . . . ?

"No, not really," I said. "You don't have enough man-power to do it, and there's no point in a partial job. I'll tell Her Majesty's people that."

"I feel bad about it, sir. We should have checked our own."

"You did," I said. "You warned them and they didn't listen. I've seen a lot of that lately."

I didn't want to start recriminations. I wanted to pick up a cold trail.

I felt compelled to get a message out to a secure code to Naumann. Randall wasn't going to search through thousands of messages for this, nor would it tell him anything if he did.

I coded a short update. *I wasn't going to contact you but things have obviously changed. He's better than I would have expected. He's had more training. Leads on where appreciated.*

I met up with Silver, and we moved to a hotel. We were farther from the operations area of the station, but had more room to lay out equipment. This was a nice area of the station, pretty much hotel quality from axis to rim.

We managed a two-room suite, which took some stress off for a couple of days. That stress was replaced with concern over where Randall was or was going. I had nothing to work with, and just had to wait for responses to my inquiries. However, I did insist on and assist with a search of the station, through every compartment and crawlway. It was dusty, greasy, messy work. Silver got dinged up worse than me. She was younger and more nimble, but less experienced.

Most of the station support had clearly not been

touched since last overhaul, if then. A couple of areas
might have been hiding places, but could have been used
by illicit or playful lovers, juveniles of station staff, or both.
DNA traces were insufficient to offer more.

We got sandwiches from a kiosk, and were on our way
back to the room when I got a call.

"Jelling," I answered with my standard cover name.

"Sir, I'm Roger Rothdal with the Royal Security
Service. I've some intel for you."

"Really. That's most welcome. What do you have?"

"A detailed search of Randall's domiciles yielded little,
but there are lingering traces on the hypernodes out of
there."

"Go on," I said.

"His comm received, and replied to two messages with
a node tag from Mtali, then a third message that he sent
out to Mtali the day before he departed."

"Fantastic. If you find anything else, please let me
know."

"Absolutely, sir."

"That is very helpful information. Thank you."

I looked at Silver and said, "And that's why we had
preplanned codes we could throw on any third-party
forum. He's hindered because at some point he has to
communicate with a client, and he can't do face-to-face
unless he's on the same planet."

"So we're going to Mtali?"

"Right now," I said.

I went to inquire personally and discreetly about tickets.
My phone chimed again. It was a recorded outsystem
message from Naumann.

Regarding your inquiry. Subject attended and graduated Cobra Joe Tactical Training four years ago. Information recent due to investigation.

Cobra Joe was one of the best private contractor schools in space. Well, that was truly succulent. I sent a reply.

Subject should have been IDed via DNA or other methods.

This was something we'd have to keep track of internally. Not just Operatives and Blazers, but any vet seeking training and employment like that. Just so we didn't get blindsided again.

The Caledonian Space Authority could handle reservations for anything. At the desk sat a very nice middle-aged lady. She looked helpful and slightly bored. No one else was around at this time.

"Good day," I said. "I need to book priority passage for two to Mtali."

She feigned dramatic bother. "Well, with all the thousands of people swarming to get there, that could be a problem." She waved and pointed at her screen and pad, bringing up color-coded options.

"Hopefully, there's space," I said.

"There is. It is a somewhat circuitous route. From here to our Jump Point Two on Royal Spaceways, wait two days, through to Alsace via Terra Nova Lines, wait two more days, then to Mtali on a cargo hauler with a spare stateroom for let, and they'll even transit you to orbit. You'll have to book landing there. There is some, but I can't find a schedule."

"'Somewhat circuitous,'" I repeated.

"That's the fastest route I could find. I don't think you'll like the price, either."

"Try me."

"Twenty-seven thousand, four hundred sixteen pounds and seven pence, assuming joint occupancy."

That was borderline rape, but it wasn't my money, so I said, "That's within my budget," and handed over a card.

She hid her surprise well, and I could see her trembling in interest as to what I might be doing going to a remote hellhole.

"Thank you very much," I said, and left her disappointed.

I find it amusing that Caledonia is a UN nation, but insists on issuing its own currency, which of course is pegged to the UN mark. Still, it's at least a show of independence.

Silver and I bagged up, loaded out, added some supplies available on station at a stiff premium, even with the government's official discount, and got ready to travel.

Our departure gate was the far side of the station, and I realized the boosted security was going to be a pain. I'd prefer not to flash the Queen's paperwork around. We wanted to resume anonymity. I had the captain call ahead on our behalf and ensure our traveling names were starred.

We took the perimeter tram around the skin of the station, past a dizzying twist of stars seen through ports, pillars, shops, gates, the lumps and tangles of intrasystem ships and the glare of Caledonia and Ness. I enjoyed the contrast between stark nature and differently stark state-of-the-art tech.

Our shuttle outsystem was the *Mary*. Like most such, she was a combination cargo and passenger craft, with the passengers gravy money. They were the cheapest leg of our trip, the price varying not by distance, but by energy expenditure.

The captain had done his job well.

"Sir, your names are flagged," the gatekeeper, Jackson, two stripes told us.

"Good," I said.

"That's not good, sir," he said with a half-chuckle, half-frown. He was wiry and bald and I didn't detect any humor.

"We're priority and trying to be discreet about it," I said softly. "Security matter."

"It certainly is," he said. "I'll have to ask you to step over to the side, please. Someone will be with you in a moment."

I shrugged and we complied. Whatever silliness it was, I didn't need a scene.

We waited.

And waited.

I was about to "ahem" and shuffle for attention when two other costumed clowns appeared, one male and one female, took us each by an arm and led us to a back room. They were larger than average but not in bad shape.

"Is there a problem?" I asked reasonably.

We entered the office and I was pushed toward a chair at a table.

"Who are you?" he asked as I sat down. He took the chair across from me. Silver was next to me and the female backup across from her. The chairs were on rails to allow travel, but prevent them slapping around if the station had problems.

"You have my ID." This was odd.

"I don't believe this for a second," he said, waving it. His name was Radernan. Three stripes.

"That's who I'm traveling as."

"Exactly. So who are you, really?"

Had he not got the message? Or, had the flag been misread as to offer me lots of special attention? Hell.

"I am not at liberty to discuss that."

"Sir, do you see this uniform?" He waved a thumb. "That means I get to ask questions, and you are required to give me answers."

He focused on me to exclusion, ignoring Silver. His assistant did nothing. It wasn't good cop/bad cop, and wasn't an attempt to play us off against each other.

I slid the Royal Warrant out of my coat and passed it over.

He snorted.

"Do I look like an idiot? That's fake."

"I assure you it's not."

"Her Majesty does not hand out writs to foreigners traipsing through the system."

"As I understand, she doesn't generally do so at all. You might want to call and verify that."

"I don't need to verify that, because it's fake. Now, you can comply with my very reasonable requests, or you can not be on this flight."

I'd met my share of petty uniformed thugs before, but this guy didn't seem to be that way. He seemed pretentious and stupid rather than conceited.

"Sir, I don't threaten worth a damn. My business is of interest to Her Majesty's government, is crucial, and you can comply with your own protocols—if that Warrant is fake, you must report it and the Crown will file charges against me—or you can be looking for different employment tomorrow morning."

"So, why don't we just sit here for a while until you miss your flight, then we can sit here a little longer until you decide to get smart."

I raised my eyebrows slightly and tried a different tack.

"May I make a call, then?"

"No."

"Sir," I said, "I've been very reasonable and tried to answer your questions. I've offered documentation and you've refused it. What exactly do you want from me?"

"ID, showing who you really are."

"How will you know it's not fake?"

How did I know Randall hadn't set this clown up with a bribe to slow us down?

In any case, we had a finite window to get aboard that ship. I figured we had six minutes to resolve it or a frantic reschedule would have to take place, which would be even more noticeable than our current urgent route.

Given that, I stopped being polite.

My hands were casually on the table edge. I gripped unobtrusively, with just tips and palm, then hooked his chair with my toe and yanked. It had stops, but they were closer in than his guts and ribs. He squeezed against the table and threw his hands down to resist. As he did so, I grabbed his jacket with one hand, floated the other toward his face, and snapped every joint from hip to wrist into it. His nose flattened and exploded in blood and both his eyes blacked and bloodied as well.

His assistant tried to jump back, and fumbled at her

weapons while gibbering. She'd just secured her stunner as I came up and spun across the table, banging my knee. I'm not chivalrous, and she was no lady, so I kicked her in the shoulder, tapped her under the chin with my toe just enough to clack her teeth and disorient her, then reached down for a carotid choke that finished her nap in about five seconds.

Silver had come around the table and bound Mr. Radernan with his own cuffs against one strut of the chair. She found strapping tape somewhere. Then she started to wrap his head.

"Don't," I said. "He might die with his nose clogged, too."

She nodded, and came over to gag the assistant instead. We lashed her separately and she looked terrified, then furious, then disgusted as she realized we weren't going to hurt her further, and were going to leave her lashed.

I carefully closed the door behind us, as I said, "Thanks again, sir. We appreciate your help." My right knee was swelling and painful by then. Ouch.

Our personal bags were still on a dolly, so I rolled it myself with one hand, letting it take some of my weight, while I called the captain with the other, using hush.

"Incident. May have been a setup or an idiot. Station security is unconscious and angry. Need it squelched."

He sounded rather miffed himself.

"That's really not good, sir. I'll do what I can, but you understand this is going to be a bother."

"I wish it was avoidable. I greatly appreciate your help, Captain, and I've informed Her Majesty of that. I must ring off now."

"Travel safely."

"Thank you, sir."

I clicked off.

There was a very brief mix-up at the boarding desk. The clerk said, "Mr. Arun, there seems to be a flag on your name."

"Yes?" I prompted.

He looked at something on his screen, then said, "It's nothing. Please proceed at once, sir. Have a good flight."

"Thank you."

Apparently, if you punch a bureaucrat in the face hard enough, the message does get through.

We made it through the gangtube and aboard with no further incidents. We had a small stateroom with bare amenities and use of the passenger diner. It was perfect for our needs, even if overpriced due to the urgency.

We still could be harassed en route, but that should be an easier fix. I still had the Royal Warrant, and I intended to destroy it as soon as we cleared system. It probably wasn't of much use now, but one never knows. Assets are kept until mission parameters dictate destruction.

I went past the passenger galley and acquired one triple of a good rum for medicinal purposes, and sat back to destress. There would be lots more of it in the future.

I felt a beep and checked my phone.

Re: Your suggestion. Yes. Should have.

I knew what he wasn't saying. Why hadn't they tracked me? All those files must have been corrupted during the war. They were now trying to reassemble them as best they could. That also explained why I'd not been found. They had no reason to look for any individual, and no reason to attempt to reconstruct a database on information they didn't want to admit existed, for future operational security needs. Oh, joy. What else had he learned?

It was a short flight as such go. The craft was fast. Eight days instead of ten doesn't seem like a huge improvement until you try it. I had to work to stay busy.

Because I can be a vindictive bastard, I kept a search out for Security Agent Radernan and the station. Sure enough, I found a note about his "hurried transfer" due to "minor personal issues" and that support was appreciated but there was no cause for concern. A PR lie if I'd ever seen one.

I coded a follow-up text for the captain, thanking him for the resolution. I didn't know if the clown was a plant, but he was definitely an ass and it seemed he was suited for different work. The captain responded that if they determined anything from debriefing him, they'd let me know.

❂ CHAPTER 10 ❂

THE REST OF THE TRIP was uneventful until the last leg, switching from shipboard to station cabin and back, with two jumps to twist the brain. We searched for possible targets on Mtali (not "In"—there's very little off-surface development), but there are so many factions and clans and interests, all interconnected, I had little hope of accomplishing much before arrival. We figured there were a hundred or so probable targets for Randall. We'd rule about half of them out after arrival, and add about the same number back after new intel.

The tramp we rode was actually quite nice. It was Freehold-flagged, as most are, and also Freehold-crewed. That's a good combination. Our flag of convenience often means someone trying to shirk inspections and safety to save money. Our crew means potential massive lawsuit for failing to comply, for which we had precedent only a couple of decades before. It was a family-owned hauler trying to make a few credits. They had three couples besides us, and one family of four as passangers.

Space travel is culturally distorting. You're looking at several months' income per person, so only the upper class ever do it, or middle-class people bent on permanent relocation who have sold most of their belongings. Passengers are almost always honest and beyond petty crime. The most you're likely to encounter is a loud drunk. There are occasional stowaways, and a few poor people who scrape up one-way funds but often run short.

The Travers had three wonderful kids from four to ten, our years, who'd grown up in space and well knew the handling of ships. The father, Thor Travers, was former Freehold Military Forces Space Branch. He'd bought a salvaged UN support boat after the War and fitted it out himself. His wife, Lari, had been a groundside volunteer for medical support.

I felt comfortable.

We made a point to join them once a day for drinks, and for meals. The galley was small but clean, aft of the controls but before the cabins. A good buffer zone. They were gracious hosts and the food was commercial but Lari spiced it up a little and improved it. No complaints.

The third day out from Alsace, we talked business a little. I'd allowed that I was a veteran, and admitted to knowing emergency procedures for space.

Thor limited himself to a single beer. "I can't drink much so I only drink good stuff," he said. He had quite a chill rack of real glass bottles with a hundred or so types on hand. He sat back with a very classic reproduction firearm—a handgun with a revolving cylinder—in a thigh holster.

"This is an unusual leg for us," he said. "Not many

people go to Mtali, and not much cargo. I gather this isn't your honeymoon, Mr. Dahl," he said to me.

I grinned. "No, we're doing research on some of the geologic formations for my wife's thesis paper, and because I like colored rocks."

Silver said, "I prefer the green, translucent kind with flowery inclusions."

Everyone laughed.

Lari Travers asked, "Are their formations unusual?"

"Generally boring," I said. "Lapis is common, which is ironic given the culture. There are various corunda and some interesting limestones. Not much in the way of gems or others."

"There are some odd impact formations," Silver said. I hadn't heard that, and hoped it was true. Cover lies have to be solid.

"Really?" I asked in hint.

"Oh, yes, didn't I tell you? A large one in the southern bay. We need cores from there."

That sounded quite feasible. Good.

"I learn more all the time. And if it's the bay, maybe we can go diving."

Travers turned to the family of passengers. "And you folks?"

"We're missionaries," Mr. Terry said. "There are many people in need of help."

I let a little more background slip out.

"I was here with our forces some years back. I do hope you've got a secure mission. Most of the people are quite nice, but a few make up for it." Their kids were cute. I'd hate to hear of them suffering.

His wife said, "Yes, that's a concern. We trust in God, but have strong walls."

"Good," I said. I hoped they did. Then, "What of you, Captain? You have cargo on this leg?"

"I do. Mostly weapon-related support equipment, I'm afraid. Stuff the UN will allow in for various enclaves to use for defense and support, without actually being lethal. It's the only thing that really gets imported here, except for occasional donations of infrastructure gear that usually doesn't last."

"That sounds like what I remember." And I suddenly wanted very badly to look at his manifests and get into his cargo holds. The odds were slim but possible that something was tagged for Randall.

I paid enough attention to the chatter of the other passengers to find out the Roulets were going to the Alsatian embassy, and Mr. Merkel was a consultant for the fusion plant upgrade in the capital, with his ladyfriend along for company.

"Dinner was good," I said, "and the beer is excellent. Thank you very much."

"You are most welcome," Travers said. "If you'd like to try a couple of rounds in the Colt Special Police, I may fire a couple in the bay tomorrow before dinner. There's a solid backstop and these rounds won't penetrate the hull armor."

"That would be quite exciting. Please."

I wasn't lying. But I was still more interested in his cargo.

I made an official but badly acted show of shoving Silver against the hatch to our stateroom, just in case anyone was looking. I did not grope or kiss her because there was no need to and I would have enjoyed it too much and not enough. She giggled as we fell through, then we both resumed professional masks.

She said, "You want to see the cargo."

"I do. It's all but impossible."

"You can't get back there?"

"I can. Doing so without leaving some kind of trace in a manifest this small is very unlikely. That kind of breech would not be discreet or acceptable. Can we find anything through the nodes?"

"I doubt they're even active at this point. We're light hours from either the jump point or orbitals. Unless you ask them to activate it, which means they'll know we're on, and any traces will be hard to cover with an 'oops.'"

"Do it when we hit the orbitals, and do it fast."

"What are we looking for?"

"Anything high tech or sexy."

"I'll try to set some protocols. We won't have long. Will you try to intercept?"

"No, but I'd like to know what to expect, and any official destinations."

"Understood."

There were no professional escorts on this ship.

However, I did get to shoot the reproduction Colt. I knew their function, but we covered it in a couple of segs in training. It was unlikely we'd ever encounter one in operations. They handle differently from regular pistols, and require a lot of hand fitting, but they do have nice lines and decent accuracy. I'd never want one as an actual arm, but it would make a lovely recreational piece. Shooting one in emgee aboard a starship was anachronistic and amusing. Echoes came back from the spaces between cargo pods, tinny and phasing in texture. Those cans were a taunt, so close, but utterly unreachable. I fired three rounds.

The recoil was surprisingly mild considering there was no recoil mechanism. The old guns don't pack the power of modern workhorses. This one barely pushed three hundred joules. I was used to pistols with four times that power.

"Classy gun," I said. "I can see why you like it."

"It does have good lines."

"Thanks for letting me shoot it."

"No problem. I enjoy showing the old stuff."

I went back to our cabin, and found that Silver had acquired a signal.

"It's still slow at the moment," she said. "I've started the search, though."

We closed into orbit in a fast pass, but "fast" still meant another full day at G. I've always enjoyed watching a planet appear as a spark and grow to an orb. It was even more fun in that our small port let me watch it directly, if at a very acute angle.

After dinner, Silver suddenly said, "Mining explosive, which would normally be produced locally under license," she said.

"Mtali is so screwed up that doesn't surprise me."

She scrolled more files while I leaned over her shoulder. She said, "Some isotope clocks."

"Go on." I could feel her breath, her hair, the warmth of her skin . . . dammit.

"Nano-tolerance bearings for several applications."

"Anything else?"

"Security cameras and sensors."

"Can you be more specific?"

"I have stock numbers but they're for assemblies and kits."

"Yeah, I know how that works." Each "assembly" would consist of several components. The numbers might or might not match the actual components. The kits were put together by packagers. Researching those would take time and require either personal inquiry, or a transmission.

I said, "Well, keep track of it and we'll see if anything suggests itself."

We docked at the only orbital station. It was overly modern for a backwater, and was administered by the UN, since the locals couldn't decide who had authority over what. Our papers were in order, though I got the impression it was largely a formality. They were more concerned that we not be transporting any weapons, because one more knife or gun on a planet of a half-billion population just might break the balance of power between factions.

There are laws against segregation and "profiling" in the UN. I can only assume it was pure coincidence that the robed Shia wound up in one section, the Sunni in another, the two Amala at the rear with the off-worlders separating them, and the Christian sects on the other side of the aisle, with the missionaries as a buffer. I thought it a good and useful coincidence, though. The whole planet is like that.

We landed, rolled out and then debarked down steps to the surface, rather than through an umbilicus. It was hot and bright despite the dim star—GRN 86 is a Ko; we were closer, and the higher ratio of land mass made it drier. We headed for cover, and waited for our baggage. It was brought on a cart and left for us to sort through, under the eyes of two stunner-armed guards. I felt sorry for them. They were the least armed combatants on the planet.

Mtali was still the chaotic, bizarre nightmare it had been a decade and more past. In fact, trouble started there within a decade of settlement, and never ended. It had an African name from discovery, then was sold to an African Muslim national confederation. From there, various power groups within Islam licensed plots and transport. Some peripheral groups like the Sufi and Baha'i came along, and some Christian groups believing the story of a cheap paradise with religious tolerance. Then a few nontolerant ones moved in to "secure a virgin planet against the rape of Islam." Then the Muslim nutjobs made themselves known, and it turned into something like the Balkans on Earth had been for a millennia.

One found a mix of garb, from skirts and bonnets to robes to dishdashas and jellabas, and T-shirts and shorts. Religious services ran Thursday to Tuesday depending on sect, and the gunfire and bombs added to the festivities at random intervals. Various settlements were monocultural, the capital was a mishmash, though currently in a truce with no major violence, just street gangs and midnight kneecappings.

The problem I faced was that there were far too many

targets worthy of assassination, and even more people willing to spend the money to do so. The planet exported a lot of semiprecious minerals and some gorgeous woods, so they had a steady economy with the ultrarich.

I recalled this was where my life had turned. I'd arrived a trained expert with no combat experience. Before I left, I had experience of combat, atrocities from all sides including myself, a hatred for the human race including myself, and a realization that some people will refuse to respond to any logical argument even if it means their death.

I did not feel well. Yet at the same time, it was familiar, and not uncomfortable. I knew how to move here, how to talk, what to expect. It had been formative for me.

Attaturk, the effective capital by being the largest and having the easiest star and sea ports, had changed in fifteen years, twenty-two Earth years. It was making an attempt at being modern, and regular infusions of capital and infrastructure made it a place that most of the factions regarded as off limits. They all placed their HQs/embassies/OPs away from the cultural and commercial areas, so violence was minimized, apart from the occasional vehicle bomb or drive-by rocketing. Another couple of centuries and they might actually sort things out.

Once outside the city, the entire main continent was a hodgepodge of "zones" mapped by culture, religion and sometimes ethnicity. This is something the UN has tried successfully for centuries both here and on parts of Earth. That is, they've successfully drawn lines on a map. Getting the locals to both concur with the lines and abide by them is another issue.

Realistically, we could probably ignore ninety percent of the planet. In fact, so far we'd been lucky. Randall was sticking to surfaces and major centers. His rates must rule out the lesser options. Here, there was the one major city, and possibly two minor ones. It was also somewhere I had much more experience than he did.

Silver and I had multiple charts, graphs, plots at this point. The victims were broken down by every demographic possible. The locations and MOs were listed step by step and by relevant characteristics. We had some DNA on him. She'd set up a bias function to weigh potential targets against the existing data.

If we could get me close, I could take him out. He varied his methods a bit, but they all had a high-tech feel to them.

When I'd done wet work, I'd gone for psychology. People died in their sleep and the person next to them woke up in the morning to find a corpse. Targets just disappeared. One got dismantled to the point where he still hadn't recovered, as a warning to others. It's very hard not to leave a signature of some kind. So far, the only commonality of Randall's was the kills were exotic, but in lots of different ways. Predicting his next method was all but impossible.

But mine had been simple. Find the person, kill them silently or without witnesses, exfiltrate. We didn't care if they knew who did it, as long as they couldn't prove it.

He wanted people to know who did it, and required setup and equipment.

Had any of that stuff we'd arrived with been tagged for his use? Or was he plugged in and planning to steal it?

Or had he brought all he needed with him?

No way to know, so we went back to trying to anticipate target first.

⚙ **CHAPTER 11** ⚙

I DECIDED TO CHANGE OUR MO a bit. Instead of a hotel, we got a cheap one-bedroom flat in a working neighborhood. Silver was dark enough to pass as one of the typical racial types found locally, especially once in a nondescript robe that fit many of the sects. She carried hardware underneath. I donned a light silk coat over an ankle-length shirt, and looked like a middle-class business rep trying to dress for upper-class clients. We stocked up on food and were prepared for a wait. I bought a used but reliable basic van, and we disappeared into the local scenery rather than the off-world crowd. In less than a twenty-five-hour local day, we looked like natives to any outsider. All the UN cared about was our return tickets and visa fees. If we were here over a month, I'd pay that at the consular offices.

That made it easy to drive around, get images, draw maps and otherwise plug into things. I held off on weapons. The UN would seize anything they found, and I'd need something good if I planned a distance shot.

I found an obvious target in a short search, one of the top of my prearrival list. The UN was holding one of its endless discussions to resolve the problems on Mtali, which had been going on for at least two Earth centuries—the problems and the discussions.

One Rajini al Alrab was a minor sheik and major financier for the Shia Nation Movement. Their agenda was a distinct nation for Shia followers, specifically, with others "tolerated" as long as they followed the official Shia law in public. Unsaid was that they wanted the choicest land and the capital, and to drive everyone else out or kill them to get it. For some reason, the other factions didn't agree to this.

Alrab was an agent who transshipped stuff through Mtali space to other systems. He personally owned an almost-completed grav-sling setup to make this more efficient, at the trailing Trojan and at two jump points, one from Earth and one from Novaja Rossia. In exchange, he did provide lots of money for development and charity, though with the environment, breeding rate and sheer numbers, it didn't go far. Still, he was no worse a bastard than anyone else. He arranged investors, he took a percentage, and everyone gained some benefit in the deal.

He was wealthy and visible, though, and the key speaker at this thing, which was in seventeen days.

We sat at the cheap extruded dining table next to the bed in our tiny apartment, with a large fan acting as background noise and hindering any scans from the window, but we had to have some cooling. It was dry, but stifling.

Silver concurred. "He does seem to be the only one who makes sense. Easy to find, contentious, has previous attempts."

"Pretty much the biggest fish around these parts. Lots of unhappiness all around about him, versus all the money he doles out and the hatred the other groups have for him."

"Would they jointly finance a hit?"

"It seems most unlikely, but it's possible. Do you suspect something?"

"No, just wondering for now."

"Well, the forum isn't the only place to tag him. I'd go for his residence, and just hang out and wait for a quiet moment. Either shoot from a distance, or slide in and look like a guest on a junket or some minor staff. However, I'm guessing Randall wants another scene. These seem to be largely message as much as kill."

"Complicated, but there is an MO there, and he's shown the skills so far."

I said, "However, this is a major event. Security will be much tighter than military, because they're expecting hundreds of people with limited access each, and their badges will be coded accordingly. Checks will be ongoing. Biometrics. We could crack it, but it would take a lot of work, and then we're caught inside if something goes on outside. I hate to abandon someone to the wolves, but as tricky as Randall is, I want to run recon and wait for him to show. Before, after, doesn't matter, though it's hard on the potential victim."

"I agree," she said. "There'll be all kinds of overlapping security. What about a distraction outside?"

"What kind?"

"Something to heighten security all over, to improve Alrab's odds."

I thought about that.

"Anything unusual outside will cause them to tighten up inside. That's a given. So we need something outside to reduce hit probability."

I thought aloud as I worked it out. "So, we can't do anything in the entry phase, or in his limo. Inside the arena is unlikely. I made sure word leaked out on the chameleon; Royal intel forwarded info to several agencies here, and there's little clear space the way the meeting is set up. So if anything is going to happen, it'll be when he crosses the plaza."

"Will he cross it?"

"It's traditional. The grand entrance. Not doing so would indicate a problem to everyone. It's also a chance for people to gawk at one of their betters and vice versa. He'll do it."

"What do you think then?" she asked. "Trap of some kind, rocket, bullet, or something more exotic?"

"I don't really care," I said.

"Oh?" She gave me a quizzical look.

"I don't care what targets Mr. Alrab. It won't be able to confirm Mr. Alrab."

"Tell me more," she said.

"Misdirection. We're going to hire some actors."

She smiled with a quirky twist of her mouth.

"Elegant and brilliant. It doesn't sound simple, though."

"I take it you haven't met many actors?"

"Only some of your instructors I met in passing. We get a very brief lecture on making the role and the documentation match."

"Yeah, I got actual acting classes. I've met real local actors. They're underpaid, love a challenge, and will do ridiculous things for a few creds."

"Even here?"

"It's universal."

The next day I called a local agency. I sought one run by an offworlder.

Acting is simultaneously pure art and pure greed. Given a role, actors will compete mightily for it, and take little money. This is why their agencies exist; to demand outrageous amounts of money. I planned to exploit the latter.

Silver set me up with an Earth suit and business flashes. They were piezo, digital and expensive. As I only needed a few, and had money to burn relative to the project, I looked like a big shot. I called ahead for an appointment, and insisted on discretion.

"I'm with Taylor and Ozuka," I said, "but this must be kept quiet. Most of our own people don't know we're doing this."

The receptionist I spoke to was a young woman, probably a Sufi of Turk ancestry, who said, "I understand, sir. Will three o'clock high work for you?"

"I really need something earlier if possible."

"There may be some time right after lunch at one high."

"I'll make sure I'm there. I can wait if I need to."

Meanwhile, Silver went about recruiting an established

retired theater actress turned teacher. There were three in the area. She found one I'd heard of, with good credibility. Sayina (Ms.) Aysa Meluki.

I arrived for my meeting promptly at ten minutes to one. The receptionist took my card and I made it a point to stand. The office was small, clean, but a few years out of date. The walls held shots of various projects and some local business markers.

Eight minutes later, the head of the agency, John Schinck, came out to greet me.

"Mr. Blenton? John Schinck." His accent was pure New York, and I surmised he'd moved here to run his own agency, cheaper and with less hassle than on Earth. He looked Earth, not local, probably for the aura of respectability. He was taller than me, smooth-headed and his acquiescence to local culture was a button-necked shirt instead of a pullover.

I said, "Pleased to meet you. It looks like you're keeping busy."

"I am, and that's good. It's a backwater, but there are some talented people here. Won't you come into my office?"

"Thanks," I said and followed him. "So I'm told. I work from L.A. myself, though it's not home. This is remote, though."

"Yeah, I was through on a documentary some years ago. It's a rough planet some places, but very pretty, and you can make your own future."

We took seats. These were comfortable, and he didn't put a desk between us. He understood the locals that much.

The feel-out talk was good. I said, "I've thought about that myself. I got a good offer in L.A., but I want to move back out when I can."

"So what can I help you with?" he asked, as he reached behind him to a fridge and offered me a real glass bottle of ice cold spring water, and got one for himself.

"A guerilla ad campaign." I took the bottle and we twisted together.

"Go ahead," he said.

"Mr. Alrab, who is a very complicated man, needs some media buzz."

Schinck chuckled. "'Complicated' is certainly the word for him."

"I thought you'd catch that," I said, establishing that we were both in this for the money, not out of any sense of clannish duty. "I need up to ten actors who can pass as him once made up, with minimum enhancement. We'll pay for training. Discretion is important. They just need to appear, wave, and disappear again. Easy work, but we want it quiet and we want skill."

"Eminently doable. What's your time frame?"

"A week from now latest to start training."

"Tight, but I think I can find them. How much?"

"I'm agreeable to two hundred a day, local lodging or mileage, and meals. We'll need them about ten days and if it's less, I can pay up to that."

"Two fifty," he countered.

It was fair. He'd get the fifty.

"I can agree to that. Please let me know soonest," I said. "More rehearsal time is better, and means more money for them."

"A pleasure working with you, Mr. Blenton. I'll have my assistant bring in a standard boilerplate."

We swapped a few more pleasantries about being away from Earth. The spring water was actually that. UVed to sterilize it, but actual spring water with natural minerals. Very tasty.

The assistant brought in the contract on a tablet. No effort at all, but Schinck didn't do his own documents. I understood that. It was a standard contract demanding insurance, compliance, default, payment, performance from all parties. I scrawled, and said, "Because we don't want any leakage on the nodes, payment will be in cash."

"Almost shady, if we weren't on a planet where most things are cash," he said with a laugh.

I chuckled back. "Yet another advantage," I said. "In L.A., *Variety* and half the competition know you've signed a contract before you're out of the office. Damned spies. It's like being in a second-rate vid in real life."

"I remember," he said.

If he only knew how accurate it was this time.

Three days later, I had my actors. Some had been without work and were eager. Others took vacation time. A couple were established locals. All had some experience at least, and I trusted Schinck, as I didn't know enough to make a call. I did, however, assume that at least one was a plant. It couldn't be helped.

We met first at Schinck's office. I took him at his word, because none of them jumped out as problematic.

He introduced me, I stepped up and gave just enough condescension to look like an offworlder struggling with the culture. They grinned rather than frowned, so I'd gauged it correctly.

"This is a marketing stunt for our new video system," I said. "You all look quite close, and after the compositing is done, there will be even more of you, and no one will be able to tell you're not one person. The portable holo units should even fool a lot of bystanders."

They all looked amused.

"We have a principal for you to work around, so the important thing is to make sure you can match gaits. Looks aren't going to be the tell, the giveaway. Movement and mannerisms are. You need to match him, and each other."

I got more nods.

"So Sayina Meluki will take over on choreography."

She smiled and waved and said, "We will be at my studio each morning."

They were all signed on nondisclosures, which I gathered from my past experience were pretty binding. This place was clannish, and they didn't care much for word outside the clan, but they knew when someone might deliver divine retribution. They'd been hired by someone apparently with money enough to travel between stars for marketing concerns, and they were from different factions themselves. It was easy to imagine vengeance if they reneged.

I'd rented a bus, and we piled in. I took the front, Silver sat next to Meluki. It was clean outside, rattly inside, like so much of this planet. But, it was functional. The clean was a fresh coat of paint, done semiprofessionally.

We dropped off a block early and I made sure the

driver got a tip and went back to the office. We walked the rest of the way, while I called Schinck and explained what I'd done.

"Give the driver another ten and tell him we're through for the day," I said.

"Will do," he agreed.

True to form, the first item on the agenda was tea. Meluki had an assistant, a cute little thing perhaps fifteen Earth years and disturbingly flexible, who had tea and honey and rice cakes ready. She also swept the studio, which was converted warehouse space with bars, mirrors, chromakeys and some basic vid gear.

You can't rush them and I didn't. I had some tea— quite good. It does well in their soil and light, and is more complex than Earth tea but lighter. Some of them knew each other, and chatted a bit. As actors, they were used to working with women and didn't stay aloof of Meluki or Silver, but I knew they would resume the charade in public. That was part of the problem for Mtali. Even those who didn't care for the outdated theopolitics went along for safety and tradition. They didn't have any problems with their sects here, either. Outside, the fighting continued.

The tea done, they changed into suits and got to practicing walking and stance.

They worked hard all day, and definitely were much closer to his gait, our "standard" gait, by dinner. I made a note to boost the pay slightly. They all thought this was a professionally listed gig. It was a put-on all around. A few extra dinars should fix it.

The next day, I had a tailor fit them for matching suits,

after which they did another four hours practice. Meluki and I pronounced their presentation excellent.

"You won't quite fool his father," I said, without saying whose father it was. They all smiled. Then I had the caterers roll in a cart with braised lamb and accessories. Actors get paid in food as much as in money.

I turned to the skillful Sayina Meluki and thanked her.

"It was a fun project, sir. I'm eager to see how it turns out."

So was I. If we were correct, Randall was fairly going to shit himself.

"Watch the vid and you'll see."

I wasn't going to key the actors in until show time. They were going to be impressed by the notoriety, though, for good or bad.

In retrospect I feel guilty. I'm sure some of them were harassed or otherwise affected by the event. Just because I needed to do it doesn't make it right. However, I hoped any trouble they had would be trumped by Alrab's survival, bastard that he can be.

It took a lot of people for this distraction. I called and reserved rental vehicles. I got a Lincoln van and a Maruto carrier plus a classic, classy Mercedes. I'd drive that, Silver the Maruto, and one of the actors the Lincoln. Once in the area, Silver and I would bail. They'd continue.

I was still taking a bet, but I was confident. This man was the big fish in the area. He was the only one someone would spend large amounts of money to hit, and he was going to be making a very public presentation, then dealing with several bureaus for a lot of money.

Still, I wasn't positive. Every intel agency in the universe was monitoring these assassinations. If they came up with a coherent analysis, they'd move to interdict and intercept. Was there a political tie? Some economic benefit to each one for a particular nation? We hadn't found it; no one back home had contacted me with anything. No one else was moving, or indicating they knew. So everyone was keeping quiet and looking for leads.

So far, he was doing a very good job. No MO, except "exotic." No connection between targets, except rich and powerful.

Unlikely, but had he won some lottery and was satisfying a personal agenda?

My mission consisted of intel gathering, protection of victims when possible, interdiction of Randall's logistics, to be followed by execution when possible. They all would have some effect. The more he was hindered, the less marketable he was, and the greater his overhead.

To be fair, if he'd been some petty mercenary or assassin of factional assholes on this planet, and never left the surface, we'd likely have never known and not cared. He could have made a quite adequate living here, too. There were some nice areas.

That fit his persona, though. He'd always wanted to be more. He needed feedback and attention as reassurance. In this case, headlines and money and offers of further jobs reinforced his belief in his competence.

So I'd keep attacking that.

We needed recon on site, and there were several ways to do it. Of course we ran into issues over it.

The first thing we did was send a coded message to the

embassy, citing an authorization number and requesting a drop of supplies.

We actually got a one word response of "denied." No reason was given. The code was good or they wouldn't have replied at all, or else queried for further bona fides.

Denial meant one of several things. It could happen if they were short of resources due to some other mission. I'd gotten nothing informing me of that. It could happen if our mission conflicted with one of theirs, but they'd not been told the nature of our mission, and our coding overrode anything less. I hated to think it was due to some self-aggrandizing cockholster clutching at power for an egoboost, so it was probably some petty little reg-wanker hoping that by enforcing "procedures" he'd make a name for himself.

That still left us without said supplies, especially the advanced drones we wanted. However, this was Mtali, and I had a standard map and one of the specialized algorithms taught to Special Warfare officers, that let me mark the location of several caches. One of those would have what we needed, and then some.

We were sufficiently in place. I was able to rent a small unitized coordinate excavator. I drove to the cache I needed, which was not the closest and was a little tougher to reach and, therefore, less obvious. It was in an outlying park in a copse of trees. With a coverall and some traffic markers, which were obligatory even if unneeded, I managed to dig unhindered; only a man and his two young sons stopped briefly to watch the machine scoop and scrape and dig. I nodded and smiled, let them watch a few minutes, then gestured from within the rumbling roar that they should keep moving. The man smiled and waved, and I returned it.

Once I had the box exposed, I grabbed stuff from within. I took a standard ruck with a variety of tools and weapons, the container marked for recon and a small, heavy satchel with bullion and readily convertible documents. It didn't hurt to have more money. I noted mentally so we could inform the embassy as we left planet, in courtesy they'd not extended to us. I replaced the lid, filled it in with the digger, pulled the markers and drove back to down.

That evening we moved to set things in place early. There was a juggling act of service life of the devices, detectability to other intel agencies who were certainly monitoring the events, placement and the moment when the cordon would be too tight for us to deploy them at all.

In addition to scatterable pebble sensors, we had two small drones designed to mimic generic birds, the kind humans took most everywhere. They had biomimetic muscles of memory spring, effective and visually passable brown feathers, small camera eyes and an energy cell good for several divs of operations with a half div (two hours) of flight time. They had limited payload capacity, and transceived on a high-speed scramble that was supposed to be hard to locate and crack. The birds' payload was more pebble sensors.

Silver kept getting better. With a local robe and a wicker basket of laundry she walked right through an office building two squares away. She ripped the locks in the accessways, ascended the roof, pulled on gaffs and scaled the rampart wall on the top level. It was 0300 and she was all but invisible on the ledge, a good hundred and fifty meters up. I drove past the plaza in the van, detouring around some construction, and keeping a tiny swivel camera focused on the forum.

I heard her ask, "How about over the entrance, in that cornice? There's a spot that could easily hold a nest if it doesn't now."

"I see. Concur."

"Light, please," she said.

I tagged it with an IR laser for a fraction of a second, which is not easy to do while swerving through traffic. I managed after several tries, and she said, "Operating."

She let it fly on autonomous for most of the way, then joysticked it for about ten seconds, flaring, hovering and settling. I couldn't see but could imagine this artificial bird landing, strutting into the nook, settling down and greatly confusing any real bird that was homesteading there.

"Placed. Second. Opposite," she said.

I drove around the entire square, swung the assembly, zoomed in and panned.

"I want that spot behind the roof buttress," she said.

"Ready."

"Tag."

I splashed it with the laser and she slapped the second one on its way.

"Done," she said. Good. I didn't want to orbit too many times. It would get noticed. I proceeded straight out along the current street, gave it three kilometers, turned, paralleled back and pulled into the alley behind the office block. Sections were fenced, barricaded and fielded against intrusion, but there was enough room to drive, and the rough and rutted ground surface encouraged that travel to be slow. Shortly, a figure in black materialized from the shadows, with a basket of laundry. I stopped, she hopped in, and I was in motion again five seconds later.

"I need a d-drink," she said, and started shivering.

"Devout Muslim women don't drink," I said.

Her voice was sharp. "How nice for them. I was on the edge of a building looking down to a very hard ground under a bunch of debris, spiky posts and angled protrusions. Please get me a fucking drink."

"Got some at the flat," I agreed. "You did well."

"I did well by not thinking about it, until it was time to come down. I was absolutely stiff and still managed to steer. Do you have any idea what the ground looks like from that height?" she asked.

I stayed uncomfortably silent. We were in our neighborhood anyway, and I pretended I was busy driving. I recalled hanging on a rope between two vertols, one with failing bearings, a thousand meters up while hostiles shot at me. That was in the nonsecure part of my file and she might have read it.

"Sorry," she said, and I could feel the heat of her blush.

"Just because I know what it's like doesn't make it less of an accomplishment. Very few can do that."

"Thanks. Stressed," she said.

"So let's get you upstairs and medicated."

Once inside, she kicked off her shoes and threw off the robe, leaving her in a snug body brief. I made one note to remind her that even underwear needed to be local for best cover, and to ignore how well it hugged her form.

Three stiff shots later, she sprawled prone on the bed, legs parted and hair a cascade over the pillow.

I grabbed a spare pillow, a seat cushion and a blanket and picked a spot in the corner to crash in. I didn't want to get anywhere near her when she looked like that, and she needed the rest.

I was unable to get the image out of my mind. I did take the time to note our progress on a coded sheet. Three stiff drinks later, I got to sleep, too.

✸ CHAPTER 12 ✸

WE BOOKED A HOTEL ROOM and stowed our recon gear in it. It overlooked the plaza from seven-hundred-sixty meters. That was close enough for good visibility, far enough for discretion, I hoped. It was flagged for privacy, and Silver had bypassed the lock from the outside so housekeeping couldn't get in. The manager key would work, but no one should need to use it.

That night we drove through the plaza for an advance recon. Already, large areas were cordoned off. I had a strictly passive camera and let it run steady video of our pass. We probably weren't the only ones scattering tiny sensors in the gutters, and I expected most of them to be swept up by some cleaner. Some would survive in cracks. Little bits of data all helped.

She said, "The birds are still in place, so no one has done a manual check of the façade. It's possible they'll throw a shield, a jammer, some kind of override or just an EMP of course."

"Yeah, it depends on how they perceive the threat

level. I'm torn between wanting them to be as good as possible, and being slack enough we can do what we have to unhindered. What do we have on DNA?"

"Nothing too specific. He could have been suited for a few hours. There are minuscule traces that are probably him, but could be false positives."

"I like that. It's easy to get caught up in ubertech and miss the obvious."

"It's all part of the process," she half-argued, half-agreed. "So let's head back and get ready."

I pulled out of the square a different way than previously. The unremarkable van shouldn't arouse any attention. It looked like a thousand other faded, distressed vehicles in the city, and there were lots of legitimate reasons for us to be there.

"We need to keep an eye on all this construction," I said, counting the crews at work. "I wonder if they'll be clearing them out in a few hours. Some are working late."

She said, "I assume some of them are security, masking as maintenance, pulling lines and checking the drains and sewers."

"Undoubtedly. They'll also want to have things neat and shiny for this, with all the outsystem press."

"News and traffic monitoring," I said as a reminder to us both. Radio and phone chatter about these projects would help determine which way to jump. The radio traffic here helped a lot. It wasn't encrypted and much easier to crack than more advanced intranet signals.

We cleared the area five minutes before the cordons went up, to avoid any interaction with officialdom. I'd like to have remained in the area, but it hadn't worked on

Caledonia and I did not want to risk the trigger-happy
yahoos in this system, or the political fallout, or the sheer
mass of bodies. The various groups on Mtali fought like
squawking chickens, but they fought like fanatical,
drugged-out, fervorous squawking chickens with heavy
weaponry.

We had passive sensors and video at the hotel, which
Silver triggered by remote. Her phone was a most
impressive little gadget, and fiendishly expensive, since
it contained a mutable ID tag for tens of systems on six
planets and the flexibility to add more. You can't buy them
in stores. Our Projects people have them custom built and
then do the hotrodding themselves.

We weren't going to get much sleep, but there was
little else to do here without being obvious and we had
scanners running, so we went home for a combat nap.

The morning of the summit, our actors arrived for the
"gig." One was late, and had me sweating, until he
dropped from a bus.

One named Khan had shown great promise and grasp
of things, so I tagged him as a driver.

Silver and I were garbed and geared like professionals,
in coarse, loose workpants, pockets stuffed and with back-
packs and harnesses. I greeted them as they arrived. Once
they were all there, I explained.

"We are going in three vehicles. Ms. Mael and I will
depart at this location. You proceed to the summit, where
Effendi Alrab is to appear. There are floatcams and
ground cameras in several locations."

They looked a bit wide-eyed. Some nervous, some

excited, a couple a bit disgusted. Not fans of his, obviously.

"The important part is to look cheerful. Wave as he does. You'll be along the route without headgear. As he steps out, don headgear, step through the line and walk along the carpet alongside him, but not too close together. You should look like ten of him. Once you reach this point," I held up a pad with a map, "disperse back into the crowd and greet people. You are to say, 'This is a great step forward.' Shake hands and bow. We'll meet back at this point after that."

One man asked, "Is this a security measure to make us targets for him?"

I replied, "It is designed to attract a lot of media attention. I don't know what he intends to announce, but my job is to make sure this is widely noticed." I had told the truth and not answered his question.

A couple of them looked really unsure. That was fine. I could manage with five, though I'd hate to have less. There were mutters.

I said, "I can only speculate, but part of the discussion is about the new university addition and the media complex. This would tie in with that. Ten effendi Alrab's demonstrate ten different buildings. I know we have a tasking for the coming week, too."

Someone asked, "What are the details on that?"

I shrugged. "The executive producer hasn't mentioned it. I'm sure you know how this works. They'll tell me on Saturday evening."

It worked. They agreed that Alrab was a celebrity, and that the proposed event was adequately neutral and beneficial to be worthwhile.

At the zero point, Silver and I climbed out with bulky multispectrum recording gear, water bottles, comm belts, floater controls, the works. We looked like experts. I handed a keyed phone to Khan and told him to expect my signals. "Here are the parking passes," I said. "We're paid for the primary zone."

He nodded, smiled and engaged. They drove as we made a show of checking gear and following along on foot. I watched as they got lost in the fleet of limos and escort vehicles, and turned into one of the upscale parking areas.

We walked briskly toward the perimeter, then turned down a side street toward the hotel. We went largely unnoticed, with hat brims covering our faces against cameras.

I had another car stashed here, which I'd recover later if possible. The duplicate gear went into there. All things included, this minor distraction cost better than fifty thousand credits.

Unencumbered by the gear, and nondescript, we moved through the lot—old-style painted lines on flat ground with no autonav—and into the hotel. We kept the hat brims down. The lobby was nice, but not up to modern standards. Things were patchy and threadbare in spots. They did try to keep it clean at least.

The elevator was wonky. I had to trust it, but it would be very ironic if it failed at this moment. I hate irony. Nor could I say anything. We might be overheard.

Silver and I kept up a natter of nothing. Overdone, it can be an indicator that someone is nervous and hiding something. Done right, just a little, it looks very casual and lets an agent disappear.

We entered the room and I cleared it, checking for anything physical—cuts, holes, anything left behind. Our own camera showed nothing. Silver scanned with her gear and nodded. No bugs she could detect.

"Okay, set up and get ready," I said. She was already working it.

In moments, we had gear similar to what we'd stowed downstairs set up and ready to go. It was stashed in normal-looking luggage, and keyed so it would lock and jam if disturbed, making resale difficult. Had it gone, we'd be screwed whether it got sold or not, but I never want to give someone that satisfaction if I can avoid it. Stealing from me had consequences.

We ran right into the kind of time crunch I used to live for, and I admit I enjoyed it.

I had a phone cued for our actors. I saw them pull up outside the barricade, get directed to VIP parking, and roll in. Perfect.

Our emplaced camera rerun at high speed showed the overnight setup, as the cordon went in place, buildings and subsurface were scanned, searched and tagged, the red carpet was rolled out, literally, from a large drum. Some media had driven in early, but they were all household names in their venues and easily recognizable. I doubt they brought any local support, and if so, those would be heavily searched. I could bust that if I had to, but it would take time I didn't have, and I'd be more limited because I'd have to stay with a crew. I was better off here.

We caught up on the overnight as we followed the real time, then went straight to real time. We had our own sensors, five different video feeds and the official itinerary, and eyeballs through binox. For the video, I was more interested in background shots than talking heads. I watched the crowds and the movements. I had a comfortable chair and a bottle of water to sip. The weather was decent outside, so the open window let in dust and an exhaust-scented breeze.

Vehicles stacked up, and I had to determine which to watch. In a motorcade, there will be the principal's vehicle with him and his personal staff, another with his support staff, one with extra security goons, several vehicles in place to scatter as decoys in an emergency, and as many additional vehicles as deemed necessary for a person of that stature. If you see a head of state with a motorcade of thirty, there are only three vehicles you actually care about. I had this times nine major muckymucks, and tens of lesser personages in 'cades of five or less, or in simple chauffer-driven limos.

We both scanned and marked and prioritized other potential targets, and zoomed in to ensure our people were there. I'd manage something if they weren't, but I much preferred the time and money invested so far be productive.

The crowd built as the morning progressed. Our cast eased their way bit by bit forward until they were at the edge of the cordoned pathway. That was guarded by bored looking officers, who pretty much stood at the rope and made a visual barrier. The rope was stiffened, so no one could push too far in, and there didn't seem to be any obvious trouble. There were protesters in a gaggle across the street, holding placards and making speeches.

However, unlike some other places, they were very physically polite, not getting in anyone's way. Possibly, they were afraid of a massive repercussion if they intruded, or it could be cultural. I couldn't place them to any particular sect or party, except for "disaffected youth with middle-aged hangers on."

The clock seemed to alternate between creep and race. The incoming crowd got bigger, additional press and observers queued up at checkpoints for clearance, and float platforms started rising.

Silver spoke while staring through her headset, "I spoofed the CNA codes and our floaters are IFFing as theirs. I have all three in cross angles."

"Excellent. It's almost time."

Would this work? It could be a disaster several different ways.

"Here they come," I said. Long lines of limos and escort trucks and police on zipcycles.

The security wasn't bad. That is, it was functional instead of showy. The motorcades were timed and coordinated, and one that missed the cue just circled the square rather than wait. It pulled up, its occupant stepped out with his two associates, there was some cheering and waving, a few handshakes and up the concourse he went.

Alrab was next. I recognized the vehicles. There were five. He'd almost certainly be in the middle regardless. Point and Charlie were just blocks. I was right. Number Two pulled up, someone opened the door, and he stepped out.

Once up, he waved. He turned, gestured the other way, then started a leisurely advance up the carpet. He wore a cheery smile, and his detail moved in around him.

Then ten men stepped over the rope and coalesced around him. The makeup was good enough to make target ID all but impossible.

Silver had her scanners running.

The media went berserk trying to figure out what was going on. Cameras on float platforms zoomed in from all over. The police stared stupidly for several seconds. This wasn't an overt threat, and hours of standing had lulled them.

Alrab's security went schizo and closed in in a box, then rushed him up the plaza into the building. The doubles did as we'd rehearsed, shook hands with people, smiled, talked about how great the day was. Three of them made it as far as the door. They were all apprehended, surprisingly peacefully, and Alrab was unharmed.

Phase One had gone well.

"I have possible traces," Silver said.

"So now we watch the exit."

One of my concerns was that the local security apparatus would be looking for people like us, especially after a potential threat of that kind. Our balcony was probably safe, and we sat well back inside looking through sheer fabric that would destroy incoming visibility. I wasn't sure where offworlders would fall on the threat list, though. They might be actively looking.

"Definitely him," she said. "Upwind that way." She nodded with her head, toward the east.

"That's where the exit is going to be. He'll have a narrow window as Alrab exits the building. At worst, he'll have goons in the way. At best, complete exposure from those windows there."

"Unless he's using remote eyes and some kind of flight warhead. He has better access to the black market than we do."

"Crap. You're right."

"This fits with it being a stale trace. He set stuff in place, but isn't going to be on hand for the kill this time."

"Neither should we. Where would he get those devices?"

"There are only three makers, if that's what you're asking."

"I am."

"ArthroLogic is in the Freehold, AnimaWings come from Stoltze BioTech—those are gene mod insects with micro implants, and Spy Gnats come from Kaman on Earth."

"He'd be more familiar with Arthro, I presume, but Stoltze stuff is übermodern, which fits his persona."

"Okay, do you want me to check purchase orders?"

"Can't hurt, though I doubt they went to him. If we're able to snag one we can try to ID it. I do want you to look for residue now and after exit."

"What are we doing about the exit?"

"Nothing. I'm going to trust Alrab's now-aware security, and look for Randall."

I used the telescopic camera and swept that building, looking for anything suspicious in line with the concourse. There were people at windows and balconies in the surrounding buildings, but none of them were him.

So, I used it to zoom for possible insects or drones. We

had our mock birds on a cornice, but any lead time was helpful. When Alrab came out, Silver would launch it, but if we knew where to send it, that would increase our probability of success.

There were definitely dronesects in the area, but some were probably media, some commercial espionage devices, some security . . . there was just no way to control everything that went on. As I'd told the captain at Caledonia's station, welcome to my world.

Three hours went by with no significant information.

"They're heading out now," she said.

"Got it." I strained to see anything.

Our bird was powercell driven to reduce noise. Silver dropped it in a sweep, ran up the drive, batted several bugs from the air, both real and recon, until it was identified. One of Alrab's guards frowned in disgust rather than fear, but they hurried the man into his car.

"They're killing the bugs and birds, but I still have our media cams," she said.

"Good."

So, now I needed to watch his car.

All the supplicants came out, each into their respective motorcades. Could Randall be staff in one of those? Hired on to some other entourage? Given the backwardness of this place, entirely possible. There were so many liveried and unliveried retainers running around, I could have walked out there with the right jacket and attitude. I watched Alrab's car, looking for someone to place a charge. I zoomed back and looked for someone to shoot. We had sonar and radar ready to track any shots.

Then I'd be on him like a fly on a fresh steamer.

The vehicles were not an official convoy, but they were in line and left pretty much in order, the drivers queuing up and pacing for both security and comfort, and then into a showy formation, each one sweeping the long drive and out onto the road. I relaxed slightly. Moving targets are a harder shot, and the drones were probably out of the equation. We'd compromised everyone when ours was seen.

Maybe he was safe.

I watched Alrab's car turn onto the main boulevard, and relaxed a little more. That vehicle was armored, and now in motion.

Then a car in the fourth entourage back erupted into the air, flipped over in three large pieces like a broken omelet, and crashed in a burning heap.

Naturally, he'd gone for a car bomb, because they were so common here who would question it? He may even have had several set up.

I snapped, "Get a residue trace!" but Silver was already out the door with a camera and a scarf.

I found a channel that showed the route, captured the vid and ran it several times. I couldn't be sure at this resolution, but it looked awfully like a painted gel. Simple enough. Have a street department truck roll through and lay down gel platter charges, coat with road surface material so it looks like a minor repair, move on. No one would question it. I hadn't questioned it, because I'd driven past that "construction site" during two recons. The dogfucker.

Only who was the victim? Were we wrong or had he missed?

I watched the news. The fourth vehicle was UN Bureau of Progressive Investment chairman of the Mtali Development Fund, Arman Lee.

Twenty minutes later, Silver was back, with a vial we could hopefully test.

"I will be fucked," I said.

"Dan?"

"It actually was a faction matter. He was favoring the Amala, who are poor and starving and would be better off dead. The Shia don't like that. At all. Nor the Sunni for that matter. Either way, one of them decided he was a bigger hassle than Alrab."

"Trif," she said. "What now?"

"Got anything?"

"Plenty of trace on the explosive."

"Confirm. We're close and hot enough we might get a lead." I hoped.

"Our drones are down; so are everyone else's."

"The caches are all clandestine purchase, usually local. Can't be traced to us. And the drone swarm was also to ID us. Or at least we have to assume it turned out that way."

"Is he stalking us now, then?"

"I hope so. That'll make it a lot easier. More likely, he'll take any opportunity he gets, but won't want to reveal the compromise. We might get lucky, though. Keep in mind I trained for this for most of a decade. I trained him for one mission. A very deep mission, but a single approach."

He was gone. I suspected we'd seen the last of the chameleons, though. The gimmick was compromised and he knew it.

Silver was agitated, lip trembling. It didn't look like fear. It looked a lot like anger or frustration.

"We keep catching the tail end and missing him," she complained. "Failure every time."

"Not failure," I said. "We're getting closer. We IDed the wrong target this time, and still got close enough for good intel. That's a positive."

"In the meantime, people keep dying."

She reminded me of myself when younger. Such things had made me furious. They violated good order.

What would she say about my position that most of the victims were assbags who deserved it? I objected to Randall making the moral call on people's deaths, and I understood the risk he generated for the rest of the community, but I had no sorrow for high-ranking politicians and their friends, all of them corrupt, becoming the centerpieces of elaborate funerals.

However, that passion was part of what drove her, so I needed to support it.

"We have managed to help limit collateral casualties," I said.

Sighing and steadying, she said, "I suppose that's something. He's mocking us, though."

"Part of the game for him," I said. "Hell, for me too. We ran a hell of a block. He ran a hell of a diversion and shuffle."

She nodded.

Then I said, "What we need is something he can't resist, with a nanotransponder. It also has to not be, obviously, something he can't resist."

"You don't want much." She looked annoyed, but

redirected back to the project from beating herself over failure.

"I'm sure it's simple. I'm just not sure what it is."

She asked, "What does he like that's unique enough he can't just buy it anywhere?"

"That's a good line of inquiry," I said. "He's getting paid a lot of money for this, we assume, or else he's an idiot. What's he doing with that money? It's not a drug habit. He isn't the gambling type and could get out of debt by relocating. He doesn't have a family that's being extorted. He's saving it for something or spending it on something."

"What were his hobbies?"

"He didn't seem to have a lot. He loved Projects work. Little socializing in his past and none while we were operating. He did read books. He enjoyed the old, bound style. Very fond of knives."

"Would he collect exotic stuff then?" She sat and started twiddling with a touchpad. She wanted to do something productive, or at least make a spreadsheet.

"He might."

"Would he rent sex?"

"Likely. I couldn't say what type, though. He made eyes at Deni, but a lot of people did. Tyler didn't seem to interest him. I recall he liked one of the dancers at Phil's. A lot. So, he'd probably go for tall women, mixed race."

She shrugged. "That rules me out."

I flared eyebrows at that. "While I appreciate your dedication to the mission, you do not want to do that. Not unless you are much better unarmed than your record says."

She shook and shivered a little. "No, I'm rather glad, actually. I always wondered what the protocol was for seducing someone for the good of the Force."

"Much like a suicide mission. Volunteers only. Anything else would be rape."

"That makes sense and reassures me," she said, with a twist of her head. "So," she continued, "I could make up a coded nanotransponder, which we can insert in several items and market at auction."

"That's possible. It requires knowing the kind of blades he'd be interested in, or the books, and making it desirable without being blatantly obvious."

"Also check out fine restaurants?"

"Less likely. He complained about the food a lot less than I did."

"It might be worth doing. He wouldn't have a secret lair, but he might be building a retreat somewhere."

"I don't recall he had a favorite planet, or that he'd been anywhere other than Grainne and Earth. It would fit him to pick a planetoid, though. It seems like his kind of exotic. Otherwise, hard to say."

"This will take more embassy work."

"Which I hoped to avoid, but I don't think we can."

"Well, there are discreet ways to ask," she said.

"Another thing occurs to me," I said. "We've blown through most of a million credits so far, between hotels, vehicles, food, ID changes, ship fare. This isn't cheap for him, either. I can't imagine he gets more than a million per job, even for such high-placed personages. So he's not rich. Well to do, but not flush."

She said, "I'll get three nanotransponders. You find

me something to hide them in. We hit a third-party auctioneer."

I nodded. "Makes sense. Meantime, let's get out of this hide before someone comes looking for us."

"Oh, right," she said, looking a bit sheepish.

We packed up our "luggage" and went back to the apartment. I'd have to make a trip to recover the rental vehicle and other gear later.

The final irony was that our stunt did serve to promote Alrab's announcement. I should have billed him for the service. All the doubles were released without charges and unharmed, with all of them repeating that they'd been hired for a publicity stunt. I'm sure the company I claimed and his own promoters had a fun time trying to chase down just who might have run such a program unannounced.

That, and the explosive actually had come in on our ship. He should have used locally available stuff. Not as reliable, but harder to ID. Silver started searching for its source and end-user data.

❁ CHAPTER 13 ❁

IT TOOK SOME LOOKING, but Mtali does have some neat stuff. I found my first item at a collectible bookstore, and it's a good thing I can read Arabic. It was a printed book, from Earth, on historical blades, published in the Pan Arabian States a hundred years earlier. I found several likely items.

I perused a bazaar for a local hour, asked a few questions, went to a little stall a few streets over, then into a dark, musty cellar, which had me rather disturbed, seeing as the last time I was here it was to kill people. An enclosed space with me surrounded by this group was not good for my mental well-being.

I had four locals in close proximity, and I was obviously an offworlder. I wasn't comfortable, but I tried to control it, while being polite through tea made with water of questionable potability. I hoped it was fully boiled. The hassocks were dusty and worn, but thick enough.

However, this craftsman did have lovely local jambiya

and a small, curved beltknife. He did work in gold and Mtali lapis and horn for the handles and sheaths.

I brought out the book and showed him a page.

"I want one of those, as exactly as you can make it, aged to be two centuries old."

He accepted the book and squinted.

"I can make one like new," he said.

"I don't want new. I want it to look old, for my collection."

"I can do that," he said. "That will cost extra."

"Of course. I also don't want anyone to know it's not original. I have a style to maintain."

"I need a month," he said.

"I have to leave in a week. I don't mind paying."

What I asked for would take more tools than I saw here, but a skilled craftsman can make things move. He probably had modern tools elsewhere, and it couldn't be the first time someone had asked him to make a fake.

My main concern was proper alloy, though I didn't want to come out and say so. I was an art collector, not a crook. However, he'd probably get it right, and the deception didn't have to last long, if all went well.

Silver got out and around, too. With a change of styles and her skin tones, she could pass as Turkic or Asian in ancestry at a reasonable distance or with a scarf. She drove sometimes, rode and walked others, and managed to bring in video of the blast area. Then she had to analyze it.

When I got back to the apartment, Silver was in the middle of a call. I walked in, she held up a hand, I paused.

"I don't mind if it hasn't been displayed," she said. "Can you describe it? Yes? Oh, that sounds precious. Is it a royal blue? Dark and rich? Yes, I know the pattern you mean. That's woven in? Oh, yes. Can you give me video? There we go. Yes, I'm sure that's what I want. Please send it at once."

She offered a receiving address that wasn't our residence, and arranged payment through an escrow house. Once done she closed camera and turned to me.

"I found a beautiful display case for a dagger. How big is the piece?"

"Thirty-five centimeters."

"Perfect, this is forty."

"Can you tag them all?"

"Easily. They should withstand most scans."

"Excellent. Do we have more video for this morning?"

"Some. I went to the library and used a public download."

"Good."

She brought up files and I leaned back on the bed, screen across my knees and studied.

Ideally, I wanted a close-up, high-res pic of the blast area, running video from two angles with a time count, and super-slow frame rate in several spectra. What I had were news feeds with buried adlinks and a horrific angle with a lot of shake. Only two cameras had been nearby, only one pointing in the right direction.

I didn't get much from it, but it was definitely the construction zone I'd passed twice and I could now see the blended edges over the millimeters-thick charge, which he'd even filled with tumbled stone and rolled out. He'd lost some effectiveness, but gained amazing concealment and the blast was disrupted just enough to roll and twist the vehicle instead of blowing it straight up. I couldn't tell if that was intentional, and I hoped it wasn't. If so, it was very sophisticated. I was betting on luck, but only because there was no reason for it not to be so. It could have been a failure with a little more disruption. The car was tough.

The car was so tough that even in three pieces, the passenger compartment was largely intact, though Secretary Shandari had lost a leg in the blast and taken frag in the torso. He'd been dead in seconds. However, a few centimeters difference and he might have survived intact.

Sloppy, Kimbo. He'd only had abbreviated demolition training, and specialty improv for mass destruction and disruption. I'd learned how to do anything from crack a window frame without breaking the sheet, disable ships, kill engines on moving vehicles without harming the occupants, and toss debris in a divided cone around a safe zone.

So he was probably behind the curve on that.

I turned off the lamp, shifted a bit to get a better view angle of the screen, and went through it again, this time looking for cues on the witnesses or observers. He or a shill or a camera might have been there to confirm.

We found some possible but nothing concrete. I did grab some faces and compare on my database of known scumbags. None were definite matches, and the only possibles were local. Of course, I hadn't updated since I left Grainne, and any data on an unregarded dump such as this were bound to be thin and out of date.

I sighed and zoned, running the feeds over and just letting it permeate. Something might jump out at me. Nothing did, and I stared at nothing.

I snapped back to alert when Silver said, "Dan." I didn't hear any tone of alarm in her voice. I dropped to normal level and replied.

"Yes?"

"Does my presence disturb you?"

"Are you asking in what way it disturbs me?"

"Yes."

I sighed.

"It's easier to list how you don't."

I clicked the lamp on and sat up.

She said, "We should have had this discussion already. I was waiting for you to bring it up."

"Yeah, I don't do well with people, and I don't discuss myself well. Partly me. Partly being alone so long. Partly the time I spent on Earth. Feelings aren't something you discuss there. And of course, we were in complete ID cover."

"If I'm stressing you, we need to resolve it."

"Okay. You're about the same age Deni was when I was on Earth."

"Deni?"

"Senior Sergeant Denise Harlett was a friend, the only real lover I had on and off for a decade, a fine sniper and tech specialist. I chose her for my cell because she was very good, and I knew how she worked. I wanted my deputy to be familiar."

I sighed, closed my eyes, and said it.

"We screwed up; she got pregnant. That's where Chelsea comes into this. Deni hid her in the building when they got hit by UN troops. I was out at the time, officially gathering social intel. Actually, I was going irrational from realizing I'd just killed three million people in a morning's work. So I left her, and Kimbo, and Tyler Jones to die. I feel pretty fucking shitty about that even now, and will forever."

"You had to save your daughter," she said.

"Yeah, and that didn't help with the guilt. I should have gotten the two of them out and made the fuckers pay. You might pick up that I'm not very happy with life."

"So me being a seventeen-year-old female is the problem?"

"One of the problems, yes. And dammit, I've had no romantic partner since then, because I was in hiding, and self-loathing, and don't have a personality most people can handle when I'm not pissed off, which is constantly. So now I'm next to an attractive woman, stuck to me like a hullsucker, no offense, for the duration. I can't nail you, I can't get away to nail anyone else, I want . . . dammit."

She sat quietly and gave me time to compose myself.

"There was a slaughter on Mtali, too. Partly my idea, partly Naumann's, but I think he manipulated me into it. Still, it's my fault. We went around terrifying villages into compliance. I screwed up and let one get the upper hand. The only response possible was to exterminate them . . . all of them . . . dammit."

I felt nauseated all over again. It had been a total fucking waste, brutal murder, and it had accomplished nothing. I didn't want to think about it. We'd made sure to destroy all the evidence we found, and now everyone involved was dead, save me and Naumann. I sank my nails into the quilt and twisted.

"So I came back . . . and I was overloaded with stress.

I went to the rec center, and I couldn't . . . I needed release, and I couldn't, because I needed a human being, and I needed it to be someone compassionate, so I could use them as a tool.

"At that point I found I couldn't.

"I am an insane sociopath. I see everyone as us or them, and I can do whatever is called for to them— complete suppression of emotion. I can't do it to my friends. If I were a true sociopath, I wouldn't care at all. That I care means . . . I don't know what it means. It means I hate myself for what I do. I'm broken."

I sat, hoping she'd ask and hoping she wouldn't. She deserved to know, but nothing would fix it.

"Go on," she said. Her body language tightened up as she sat back. Dammit, that was bad for our cover.

"Yeah, I'm sexually stressed, among other emotional overloads. It would be unprofessional to grudge fuck you. It would be unfair. It wouldn't make things better, and I can't do it. Part of me is overcome with lust, part is fighting it down, and all of me is hating me, and I want the entire universe to die, except I'm the one who should. And it's possible I'll need to do something that gets you killed to accomplish this, and it's between me and Randall and Naumann, and even if you volunteered, you deserve better than to be in this cesspool."

There was more silence. After a long pause, she said, very softly, "There is nothing I can do to help."

"I know."

I could hear the hesitation as she said, "I have a question, which is mission relevant, but probably very painful for you. I don't know how to phrase it."

"Go ahead," I said, with my stomach eating its way out of my belly.

"Why aren't you a contract killer? From what you describe, you fit an appropriate personality. But you're not, and he is. That's important to defining his personality."

That really, really hurt.

"I don't know," I said. "I don't want to hurt anyone. I never did and never do. When I have to, I shut down and . . . except I used to have furious hatred. The illogic. I became exactly the things I hated so I could fight them, and I can't get back."

"They broke you," she said. "I'd say it's not your fault, but that's not going to help."

"I'm glad you realize that," I said.

"I'll sleep clothed. Should we have space?" She looked serious and professional, her face in stiff lines, and fuck me if that didn't make her more exciting.

"When possible, just like we have been," I said.

"I'll make it possible. I hadn't realized until we started this mission how it differs from battlefield. Battlefield, everyone's a unit, and some have different plumbing. This . . . is intimate and personal, even as an act."

"Acting's like that, as you saw."

"No wonder so many celebrities are freakos. We've got that, and combat, and politics."

"Yes, it calls for special people."

That stern look again. "Please advise me of my performance so far."

It helped. I knew she was doing it to push me into a useful mindset, and . . .

Wait, I hadn't told her much, really, since we started.

Crap. Yeah, self-centered is Ken.

"You've saved my ass several times directly. Your technical skills are amazing. We have good rapport and work well together, despite my early misgivings—unwarranted—and no lead-up time. The problem here is me, not you, in any fashion."

She flared her eyebrows and said, "Thank you."

"It's fair," I said. "You were right that you could handle it emotionally. You've waded in where needed without hesitation."

"I still get the shakes. A lot."

"Shakes afterward are normal and expected."

"Yes, I knew that. It feels different. Then, I sort of retreat behind training when I have to confront people. It helps."

"I know," I said. I must have grimaced again. I'd done that retreating myself, to an extreme.

"Sorry."

She stretched slightly, said, "Try to sleep. I'll sit up a while."

"Thanks," I said. It was a nice gesture, but I wasn't going to sleep.

Still, I lay down to try, and had to rehash the discussion, even though that would keep me awake. She sat at the cruddy little table, researching more of something she'd compile into the files.

That had been easier, in the sense of a straightforward explanation, and more horrifyingly violating for my psyche, than I'd expected. I could never forget it, because the survivors of what I did could never forget it. I doubted most of them were very forgiving, either.

I half dozed in and out until dawn. Then I gave up and rose. She was asleep, on the far side of the bed. Even dressed, she had an elegant curve to her hip and a pretty face. I sighed.

I promised myself I'd do whatever I could to get her home in one emotional piece.

⚙ CHAPTER 14 ⚙

THE JAMBIYA WAS LOVELY. It looked and felt centuries old. The goatskin on the scabbard was tattered in spots. The wood was crumbly. The horn hilt even looked bug bitten. Amazing.

"It is beautiful, and you are a craftsman before Allah," I said.

"You flatter me. Any praise should be to Allah, for gifting me with my poor skills."

"I am most pleased. It will make a fine addition to my collection. It is so hard to find an original."

We swapped tea and pleasantries and then I made my goodbyes. They don't hurry in that culture. You must exchange tea and pleasantries. I kept it under a half-hour, barely.

Silver was likewise stunned.

"I wonder how it would hold up to genetic analysis of the organic material," she asked. "I'm impressed."

"Well, I figure to sell it as 'provenance unknown.'

Which is accurate. Buyer can make their own conclusions. Now we need a high starting bid to rule out poseurs and locals, but low enough to inspire interest."

"After I tag it," she said. "I'll put microtic xceivers in the scabbard and inside the hilt plate there."

"Bolster," I said.

"If that's what you want to call the hilt plate, I won't argue with you." She smiled.

"Fair enough," I said.

"To sweeten the deal I had this belt cut and beaded across town, and it goes with the case I ordered." She laid that out again. Yes, it was amazing.

"Package listing?" I asked.

"No, separate, and a few hours apart, at three different houses in this area. The idea is to confirm he has at least one of the three."

"Makes sense. Do you have dealers set up?"

"I do, all on commission. As a minor benefit, we should get better than half our investment back, perhaps more. We also hope to get it from him."

"I see nothing wrong with that."

She seemed a bit distant. I could guess why. Covert covers are always messy, or at least, have always been so for me.

We had a two-week hiatus before ships arrived. There were few regular routes, this being a destitute backwater. There were sporadic charters and tramps with cargo, such as we'd arrived on. There were UN-sponsored relief ships, and some contract haulers for industrial stuff. If we could pin Randall down a little, there was a good chance we could intercept him as he left. I had no moral issues killing him in public in front of a crowd. Well, one. My daughter. Still, if it came down to it, she was old enough to manage on her own and Naumann would ensure she had a guardian for whatever time she needed before she declared herself an adult. Then she'd have all the assets I'd acquired. It was also very likely he'd have me sprung before I actually got to arraignment. I could trust him that much.

I found a discreet agency that catered to businesses that needed flexible transport schedules. For a mildly extortionate amount of money, I bought into a pool of departure slots they kept open. There were fees for each rollover, and occasional expensive hits if no one in the pool used any of the slots, and I figure those slots were all actuarial, based on statistical planning of how many people would leave at once. A serious disaster would prong the dog, but that would be trouble for everyone.

I assumed this pool consisted of smugglers, military recon, diplomatic protection, lobbyists wanting deniability, business shills trying to keep ahead of the competition, and at least one assassin. The group would probably make for a great bar crawl. Hell, Randall might be the assassin. There was no way to check, though.

Someone bought our devices, all three of them, in close timing. It did make sense. They fitted each other nicely enough to make a set, and it's not unknown for sellers to break sets up to generate more income piecemeal. We'd have to track them periodically to determine movement.

We had three bags ready for departure. One each personal bag, brandname but low-end, worn and discreet, with clothes, one ID, phones. One full of deniable stuff we'd have to dispose of in a hurry, rigged accordingly. If they actually searched our phones we were in trouble, but we had to have data and tools. We each had a pouch with carefully camouflaged and concealed lock coders, sensors and extra currency and bullion. A detailed search would make it clear we were criminals or spies. However, the mass of stuff was small enough to not spook most border agents, who generally looked for smugglers and known criminals. Truthfully, they were more concerned about deadbeats moving into the system, and wanted to check your accommodation reservations. Only actual intel agents would care about the stuff we had. Except for the one stunner I'd broken down and packed.

I sent a coded message to the embassy via a throwaway pocket unit, into a library and then through. It invoked a clearance, told them I needed a worm into the Earth nets to draw data, and a code I could use to pull said information. The code would be left on a node with nothing to ID what it was for, buried in an inane post. This message went straight to the intel branch, not through any diplomatic staff, so I had a reasonable expectation that would be accomplished and ready wherever I went.

We were busy as hell, tracking what data we could, trying to determine if he might go offplanet or pick another target, and who might have bankrolled the hit. We didn't get much. He didn't seem to communicate directly with employers, though he had at least once. I also had to drive around and look busy for my neighbors' benefit.

I wanted to interrogate people from the major factions who might have leads, but it would take time to develop a source, and I could not attach myself to anyone at the embassy, nor at this juncture, the Caledonians. It would point right at me. I had to infer everything from secondary data.

I did find out the locals were very agitated at the number of drones and platforms, and the discovery of "several types" of espionage devices. We weren't the only ones intruding. Mr. Schinck claimed anguish and denial of our unethical hiring of his actors for deceitful purposes, and claimed he'd had to pay them out of pocket. Naturally, the cash I'd delivered was not going on his taxes, and he was going to claim the loss on insurance and taxes as well. More power to him.

Silver managed her analysis with chemicals, charts and a number of inquiries. Some explosive had tagged molecules for this purpose, but not all, and I assumed the trail would not lead conveniently from manufacturer to him.

She did find something, though. After hours buried at her screen, taking in nothing but water and cursing periodically, she looked up and caught me.

She said, "The explosive on Mtali was sourced by a company called Chongu Chemical."

"Okay."

"They're widely believed to be a public arm of the mob in Novaja Rossia."

"Then that's who I need to talk to if this doesn't go through."

Serendipity struck. A message popped up and she glanced at it.

"Guess where our little devices are?"

I quivered alert. "Starport?"

"Yes."

I said, "We need to be on the next lift."

She already had her coat and bug-out bag. Anything else we could leave behind. We pulled on pants and shirts, since we weren't going to be locals. We bounded down the stairs, jumped in the van and rolled.

"I'm disposing of hard evidence," she said, while running the window down. She held up a large duffel. "Say when."

"As clear as it's going to get," I said.

She pulled a striker, ensured the fuse caught in a cracking puff of sulfur over the spark of voltage, and shoved the bag out into the alley. In seconds, it was a roaring inferno of flame. Any data or ID should be effectively fried in two ways.

Once again, discretion was gone. I drove quickly, we reached the port and didn't bother locking the vehicle. I even left the key in plain sight, because if it got stolen it was one less piece of evidence to point to us. We hopped on the tram as it rolled past, entered the station with only our bailouts, walked briskly to the counter, I slapped down a card, and we had boarding passes. After being scanned, harassed and ignored by security, we boarded the shuttle.

Silver sat next to me. She smelled a lot better than the stale, musty fabric of the seats. It couldn't have been cleaned in months to be that saturated with sweat and grime on modern duralon.

She leaned close and said, *"Kamu bisa bicara bahasa?"* Do you speak Indonesian?

"Lumayan." Reasonably well. She kept her voice quiet. I wasn't sure if she knew there was a small community of Indonesian Sunni on Mtali.

"Kita harus segera naik kapal. Kita harus cepat." *We can just make it aboard. We'll have to run.*

"Kemana?" *Where?*

"Kapal selanjutnya menujui ke NovRos." *The next ship is for Novaja Rossia.*

"Kamu yakin dia dikapal itu?" *Are we sure he's on it?*

"Tidak. Tapi kita yakin karena dua dari peralatan kita menuju ke arah itu. Saya dapat mengecek kalau ada waktu. Bila kedua peralatan itu menuju kearah yang sama, berarti seseorang menguasainya. Mudah-mudahan dia." *No. We're sure two of our devices are heading that way. I may be able to check in orbit if there's time. If they're both going the same way, then someone has them, hopefully still him.*

I did not want to be on the wrong starship while he laughed at us.

Docking seemed to be interminable. I could see the station, alongside. I could see the gangtube. The mating arms swung out, and paused. Some minor software issue kept us sitting.

Then the arms banged down and we were secure. It swung us to horizontal relative to the spin of the station. I waited, gripping the safety harness, staring slantwise at Silver, for the *whuf* of the airlock. There it was, and I was on my feet in the centrifugal G, clutching bag and ready to move. The people ahead weren't moving fast enough to suit me, but there was nothing I could do.

I joined the shuffle down the aisle and through the gangtube, pent up and coiled like a spring. As soon as we burst into the station and fanned apart, I went to a brisk stride around and between people, bounding in the .5 G until I got it under control, and headed for a Comm Cubby. Silver went past me and sat down, I blocked the entrance with my bulk.

She pulled out her tracker, built into a standard pocket roll, and brought the system up.

"Still here," she said, and I exhaled in relief. Ironic. Relieved that I was about to go face-to-face into combat.

"Talk to me."

"He's nowhere near anything at the moment," she said. "Far side of the station is all I get."

"Well, let's perambulate."

"Do you actually use words like that?"

"For emphasis."

"Should I leave it open?"

"Can you keep it hot and stop the signal until we need it?"

"I already am."

"Do that."

"I already am."

"Less talk, more walk," I said, though I smiled.

We took the high speed slideway, which went around in quarters. From the low speed between gates, we took the midrange between termini, to the fast one, that even at twenty-five kilometers per hour was not fast enough for me.

We debarked at the quarter, stepping onto the deceleration ramp and then to solid deck. We moved to one side to avoid other travelers, and she brought the signal up again.

"About an eighth more. He's taking a slow one."

"So we'll take this again."

I was twitchy. This was it. It was probably far too public. Still, his retreats being limited was a good advantage. Or it was, until we finished the next leg.

"Pulled ahead. He's on a fast one now," she said.

"Are you sure? Can you read enough for station width?"

"No, I have to deduce. Too many echoes off these surfaces."

"Dammit. I'll go the other way. Slip me that item."

Her eyebrows flared, but she bent down as I did, lowered a bag, fumbled with another, and when we stood we'd swapped nondescript personal bags. Mine had the disassembled stunner in it, of a sort.

I said, "Okay, I'll catch you at the gate. Wait a moment." Then I dragged her into a kiss. It was partly for show for cover, and partly because if I might be about to die, I wanted something to take with me. Her mouth was spicy, hot, fluttery sweet, and she played along almost too well.

I broke, waved and started quickly back. She waved with a sad smile.

Great. All I needed.

I wished we'd had time and resources for two weapons and two trackers, but each was a security risk. We'd have to make do. I got off the walk at the next terminus, went into a restroom and found a stall. I latched the door, hung the bag, ignored the huge, stinking grumbly someone had left that the system hadn't flushed yet. Nothing here worked right. With my body shielding things, I reached into the bag, slipped several components together, and twisted the locking knob by hand. I had a two-shot, handheld flashbang, basically. It would crack, light off two thousand lumens, and direct forward in a large arc. All I had to do was blink as I shot. I figured more to use it to stun bystanders.

I got it into a pocket, made a show of reaching for my pants, said, "Ugh. Damn!" as I "noticed" the filth—always make use of free resources—and walked out of the stall. Checking my phone, I muttered and headed for the door quickly.

I didn't know that they had cameras in there, but I was going to assume they did and protect myself accordingly.

Outside, I flipped a phone, called Silver's code. She said, "Yes?" and I said, "Where?"

"Radius eight seven."

I was at seventy-two.

I walked along next to the slides, ready to jump over the barrier when I saw him. Faces . . . rule out the females, the very short or tall, the young, quick scans of families, focus on the singles. Had I missed him?

I raised the phone. "Where?"

"Eight zero. I'm at one two zero."

I was at seventy-nine.

He could have changed skin color, had minor surgery, be wearing makeup. I checked people with hats or keffiyeh.

I didn't want to turn too soon, but I should be right on him. There were only a few people. None looked like him. Only five males, none a close match.

Had he passed the bags off on a shill?

I caught the buzz, raised phone, and said, "Yes."

"He's at seventy, slowed down, on foot now."

"I didn't see him. Seventy?"

"Yes, right at the gate for NRS."

Dammit. Now he was going to board.

"Go there now."

I started jogging, working the low G against the gentle arc of the deck for an efficient but quick gait.

There was a cluster of people boarding. They'd been boarding for an hour. We had only a little time left.

Silver came up behind me.

"Are we sure?" I asked.

"I don't know. He could be lurking and waiting for us to board."

She looked frightened.

I said, "Buy the tickets. If we have to fight our way off we can."

She nodded, switched panes and pushed a button.

"Ready," she said. She stepped over to a kiosk and pulled two keys from the printer.

"Let's go."

We made our way across the arc. It was amazing how immense even a third-rate space station could be. Five hundred years ago, this type of construction would be unthinkable.

"Time frame?" I asked, checking my phone.

"Nineteen minutes," she said.

"We're pushing it, but that hems him in. Still got him?"

"He's at the ship, if that's him."

"It would be great to see him right here," I said. "That would conclude things easily."

We were almost home. I could feel it.

She said, "He's not boarding. He's in the downward waiting area."

"Slow, then. I don't want to spook him. If he misses and is stuck here, good. If he misses us and we get aboard after him, better. It gives me days."

"We can duck into that shop," she said.

"Good."

Twelve minutes. He was cutting it really close.

"He's not moving," she said. "I've got him that way, two hundred meters."

"Luggage transfer. Dammit."

I dithered. Was he there? Or just the bags? Those were good transponders, but they were active now . . .

"Let's get him."

She split with me, keeping enough distance to expand our net, and to be backup, and to be able to give hand signals, without being so close as to make us a unit for tactical purposes.

"Within meters," she said

Dammit. He wasn't here, and we needed to get to the ship. Except, if he was, and we were aboard . . .

I started opening lockers. I worked around one side of an island and found nothing but some food wrappers.

There was nothing to be lost by multiple pings, so she dialed in, and pointed.

"In this locker."

It was locked. I shrugged. She fished into her pockets and pulled out tools.

In a few seconds she had it open. Sure enough, luggage.

"He abandoned his bags," I said, uselessly. "Run."

This was an old game, and I was furious. He'd

wandered around waiting, almost certainly observing us, able to dodge either way, as I was now doing.

We had tickets. All we had to do was board. All we had to do was get there. We were at a full sprint, and I was about to Boost, when I saw it was too late. The hatch was closed, and the lines dropped.

If he was aboard, he was gone.

I thought about an insystem ship and transfer at the jump point, but this Mesolithic hellhole didn't have the infrastructure. Ships went directly.

I was incandescent in impotent rage. Brilliant misdirection. Now we had to play catch up again.

"He's bound for Novaja Rossia, assuming he is aboard. Find us a workaround."

She nodded, looking frustrated and worried. Was I scaring her? I might be. I forced calm. The situation was what it was and nothing I could do about it now.

She strode over to the public terminal and logged in. Ships didn't leave here often, but there were a couple.

"Got one leaving for Celadon space, in nine hours. We can disembark at the jump point, take a cross-system shuttle to the far side for Alsace, then across there and to Novaja Rossia."

"Time frame?"

"Twenty days."

"And he's going to be there in fourteen. Blast. He could even light out again before we get there."

"Do you want to try to hold at one of the stations for him?"

"I am not holding. I am intercepting, one way or another."

"I'll book them. Can we try to get the ship stopped at the jump point?"

"Citing what grounds? We'd need to persuade a UN judge, then he'd be in a ship full of hostages."

"Understood. Passage through is thirty-seven thousand and change."

"And comes with capsaicin lube?"

"That's what we have, okay?" she snapped in a whisper.

"Aggravated. Not you."

"Sorry," she said. She was taking this personally. He'd defeated her trackers.

I said, "Those were excellent devices. It happens."

"He's better than me."

"He knows he's being followed. Remember, he only has to make one mistake."

"As opposed to the tens we're making?"

She was steamed.

She was even angrier a moment later.

"Dammit, this line has a purchase window. We can't get on that one, either."

"Yes we can," I said. I motioned and started walking. That line's office was only a hundred meters down.

The counter clerk didn't seem very interested as we approached.

"Yes?" he asked.

"We missed our flight, and are trying to rebook now. Family emergency. But we're inside the cutoff window."

He shrugged.

"You will need to get on the next flight."

"We really need to hurry," I said.

He shrugged again. "What kind of emergency?"

Silver gushed tears.

"M-my father," she said. "Please?"

I was impressed. She really looked as if someone had died, rather than that someone was about to die if she didn't get her way.

Grudgingly, as if he had other, pressing matters, he leaned over to his comm, tapped in a few characters, filled in a couple of blanks, and said, "There is a ten percent surcharge for flights booked within the window."

"That's fine," I said. I turned to Silver. "Hang in there, Meg. We'll get there."

He took our info and my card, which would once again be disposed of. Shortly we'd have to funnel all those loose funds somewhere we could use them.

It was wrenching. He could be debarking right now, for the surface, or for another craft elsewhere. He could be well on his way, and we had to assume he was. His funds were not unlimited. He had contracts to keep. He couldn't afford to detour all the way up here, even without a ticket, then drop back down. Disposing of luggage . . . he might have had something else in the bags that would have aroused security, and decided to dump it. Or it could have been a DNA spoof.

I assumed he was on there.

In the meantime, we had hours until our new berth. We took the tickets and left. I didn't thank the guy.

"Search again," I told Silver. "On foot. I go up, you go down. We meet back here. Check for lurkers in shops. Check any available maintenance passages."

"Will do."

I'll spare you the details. We found nothing. We did

arouse suspicion ourselves for poking around things, and the third time the same officer questioned my flight and asked to look at my itinerary, I called it off. We grabbed a toasted sandwich and went to sit and fume.

I didn't see any reason to risk another miss, so we boarded early.

❁ CHAPTER 15 ❁

THE TRIP WAS YET another combination of boredom, frustration, strained eyes from searching data and cabin fever. News updated through the Point regularly, but there was still a lag of minutes to hours to reach the ship, and then back. Whoever develops an FTL transmitter is going to be rich, though probably more from frustrated teens and stock-watching business drones than from spies.

On the plus side, arrival was easy. Customs required a small fee, a cursory glance at our documents, and a declaration of purpose. That was processed via comm aboard ship. We traveled directly to the orbitals, transferred to a lander, and swung down on a skywhip before landing in a long, screaming hypersonic approach. The commercial port was unremarkable, just gates, slides, tunnels under the ramps, with the usual stores selling overpriced souvenirs and travelers' necessities. We found our luggage and sought lodging.

Novaja Rossia was modern without being a rat maze. It

wasn't as open as the Freehold, a bit more so than Caledonia, and as much better than Earth is as lobster steamed in wine is over raw cockroach.

If only I had time to sightsee, I'd be having the time of my life. Novaja Rossia, despite its name, is largely Western, with Germans, Brits, Americans, quite a few Aussies and Canadians and a large South American heritage. The Russian planetary development company sold stocks to a Swiss consortium who'd sold the hell out of the idea. All the commercially based colonies turned out rich and cosmopolitan very quickly. All the idealistic ones sank into the mire for lack of interest and lack of purity. There's a lesson there somewhere, I'm sure.

Grainne is beautiful, but we have high coastal hills and young, craggy mountains as the prime natural assets in our most populous areas. NovRos has staggering fractures unseen elsewhere. It's a very active planet, with lots of tectonic activity. Noglomsky Hrebet, the Legbreaker Range, was a mix of volcanic rifts and vertical shards. Oozing magma with steep basalt in between is very pretty, at least from a distance. What looks like dug terrain is actually ragged lava, and uncrossable by surface means. Gravity is .93 standard, metals a little lower and the planet marginally smaller than Earth. UV is moderate.

While the nation is modern, that terrain restricts expansion. The lush bowl of the capital is surrounded by two long arms of the mountains, with a broad river running to the ocean.

There were lots of small towns, one hundred K and under, scattered across the continent, around landing pads. Those patterned out to smaller towns and ranches before reaching an "older" range like the Dragontooths on Grainne, or Earth's Rockies. The coastal plane was mostly arid semidesert.

So, unless he sought someone in their home, which he might, any target would be here in the capitol.

Our target-predicting algorithm was better at narrowing down the choices, and showed me its nonchoices separately in case I wanted to feed them back in. I appreciated that. An MO could suddenly change. Hell, mine definitely would.

We took a room at a Hilton, out of downtown Karlsgrad but within easy driving distance. A rental vehicle, just a basic commuter, lasted two days before I found someone selling a used but reliable six-seater sport sedan. The load looked good, it was adequate in person, and I handed over cash and false ID. Silver had it registered and with a new, legal transponder the next day. She also had two other transponders, illegal but passable, that wouldn't show on any database if examined.

We still weren't positive Randall was here. It was all betting and guesswork. He could have slipped back to Mtali and gone some other way. However, I knew he'd been here before, and the explosive he'd used had probably come from here, via a shipping company with ties to the crime families.

I was confident. Bits of data, patterns, events, all inexorably drew together. At some point, the puzzle would be complete enough, I could intercept early.

Still, we were going to have to recon, and he probably had a five-day lead.

I told Silver, "We need to plan on being here awhile. If

we have to abandon stuff we can, but this seems to be at least a landfall if not an operating base."

"I'll work on the vehicle," she agreed.

"With defenses."

"I like hearing you say that," she said with a smile.

"I want our car rigged as a chase vehicle. We may be here awhile, I'm actively seeking him now."

"That's pretty straightforward. I'll do that first."

"Thanks. I'll be looking for targets and leads."

We settled in with supplies, including a variety of real food with fresh vegetables and fruit, extra clothes of several types, miscellaneous hardware and tools for fabrication. I wanted to find a rental house with attached garage we could use. With that, we'd be set for quite a few things.

As we organized, I mulled things over. If he was getting a mil a hit, his overhead was about fifty percent. Otherwise, the contractee was paying expenses and he was making less. There was no way anyone would pay more than that even for such high-placed victims. So, he was racking up about two million UN marks per year. Then, he had to stash that money somewhere safe. Our system would be best, but he wouldn't want it there for obvious reasons. Any other discreet system was either unreliable politically or had some means and desire to stop him. However, our system was not only best, but he'd never taken a contract there. So my working hypothesis was that it went to our system. It would do so in physical form, either bullion or a paid draft. Large amounts flitting around were traceable.

Although, he could do it as lots of little drafts through different "purchases," accepting more loss in processing in exchange for safety.

We needed to look for such a business in our system. The odds weren't good. There were lots of them, mostly legit, some simply evading tax somewhere else.

I ran through that theory with Silver.

"It's doable," she said. "Not really my specialty, but I can learn and get more info. Basically, we look for patterns of transfers right after his hits. Those are also going to be transactions for services rather than goods. Cheap goods don't ship out of system."

I said, "Good point. That actually means it might be traceable. Assuming it's in our system and we're correct."

"Absolutely. You realize you keep loading tasks on me and expecting me to keep up with your physical ops as well."

"I do," I agreed. Yes, I'd noticed somewhat, though obviously not enough if she needed to mention it. "I'll help wherever I can, whenever I can."

Then I said, "Next, if he might be based here, we need to locate that base. He might use several, or be arranging them now. In which case, his oldest will have some kind of intel. The new ones are still useful, though."

"Can you do that? I've got the vehicle to handle."

"Yes." There was too much work for two people. But a team's movements were too likely to be exposed. It was a good thing I was multiply trained in several relevant support skills.

I said, "I'll go out for additional tools."

It was almost like being home. The vehicle was an

identical design to the same model on Grainne with minor mods, license-built here. It seated six comfortably, eight if necessary, and had several stowage compartments for supplies, as well as cargo space with the seats collapsed. Many of the stores were of the same conglomerates, with local industrial support. The biggest thing that traveled in commerce was information—patents, designs, processes. Material goods didn't ship much, except for custom art, unique natural products and minerals, or to places with inadequate infrastructure, at extreme prices. That was changing, though. Phase drive continued to get cheaper and more manageable, and within a couple of decades I expected transshipment to increase, thereby destroying most of the unique flavor of these systems. Don't laugh. It's happened before throughout history.

I guess I just like to see the bad in things.

I found several tools, paid actual cash and used anonymous cash cards, and went completely unquestioned. I said little enough that accents weren't a problem, so I didn't even have to attempt one. I boxed up wires, control modules, some drills and other brute force items, tubing, a small welding rig. We could fabricate a lot here if we needed to.

Assuming he was here.

When I came back, she said, "There's an interesting death on the news."

"What?" I asked.

She toggled from screen to wall holo so I could see.

An Ivan Janich, the owner of KnoledgeKnode had been out in his personal lifter, and it seemed that there was a malfunction with the pressure system. Somehow, the oxygen filter had been swapped the wrong way. He'd breathed pure nitrogen until he passed out. The craft continued until pinged by flight control, which realized there was an onboard emergency, and landed it. Two rescuers passed out and needed help while trying to treat him. Too late, he was dead.

Silver cut the sound and zoomed in on what imagery there was of the relevant components.

She said, "You can't install one incorrectly. Safety feature. You have to physically remove the housing, and install a replacement one. They don't make those, for obvious reasons. It was a custom job."

"Fascinating," I said.

That was a ninety-nine percent hit on him being here.

"Okay, usual stuff. DNA, any specific purchases. Victim is owner of a moderate market business. This is new and significant. He's not got fingers in everything, and he doesn't have tremendous amounts of capital. Who pays high dollar to bump off an entertainment nerd?"

"Someone with gambling debts, or who wants a chunk of his action."

"Good," I said. Yes, that sounded likely. "Watch the stocks and any sudden offers his heirs take."

"That might be months."

"It might," I agreed. "We do what we can.

"Meantime," I said, "we have to assume he's using our same techniques to track us. He had a four-day lead, yes?"

"Four and some hours."

"He could have got into their port cameras, or set up drone flies."

"I'll sweep regularly and repeatedly," she said, sounding

tired. "Look, I realize I have to do all this, but I only have so many hands, so much time, and so many comms."

"It'll get worse as we get closer," I said. "Prioritize as you need, ask me if you have to."

"I will." She slumped, sighed, stretched and arched, her breasts amazingly taut, then bent back over touchpad, controls and mic.

She actually didn't grumble nearly as much as she claimed she had. She managed to get past it fast. Unless it was because I scared the hell out of her.

"Silver, question."

She looked up, and I asked her, "You don't complain much. Is that because of me?"

She looked a bit surprised.

"No! You treat me very well. Most officers can't help being a bit condescending, or presumptive. You've treated me as an equal, and I don't have nearly your qualifications." She smiled with a quirk. "This excludes those first couple of days, when you were acting the psycho."

"I wasn't acting," I said. Then I realized that's not what she needed to hear. I couldn't manage to joke well enough to get past it. I just continued. "I don't want my only team member getting burned out. If you reach any limits, tell me."

"I will," she said. "I think what's got me is the urgency, the time constraints, the increasing risk."

"Those will burn you out, too."

"Noted. Please let me get back to work."

I pointed and smiled.

Almost at once she said, "News reports his car was in the shop. I have a location."

"We'll drive over," I said.

Actually, I dressed and drove over while she mined more data, after I had her diddle the car so I'd have an excuse to be there. She did so with a pry bar and a grunt that told me she wasn't happy about the distraction.

Traffic wasn't great. These people didn't have the automatic controls Earth had, and they weren't as sophisticated as we are. They mostly drove safely, but dully. A few tried performance driving, so they were idiots and reckless. Still, it was better than Mtali and I prefer the freedom to the locked-in driving of Earth.

In thirty minutes I saw it. It was a very upscale garage with shrubs and color-shifting light tubes. Very nice. As I pulled in I saw they even had a fountain.

I parked on a broad apron surrounded by manicured shrubs punctuated with flowers. The grass was maintained with a combination of nano-trimming and regular caretaking, and stopped exactly at the edge. The surface was cut gray granite flagstones.

I walked inside, and the treatment was first class. Their counter rep was a very classy looking young lady.

"Welcome to Empire Repair, sir, what can we do for you?"

"Yes, I appear to have an imbalance in a wheel. Very straightforward."

"We can get to that in about half an hour."

I made a show of checking the time in my glasses. "I can wait, I suppose. It's pushing my schedule." I was aiming for pushy but not obnoxious.

She smiled and I couldn't tell it was fake. Well done.

"I'll try to expedite it, sir. I'll need a key, please."

I offered a chip that had access and fake contact info. She plugged it in and we were set, as long as they didn't notice it was sabotage. Silver's "wheel imbalance" would require replacement. No one was going to thank us for helping the local economy, either.

"Then I'll wait. Thank you."

I stepped out, acted very casual and relaxed, and strolled along the apron, far enough from other vehicles or the buildings to avoid any suspicion or notice, and out of traffic. I sauntered along and casually drew my phone.

I had a few small sensors in my coat, encrypted and remoted to the unit, and did a DNA scan. Yes, he'd been here. A moment later, I put the tools away. A large, used tool rack labeled "Rognan" sat at the end bay. Doug Rognan was one of the names he'd used on Earth. The little bastard had a job here.

I expected he would not be in today.

That gave me all the lead I needed. I walked back to the office and stepped in again.

"Pardon me, miss, isn't the end bay open?"

"Sorry, sir. It's not. That technician wasn't able to come in today."

At that moment, the police showed up. I'd even beat the investigators in, with the aid of my lovely assistant. To be fair, though, they had to arrange warrants and brought a lot more gear than I did.

There were three cars and a scene van. One suited detective got out of his car, as a young female patroller came around the other side, and two others.

I said, "I guess I may have to reschedule." She wasn't

paying attention to me, though. She was watching the approaching interference.

The lead man came up, displayed ID quietly, and laid down a sheet. The supervisor nodded, the manager came through, and in a few moments the staff from senior tech to tire wiper were all paraded into the office area. Three other waiting customers, or at least the drivers of the actual customers, sat back and watched in fascination. I blended in perfectly.

I overheard, "Is anyone missing?"

"Technician Rognan is new, but did not come in this morning."

"Who worked on this vehicle?" he held a print with information that was obviously of Janich's car.

"That would be Rognan."

There was a momentary tableau as everyone figured out the implications.

Inside my pocket, I flipped on my phone. They had some good sensors, though, as someone turned and said, "No phones inside at this time, please. You'll need to go outside."

I flipped it back off. Well done. They might actually track him. That presented some issues.

I stood, stepped forward just enough to be noticed, recognized, and cause a break in conversation.

"You're obviously busy with something important. I can wait and will bring my car in tomorrow."

With some relief and sadness, the manager said, "Yes, sir. I do apologize."

"Not at all. I'll see you early."

I planned to. I wanted my own hands on this.

I did a little evading on the highway, just to make sure. It wouldn't stop anyone following me, but it would delay them, and I'd recognize a tail. Of course, they might have me painted from high overhead, or by drone. The most effective solution to that was a pass through a parking elevator. I took a spur into the city, found a nice new one between blocks of office and shops, and let it raise the car into a bay. I found a vendor, bought a cup of pirogies and ate them on my way back. I signaled for recovery, and the forks pulled the car back down.

I took a leisurely pass around the downtown on the elevated highway, then headed back out to the hotel, alert for tails. I called Silver for an update, and she didn't know of anything obvious on the nodes or the police net.

Once there, I filled her in on the day's intel.

"Sounds productive," she said. "I have some intel, too."

"Go ahead," I prompted.

"The main purpose of KnoledgeKnode is data sharing. Proprietary industrial processes, vids, presentation transcriptions, the works. He's gotten periodic threats for years. Someone finally followed through."

"Very interesting," I said. "No government stuff?"

"No, just private industry and commercial material."

"Very interesting," I repeated. "No one came after him before, because of the risk of it being tracked. So Randall's marketable enough to expand. Very bad news. At the same time, those outfits are not going to be interested in paying extreme amounts of money. It's just not worth their time. This means his rates are palatable. I'm not sure where to price it, but I'm going to start with an estimate range of fifty K bottom and a mil top. I doubt this project was over two hundred K."

She wrinkled her brow and thought while I spoke, and replied, "I can try to find who's made recent reportable threats. They may not have been public. This also suggests he's trying to keep the jobs going and as you say, expand them. He wants or needs more money."

"Yes, we're closing in. I know I keep saying that, but we have to expect a point where things will start to move very fast, and we may not have time to plan for it."

"Understood," she said. "And the visit on the shop was productive, too?"

"Somewhat. I need to get back there and do more, but not while their crew is on site."

"Yeah, that's impressive." She grinned. "I'm proud of myself. We beat the local cops on scene."

"You should be," I said. "Dinner when this is all done."

"You're gracious," she said.

"I appreciate my troops."

The mutual cheering came to an end when the room comm chimed. That was unexpected.

I gave Silver a nod, and I ducked for cover in the bathroom. I nodded, and she clicked the intercom. "Yes?"

"I need to speak to Mr. Jelling, please."

That got my attention. I nodded. Silver gave our room number.

She turned to me and said, "I'm nervous."

"As am I. Let's see what this is." I indicated the door, and I stayed back, weapons handy. If they wanted me, a pro shouldn't kill Silver. It would slow them down and alert me. If they wanted me, she'd be behind them.

☸ CHAPTER 16 ☸

SHORTLY THERE WAS A CHIME at the door. Silver looked to me, I nodded, she opened it.

A young woman stepped in. Average size. Pretty brunette. Business typical with ringneck shirt and jacket. She held ID.

"I'm glad to have caught you," she said. "I'm Courtney Petersen with the embassy."

I stepped out, took the ID, examined it, handed it to Silver, who scrutinized it in detail. She nodded and handed it back.

"How can I help you?" I asked. I was not happy with any contact. It could only serve to mark me.

"Your target has been apprehended. We're trying to lower the recognition footprint, and want you to come in. We'll do another ID change and get you home."

"Really. Someone else brought him in. Who?"

"Sir, I don't know. I was simply told to locate you and relay the information. I don't even know your real names, or that of the target."

It was possible, I suppose. Though I couldn't imagine Naumann doing so. He'd tell me . . . how?

That was a problem. He hadn't said there was another team out, but of course, he wouldn't, and multiples did offer some advantages. I could also easily see a diplomat wanting to do something like this, to reduce "tensions." They tend to hate secret ops. Reasonable, from their point of view.

"Who is the ambassador at the moment?"

"Citizen Cambara."

"I know him slightly. How does he handle repeat or obnoxious calls?"

"He tells his assistant to 'tell them I'm dead.'"

That sounded like him.

"Who's head of security?"

"Lieutenant Riggs."

I'd never heard of him or her. No reason I should have. She was comfortable offering answers, though.

"What's your official position?"

"Military Liaison Office. I'm the junior coffee girl."

That didn't sound right. Coffee isn't all that popular with us. We prefer chocolate. Her accent was very good, but that can be learned, and I'm not in a position to study them.

"What unit did you do Basic in?"

"Second Recruit Training Regiment."

That didn't sound right either. When you ask someone that, they rattle off their platoon and company. Recruits are only barely aware that Regiment exists, except as a fact to be memorized.

"Who was your instructor?"

"Sergeant Instructor Abernathy. Look, sir, I'm happy to answer questions all day, but can we do so on the way to the embassy? Our schedule is somewhat tight."

"We have fresh ID," I said. "With that noted, we can make our own way out. It'll be less apparent than the embassy, which is certainly observed by multiple parties."

"I don't know, sir. I was directed to deliver the message."

There was nothing concrete here, but I was suspicious. "I'm only the messenger" is an evasion I've used myself. She had a pretty good knowledge of some cursory details, and seemed confident enough. It did fit in with the fact that I only knew my part, and didn't have any current codes or other info to use to verify things. However, going to the embassy was not a necessary part of the equation. I was perfectly trained and experienced in the art of changing identity and E&Eing an area.

I could see an ambassador with limited military experience wanting to ensure discretion. I could see them wanting to meet me. I could also believe there was something larger and more critical—intel I needed or such—at the embassy, and this was a misdirection to cover that.

It was also quite possibly a setup to funnel us to a kill zone.

"Can I see your ID again, please?" I asked.

She handed it over at once. She presented as very comfortable with it being examined. So, it was either real, or a good fake, or she at least thought it was.

"Where's your sidearm?"

"I'm not carrying one."

That was three discrepancies and prompted me to try

a test. I lobbed a punch, fast enough to cause someone to trigger, slow enough for interception. She ducked back and cringed but did nothing practical.

I grabbed her, shoved her down into the chair. That clinched it. She had no knowledge of any combat martial art, certainly no Freehold Forces form, and I levered her down. Silver moved fast, handed me a cable tie, and I bound her to the back of it.

"Okay, so where is he?"

"Who?"

"The man who hired you. Dark skin. Slightly Afroid features, eighty kilos. Sound familiar?"

She said nothing. She knew she couldn't bluff on it, so she just stared sullenly.

I pointed for Silver to watch her, grabbed a couple of items around the suite, and came back. I carefully and neatly laid out a knife, a pair of pliers, a bowl of water and a friction buckled belt. I looped the belt over her throat and snugged it just enough to get her attention, grabbed the pliers in one hand, then used that hand to shove her face down into the bowl.

She was smart. She held still, saved oxygen, and lasted twenty seconds before she started thrashing in panic, surging against the restraints. My arm was stronger than her neck. I gave her another fifteen seconds, watching to see if she actually aspirated any, then let her up.

I put the pliers about a millimeter from her right eyelid and asked, "Where?"

She shook in fear and spewed intel in a hurry, nerves broken. She spluttered through the water.

"GenSuites Room one oh five, north side of town, I

don't know the address. Yes, that's what he looked like, close enough, he paid me a thousand and you can have it if you let me go unhurt, please. He said it was a scam and it sounded a bit intense and this is some high-end spy shit and I really don't know a fucking thing more and don't want to, just please let me go, I never saw anyone, I'll even scene with you if you like but I want out of it, okay?" Her eyes remained locked on those pliers throughout. She was afraid to pull away in case I took it as a hint, but clearly didn't want to face them. A moment later, she started shivering. I could sense her pulse and blood pressure rip off the scale, and smell fear. She trembled all over and her lips quivered.

"Tell us everything and you can walk out of here. Lie and they find you in the river."

She nodded vigorously as her lips trembled and eyes watered even through the rivulets of water from her hair.

Silver asked, "Where did you get the ID?"

"He made it," she said. "Capped an image and took ten minutes."

"How did you find out about the embassy?"

"He had a map and some names."

That was interesting. Good thing we were avoiding it. Either there was a leak or he had probes.

"What did he tell you to do?"

"Drive you to the embassy, park a couple of blocks away. He named a garage. Walk the rest of the way and we'd meet at the front gate."

"He'd kill us, and you. I just saved your life."

She didn't seem to doubt me at this point.

I said, "Okay, Courtney. This *is* some high-level spy

shit, and you don't want to be involved. You're going to lie face down in that pillow and count slowly to a thousand. Then you're going to sit here thirty minutes and do nothing. Then you can go. We still have bugs on everything, which will deactivate at that time. Don't beat the clock, don't try to call, don't get smart. You do that, you walk out unhurt and keep the money."

She nodded vigorously, and I spun the chair and cut the tie. She moved quickly but made sure I was aware of her movements, sprawled on the bed and stuffed her face into the pillow.

We grabbed bags and walked out the door. We moved briskly, because we didn't have bugs on everything and I don't ever trust a criminal. For all I knew, she really was a high-end spy herself, and had conned me.

We were in a rental vehicle soon enough, and rolling. The one I bought I'd abandoned, with contents. We needed to relocate a good distance and clear DNA traces. That would take a bit of work.

Silver was silent for several segs. When she spoke, she asked, "Would you really have forced it out of her with the pliers and knife?"

"Yes," I said.

I looked at her and noticed her expression.

Goddammit.

We said nothing very loudly for awhile. I realized I had to offer something.

I was surprised how soft my voice was.

"Silver, I've interrogated people in the field before. I've killed before. I've personally killed several hundred people, directly caused the deaths of fifteen million or so, indirectly killed a couple of billion. I'm an asocial, self-centered thug with egotistical tendencies. That's why I got where I am. I don't like hurting people, but I'm able to compartmentalize 'enemies' as not-people, and do whatever needs done at the time. Then I realize afterward that they were actually people, and hate myself for it."

There was silence again for a while. When she broke it, she said, "I feel very sorry for you."

She meant it. That hurt.

"Thank you. I'm glad someone does."

Yeah, I'd never been very sociable. After I enlisted, I cared about Deni and a few friends, and less about anyone else as time went on, partly because I'd had to treat everyone as an intel threat, had nothing in common with most, and spent a lot of time among enemies. Then I'd infiltrated a society I hated, become part of it, wound up hating my own because of it. These days, I cared about my daughter, Andre, and now Silver. Not much else in the universe mattered to me.

I didn't want to hurt her, and I didn't see any way not to.

You know those dogs they rescue from illicit fighting rings, who have to be kept in a cage and only warm up to the person who brings them food every day after a few years? I envy them. They don't have to think about the philosophy of their past.

We found a light industrial area near the regional airport on the west side of town, and called in another car rental. Across the street was a hauler stop with a cheap inn. We checked in with cash, showered, wiped down with enzyme-soaked rags, bundled back out with sealed luggage, walked across the street, grabbed the new rental, and got back on the road.

"South," I said. "Near the starport is useful, and we already have traces in the area."

"Got it," she said.

At a small chain hotel, we set up shop. The port was five minutes by car, rail or taxi. We had a nice little kiosk for groceries or franchise food and good access to civilian communication.

"What now?" Silver asked as she threw her bag on the bed.

"Either find some more forensics, or wait for another kill to track him."

"How hideous."

"It's all we have. Hopefully, we can keep narrowing the gap, reduce his options, put him under stress."

"You're enjoying this, aren't you?"

"Only as an intellectual challenge. Okay, yes. I'm an assassin and this is a tough one."

"The only moral difference is that you have government sanction." Her tone had a clear tinge of disgust.

"Yes," I agreed. "And I don't like governments. How's that for irony?"

She said, "I feel frustrated. I wish this would move faster." She looked around at everything and nothing.

"It's one of those things we have. Months of boredom, moments of bowel-emptying terror."

"I know," she said with a sigh. "How am I doing?" she asked again.

I repeated, "Still great. You're discreet and professional,

and your support is first class. Keep working on your nerves."

"Thanks," she said.

I understood the need for feedback. Myself, I either like detailed feedback, or to be left alone. I hate someone asking for regular status updates, but I sometimes preferred to give them. Or I had, before I took on a position that made me a solo artist.

A thought occurred to me.

"If we do trace his money, I could go into competition with him."

"How?" she asked. She was changing clothes. I kept my gaze elsewhere.

"Put the word out I'm available for kills, boast of a background, work cheaper. Prove to be incompetent and wait for 'replacement' by him, because I've blabbed a bit. The bad news is, I make our vets look bad. Good news is, that dilutes the market."

"What if they then just ice you themselves?"

"There is that. I can almost certainly beat them, but that blows my cover spectacularly. Let's save that one."

Something else occurred to me.

"He's hunting us, now."

"Um, yes," she agreed.

"Okay, we need a massive DNA distraction, and use vehicles only once."

"Urine?" she asked.

"Yes. Piss in a bucket, pour it all over the landscape as we drive. Saturate the area."

She said, "I'll visit the hardware store."

I hoped he'd make the amateur mistake of trying to

catch up with me. That's exactly what I wanted. He might manage a clear shot from a hundred meters, but his MO was to get close and personal. While I couldn't predict what trick he'd use, I was confident of knowing them when I saw them.

Given that, I went out to conduct a reconnaissance. I needed to know the area, so I could look for anything unusual.

You probably don't see things the way I do. To most people, this was an area of comfortable but basic inns, franchised restaurants, fuel and charge stations, and a few hectares of weed-covered basalt awaiting development.

I saw it as a combat environment.

It would be difficult but not impossible to advance on foot through those weeds. It would work better at night, and take heavy clothing. It would also be too slow. Still, launchers could be hidden in cracks, though they'd be compromised in use.

All these inns could be sniper points on any facing window. Some didn't open, so that would require drilling a hole. That reduced their efficacy. It would take time to track said hole, but there would be some DNA and probably other evidence. The ones that opened were prime positions. I took some images, so we could assess angles and risks. There were the roofs, of course. A couple of video pans would establish shadow areas and cover.

Trash receptacles and privacy and sound barriers offered locations. There was the power terminal that fed the area. These were easy places to stash gear in discreet packages for later use. I'd have to make sure they were stirred up or examined.

There was a slim risk of toxins being slipped into food. We wouldn't eat in this area.

I walked through the lot, examining the vehicle charge posts. One could be boobytrapped, so I would not take a convenient slot, or the last one left during busy hours.

Just in case, we'd need a distorter on the window of the room to obscure our conversations from a vibration reader. We'd keep the dark screens down and the window polarized. We'd do our own housekeeping.

I felt comfortable. I knew what threats we could face and how to prevent them. Of course, feeling comfortable indicated I'd missed something. I'd keep studying.

By the time I patrolled the area, just a couple of kilometers by eye and a kilometer radius on foot and returned to the room, Silver was done. I noted the vehicle's presence, tapped on the door in code, opened it by key, nodded at the stun wand she held, and closed it.

She pointed to a couple of buckets and some spray bottles. Good. We'd dissipate our scent all over the valley.

"In other news, I have this." She pointed at a graph, gestured and elaborated.

"This account opened right after the first hit we've tracked back to him. It got a large initial deposit. It gets occasional trickles of dividends, other small deposits, then it got another large one here, after his next kill. After that, he got smart. As you said, he started having the funds trickle in, from several alleged contractees. It's ongoing, but there are noticeable peaks after each job. No way it's coincidental."

"Why hasn't anyone found this before?"

"We may not have been looking. But, there's not

enough here to justify what you speculate. Either he gets paid a lot less, or he has other resources."

"Other resources," I said. "He'll have some in Earth cash cards, some in bullion, some in tools and other infrastructure. He's likely living high when he can. However, this is his nest egg. How much is it?"

"Currently about eight hundred thousand."

"That is a not lot of money, really," I said.

"I have no idea how to seize it, with our laws," she said.

"We don't need to. The government will. It'll be snagged for escrow, put to earning interest, and if the owner comes forth and identifies themselves, he gets it back. Otherwise, it'll default to the Freehold along with the interest. It'll take a Citizen's signature at the very least, but it's doable."

"How is it possibly constitutional?" she asked.

"That one rarely referenced section that prohibits entities from creating local government not respecting of the Constitution, exploiting minors and acts against the Freehold. Easy to prove he's not the former, all he has to do is ID himself, show up and claim the money."

"Since he's doing one of the very few things our government would frown on, he can't. If he were selling drugs, or pimping widows . . . "

"Exactly. All legal. But exploitation of minors, espionage or acts against the Freehold, which this is, are proscribed."

"What do we do?" she said.

"I send a message to the boss and we wave bye-bye to his bank account. I wanted him stressed. This should help."

So, was he getting less than I thought he was?

Failing to save enough? Having a lot of overhead for his gimmicks?

Likely money was not his major motivator. A means to an end, and he'd want a pension. He probably was doing it for the thrill, hence the risk-taking on the jobs.

There was only one way that could end. If he was at all rational, he knew that.

So I guessed he was living for the day. Whatever he enjoyed was the finest he could afford. The savings were to tide him over between jobs only. He didn't expect to retire.

I understood it, at least. I'd made my career increasingly challenging and exciting. I'd retired because I had a daughter to raise who, despite being an accident, was the most wonderful thing that ever happened.

He didn't have that. We'd all been loners and social misfits. We barely got along with our own type, and the more we advanced, the less we had in common with others. Those of us on that mission really were in it for the sheer challenge. Most had died, a few had lived.

I needed to find out who else had survived and what they were doing. That would give me insight into Randall.

I could easily see, though, that someone would want to maintain that rush as long as possible. Randall had that type of personality. They'd been trying to admin him out over some silly stuff when I found him. He was loyal in return for fair treatment, aggressive against attacks on his persona—his pride, his intellect, his capabilities. Always edgy and wanting to prove it. Now he was proving it.

I felt sorry for him.

※ ※ ※ ※

Covering our DNA trace was messy and nasty, but just business. We both used the bucket for urine, brushed our hair over it, chopped up underwear into shreds over it, then snuck out with bottles and tubes to splash it over every tire and front deck in the parking lot, along with the exhausts of engined vehicles, so the heat would help disperse the material. She took one side of the lot, I the other, and we wandered around looking foolish whenever someone walked through the area. I should have thought ahead and dressed like scapers.

I had one close call as I bent over and started to spritz the tires on a Mercedes. Someone behind me called, "Excuse me!"

I looked up, feigned confusion, scanned through my memory and said, "Oh, sorry. Mine's over there. I wondered why the tire looked clean."

It worked. He assumed I wasn't a thief, and he was correct. He drove off as I went to vandalize and contaminate another vehicle.

In short order, we could be traced to this lot, and then all over the capital. Our actual location should be lost among the noise, or too dim to place easily. He could verify our instantaneous location if he were in the immediate area and we were outside, but he'd have to get there first. My plan was not to let that happen.

I nodded to Silver when I was down to some puddles in the bottom. A quick look confirmed no one else was within view this late. I slung the bucket underhand into some bushes, where the real scaper could dispose of it later. We walked out of the lot and down the road. Cars passed us, disturbing the fresh air with exhaust or hints of ozone, which also disturbed hints of residue on us. We took hands and strolled as a couple into a Rabbit Hut restaurant. An hour later, we'd scrubbed, ordered, eaten and returned to the room. To the best of our knowledge, we were clear.

Next was to egress the area and get more discreet.

As soon as we were inside, Silver hit the comm to reserve two other rooms elsewhere. I packed our stuff. Tools, gear, the other comm, my basic slacks, kilt and shirts, shoes and boots, her tunics, unitards, blouses, lingerie. I treated it as any professional task, but I knew it would be a reminder later. I don't have a problem not treating a female sexually. I do have a problem pretending to be intimate with a sexy, sensual woman while actually being a monk.

I cleared drawers, beds, curtains, for anything incriminating, hosed out the shower and wiped the tub and commode to minimize any traces.

Silver suddenly announced, "Hello."

I stuck my head into the main room to look.

There was a banker on the news. It seemed someone had spooled the axles of his vehicle with monomolecular wire, even while it was parked in his secure compound. As the car drove, the wire wrapped around its special drum and sliced right through the undercarriage, the seat, and well into him. They noticed when he fell into several pieces and screamed as he bled out.

That was an impressive method, but silly. There were several things that could go wrong with it, such as the wrong victim, a failure of materials, being IDed on entry or exit, vehicle changes. It certainly was visually outrageous, though. That was the MO

The problem I faced is that there are just too many thousands of exotic ways to do people in. I couldn't possibly plan for or even list all of them.

How many jobs did he have lined up here? At what point did he plan to retire, and where?

◉ CHAPTER 17 ◉

I WASN'T KEEN ON A HOUSE ANYMORE, given the recent tail and other issues. I wanted to be able to fly in a second, and have the protection, distraction and concealment that large crowds of people provided. However, we needed somewhere to fabricate tools. I found a small house in a quiet, lower-middle-class area just in from the port. It had one bedroom, one common room and services, a starter house for a couple without kids. I left enough cash to cover two months, and called it fair. Then I bought another car, and we repeated the registration scam. That made me nervous.

It had a covered garage, and Silver went to work, as did I. We installed a "barbecue" we could use for disposing of evidence and with a controlled air feed so we could do some basic metal treating. She adjusted, dismantled and modified parts of the car for better chase functions. I worked on some weapons. In between, we followed data and tried to figure who was next. We moved our car into

283

the garage, our few possessions inside, and I made a quick trip to the store for an airbed and some thriftstore utensils.

NovRos has some weird laws. They do allow weapons, unlike Earth. Their restrictions are all over the place, the requirements can vary by model, and the difference between a "sporting" arm and a military arm can be purely cosmetic—color or style of stock.

At an outfitters, I looked at a "sporting shotgun." I'm not sure why it's more "sporting" to shoot at targets or game with a five-hundred-year-old design rather than a new one, but I don't make the stupid laws. Again, due to a quaint local custom against anything effective, it had a two-round magazine. The barrel was seventy centimeters, which was fine for hunting, but far too long for combat work. While asking about it, I found out that there's a law against camouflage clothing. Apparently, if terrorists and rebels can't buy camouflage, they grow despondent and won't fight. At least I assume that was the logic. These fools held to the insane theory that inanimate objects create disorder and chaos. I nodded politely about how pretty it was. It actually was a very nice gun, just useless to my needs. It also had ID plates embedded in every component. I thanked them and left.

But I had done the basic improv weapons course, and I did have machinist experience, a Special Projects instructor, and a shop full of basic tools. We'd grabbed a pocket coordinate machine with lathe head at a farm supply store.

Steel or ceramic of a grade to make weapon barrels or liners was available in town, but I wanted to be discreet, so we settled for a shaft from a vehicle transmission from a cannibalizer. I straight-bored it and turned it on the lathe, not worrying about a forcing cone, rifling or choke, as this was a close-range combat weapon. A few strokes with the mill and a welded ring made it fit the receiver, then a pass through a fire while wrapped airtight in foil, and I had a forty-centimeter shotgun without filing paperwork with the government. It was not the lightest, strongest, most accurate barrel I've fired, but it would work, and safely.

For the receiver, we chose plain steel. It wouldn't be as durable as a professional product, but I didn't expect to need more than a few shots before I abandoned it.

In the 1920s C.E. by Earth reckoning, Hiram Maxim created the first "silencers," correctly called suppressors. His goal wasn't to overthrow a government or enable assassination. Instead, he wanted to quiet a shotgun so he could hunt ducks without the flock scattering at the first blast. Also, no effective hearing protection existed back then. Suppressors are a very practical device and used on most projectile weapons today . . . except on civilian weapons in nations where people are paranoid about such things.

All I did was drill a series of slightly rearward-facing holes around the barrel and back ten centimeters from the muzzle. I added several narrow, helical slots in among the pattern. We built a can with inner baffles and vent holes, stuffed it full of wire wool and slid it over the holes in the barrel, tacking it in place with a fusion welder. It protruded another ten centimeters. Not elegant, not efficient, not low profile, but it would quiet a kaboom down to a loud thump.

The receiver was a problem. It took several passes, and I finally stepped aside and let Silver do it, swallowing my pride. I'd never been formally trained, but relied on my wits, and I'd never been trained to build guns. I did, however, mill the internals. Then I cut a small bag and wired it with hooks. No need to leave shells around that could be traced to this weapon. All of this took about a local hour, plus time waiting for the heat-treat. While that happened, I folded two new sheet-steel magazines with bent wire for magazine springs. They loaded and cycled flawlessly no matter how ugly they looked, but we'd have to see how they handled combat. The originals held two shells, as I've said. Mine held five.

As soon as any decent product comes out, someone will make a knockoff. Thus it was with the crap at the store. This stuff was certainly fourth rate. I had a "field knife," so-called because "combat knives" are illegal in NovRos. Twenty centimeters of steel is twenty centimeters of steel, as far as I'm concerned, but the people who obsess over such things will accept one and not the other. It looked a lot like the standard issue military knife, but that's where the resemblance ended. This thing was decently constructed at least, but of third rate materials. The hilt was nylon and glass instead of boron fiber, the blade was a cheap utility steel instead of a good tool or cutlery steel. The sheath was neither a decent plastic nor fiber nor leather, but was flimsy vinyl. On a scale of one to ten, this rated perhaps a three.

The knife simply needed a molded thermoplastic sheath with a fabric liner to quiet it. That took a few segs. Sharpening it barely took longer. It was ugly, but workable.

For camo, I got some old workclothes, dyed them with carbon dust and grease, then washed them with strong soap and a little bleach. They came out a mottled gray-black. Perfect.

I was ready to go hunting, or to fight back against any intrusion. This was getting closer to my preferred environment.

Silver had a place to lay out tools and upgrade the vehicle, stitch armor if we needed it. She had encrypted channels to a remote booster, which I snuck up the side of a warehouse two hundred meters away, along with a spherical eye to watch for detection.

The one really tiresome aspect of this job is always having a bail-out bag and three escape routes ready. Every time one enters a building, one has to look for ways out, and assess everyone else. If you're not paranoid when recruited, you are within a year. I remember one time, six of us went out for lunch and had to wait for a corner booth because no one was going to sit with their back to the door. Accordingly, our seats, desk and bed all faced out.

This also meant a lot more time working, but Silver and I could rest right on the spot, and generally in shifts. There was little overlap. I found it much easier to sleep, and I don't think it was just the distraction of Silver's body. I'd never had a regular sleep partner, and part of it seemed to be security tension; my hindbrain never believed I was safe with someone that close. Add in the sexual tension and it had been awful. I was much, much more relaxed and rested. It's amazing how hard some things are to notice. Maybe it's just me.

I did make a point of going out every morning with a stack of boxes to mail. It looked like we ran some home business or other.

This probably sounds like a major tasking, but we had most of it done in a local week—seven days, not ten.

The cargo hatch of the car was something we wanted to keep hidden. We lined it with some tools and scrap to make it look like a working car, to hide the guns, knives, spare clothes both camo and suit, node scrambling and spoofing gear, and other mayhem the police wouldn't like if they found a reason to scan us. All we needed now was a lead on Randall.

The next day, we made a patrol around the town, seeking signals, DNA traces, listening to news and getting familiar with the area. I felt good generally, but antsy.

Silver asked, "How long do you think he'll be here?"

"Another couple of weeks. He seems to be on a cycle of about an Earth month, thirty days."

"When does he run out of planets?"

"Yeah, there is that. He hasn't gone too far afield yet, and Mtali seems to be an aberration. Everywhere else he's been have been wealthy systems. Eager to get home?"

"Eager to be done," she said, and stretched. I stared at the road. "Home would be nice. This accidental tourism isn't fun."

"No, it's not. I just realized I've never asked. Do you have family or a relationship back home?"

"Nothing long term. Couple of guys in the unit I go out with. They won't say anything."

"Good," I replied, though that wasn't what I'd been

asking about. It said a lot about me. She assumed I wanted a tactical brief. I was trying to take an interest in my subordinate's social well-being.

She continued, "My parents and sister know I disappear for long periods on duty. I'd like to ping them via repeater, but I'm sticking to the letter of the reg. This guy is not someone to mess with."

"Good. I'll get you home as fast as possible. I wish I'd asked sooner."

"Yes, you focus on yourself a lot," she said. "Given your history, it's probably a healthy and necessary adaptation."

"I hope so," I said. Except I'd been the same way before all the crap on Earth. It was just the nature of me. It's not that I'm not interested and compassionate, but I really don't notice other people except as resources. I do care when they get hurt, but it's a responsive act, not a natural interest. I don't even know if that's environmental behavior or instinctive.

Just then she said, "We've got one!" and brought audio up for me.

"—collapsed dead over dinner, apparently from a neural toxin. We will bring you other details as they become available."

"Where?" I asked.

She popped up a map. I said, "Directions." she keyed it and off we went. I exceeded traffic laws slightly, but generally complied, twitching in frustration as we went. If we could get there fast, we could try for an intercept.

The place was cordoned, barricaded, had remotes up to first inform and then intercept vehicles, and a quickly building ring of press. Without a word, Silver handed me a press badge and grabbed two headband cameras from her ready bag.

I parked, we hopped out, and no one should question us rushing over. I looked for any kind of entrance, but there were too many cops and I didn't want to be noticed. He was likely in the area, and might even have had a boobytrap waiting for me.

I walked around the whole building quickly and kept alert for him. Unlikely, but it could happen that I'd just run into him. The place was a restaurant and garden with a wall at one end of a block of upscale shops and eateries. It had ironwork and nice bricks.

Silver took my cue and scanned around. She was looking for facial features, transmissions, signs of similar recon gear—that last had to be hard. I expected several of the news crews to be placed there, and that would complicate the search.

I didn't see him, and Silver reported nothing at her end.

That done, I sought a gaggle of press on a grassy island overlooking the entrance and oozed in. There were ongoing mutters but I wanted something solid.

A videographer from XKC nodded as I wandered closer. He glanced at my badge and deduced I was private. I nodded back and walked through obstacles of feet and bags, professionally not stepping on anything.

"What did you hear?" I asked.

"Binary poison," he said. "They say the wine and his food were contaminated. Someone had it in for him."

"Apparently. Who?"

"Alec Lenz."

I was supposed to recognize the name and said, "Damn." I found out later he was an investigative reporter. That could be useful.

Binary poison. That was interesting. Not as flashy, but I was sure it was him. Doctoring the wine would give him a thrill, and tweaking the right glass or plate another. It was very tricky.

I didn't want to stick around too long, so I nodded and we headed back to the car.

I drove. As I pulled into traffic I said, "I'm going to orbit out by streets. We might see something."

"Understood," she said. "What do you make of him? Settling down here?"

"Hired here," I said. "The mob is using him. Either he got a long term contract to eliminate their problems, or the previous ones were tests, though I expect pay was involved. You don't hire someone to knock off major players in your backyard without bona fides."

"Reasonable," she said. "We can try again to trace the money."

"Yeah. I don't see anything so far, but I do see a Gem sedan that's been behind us for two turns. Watch it for me."

"Got it," she said, and looked into the mirrors and screens.

I made another turn, and she said, "We're definitely being followed."

"That's interesting. They are definitely not him."

"Hirelings."

I grinned. "That's eating into his capital. Good."

"Yes, well they're gaining fast."

"Let's take the upcoming right toward the mountains. I want a quiet area. We'll try for a collar."

"There's a park about five kilometers out," she said.

"Good. Can you distract them?" I asked, revving the turbine while feeling and hearing the tires shiver on the edge of traction. I powered out of the bend, and counted four cars all matching speed.

"I can do more than that in moment," she agreed. "Do we have another curve?"

"Just ahead."

"Tell me when you start in."

"Now," I said.

"Distracting," she said.

A glance at the screen showed a pall of greasy smoke behind us. She'd rigged an oil injector on the exhaust. Standard, and effective. There's not much you can do against it.

"That slowed them," she said. "Want more?"

"Yes."

She said, "Caltrops and oil. I cut some large size ones while you were working on the barrel." She fumbled and shifted.

"Excellent." I assumed they had typical reinforced tires, but what she had would tangle in the undercarriage, and from a look at the screens, was. The first car careened, skidded, spun and crashed off the side into the growth.

"He must have paid them a lot," I said.

"Good. Logistical win? We eat away at his funds?"

"That won't stop him, but might make him more desperate."

The second car swerved around the first, accelerated and came for us. They were still smart enough not to bother trying to shoot from moving platform to moving target, though I wondered about a directional EMP or some such. Hell, I wondered about missiles. If I could rig a launcher in a car, so could someone else.

Local laws might have hindered them. He likely called them on short notice, after determining we'd arrived. These were pros, but probably didn't keep missiles around on the off chance some desperate military types hired them. Still, they had four vehicles to my one and several people to our two. Amateurs can be even worse because they're clumsy and crude.

They still hadn't shot at us, either. I figured it would be a good idea for me to start those hostilities. They wouldn't want attention any more than I did, and I'd be better at evading.

"That park you mentioned," I said.

"Fifteen hundred meters on the right," she said.

"Noted. Can you climb into the back and get the gun?"

"I can," she agreed. She sounded a little unsure, but didn't object.

She climbed past my shoulder, as I tried to gauge pursuit. They were faster, and gaining. The park came up quickly. Sign, signal on the dash . . .

"Turning," I said. "Get ready to deploy right."

I swung into the turn, she swung into me, tires protested, I nailed it as we straightened, and braked hard to turn again into a parking area. All three cars turned in after us and the fourth one was visible a ways back. I spun and barreled back as they dodged, and I could see guns now, though they hadn't fired and didn't try to wreck. Interesting. Was it possible they weren't hostile? Except they had guns out.

Then one of them did fire, and perforated a window. Silver yelped. She was just straightening out, and had the shotgun.

I gripped the yoke and drove down an access road that ended in bollards. I leaned into the brakes, unlatched the door, said, "Gun!" and leaned more.

She passed over the gun, I reached a stop, let momentum throw the door open, and tumbled out fast, tucked around the comforting feel of large gauge firepower. I rolled into some brush and confirmed I heard her door, too. Good.

I heard their cars screeching to a stop, the tire compound melting instead of grabbing. That took effort, given the modern materials coming out now.

The park was pretty generic, really. Lots of Earth grass cut short, some stone walls and a couple of cairns. Those were carved from local lava, as was most stone here. There were some walkways through the trees, like the one where I'd slammed to a stop. A couple of pavilions for parties and meetings, a restroom block and a utility shed rounded things out. In the misty distance I saw a children's digging pit and some kind of climbing toy with slides and things.

I cleared the brush and stood to see several thugs coming toward me, lightly armed with pistols and bars. Sixteen, at a gestaltic take.

I love operating in a society where few people are armed. The psychological effect of a weapon on the rabbits is quite gratifying. Back home, it barely would have caused a raised eyebrow. Here, however . . .

I whipped it out from under my coat and jacked a round. They recognized the threat and scattered. That wasn't entirely the best outcome, but it did mean, unless they were very professional, their attack wouldn't be coordinated.

I reviewed where each had run, chose a direction, and took back off into the growth. Two had chosen the foot-paths over this way, and I was between those.

One of them heard me and took a shot. That was excellent, because he got nowhere near me. I heard the *crackzing!* of the round about four meters ahead, saw a very faint but definite muzzle flash, and heard his buddy to my right curse. They were perhaps five meters each way. I fired left first, figuring the one on the receiving end would need a moment to recover. Then I fired at the other. I heard him yelp, so that was a wound.

The other one fired again at the *whamf!* from my gun. I can't describe it better than that. A bang, but softened at the edges and lowered forty dB. I'd moved as I shot, so he missed; I fired again and didn't.

I slid another shell in the breech to conserve the magazine, looped around to the man I thought I'd injured to find him clutching a leg. He tried to stand, I kicked him in the head and kept running.

The woods were my friend, but the goons did have numbers and could set ambushes. I decided to relocate to the service building. I crossed the path, bounded twice in the woods, then out onto the grass and forward through the open.

I wiped out as I hit the parking lot. It was ringed by a "decorative" chain fence about thirty centimeters high. I ran into it at a sprint, which made my shin scream. I stumbled and rolled, and that's when I did the rest of it. I tried to land weapon-butt first and roll, but missed the timing and landed on my little finger. Let me say that again: I put close to one hundred kilos down on one little finger, second knuckle, at a dead run.

I thought I'd pass out from the pain. Not only was it certainly broken, I skinned it to the bone and then some. Then my head slammed down, as I'd not tucked enough. I lost skin and hair and jarred my neck. The pain between those three was so great that I saw spots, blotches and streaks, and just managed to divert a heave from becoming vomit which I would have aspirated. I Boosted, swallowed, clenched my teeth, went into recovery breathing, and let the tears flow as I keened as quietly as I could. I staggered two steps and threw myself alongside what looked like one of a pair of public restrooms to catch some breaths and deal with shock, sitting with my tortured skull gingerly resting on the bricks. My ribs started hurting, too, from the strain and tumble.

I realized I was in light, not shadow, and moved sideways quickly. When you do something stupid, it's time to stop and regroup, only I couldn't. I heard steps, knew one of the thugs was approaching, and stood ready. As he came around the corner, I shoved the muzzle up under his ribs to increase the suppression, and fired a shot straight through his inferior vena cava, liver, lungs and spine. There was a _whump!_, his exhale, and a thud as he hit the ground. I scooped up his pistol and jammed it into the other pocket. My finger was on fire, aching and throbbing, and had gotten dinged again as I shot. I ignored it, turned, and ran around the building, hearing his buddy approach.

I cleared the building with my back to the wall, saw one guy disappear between the buildings. He gasped, swore, and knelt to check his buddy. I came around behind him and fired a load right up his ass, balls and spine. He squealed slightly and dropped. I dodged around him and then cleared the other building, low and slow. As I snuck around the corner, I saw two more of them bringing up the rear, then a third behind them, as they spread out to look for me.

I reloaded gingerly, using only two fingers. Carefully then, I eased the muzzle past the corner, shot number five, and waited. The sound echoed between the buildings and the concrete walk. This combined with the sound when the previous victim dropped, caused their attention to be diverted toward him. Not being chivalrous, I shot two more in the back post haste, and departed the field at a low run.

Shots cracked past, a couple of them frighteningly close, but I was alive and they had seven down of sixteen.

As I ran, I reloaded with the fresh magazine. The depleted one went into a pocket, and I reached in to slide five more shells into it with my good hand. The damaged hand could support the weapon and would have to fire while my left did most of the heavy and fine work.

Silver whispered in my earbuds, "Approaching," and I took a moment to figure out she meant herself. I saw a hand wave behind the gate cairn, and I angled that way.

I low-pitched a pistol, dodged the other way and took cover.

She didn't hesitate, but scooped it up, glanced it over, raised it plane over the stones and shot. She got one, who staggered and snarled and tumbled to his ass. Then she winged another, as I got one in the face, pointshooting as I stood.

This caused them to reassess, and they seemed to have some training. They pulled into a group while unloading suppressing fire.

I wondered how long it would be before the cops showed up. We were rather remote, but someone had to have heard by now.

Silver sprawled prone and low around the rock, fired twice more, and another one dropped. I think she got him in the leg, but he didn't like it. Dirt kicked up around her, and she flinched, then I stopped watching as I whipped around and fired two more quick shots for a wound.

It really hadn't taken long. I'd killed five and wounded two, she'd killed at least one and wounded two. That left five functional, and they'd retreated in a group into one of the cars. They ripped out throwing gravel and I let them go.

There were five wiggling wounded here, though, and they varied from critical and alive to barely scratched. It wasn't over yet.

Once again, my training proved useful. Some of the most ridiculous exercises have real world applications.

My survival course was much like that which pilots and combat rescue teams got, with one difference. I had to survive, and I had to keep four of them quiet for ten days.

They'd get recovered as soon as they could signal a search party. My task was to stop them from doing so, keep control of them, and keep them alive, then get us all out together. I'd been given a uniform stripped of fasteners, and my wits and viciousness.

This would be easier. I didn't particularly care about this round of clowns, nor did I need them alive. I grabbed the one with the shot thigh, wrapped a sleeve over his mouth, and dragged as he twitched and tried to scream, in muffled gurgling squeaks.

I whacked him in the skull, grabbed a cable tie from my pocket to attach him to a corner of the railing on the forest side, and went for the others.

The second one's guts were peppered with 6.5millimeter shot. He moaned rather than screamed, and I dragged him to his buddy, but placed him an entire railing length away.

The third one had a shattered ankle, and after two kicks and a whimper, he passed out and wet himself in a muffled trickle. Yeah, I bet it hurt. Well, so did the remains of my finger, so prong him.

Number Four was near dead. Five had been stunned and was upright and scared but decided to put up a fight when I got close. I let the fist hit me, rolled aside and caught his elbow, hooked his wrist in my elbow and bent. It didn't shatter, but it did throw him to the ground. I kicked him hard in the kidney, balls and anus, then in the solar plexus as he thrashed and twitched over. Then I just grabbed the back of his jacket and dragged.

Four of the five were mostly conscious, all wounded, and mentally stunned from the fight. They'd started with sixteen-to-one odds and now I had the upper hand.

Number Four was pretty well gone, but he still might save a couple of his buddies.

I looked at his hemorrhaged, concussed eyes and asked, "Who hired you?"

I gave him a three count, as he tried to track and follow me, then reached down and punched the knife into his throat. He gurgled, his legs frog-kicked, and he died in a spilling pool of blood.

Number Five was not the boss, and had put up a crappy fight. I walked over to him and repeated the same question in the same dispassionate monotone. "Who hired you?"

"I don't know! I really don't know!"

"Who does?"

"Him! Krensky knows!" He wiggled his hands and pointed with his chin.

"Thank you," I said, and sliced his throat out with a swift flick. He gurgled and sighed and gargled and strained, then died.

"Krensky, I don't need to kill you all. I do need the information. It's all up to you."

He couldn't talk fast enough. His voice was animated and high as he said, "Dark-haired goz, mid-thirties, very fit. Roll of cash, some bullion."

"Where?"

"Inn Seven, north side, room twenty-three."

"When?"

"Monday." Today was Thursday. That was pretty fast.

"How much?"

"Five thousand each."

Eighty thousand to do me in. I was flattered. That might be ten percent of what he had left.

"Instructions?"

"He said where you were staying. Called when you were on the road."

"Instructions?" I repeated.

"Uh, hold you for him, kill you if we couldn't. Said to shoot first and bandage later."

Good to see he still respected my abilities, and kept his ego out of his wits. Yes, broken or dead was the only way he'd get me.

"When did you last talk to him? With that phone?" I indicated the flat unit static-stuck to his belt.

"Yes, take it. About three hours ago."

It was good he could be reasonable. It also wasn't going to save him, because I couldn't have him blabbing to Randall, nor to the cops. I also wanted to dissuade any competitors from taking the job. I reached down and took the phone.

Then I stood, hacked, stepped over, hacked, stepped and hacked again. The last one almost got a scream out before I reached him, and he did a most amusing dance considering his hands were lashed at ground level.

That done, I detached the sheath from my coat, sliding the knife in. I gingerly reached into my pocket with three fingers, drew out a bag and dropped the sheathed knife into it. I made my way back to the car with a couple of staggers. Silver had the trunk open, and I tossed the knife into the disposal bag. She'd scavenged several pistols and a rifle as well.

"You drive," I said, and made my way to the passenger seat. I collapsed in a heap on a polymer tarp she'd thoughtfully laid out. Once down, I reached for the touchpad and reclined.

She tidied up, climbed in, and we pulled out.

As she turned onto the road, she said, "That's quite a pool of gore for a good guy." Her voice was flat, but I caught the moral jab in it.

What brought that on? "Hey, they tried to kill me first, for no ethics other than money, so prong you."

"And you were as cold and heartless as they."

"I'm chasing a killer." It had to be reaction stress from the fight. She'd done well, but it was her first firefight. Well-prepared, but it's always a shock.

She said, "They were chasing a killer."

I had to stop and integrate that.

The rules said I was the good guy. So why did I keep doing the same things as the bad guys?

The thought physically hurt my brain, and triggered an explosion of anger.

I wanted to hit something, smash something, but she was right, and that made it worse, and it was irrelevant dogshit to our mission, and her job wasn't to psychoanalyze me, nor teach philosophy, ". . . it's to build the goddam tools I need and provide technical support and overview, is that clear?"

"Yes, sir," she said; with an icy lack of emotion.

I wasn't sure when I'd switched from thoughts to vocalizing, either.

This was not going to help me sleep.

"You're shaking," she said.

"I was just shot at. You're shaking, too."

"Yes."

Well, I was glad we agreed on that.

She added in a hurried shout, "I'm shaking because

you're scaring me." She gripped the controls rather tightly.

"I couldn't leave them alive."

Calmly now, she said, "I know. It's not that."

"Too dispassionate for you?"

"Dispassionate? You've got a fucking erection." She nodded at my crotch.

Yeah, I did.

Damn.

Thrill of the hunt, pleasure at surviving, massive endorphin dumps.

"When?"

"About the time you had them secured and started asking questions."

"It could be coincidental with ending the shooting."

"It could," she said. She didn't believe it.

I wasn't sure. However, the more intense things got, the more I did enjoy them.

Sadistic tendencies? Maybe.

I was supposed to be the good guy. I think the only thing that told me that was I had national sponsorship.

That wasn't a definition I liked.

❄ CHAPTER 18 ❄

SHE DROVE WELL ENOUGH, and I directed her through several turns at random to dissuade pursuit. I hated that we'd used our own vehicle. Sooner or later that would haunt us. However, the evening score should dissuade most thugs. That they'd had eleven shot and hacked to death spoke well for me against him. Silver's complaints aside, and she was right about several things, I'd done what was necessary. Also, he'd be the first suspect, not me.

I wondered if he was scared yet.

Back at the house, I stripped, and all my clothes went into a burn bag. I wiped off with bleach, the wipes went into the bag, and I showered, my ruined finger screaming in the flow. Then I wiped the weapons down, washed them, wiped them again, and showered again. After that, Silver peeled, we dumped her clothes, she showered, washed guns, showered again. We got the burn bags into another one, then wiped down one more time before getting dressed. I wanted the minimum possible evidence against us if questioned. I managed to focus on work and pain and ignore her naked and wet body. It didn't help that she was shivery after her first kill. She distracted herself by making discreet arrangements to have the shot glass replaced in the car.

My ribs hurt again. My scalp was bruised, but minor, and luckily under my hair. My finger was on fire, and I'd need to see a doctor, but not soon enough to attach me to the crime. I still hadn't seen a doctor about follow up on my ribs either, and the rolls, combat and general crashing around was something for teenagers, not guys my age. I popped some analgesics and sat down to think.

I needed more analysis of Randall's motivation. I had a summary I'd glanced at but not paid attention to yet.

Two hundred of us went to Earth. Ten died on the insertion. Five had to be withdrawn for various reasons. One hundred eighty-five of us took down the infrastructure of a planet, rendering the inhabitants physically and morally incapable of further fighting, and terrorizing the hell out of the survivors so much they were still having panic reactions half a generation later.

Of the survivors, twenty-four were still alive. Minus the two of us was twenty-two.

Three stayed in the military in Special Warfare, though all had gone on to less strenuous acts now. Four others went straight to non-SW slots and showed little interest in returning—all were non-SW before I recruited them. Five transitioned straight to boring civilian lives, safe and comfortable. One ran a tactical school—former survival instructor. Four were security contractors and bodyguards—they'd come from Blazer diplomatic protection. Two did spaceside rescue, three did wilderness rescue—those five had all started in combat rescue.

We stuck to our backgrounds mostly, except for Randall and me. I'd probably have stayed in if the circumstances had been less horrific. I was getting a rush out of the project now, and that was disturbing on several levels.

So yes, he was doing it for the thrill, the challenge, to prove to the universe he was every bit as good as his friends growing up had said he never would be. The money was nice. Beating the entire universe at the game was better.

I'd had second thoughts about recruiting him, as I've said. I needed everyone I could get and didn't expect him to survive. So in that, he was even proving it to me. That was probably important to him. I'd keep that in mind, too.

This did reinforce the fact that he had to be stopped. Outside agencies would keep underestimating him. He'd get better with practice. End game, he'd take out one or more heads of state. Then he'd likely retire, with entire cultures in chaos. He was probably okay with that.

With that presumed, back to the hunt.

I didn't sleep well, woke early, and Silver took me to a clinic for the finger. They weren't overly concerned with ID, just with payment and a statement. I said I'd abraded it under a stuck wheel, and they accepted that. I made a point of not watching as a medical assistant debrided the wound and wrapped it with some nanos and bandages. It was ugly, but should heal.

❋ ❋ ❋ ❋

Given the number of hits in this system, the smuggled explosives and connections, I had to give strong credibility to the possibility the local crime families had hired Randall. Could it really be as simple as him being hired by the mafia? Well, not simple. Some of them were *vory v zakone,* literally "thieves-at-law," well-connected. However, they were unlikely to hire Randall. They'd just arrange suicides where someone shot themselves in the back of the head twice. It didn't happen often, but there were one or two here.

Viktor Toptygin was one, officially connected. Mean, Earth ex-pat a couple of decades back, when he got too corrupt even for them. He was responsible for better than thirty assassinations that we knew of, plus a hell of a lot more nonfatal violence. He got away with it because he was giving the UNBI information. Useful information at first; info that put his main competitor, a Sicilian mafia don, into prison. Later, just tokens. He was giving his handler-agents some quite generous bribes.

The fun part is that he had a younger brother, a Russian assemblyman, who effectively ran a large chunk of the country on his older brother's behalf. In fact, we confirmed that government investigators were pulled off probes that might have led to Viktor. There were also favors the other way, including intimidation of people who might have voted against his bills or opposed him for leadership positions.

When even Earth's system decided enough was enough, he'd moved here. Apparently, some kind of lesson seeped in. He was much less blatant, and none of the official parties wanted to deal with him. They reached a semitruce. However, assassinations happened from time to time. There were import laws here, so there was smuggling. Political favors came into play. Eventually, bribes and pushes and hits. It's something we don't deal with well in the Freehold, because we don't have a need to. Merchants bring product in, we let them. We're simple people that way.

Still, that was the environment we faced here. Rarely did anyone die, rarely did the public even know. The mob and the government and the CEOs played their games, and everyone else was mostly happy. They'd see something in the news occasionally, and not realize that years of politics and deception went into that occasion.

What this was, I suspected, was someone challenging Toptygin now that he was old. They'd hired Randall, sent him on some remote tasks to check his bona fides, and to handle some exterior business. Then they'd brought him here. It was entirely possible they rented him out as well. He'd generate income for them, and perform inside cleaning jobs. He got good money without a lot of capital, they got income and work.

However, Randall was getting flashy. The chameleons were high tech. Some of the other hits were just sophisticated in approach. A couple of recent ones had been outrageously over the top.

I suspected they were finding him tough to handle. They might also find him tough to get rid of.

It wasn't a safe tactic, but I decided to offer my services. I'd need to guess as to whom.

The general consensus in news and reports was one Timurhin, who also had a small holding on Grainne. Well,

well. That tied things in interestingly. This could be much closer to home than we'd expected.

Of course, I had to consider that Randall took multiple contracts. He may have just gotten greedy. That could also cause stress with any primary contractee; conflict of interest and all that, as well as visibility being a bad thing. You wanted your enemies to know and bystanders to be clueless, for really high-end stuff.

I wasn't sure I had the right outfit, but they'd likely direct me or hire me anyway. This was the kind of thing that turned into an arms race, which was another risk. Once Operatives or Blazers knew it was possible, not only would others consider it, but some recruits would enlist for the chance. That was good, if the post-military career was demolition, rescue, security; bad if it was assassination. Yet another reason he had to go down. Worst case, the mobs would start sending recruits to get trained. That would avoid all the issues we all had with Randall by keeping it in the family. It had happened in other militaries throughout history. Your veterans-turned-mercs needed some national loyalty.

This was at a cusp where it could all go to hell, with repercussions for years.

Timurhin and his crew ate out regularly. He owned the restaurants, so he might as well benefit, and it kept his eyes and ears on happenings. Not a bad move, really. He was also fairly easy to track, in that big Skoda limo he favored. It was dangerous to get too close, but easy enough to watch from a distance.

So I had Silver purchase and tailor some garb for me, found a spot from where I could stake out his departures.

That evening, his limo pulled out and Silver tracked him with a couple of carefully placed remotes. We pulled places off the list as he traveled, narrowed it down to two.

I drove to the area in a rental car with fake ID and transponder, orbited and waited, until she called and IDed Lava Creek. I found parking, stepped out and across the evening street, heavy with humidity and clutter in the twilight. I carried a small bag.

I crossed the street, approached down the service road behind the place, sort of an oversized alley, but reasonably clean. I pulled the apron and vest from the bag, pulled them on, tossed the bag aside. I tied both, turned and climbed up the steps and walked in the rear.

The technique I used is based on confidence. If you act as if you belong, people assume you do. Routine and standard are comfortable. Stepping out of those bounds is not. Blend in, act normal, and most people are reluctant to raise a fuss.

So, wearing the appropriate clothes, I walked into the service area. A few seconds found me what I needed, and I scooped up a tray and accessories. They actually taught us this in training, for cover and for poise.

With a tray full of frosty water glasses, two bottles of mineral water and some menu pages—the place ran a single sheet of entrees at a time—I stepped through the staff door, scanned the screen and found table four. I spun the tray up over my shoulder and headed out, just as someone said, "Excuse me—"

"I'll be back in a moment," I said with a cheery wave.

Then, of course, I had the dining room for cover. Staff are taught and ingrained not to make a scene in front of the customers, and that's more the case with an elaborate establishment.

I got only two quizzical looks as I walked across the room, and had no trouble with the broad spaces. Classier establishments tend not to crowd tables together.

"Good evening, gentlemen, and ladies. May I offer some lemon wedges with your water?"

Timurhin said, "Thank you. I'd like a bottle of Remington Fifty-Eight, the lady would like an Effervesca, and anyone else?"

His goon, much classier than most and probably a veteran of some kind, said, "A Coke is fine for me, please."

"Coke, Effervesca, Remington Fifty-Eight, at once, sir."

I placed the glasses, slipped a bottle under my arm and flipped off the cap, poured for all, placed the tray of lemon down, slid the note under the corner of Timurhin's napkin. I gave a brief, courteous bow and departed with the tray.

I walked through the door, right through the damping curtain, and the first person asked, "Who the hell are you and what are you doing here?" He was one of the cooks, sweaty and a little pudgy and right in my face.

"I just served Table Four and they need a bottle of Remington Fifty-Eight, a Coke and an Effervesca." I smiled and kept walking.

I wasn't stopped.

Ideally, of course, no one would have noticed me at all. However, no one was going to mention anything to the rich, dangerous guests if they didn't complain. It would be assumed I was some kind of mob messenger, and no one would say a word. Randall might have a plant, but he knew I was after him, and another turn of tension would be beneficial to me.

So now I had to see how it played out.

Back at the house, I watched the news while Silver dug news and police nets for connections that might lead back to us. I was always nervous about her doing that, but she'd never had a trace that we knew of. Her passive receivers were tiny but molecular-edge tech. We'd get nailed in any system if caught with them. Still, she was able to find leads on many networks, both digital data and old-style direct RF.

I didn't see anything of note, so I crawled off to bed. Not masquerading as a couple was a lot easier on me.

The next morning, I made my run of "packages," bought some supplies including soft drinks and some wonderful dark, heavy bread, and made a couple of passes against possible tails. I was actually on the street on my way back when she buzzed.

"Yes?"

"Another one," Silver said.

"Stand by."

Damn. That was interesting. Two hits, hard attempts on me, and another hit. I decided to consider better defensibility. Though where could we go other than a military installation?

I walked in the door and said, "Three in one system? That's not good."

"A sign of desperation?"

"More likely a sign of competence. He's proven he's the man for the job. It's more cost-effective for him to stack up projects in one system."

"Well, this one was messy. Someone blown up."

On the vid, the story was, "—Roberti was a well-known commercial property developer, and—" and little of substance.

He was a commercial developer, but he used very modern technologies for building, and tended to acquire property during various disasters; economic, structural, traffic. There were rumors he tweaked the traffic himself to impoverish his marks. Then he moved in, bought at fire sale prices, demolished—he always demolished, it was a trademark—and built new. An economic rape of a troubled victim. I could see why people would want him dead.

What they did show was a lot of cops and beacons and forensics vehicles and the words "blown up."

"Explosive?" I asked.

She said, "Not as such. Localized to the individual and no collateral damage at all. It's nearby."

"We need to examine it. Got ID?"

"I certainly do, Investigator Gold, licensed by the Citizen's Council."

"Let's go."

I just set the car to shortest route and let it go. I didn't know the map well enough to override. The car took us through several main streets, two detours through residential loops, and then I had to take over manual because we hit the crime scene. It was an entire square, with tens of cars, trucks, lights, warning beacons. The car's systems flashed warnings to avoid the area and I had to argue for manual control.

I found a spot to pull in, and was immediately faced

with a uniform shaking his head, waving at us, and trying to override the car with his wand.

I swung out quickly but smoothly and said, "I'm here officially." I wanted to distract him from the fact that our car was immune to his control.

"Who are you?" he asked, politely enough. He was about my age, good bearing, a little gray. He did have a name badge. Yazrikov.

"Gold. Contract investigator to the Freehold Council. I've got reason to believe this is one of ours."

"Oh, do you?" he said. He examined the ID and even ran his reader over it. It was good enough for that scrutiny. "We're guessing he's a veteran."

"Then he's probably the one I'm looking for," I said.

"Great. I served near some of your people on Mtali. I'm not happy with the idea of one turned to crime."

"Well, I'll have to see what I can find. This is my assistant, Gretchen Wickell."

"Ms. Wickell." He nodded, and gave her ID the same going over.

"Very well," he said, and keyed his phone.

"Seven to Two. I have two investigators here requesting escort."

I didn't hear any reply, but a few moments later, a young woman officer came over. She looked a little ill. Her uniform made her Patroller Meyerson. She wasn't particularly small, but presented as rather meek for the moment.

"It's ugly enough they sent me to be escort," she said to Yazrikov. She looked at us. "First violent case I've seen. I'm a bit out of sorts. I apologize."

"We've all been there," I said to reassure her.

"Please come with me," she said.

It was a very pretty building: a monococque cylinder with a oblique roof, the outside a spectral translucent that shifted from violet to green in sunlight. It was opaque from outside, the appearance coming from prismatic effects. The landscaping was coordinate-neat but warm and not mechanical.

The walkways were well-laid out in cobbles, and the parking aprons back just enough to give a sense of distance and space. There were field-supported molecular weather screens over the walks. Classy.

Inside, I could see cops at the door, cops down the hall, cops back and forth, cameras, DNA tools, bio isolation gear, everything. I could hear casualties talking softly and occasionally moaning in the other direction.

We were stopped again at a checkpoint halfway down the hall. I could see trails of debris from panic flight. People had run screaming, if I made my guess. It stank. I've smelled better morgues.

A senior detective checked our IDs, made us pose for pics, which I strained to stand still for. My cover was pretty much trash at this point. I'd have to hope that everyone would continue to vouch for me, rather than trying to get clear of the pending blast. My choice was be imaged, or start a scene. I needed the intel. I let them do it.

My image didn't trigger any alarms. Detective Marquardt waved us over, and in a slightly muffled voice said, "I saw you at Empire Repair the other day. In a recently abandoned car. So I can stop worrying about that connection in my investigation." He glowered over his mask. I guessed he was a tiny bit annoyed, in that he'd had a false lead, and been unable to trace me. Not an auspicious start.

"That was me," I admitted. "I was only seeking information, and didn't touch the scene."

"Fair enough. I'm not happy, but I know how these things work." He turned, pointed at a couple of things and nothing in particular. "Please be careful. There's considerable dispersal and we need to preserve as much as possible. Some of it will have to be compromised, I'm afraid. You'll need masks."

Meyerson whimpered softly behind us, and handed us some medical masks. Silver followed Marquardt. She seemed eager to get into this one. I pulled the filter over my face and followed her.

He pointed to a desk set up as a collection and monitor point and said, "We found this halfway across the room. It's mostly intact. I'm calling that the murder weapon for now. You'll need gloves or . . ." He grabbed a pair of tongs, grasped the item and handed it over.

Silver took it, raised her eyebrows, and carefully passed it to me.

I examined the projectile. It was just crude enough to indicate it was custom made, but of sufficient quality to be professional. And it was a creepy little thing.

I passed it back to Silver. "What do you make of that?"

She took it, held it carefully and examined it, then said, "Great Goddess." A few more turns and long looks and she punctuated it with "Holy hell!"

It was a syringelike dart, with a reservoir in the body. Said reservoir had been breached on contact. Then it had dumped a large volume of ultracompressed fluid—my guess was about a liter—out the syringe and into the target, in this case, the target's abdomen.

It had been a hypergolic fluid or fluids.

"What was it? Any idea?" I asked.

He said, "Residue indicates chlorine trifluoride."

All I said was, "Daaamn." Silver handed it back very carefully.

There really wasn't much that profanity could emphasize. The substance in question is more reactive than straight fluorine, self-oxidizing, and the decay products are hydrochloric and hydrofluoric acid.

What followed was a low-order deflagration burn. You might know it as a "fuel/air explosive." I'm very familiar with them.

Only this one had been *inside* a human body. Inside the lower GI tract. Hence the reeking mist of blood and shit pervading the atmosphere in this locale. A liter of outrageously reactive gas inside his guts had flashed them into burning vapor, blown him into cooked shreds coated in acid, and splattered those shreds on the walls, which were now etching bubbling pink paisley moirés into the surface. It was beyond excessive or obscene. It was awe-inspiring.

The body stopped just below the shoulders, with the arms hanging from muscle around shattered joints. One leg wasn't far away, the other lay below a trail of blood down the wall it had hit in flight. The entire torso had been gooified.

Among the smells, though, were things I knew, even through the mask. "I can smell the chlorine," I said. "The acid level seems rather high. The victim eats a lot of seafood and bitter vegetables."

Behind me, Meyerson overloaded again and mumbled as she staggered back a few meters.

Marquardt watched her leave, then turned and said, "There've been a number of really sophisticated assassinations the last few months."

"So I've heard," I said.

"The rate seems to be increasing, and this is the third one on this planet in a few days."

"Yes, it's disturbing."

"You don't mind if I inquire with your embassy as to why you're here, do you?" he asked.

"You can ask. They can confirm my ID but that's about it." There was a code in the choice of names, numbers, etc., that would tell the embassy it was military. If they asked, the military, meaning Naumann, would confirm that.

"Well, I'd certainly like to know why important people are getting sliced up, suffocated, blown to paste, and you're on the scene within minutes, obviously familiar with the matter."

"I'm here to investigate," I said. "I wouldn't be a very good investigator if I wasn't on track in a hurry."

"Be advised this has to go through the Dominion Police. I expect they'll have some questions, too."

"Hopefully, we'll all have answers very shortly. What's next after sponging up the DNA?"

Down the hall, poor Meyerson made gagging noises.

"We're trying to determine delivery method. We presume a pneumatic method."

Silver said, "Subsonic pneumatic. Probably ten meters or so. He'd have been dressed as a cleaner or maintainer and carrying some kind of tool approximately a half-meter long." She indicated with her hands.

"That's interesting," Marquardt said. He turned to the staff working over the debris crumb by crumb and said, "Vitkin, you heard. Interview the witnesses."

He didn't question how Silver had that information. It was obvious to all, but would remain unsaid, that we were probably military, and why we were after this particular suspect.

We went through the entire scene, escorted by the locals. I couldn't fault their willingness to share information. I think the high-profile and exotic nature of the assassinations had made them eager to put aside any jurisdictional or other issues and get what they could. Silver had already given them a nice lead.

Vitkin came back with Meyerson, who looked a bit less green, though she made a point of looking at us and not the scene. It was hard not to. The walls, floor and ceiling were the scene, and it had been so efficient a blast nothing dripped from overhead. It was just paint.

He said, "I think we have a match. Three witnesses saw a caretaker come down the hall with a cleaning buggy. Two say they remember him wearing a protective hood. It could have been reinforced with flex armor."

"It would be," Silver said.

"Two box trucks left the area right after that. Janus Janitorial and Leonov Electrical."

Marquardt said, "So we're looking for two vehicles."

I said, "Double check witness locations. I expect it was

one truck with a different logo on each side. They'll both be real companies, the logos will match, and he's already scrubbed them off. You'll waste time and manpower investigating each while he goes a third way."

"I'll pull traffic records then."

"You're looking for an anomaly. Either it was reported as a fault, or it was reported as on zone control but actually wasn't."

"I certainly hope information like this will keep coming."

I said, "Whatever we can, though I'm an investigator, and not up to date on a lot of this. Ms. Wickell has more recent information, but is only a technical specialist." Once again, everything I said was true. It's an important skill.

Marquardt said, "I get the impression this suspect is a former member of your Blazer units?"

"That's what I'm told, yes."

"This also reminds me of a recent incident on Caledonia. There were a lot of bodies involved, all good officers I'm told."

They might not all have been good, but I wasn't going to speak ill of the dead and none of them had deserved that ending.

"Yes, we suspect the same perpetrator. My goal is to try to locate and cordon him. Then I'm going to try to negotiate a peaceful ending. Otherwise there will be diplomatic requests over status of forces."

He raised his eyebrows as he understood that, sighed and shook his head.

"This is not a good thing, you understand. Especially as our nation was actively neutral during the War, unofficially supportive, and helped with a lot of rebuilding."

"I know, and I appreciate it. That helped my family. That's also part of why I'm here now."

"Well, let's get this resolved. I also want to know about that incident in the park last week. Him?"

"I'm pretty sure he was involved."

"Were you on scene?"

That made me a bit nervous. I had to offer something, but didn't want to incriminate myself.

"I didn't see him. I did see some of the aftermath."

"I expect that you will consult with me on these matters, not intrude on my crime scenes, and inform me of any such incidents at once. Otherwise, I will see about having you removed from the system. Am I clear?"

"Yes, sir. I respect that. I'm shackled by my own orders and need to keep it discreet."

"I understand. I hope you understand I can't care about that."

"Yes, sir." He was quite reasonable, really.

It was an hour later before we left. Marquardt seemed somewhat mollified due to our information. He agreed to keep providing data as they sifted it.

We still didn't have much, though. Randall's techniques were a mix of mostly old with some new from Cobra Joe and study.

As we drove, Silver said, "That was pretty revolting."

"Yes. Are you okay?"

"Mostly. I almost leaned against the wall once. I need to shower for my mental health. I want to just run hot water over me until I feel clean."

I wanted her not to put those images in my head.

So I asked, "Why the hell go to so much trouble? Any

bullet would do. Or a bomb. Why this?" It was rhetorical.
He liked the show. Still, this was outré even by his
standards.

"To send a message," she said.

"What message?" I asked. "It's excessive, crude and in
that context unprofessional. None of these people care
how they die."

She stared at me for a few seconds, and I knew there
was something I wasn't getting. "The message was for
you," she said.

That was not a pleasant thought. "Hell," I said, "I don't
care that much about how I die, either. It's not any scarier
than any other way. Relatively painless, in fact." Actually,
it would likely hurt enough one would beg for the
inevitable death. But I wasn't going to say so.

"I'm not sure it's you he intends to shoot with it," she
replied softly.

Oh, shit. I didn't want to go there. I *really* didn't want
to go there.

She needed reassurance, though. She looked at that
goo and saw herself, young and healthy and attractive with
a long life ahead, in the middle of a fight between a
sociopath and the insane narcissist who trained him, herself
considered tactically expendable by each to get the other.

"I can't see it. He's not going to stop me with a message.
This ends when he does. Nothing else. He knows that."

However, he might be sociopathic enough to do it as a
fuck you gesture on the way down.

I didn't mention that, but there was a good chance she
guessed.

I'd have to keep her reassured as best I could, because

I needed her attention on her duties, and I just might have to throw her out as a decoy.

If it came to that, we all died. I'd take him down, and then I'd finish myself, because she was competent, decent, attractive, a very nice young lady all around. She didn't deserve this.

I shouldn't care that much about tactically speaking, but I did.

Shit.

Intellectually, I knew some of that was just the stress and proximity. Any combat relationship has a certain intimacy of a unique type. However, she had a personality I meshed with, and accepted me as a human being even with my legion of flaws. Add in that incandescent body I could only pretend I was carnal with, and it was a recipe for emotional disaster.

And yet I was friends with this man.

I didn't know why any of this mattered. It shouldn't. It did.

❀ CHAPTER 19 ❀

I IGNORED SILVER SHOWERING, though to be honest, it wasn't that sexy after the human tartare.

Randall was really dialing it up. This had to stop, and soon. The sheer mess and body count were noticeable. Also, if he escalated, he'd find out I could escalate more. Naumann would probably sign off on a few hundred kilos of hyperexplosive and collateral damage. I wasn't ready to go there yet, but realistically, there was a break point. That made me furious again. More innocent people could die. The War had been over for a decade our time. Just stop.

One of the phones buzzed. It took me a moment to determine which one. We'd gotten several disposable ones for this purpose.

I answered, *"Dobrij den."*

"I am calling about a dinner service." The voice was very cultured, with definite Russian overtones.

"I remember. What can I do for you?"

"We should meet. There's a business matter we might talk about."

"I'm agreeable. Where would you like to meet?"

"North Line Park. We can decide where exactly once we get there."

I said, "Nineteen hours."

"We shall talk then." He disconnected.

Well, that was interesting. I'd got the mob's attention. Were they running him and wanted more? Wanted better? Wanted to eliminate me? Not running him and wanted parity?

We'd find out.

Silver came from the shower, dressed with wet hair and looking fresh. I told her about the call.

"You're insane," she said. "It's a setup."

"Possibly," I said. "I'll be armed, with what are likely their guns."

"As will I. I'm just hoping we don't die in the process." She looked scared.

"It's traditional. They like to see who they're dealing with, get a feel for them. It also gives them some control, or so they think. I'll do it."

I rented a vehicle, since the police had contact with us. We took a rifle—a professionally shortened hunting job that made a decent carbine—the shotgun, two handguns each, knives and light armor. This could be more flat-out combat. The gear was in a bag in the rear seat, not really hidden, so I drove very moderately.

At the park, we chose one end of the lot, so I could figure out which car was theirs. There were civilians out, children playing, and I assumed there was some attention after the shoot-up across town the other night. It was probably safe enough.

Ideally, Silver should go talk while I covered her with a good rifle, since I held the Master rating to her Marksman. However, I had to be the one doing the talking. I reached back and slid the rifle low under her seat, and said, "Cover me. If I throw prone, kill him. I'll be shooting with a pistol."

"Yes, sir," she said, a bit too formal. It was still getting to her.

I climbed out and walked across the lot, and my opposite number did likewise. I felt safe enough, though it wasn't impossible a sniper would drop me. There was also nothing I could do about it. It was a nice day, though, and some plants in bloom. It wasn't a day to die.

"Good day," I said.

"We need to discuss the future," he replied, and indicated a curb. I checked the bush nearby then sat, as did he.

"Go on," I said.

"A certain associate of yours works for us. He's becoming unstable and less reliable. Stress."

"I can't imagine why," I said.

The sarcasm was lost on him.

"Exactly why we'd like to discuss employment with you."

"Can you afford both of us?" I asked, though I suspected what he meant.

"We can, but we only need one. You'd take his position."

I wasn't going to play stupid. My brains would be one of my assets for said task.

"Go on," I prompted.

"You replace him, we continue the financial arrangement, including the prior assets. If you can find the account he used for previous activities, we'd be agreeable to sanitizing that, too."

That was quite an opening bid.

So, for some time he'd had an agent, rather than being truly freelance. It did make sense. It also meant he could call them for resources, such as official ID, flights and passage, raw materials.

I wonder how tempted I'd have been, without my daughter and a military obligation. A decade ago, I might well have considered it. I had the personality for it, the skillset, and the lack of attachments.

The problem with being so dispassionate was that I could see how it would end for me, too. One has to sleep sometime. Sooner or later the odds catch up with you, or someone hits you from behind, or you have to go into permanent hiding, which doesn't fit most personality types in this field. Randall had set himself up for the mid-term, without a long-term plan. That fit his youth and personality. He'd gotten into it a little late, but he'd always been a little immature. I snagged him for the team for several reasons, but I kept him where I could watch him because under his brilliance, he was abrasive, too clever for his own good, and liked to show off, as he continued to do in every hit. If I'd needed fewer bodies, he would have been one I'd done without.

Basically, I'd killed him on duty. He just didn't know it yet.

Timurhin was looking at me, wanting an answer, and probably wondering what that expression on my face was.

"Definitely worth considering," I said.

"Worth considering? It's a fortune, and not a small one."

I needed to stall, so I said, "You're asking a lot, though. I don't really need the work, and there is an element of risk or you wouldn't want someone like me."

"Yet you contacted us," he said. "Ten percent incentive is doable."

I didn't even know how much they were paying Randall, though they seemed to think I did. Well, well.

"It's not quite that simple," I said. "I have an associate who works with me. That's one of my force multipliers, and part of the package."

"Not a problem," he said. "We trust your judgment on how you do your job."

"How much?" I asked. I leaned back and looked relaxed.

He shook his head. "Paying subordinates is part of your operation, too. That's why you get the perks, eh?"

He actually thought I was sexually involved with Silver, as some kind of dominance ritual. Well, that still happened in their organizations. They were clannish, misogynistic and very outdated. They were just too large and wide-spread to eliminate easily, and they did accomplish a lot of business. It did reassure me as to levels I'd deal with, though. Trained thugs, not trained troops.

"Obviously, I'll have to ensure my associate is on board. The offer seems fair, though."

"Take your time," he said. "Shall we meet for dinner tomorrow?"

"I have your phone code," I said.

He laughed deeply.

"Suspicious man," he said. "Smart man. Your predecessor wasn't quite that tricky."

Very interesting. Randall had likely figured he was a match for them, and wanted to scope out the odds. He'd met them at their convenience.

They referred to him in the past tense.

"You did say you wanted to upgrade, yes? And obviously, my calls will be discreet."

"Indeed. Also, we would want to review any competing work for the duration. With a running contract we'd want first refusal of course." Interesting. Randall had gotten cocky and was taking all offers now, possibly including some set up by the competition. They probably weren't billed that way, but he was being played. His primary employers wouldn't like that.

I expected he was arrogant about it, making sure they knew how awesome he was and how hard to replace. If they were aware he'd tried for me twice and failed . . .

"Obviously. I assume there's some retainer fee when business is slow?"

He chuckled dismissively. "Haha. That might be arranged, if business is slow. These things have a way of continuing."

I knew I was a match for any of them, but they had a lot of resources. Beating them was possible. The lifestyle price was one I wouldn't pay. I wasn't going to say that here, though.

They also already considered me to have the job, contingent on eliminating Randall, whom they already referred to in the past tense.

That threw more sand in the machine. I had to kill him, and be close enough to get down, so Naumann could send the current professionals after these lice. He'd be happy. He'd get his live-fire training exercise, and we'd get rid of some thugs.

In the meantime, I'd have to play it very carefully.

To my advantage, they appreciated the discreet touch.

I stood and stretched, plastered a light smile across my face, and we shook hands. He feigned similar cheerfulness, and we raised voices slightly.

"Good to see you again," he said.

"Absolutely. I'll get a prototype set up sometime next month. Sounds like a fun project."

"How much do you think?"

"Oh, I won't charge for that. You're a friend. Just keep me in mind for production bids, eh?"

"You're worthy. *Danya*."

"*Danya*."

I turned, started walking, and then breathed a sigh. I also kept hyperaware. Even if they weren't setting Randall up, he could be here hoping for a shot.

I felt better once in the car, and more so with distance. I let Timurhin depart first, gave them three minutes, then followed. I kept a clear eye for pursuit. Then I brought Silver up to date.

"I think he's been telling them what a hot commodity he is, taking side missions, some of which interfered with their plans, and they may be aware he's tried for me and missed."

Silver said, "Here's a theory. They started using him outsystem to gauge his effectiveness. Then they brought him here. He was fine then, but the acceptance made him cocky."

"I'd thought that myself, and it does make sense," I agreed. "You don't test weapons in garrison."

"He was fine at a distance, but the elaborate schemes are noticeable."

"Yes. Hence the problem they face."

"He doesn't want to stop those."

"I'm not sure he can," I said. "He was always driven by gadgets. He made me some really trif ones. To avoid having a typical MO, he's continually developing new methods."

"They're his downfall."

"Also, he's not getting paid as much as we thought. They are. He's taking a percentage. He was never good enough with people to negotiate things like that. I suspect he underpriced himself to start, and hasn't raised enough. He's established a price and can't justify a large increase."

"How would you have done it?"

"I'd have started at a million and negotiated down no lower than seven fifty for an opener, contingent on success. Money in escrow with a drawing account for expenses. I expect he started at fifty thousand and is maybe at a hundred. You heard the discussion. A lot of it's going in overhead."

"That's depressing," she said.

"Yeah, he was always smart enough to get into trouble, not enough to avoid it. He has some temper, too."

"You've mentioned."

"Not so much temper as pride. I'm going to keep using it against him."

"Are we getting close, then?"

"Yes. No breakthrough yet, but there will be one. He's good at your job. He's half-trained at mine."

"That's scary in itself."

"Which is why he's being stopped. It's not even really an object lesson for others. It's to protect our government from the political fallout if others realize just how dangerous we can be."

"I thought you proved that on Earth. Sorry." She looked embarrassed at bringing it up.

I shrugged it off. "Yes, but governments have short memories. This is ongoing and indicative of threats to *individual* members of state. Politicians at heart are usually cowards. They rarely do for themselves what they can have someone else do."

"How long have you been this cynical?"

"Since one bunch of them ordered me to hurt another bunch, but not in a way that would result in reprisals against them personally. There's historical precedent in the early eras of not targeting commanders in war, because that would leave troops 'undisciplined.' Fine to kill them, but not the guy managing them. In reality, we learned that if you take him out, the fight gets a lot shorter. This still doesn't apply to politicians, but it should."

A circuitous route back to the rental agency made me feel better, and I took several turns right as the traffic signals locked, ensuring nothing behind me at that moment. Was I paranoid enough?

Silver had a jammer running, but the power was quite low, since that itself could be traced if it put out enough. There was also the emergency transponder, if they knew anyone at the response company or rental agency.

I was paranoid, but it might not be enough.

We made it home, checked our seals, checked our cameras, determined some city services had coasted by; trash and street cleaning, and that everything seemed safe.

I might be overreacting. I didn't know where his safehouse was. He shouldn't know about mine. I'd taught him what he knew. I had Silver for backup and we both knew our lives depended on perfection. With luck, he might outmaneuver me, but he shouldn't be able to flank us both.

We cleared the inside with pistols out and determined nothing had been touched. I'd still want to do another DNA spray across town soon, though.

Randall was probably equally paranoid. I wondered if he'd yet figured out his employer had turned on him. Not allies of ours, though. Mutual enemies, but we were not allies.

Silver interrupted my musing.

"Here's a real wrench in the works," she said, and fronted the news load.

"The God and Goddess are on my side," I said.

"It looks that way."

Buckley Bank had massively overextended itself on mining speculation in Theta Persei. Meanwhile, they'd been marketing the investment for more income to roll in. A risky proposition, against the typical bank charter, and certainly unethical. There were links to hundreds of opinions on the legal ramifications, satisfaction and settlement, long-term repercussions and why their underwriter/inspector hadn't caught this. Especially as it was a repeat of a similar event a decade before. Greedy people never learn.

That was all fascinating, but the important part for me was that the confidence drop had caused two other banks to pull credibility from their money. Then a couple more. Then an outsystem bank here, actually. Then more. Remember, our currency is a private issue by several banks in concordance. There's no national backing. The other banks were pulling their reciprocity and leaving Buckley alone and unloved.

No one would take a penny of any currency produced by Buckley. It was being melted down for scrap value, about a quarter of its previously valued worth.

So, about a quarter of the Freehold money we had along was now worthless except as cheap bullion in coin form, totally worthless in card or paper.

And Randall's account was an "asset with a claim." It would be settled in a few months for cents on the cred, and paid by whoever bought out the smoking ruins of Buckley. In the meantime, he had nothing.

It was a gratuitous stroke of luck, but it was to my advantage.

Even if he had hard assets or other accounts, this had to hurt. He was earning less than our initial predictions, spending more, and had just taken a hit. If I could pile on a few more, I could finish breaking him.

An hour later we had more. Marquardt called us.

"We have a murder that looks like a chameleon job. Joseph Rosencrans. The banker."

"We'll be right there."

I drove. It was at the far north end of the valley, in

foothills that were strangely sharp, as linear basaltic extrusions.

The house was an impressive mansion, as I'd seen from the nav, but that didn't do it justice. The foundation was carved basalt blocks. The main level was fired clay brick. The upper floors and buttresses were solid hewn timber. It was part Tudor, part Classic American, and all Modern Ostentatious.

I pulled into the apron, then had to park on lava gravel. Every space was full with police and support vehicles. Silver hopped out, I followed, and she looped an ID over my neck.

Apparently our pictures preceded us. Damn. I appreciated being waved in on sight, but it didn't speak well of perimeter or operational security, nor opsec for us.

Marquardt was in the foyer, awaiting us.

"Gos Gold, Ms. Wickell. You'll pardon me if I'm not glad to see you," he said.

"Likewise," I offered, while looking around. They'd taped and lit a route to the scene to minimize traffic elsewhere. The scene had a field around it, and a full evidence crew at work. Patroller Meyerson seemed much more relaxed with an intact dead body. I expected she'd be fine from now on, if we could finish this.

Marquardt led the way left into a large front room with bay windows, and pointed.

"A classic clubbing with a blunt instrument. It doesn't appear the victim saw anything. It would be someone familiar or invisible. He was well-liked by his staff. I'll question them, of course, but I have no reason to doubt that they just found him like this, after hearing a thump."

"Likely," I agreed.

The body slumped in a chair at a desk, head over the table and slightly misshapen. Next to the head was a blood-greased candleholder, either gold or gold plated, and obviously massive. On the desk were old-fashioned books, two reading tablets, a partially eaten sandwich of what smelled like roast beef on pumpernickel, a bowl of plums, and a jar of Curry's Cracked Kernel Mustard.

"Actually rather subtle and elegant," I said. "It minimizes traces."

Marquardt said, "A rental vehicle came into the area, parked about a kilometer away in the crumble. A single person got out, visible on thermal and visual. His signature was small, and he began taking evasive maneuvers, then disappeared about two hundred meters out. He appeared again before we were called, about a hundred meters out, and seemed to mount a small zipcycle. It was abandoned closer toward the city proper. Both vehicles were rented under different assumed names."

"Well done," I said. "Do those names attach to anything else?"

"Not that we've found so far."

"I expected as much. Well, we can look for any residue off the chameleon, or any evidence outside."

"We're working on that, and will do more in daylight, of course. Floodlights have limits, but we're starting."

"I expect he's far in toward the city by now, and anything he used has been destroyed. Those chameleons aren't cheap, though. They're also a screaming banner to any port security."

Marquardt said, "It seems to me he's showing off. A

grenade through the window is as effective. Messier, maybe, but that doesn't bother him. Except last time it was messy and not elegant, and a lot of work for something that could have been done easier. This also required serious infiltration. Do you care to give me a bit more on his background?"

I hadn't given anything, and didn't care to.

"He's a veteran with some issues."

Marquardt accepted that, and seemed to chew on it. "While we didn't exactly wade in on the surface, our nation helped yours in the War by providing flight data, pushing our neutrality—which only affected UN ships; yours didn't come through our system—delaying them when we could, and offering safe port and passage to any of your flagged merchant vessels who did make it. I'd hope he'd be angrier at Earth than us."

"I don't think anger enters into it," I said.

"Yes, it's clear he's for hire, and apparently not cheap. The messages these activities are sending must be impressive. Whoever hired him is looking to terrify the competition."

Patroller Meyerson said, "He's terrified me. The motion sensors were active. There's a stun field. He made it through both, with little hesitation."

Marquardt looked at me. "Can you guess how he managed that?"

"I cannot," I said. I couldn't guess. I knew exactly how he'd done that because I'd taught him. I was not going to share that information.

Instead, I offered, "We suspect some of his financing was damaged in the Buckley Bank matter. That may make him desperate to take anything he can get, or he may be frugal and austere. We'll send some info."

"That's useful," he said. We stared at the body for a few moments. Surrounded by his books, fine food, a lovely view, then clubbed to death with a single massive blow. There are no good deaths, but this probably wasn't a bad one. Perhaps "ouch," then nothing.

"Well, there's little else here," he said. "His widow is distraught and sedated with a friend on site. The evidence crew will be here all night. He's not going to be coming back that we can tell. We'll just compile the data tomorrow and go from there."

"I think that's all there is," I said.

Apparently, it wasn't too nice a day to die.

◉ CHAPTER 20 ◉

THE NEXT MORNING, I called Timurhin.

"*Dobrij den,*" he answered.

"Yes, we spoke earlier about a prototype contract. I've got some time in my schedule to work on that for you."

"Where should we meet?"

"Your Café Americain, in an hour."

"I will be there."

We cut the call.

Silver asked, "Do you feel safer?"

"Yes. They've got too much time tied up to dissemble now, and Randall's making the news weekly or better."

"There's that pending news special on the High Tech Assassin," she said.

I nodded, "Yeah, I'll bet they hate that visibility. I bet Randall loves it. I doubt he'll interview in person, but he just might throw some comments at them."

"Is that dangerous for us?"

"Depending on what he says, bad for the Forces and

341

the Freehold. I don't think he can do much to me." I changed subjects. "Bring a demo kit of basics."

"Really?"

"Yes, we want to broker trust and money. You should act like my squeeze a bit, too."

"I'll keep it low key and implied. Are they really that backward?"

"Yes, in some ways. Don't underestimate them, though."

"Understood." She went to the kitchen and rummaged around, gathering packets. "Let me dress."

This time we drove to the restaurant more or less directly, parked a square over as our car was a little old and not up to the standards of the clientele, and strolled in, dressed appropriately. I wore a high-throated blazer over a ribbed shirt, with a single silver chain. She wore slacks, her breakaway heels, a bra she didn't need that domed her breasts just enough under a satin ultraviolet top, and some chrome diopside that looked very much like real emeralds, at throat, ears and wrist.

We were shown to a booth at the back, with a curving, padded seat that let us all face the door. I was amused. I arranged me at the outside, ready to move in a hurry, Silver next to me, then him, then his goon. Though perhaps "goon" was unfair. He looked alert, competent, genial and not hired for more muscle than brain. He was bigger and younger than me, and I was sure he was a veteran. I was also sure I could take him. More importantly, both of us plus Silver could easily take Randall, unless he bombed the whole place. There was no room for a chameleon in here, either.

"Thanks for joining us," Timurhin said politely. He was quite classy, and from all I'd read, tried not to kill over small matters. He'd just arrived at the restaurant himself; the water glasses were just starting to bead and the condensation rings hadn't broken surface tension yet.

"You're welcome. If I may, I have a suggestion on ordering, and would like to place the order for us."

"Go ahead," he agreed.

I noted everyone's taste, from braised shrimp for Haken, his guard, to ribeye for me. We agreed on two wines.

The waitress came over shortly, and I smirked inwardly at her outfit. Plenty of cleavage, blouse cut to show it with a ruffled tie at the throat leaving a nice diamond, and when she bent for a water glass I could see clear to her nipples. Fishing for tips, are we? It was a standard uniform, she'd just sized the clothes for best effect.

"Good evening," she said. "May I start you with an appetizer?"

"Actually, I'm ready to order for us, miss," I said.

"Oh, please do," she said, and smiled.

I rattled off the orders, displacing each meal by one space.

The waitress said, "I'll put these right in."

"This is a nice establishment," I said. "Attentive without being clingy, smells very nice, and the staff look good too."

Timurhin smiled. "Yes, I like upscale, but I don't like having the staff lurk like vultures. It makes it hard to talk. We won't be bothered unless we ask."

"Excellent. Then my assistant has a portfolio for you," I said.

"I'd like to see it," he agreed.

Silver drew a folder from her bag and passed it over. He opened it and perused it. I knew we'd scored because he kept looking.

Silver had several ID cards, passports and key cards in there. He examined a page of the local ones, with perfect production of watermarks, polarized frequency shifts, the works. He glanced at one for Alsace and one for Caledonia.

"Beautiful work."

She said, "Thank you. I've studied as much as I've had hands on."

After a few more moments, he handed the folder back, almost wistfully.

The food arrived. I let the waitress set it all down, took another glance at the awesome scenery—if she wanted to show it, I felt no qualms about watching it, let her uncork the wines, pour samples for me and step back.

I approved both. One was a hearty red with a little sweetness and none of that earthy taste wine snobs claim to like. The other was a local fruit mix, dry and complex, that they drank with everything.

"Thank you very much, it looks excellent."

"You're welcome. Please wave or buzz if you need anything."

As soon as she turned, we all slid plates one space clockwise, and then I moved my glass the other way. The rest caught on and did so. In case of binary poison, no one had the same meal or glass as had been set. The remaining possibility was that the glasses had one agent and the food the other, so if Randall wanted me or Timurhin, and had managed to doctor something, either the goon or Silver was about to fall over dead. I was a bastard. I didn't mention that deduction.

We took a moment to sip wine, take an initial bite of our meals, and yes, they'd done the ribeye perfectly. I had trouble holding a knife with my hand macerated, but I made it work.

Between my caginess, Silver's artwork, and probably the takedown in the park, we'd made a good showing.

Timurhin said, "I'm glad to have you aboard. I wonder if you can guess what we'd like from you."

"You want the previous representative to be secured, and you want it done discreetly."

At no point did he ask for a kill, and at no point did I offer one. This was how the game was played. Total deniability all around, until the event happened. Then favors were exchanged after the fact, if all went well.

He continued, "That's correct. He's a liability, and the attention is unwanted, as he's been told. So you need to ensure he understands that in most definite terms. We'll then discuss other discreet meetings."

From his point of view, it was very safe. I would kill Randall, so at the very least, they reduced the security risk. Killing him would prove I was serious, and provide testament of my bona fides. They'd also try to acquire evidence of me performing that act, or admitting to it. They'd hold that close for a later threat, if needed. Investment at their end, minimal. With that out of the way, they'd negotiate with me for future kills. If I was a plant, they'd deny all knowledge, and parachute in a platoon of lawyers. I or our government would take the hit. If Randall killed me, they'd use it as an excuse to pay him some severance and cut him loose. He'd have to go freelance to lesser venues. Win-win for them regardless of outcome.

From my point of view, they were asking me to do what I'd already been tasked to do, so I had no moral qualms. I wasn't being asked to kill some innocent bystander to prove myself. In that regard, they were professionals, not mere thugs. That's how they'd stayed in business for several centuries.

The only question was if they suspected that was my mission and were playing along? Well, not the only question, but that was the relevant one. This could be a setup, with them feeding Randall whatever intel they acquired. So I'd have to proceed incommunicado again, for everyone's benefit.

"What is the rate?"

"Seventy-five," he said.

That was ridiculously cheap, in my opinion.

"You're aware of his abilities. That's not enough."

"You need to demonstrate your proficiency in the task."

"Certainly. At a discount, not a buffet special."

"An even hundred then."

"Is he really working that cheap? I'm disgusted if so. He's stupid as well as inefficient."

"It seems quite fair."

"For really high-profile or dangerous tasks? You don't go to Lola Aerospace for an orbital tug."

"One fifty is as high as I will go, no matter."

"That'll work as an opener. After I've delivered your message, we can negotiate on future deliveries."

"Acceptable," he said. I couldn't see the smirk, but I knew it was there. He figured to blackmail me at that point. He also had deniability. We'd discussed "messages" in hundreds of marks, not assassinations in hundreds of thousands. I'd get paid the proper amount, but he'd try to hold it at that level.

"Then I will tell you when the message is delivered."

"It must be soon, and quietly," he insisted. "The last rounds were too public and visible. That's a breach of etiquette."

"Noted," I said. "I'll get on it. It will still take several days."

"There is a time frame here," he reminded me.

"I appreciate any information you have on location or meetings."

"He doesn't meet in person anymore. I have been unable to locate him. That is why I am hiring you."

Well, the tone had changed here rather rapidly.

"Then I shall get on the task, after dinner."

The meal was a little tense, though we did manage small talk about the food, the lava formations and the climate.

I hadn't actually gained anything from this deal. I had a snoopy thug who thought to control me. I wasn't sure that was worth knowing Randall was on the ropes. We'd already deduced that.

Now, though, I had to worry about them trying to track me, if this went on too long.

We finished, excused ourselves and left. The cool, pleasant evening was hindered by the cloud over the deal.

They had contact through a disposable phone. I had

contact through whatever they chose to give me. There were implied threats against me if this didn't move fast enough.

Once in the car, I told Silver, "Ideally, we wrap this up and they forget about me entirely."

"I'm not sure," she said. "That leaves them without an enforcer."

"And without a problem."

"I'm not positive Timurhin's that logical."

"Maybe. He's got limited intel on us, though."

"He might have gotten something from Randall."

That put shivers through me, half of them because I'd forgotten to account for that.

"Change everything," I said. "Clothes, IDs, the works. Assume they got some DNA from that meal."

"I already did," she said. "That's part of why I'm surprised you agreed to meet in person."

"It was a risk, but I think we came out ahead. He's cut off again and they'll throw any intel they get at us, I hope."

"Yeah," she said. "They may have figured you were a threat and be setting you both up."

"That's sort of what I want," I said with a smile. If only I could believe it.

"Can you really get paid twice for the same job?" she asked.

"I know someone who got paid three times for the same job. But I only care about cutting Randall off from resources."

Still, after a convoluted detour around the city and back to the house, a check of the sensors and boobytraps, and picking up a couple of pistols to hold in my lap, I felt a bit better.

The tactical summary, again, was that Randall had lost his primary underwriter and employer and now had to scrabble. He'd lost his primary bank account. He had intelligence agencies in three major systems looking for him. He had me after him. He was panicky and insecure. He'd thrown blocks at me and missed. We were closing in inexorably, and he had few options left.

Realistically, if someone else bagged him, I didn't care. It would be easier for me, morally. An accident wasn't desirable, though, because it wouldn't send enough of a message, and dammit, as much as I hated the notion of sending messages through killing people, this time it probably was justified, one on one. I knew Naumann would feel validated by it, though.

Having done all this, I pondered what else I could do to hinder Randall. I didn't want too much publicity. That would be bad for us as well. If I could damage his reputation further, by hindering more hits . . . but that assumed we didn't end this.

Silver interrupted my haze.

"I've got a DNA match and image!" she almost shouted.

Antigravity exists. I was two meters above the bed in a microsecond.

"Where?" I called back as I landed and ran over.

"Port. Marquardt came through with what we provided."

"What's he doing?"

"Already departed. It took some time to get sorted through the system."

I remembered the trouble we'd had on Caledonia.

Here, they'd actually had people scanning the images of every passenger the last two weeks.

Yeah, Randall had pronged the dog by getting flashy.

"Departed where?"

"He lifted ten hours ago, could be on a ship or deep space shuttle now. Marquardt wants to know if he should alert the ships."

"Sweet gods, no. He'll fight like a wounded leopard. Just tell us where the hell he's going."

She dove in with mic, keypad, optical trackers. I'm fast, but she fairly flew, with several screens at once and audio. She sat there and pulled data, made notes, called Marquardt's office, deleted, tagged. It was most of an hour before she turned and said, "Ninety-five percent chance of Earth, five percent of Mtali."

That was so insane I had to ask her, "Say again."

"Ninety-five percent Earth, five percent Mtali."

My first thought was that he was desperate if he was going to Earth. If IDed there, he'd be ripped to pieces. Of course, so would I.

Had he found another patron with a lot of money? Or was he hoping to use the massive government system to shield himself from me? Was he suicidal and trying to take me with him?

We'd missed the launch, but there were a lot of ships for Earth. That wasn't a problem. I knew Earth, had money, had backup. I also found I had a neurotic fear of going there. They didn't know my name, but I was the most hated man in the world's history. If discovered, I'd be lucky to just be ripped to pieces.

"What's your deduction based on?"

"He was there just in time to board an Earth ship. There was a Mtali ship that left about two hundred seconds after they opened the hatch on the shuttle. At a sprint, he might have made that one, but there's no report of anyone doing a breakneck rush through the station, and no images on file. The Earth ship is well en route now."

"Is it an Earth flag?"

"Yes."

"Shit." Yeah, I couldn't call up the UN and give them that info. Call me a coward, but having the largest government in history aware of my presence after I'd killed six billion of its subjects was not on my list of things to do.

"Get us on the next one. Fast. Use the best ID you have. They will check it."

"How are we traveling?"

"Married couple. Museum tours. We'll need to be mid-wealthy."

"I have one we can make work." She opened a screen, grabbed fresh ID and ran a charge.

"We need to lift in two hours. So we need to leave now."

"Only essentials, and be leery even of the papers. Can you fab more on Earth?"

"Not easily, but yes."

"We want nothing questionable. Dump it all. Save two spares you can easily conceal."

"Are we calling Marquardt?"

"Yes, after we abandon the car at the port, right as we lift. Delay time the transmission."

"Understood."

She rose, went over and grabbed a bag. I had mine,

both a common garment hard case and a basic shoulder bag. She threw clothes, tossed gear, and in two minutes said, "Ready."

This is why I can never get along with civilian women.

We gathered up everything dispensable, stuffed it into another bag, and I tossed that into the car's hold. We'd abandon it en masse for Marquardt. The IDs and other technical items I tossed into the burner, lit them, and stood there for five minutes dousing them with fuel to ensure adequate destruction.

I drove, she watched for threats. That was just the state of things now. I didn't think we'd be any safer on Earth, though, and this was going to be a mental ordeal for me.

We parked in the exchange area—set up for meeting arrivals—then took a slide into the terminal. We cleared the process in minutes; the NovRos are nice people.

When we reached the station, there was a message waiting from Marquardt. It was cordial enough, but pretty clear that he'd prefer we not come back. I understood his point. We'd left a mess for him to clean up and hard evidence he'd have to carefully explain away.

☀ CHAPTER 21 ☀

WE WERE CLOSER. We were now only a day behind. Still, it was aggravating to not yet have found the man, and terrifying to be going back where I was considered history's greatest monster. I lay awake in our stateroom craving human touch.

Earth ships are not as nice as many others, though adequate, and better than they used to be. We couldn't do any research, though. All activity is monitored and we'd get flagged instantly. We stayed locked out of the ship's node and committed nothing to paper either. We pass-locked our comms and phones and secured them in luggage when not on our persons.

Earth changed security protocols after my attack, like closing the barn after the horse is loose. They've been tightening it ever since, and now it's flat out ridiculous.

All ships stop at the jump point stations, and everyone is sequestered and cleared through Customs there. They do nothing outsystem or in orbit. Fair enough. It limits the possibility of them letting someone slip through.

However, it's slow. It's intrusive. They scanned everything with sniffers, and I was very glad we'd used new luggage against any propellant or explosive residue. Those are actually quite common if you travel outsystem; the luggage is jumbled together and you get residue from other pieces. They're supposed to be able to tell the density, but that assumes they hire people with more than a room temperature IQ. The luggage went down a chute, through a door and off to be examined.

That's a problem. It's compounded by the fact that all the luggage gets held up while they do this dance, rather than forwarding other pieces. I supposed they're afraid it will strain their intellects. That, or no one wants to risk signing off in case it comes back on them.

We waited a long boring time for that, during which we made couplish small talk to look "normal," then had to go through and make declarations.

I stepped up to this typically soft Earth-type in a rumpled blue uniform who asked, "Has your luggage been out of your control?" without any kind of preamble or eye contact.

"Yes," I said.

He looked up in shock, and asked, "When?"

I said, "From the time it offloaded from the ship and into your scanners until now."

He got this disgusted expression and said, "That's not out of your control."

"I didn't see where it went, so I can't tell what happened."

"Are you trying to be smart with me?" he asked, and I choked back a response of *how would you know if I were?*

"I misunderstood, I guess," I said.

He snorted and then read from his screen, "Have you acquired or are you carrying any fruits, vegetables, live plants, unsterilized soil samples, unpackaged meat or animal products, leather, horn, bone or other processed animal products, recreational pharmaceuticals, inflammable materials, live animals or insects, non-UNSC-rated power supplies or energy cells, radiation sources, firearms, blades over eight centimeters, electronic, neural or chemical disabling devices, unapproved/unlicensed entertainment or educational or other media, bullion or more than ten thousand marks in cashable cards?"

I caught most of it and filled in the rest from context. He clearly didn't care. I didn't see any point to the question as they'd already scanned the luggage. Incriminating question? Intimidating question?

"No," I replied.

"Step through, please." He turned to Silver and started his routine.

I walked through the gate, and then two others snapped at me like cops. "Stand up, spread your legs on the marks, hold your arms up. Stay still."

It was easy enough to hold my arms up in .4 G. Three different scanners ran around in spirals, searching me for something, and apparently found nothing. I exhaled in relief, afraid it would recognize my facial bones from long past. They let me out and Silver got the same treatment.

After that, we were handed necklaces.

"These identify you as visitors and coordinate with Safety Personnel. Please wear them at all times when not in lodging. If you don't, the security systems will alert an officer to identify you. This can delay your activities."

We politely agreed, looped them over our necks and left.

I was glad they were necklaces. They'd used rings for a few weeks, until one had trouble coming off for a mugger. He'd hacked the finger off to get it. Silly, because they killed it at once and it screamed for pickup. They arrested him, did something or other and released him in a couple of months, and the victim had to get regenerative surgery.

They actually hadn't asked about our purpose, so all the creative evasions I'd come up with were wasted. Really, I don't know why they bother with this stuff. It's not cheap to travel between stars, and almost no one does so with criminal intent. Those of us who do aren't deterred by their procedures.

We'd agreed before debarking to go straight to lodging. He might be here. He might have hopped cross-system. He might be groundside. We didn't want to jump until we knew.

To our advantage, maybe, were the cameras everywhere. If Silver could find a way into them, we'd have shots from the entire station, all angles. We had the pictures from NovRos and could work a recognition algorithm. It might work, but we should move fast.

The Starlight Habitat at Earth's Jump Point Four was an inflated planetoid with centrifugal G. It was one of the oldest, of course, and roomy, well-worn and well-occupied. It was quite a city, and had most of what travelers, ships, merchants and businesses would need, at reasonable rates. Stuff came in on every ship.

Priorus Hotels had a franchise here, and even though this habitat was theoretically held to higher standards than the Freehold jump point rocks, I prefer nicer places for safety and security. The staff are honest, and far more willing to ignore nonviolent activity than cheap places.

We signed in, arms around each other, a kiss and bubbly comments about the Smithsonian and Hermitage. I'm told they're both wonderful. I'll never be able to see them.

We made it to the room, opened the luggage and got to work. I never use hotel drawers, but I did appreciate the two office chairs.

Silver started swearing.

"Those fuckers," she said. She didn't curse often

"Yes?"

"They took some of my circuit cards. Nothing we could get arrested for, I hope, and I'd deny them now, but good pieces."

"Petty theft thinking they were valuable?"

"Possibly. I need a comm store."

"Can you get what you need discreetly? And will it work?"

"I'm eighty percent sure. We trained on Earth systems."

"Go," I said.

She left. I kept occupied by scanning the news. That was unremarkable enough. I looked for events, people, potential target for Randall.

I wrote down several possibles, and some were quite high profile. I didn't think that was a bar anymore. He needed cash, he'd broken from the ungrateful goz and could charge more, and liked a challenge. Sooner or later, this was going to end in a mess. My job now was to make sure it was sooner.

Silver came back, knock-coded, opened the door, and smiled.

"Luck?" I asked.

"Yes, quite a bit of stuff is available. They deal with travelers from outsystem. All I had to do was sign a screen saying I wouldn't use it for espionage."

I said, "You have got to be fucking joking." I could tell she wasn't, though.

"Our intent is to find one of ours. That's not espionage. I signed."

"Good girl." It was a technicality, but if ever questioned, we had a truth we could stick to.

There wasn't much I could do while she built the gear, so I did some calisthenics, then researched places I could shop for groceries. It was also time to change soap and deodorant again. Anything to change chemistry.

With the advantages of modern nanocircuitry, she was able to put together a replacement device to spoof credentials. The software was more important. While I don't know the details, the summary goes as follows: her device quietly listens in on as much traffic from the security network as possible. They had a choice of hard wires that we could tap and that they'd have to check constantly, or wireless that would have encryption changed regularly. The latter was easier. Her gear lurks and pulls enough data to determine the algorithms used.

With background on protocols, she could instruct the device to send the router a false route to the authentication server. Then our unit requests authentication, and the terminal responds with the correct key. Then it calls another node, logs in with that password and connects the two.

The terminal queries the ID. The network tries to confirm with the server. Her gear insists it is the server, and validates our ID. Once she had access she could draw information from the terminals to keep updated—they had to offer authentication to her.

With that information, we could then both hack into their network and acquire intel, or spoof the network when queried. That's how we could have false official ID on Caledonia. When it queried the net, it was querying the one in Silver's shoulder bag, which was spoofing the official one. Of course it validated us. If I'd had that with me when I got picked up, I might have walked.

My concern with the Earth network was that they'd toughened it up since the War, and were very aggressive against intrusion.

"We're in," she said, and I heaved a sigh.

She turned and smiled. "Worried?"

"Yes, I was," I admitted.

"No serious trouble," she said. "It flagged us as an advertising hack on the second query, but I set it to present differently and it went through again. We're one of fifty portable units the station police use. As long as we're not on at the same time as Number Forty-Eight, we're fine. If so, it'll disconnect and try to log as Forty-Two, Twenty-One or Twelve. However, we can observe only. I have no access to the controls and I'm not sure about ID readers."

"That's fine. We can be ourselves for now, or at least the selves they think we are."

She said, "Assuming they don't have audio built into these tourist chips."

I rippled in shock. Oh shit. That was simple, possible and a threat.

She saw my expression and said, "That was my thought, too, once I figured it out. There are hundreds of thousands if not millions of visitors at any time. Even if they do so, they're likely using an AI to listen for patterns. Mine's under the pillow."

I had mine off in a second, and felt like an idiot.

She said, "Okay, I'm going to bring up screens and throw images. This is a little easier since we have description and photo to work from. Ready?"

"Yes," I said, taking a seat next to her. It was well-padded and very comfortable. One of the advantages of a decent hotel.

I hoped to find something fast. I needed to know which way to move. I'd also rather it was out of this system, where they hadn't quite gotten around to cameras in the toilets yet, but would any day. It was a dehumanizing, outrageous environment, one that contributed to my mental state, and coming back was not healthy. I was running on adrenaline for no reason at all.

"Found his entry," she said.

"Right at the gate?"

"Yes, as he debarked. Is that him?"

I looked over.

"Yes. Absolutely him." Older, but not changed a lot. A little more mass, mostly upper body. Decent shape. He'd styled hair and beard and changed clothes, but I'd lived with him for over a year. It was him.

"Refining," she said. "I think I can follow him."

This was exciting, tense, twitchy. This was it. We were twenty-six Earth hours behind and closing.

"Following," she said. "He was on foot, took slideway, off at a stop here. That's on the other side of the Habitat. He went for Budget Stay. Scrolling. Also slugging info to you."

I started from right now and worked back on departures. Insystem were every hour or so. There'd been three interstellar. I scanned from departure time back on each.

I watched the time tick on her screens. Assuming he came back out, we were now twenty-two hours apart.

"He's back out of the hotel."

"Understood," I said. I ran from my end. Another hour.

"He walked into the industrial and service areas."

"Really," I said. "Interesting."

"Hiding? Or shopping for weapons?" she asked.

"Either."

I ruled out two more flights. Nineteen hours.

She said, "I have his chip code. Stand by."

She tapped and pointed and scrolled, and said, "He did not leave using that code."

"I'll keep looking," I said. "He might have faked one. Also scrolling back from right now."

We had location and time narrowed down. Then I got past the most recent starship, and the cross-system transfers.

"He's insystem," I said.

"Confirmed," she said. "I think he's still on station, too."

"Still running shuttle docks," I replied.

Twelve hours. We were close.

I kept running back, she ran forward. We crossed.

Simultaneously, we said, "Still here."

I said, "Try to find any departure he's got scheduled or reserved."

"Yeah, kinda obvious, already have," she said with a high level of snip.

"Sorry. Excitable loner."

"Understood."

"Okay, he's still here, and in the maintenance areas. I think I need to go take a look. I'll grab a disposable phone—"

"Bought four," she said, and pointed.

"I'll take one of them," I said, snagging it and letting her copy the code. "I'll call if I need to."

"Be safe. You know what he can do."

"Yes. He doesn't know what I can do," I said. I threw on a dull blue shirt and found my notepad. I grabbed my chip and walked out.

It wasn't hard to get into the maintenance areas. I just walked. My concern was that I was tracked by this stupid necklace and someone might notice. What I recalled from my last mission here was that not all were tracked all the time; only specific events triggered even an AI monitor, and very rarely a human one. As most of the people here would be transients, and the cops would be busy with drunken Mtalis who left their chips in lodging, I should be okay.

No one stopped me at once. The corridors were paneled except where they met the outer rock hull. Gravity here was .63.

It was a familiar environment. This was the works of the station: power conduits, service corridors, safety hatches, controls. The environment units, attitude jets and power plants were secure, with redundant checks and gates. That was reassuring. I wouldn't want him taking out the station. I recalled they'd been fairly well equipped during the War, which is one of the reasons most of our attacks were on the surface.

I got a message buzz and looked. Silver said, "Departure confirmed for 1500 Station time."

So, now I knew the stupid dogfucker really was headed groundside on Earth.

Unless, of course, he either held over for the next flight, headed for another ship, or had some business here.

This area handled maintenance shipments. They were rolled in here from the dock near the passenger gate where we'd debarked. Here they were opened, accounted, sorted, separated, packed and sent around this station, the jump point control post, and other support elements. Had he arranged to send himself something? Like another chameleon, explosives, comm gear?

It was actually rather quiet, this being third shift, and I tried to skulk while looking semiofficial. I wanted to be unseen if possible, discreet if not.

I peered around crates, pallets, shelves, belts. I walked past two offices, nodding and waving the notepad at the occupants of one. They nodded in return and went back to their games or nodes or actual work.

Some stuff I identified by smell—industrial machinery, solvents, food—all came through here and then moved out in the quiet hours. There were limited service corridors in the main station, so lots of stuff had to be broken up small.

Nothing. If he was here, he was doing a good job of hiding from me, and from the internal, separate security net here, run by the contracting companies.

I took the search up one of the other corridors, which led to the rear of several businesses. Up this way were cheaper lodging, some restaurants that catered to the staff, and some light industry such as packaging, gas transfer and tool maintenance.

It also housed a few homeless people.

That's one thing our stations in the Freehold get a lot of. People manage to scrape up a transit fee or stow away, or jump off a ship at the stations, hoping to wangle transit insystem. There's no government interested in helping them, so if they don't have a marketable skill, their odds are zero. Our safety officers round them up occasionally and ship them on any national carrier we can match them to. Otherwise they're disposed of when they die. Ugly, but unavoidable.

Here, there are far fewer people, often retired from jobs in the station and wanting to hang out for some weird reason. Otherwise it's people looking for adventure and trying to get out of Earth and end up stuck. There are kitchens and clinics they can use, and the weather in a station is nominal, so they stick around. Not as many, because they can always get a ride insystem and welfare, but a few.

I saw a couple in an alcove, one sitting on the edge of a dock, and one under a platform in a cubby. Farther ahead, it became a spaceside alley, behind establishments of marginal quality. There were strict loitering laws, but I suspect most of the homeless paid off the inspectors. This was hardly a choice assignment for any government employees. The math was easy.

Between here and there, though, was an unlit and darkened section. It offered visual separation between the businesses and the grunge, though I suspected it wasn't intentional. I looked and saw where some light rods were missing.

Then I saw the figure walking past an alcove. I recognized the walk before I saw any features. He took a moment longer to react.

He was facing me. Had he been back to me, I'd've killed him and been done with it. But he saw me and slipped into a good fighting stance, so I decided some address was in order.

"Hello, Kimbo. How are you doing? You were supposed to be discreet." I Boosted.

The expression on his face was priceless. He'd known I was still around, but coming face-to-face with me was something else. And, I was always in adequate shape, now back in good shape. He'd aged a bit, too, and hadn't quite kept up on it. Not fat, but no longer a warrior athlete.

I could see him consider running, and realize he couldn't turn or back fast enough to avoid me. He almost went for it, then realized that would leave him unguarded for a moment. Each of these was a bare twitch, but I could read them.

He was not a confrontational person. He was a lurker. Still, he had a good block up, and was slightly younger than me and a little taller. I didn't want to rush in. If he made a move, I'd take him down, otherwise I'd psych him out and wait for an opening. We had a loading alcove next to us, and he tried to slip into it.

He didn't panic. He was steady, but I managed to maneuver him into the box and he tried for a feint and a rush. I let him come, twisted around his punch, leapt above the foot sweep easily in the light G, and wrenched.

Then I had a grip on his wrist. This fight was about to be over. I reached out and dislocated his elbow.

I saw his other hand flash back behind him, then come forward. He wasn't going to dislodge me like that, and I started to twist his damaged arm as he shrieked. My options from there were to strike his rear, force him to his knees and down, break his neck or just shatter his wrist, shoulder and elbow and step back.

Heated pain and wetness splashed over my knuckles. I assumed it was acid, or maybe he had a self-heating vial of something. It was a fast but clumsy reaction on his part, but I wasn't going to let go.

Except I was. He was twisting free and I couldn't get a good enough grip. I clenched, but he slipped free. Whatever was over my hand was slick. Hot oil?

Blood. I caught a glimpse of it. Lots of blood. It might be either his or mine, but it wasn't important right now; he was turning. I followed his hand with mine to keep some semblance of control and shifted to kick his ankles, hopefully shattering one. All I had to do was slow him down.

This kid was *fast*. He didn't have a CNS bioplant, and he was almost keeping up with me. I couldn't have slowed

down that much over the years, and he was only a couple
of years younger himself. Okay, five. Still, he wasn't
young.

He came back at me with that left hand, and I saw a
flash of something dark. Then the nerves in my arm
stopped sending signals. Then they sent lots of signals.
Pain, heat, cold, electricity. Massive trauma has a same-
ness to it, though every particular type has its own subtle
spice. But I'd been injured and he was disengaging like a
pro. I threw a foot out as a trip or strike, and *he* kicked *me*,
making me yelp and causing my calf to seize up with
cramps. Shit, that hurt. Then he was running as I tried to
limp upright. I forced through the pain ripping through
my ankle and right arm and pumped my legs after him.

There was too much blood. As we clattered along a
depressing gray corridor, it all coalesced. He'd opened me
up with a korambit. It's an old Filipino and Indonesian
weapon, consisting of a ring for the finger, a short grip and
a double-edged sickle blade. It cuts coming and going.
And it's even under the eight centimeters legal limit for
personal possession here. He'd sliced it across my knuckles,
which was how he could get free—I had no tendons there
anymore. Then he'd ringed my forearm just below the
elbow, severing veins, muscles, tendons and nerves. Three
quick cuts and that was that. Two outside curves, one
inside, and Ken Chinran is crippled and leaking like a
hydraulic press with ruptured seals.

I'd been banged around from day one of my career. I'd
been scared, beaten, gassed, abused, tossed out into
vacuum, kicked, whipped, crashed into trees, left to freeze
in ice or cold mud, cooked in hot Sun/Iota/name your star,

starved, sleep deprived and just smashed myself in a hurry to take cover. But in all that time, I had never been seriously injured or wounded in combat. A few close calls had torn at body armor or helmet, but never me. It was frightening.

I triggered Boost again, to deal with the shock and pain. That was good, except it also increased circulation. As I recalled from my medical training, I wouldn't likely bleed to death for several thousand seconds. Call it sixty minutes or thirty-five segs. But it hurt like hell, it was making me nauseous from the thought and from the gouts of red running down my arm as if from a small hose. It was a psychological bombshell. I needed some time to recover. And I was seeing splotches in front of my eyes from the injury, exertion, and overuse of Boost. Three times in a row is the safe max. Beyond that you're looking at a hospital and nanos to repair the damage to the cells caused by overexertion at the mitochondrial level.

I staggered and slowed. He'd gotten away, dammit, after I had him in hand. I swore through clenched teeth, held up my arm to examine the running crimson river cascading through white, striated and marbled flesh with gray veins and realized I was about to pass out. I was just aware enough to keep the arm atop me to prevent further damage.

I woke up in only a few seconds, but it hurt like a dog-fucker. Or maybe that was why I woke up. There was no way to touch the wound or support it to reduce the pain, either—it was almost totally around my forearm, about three centimeters below the elbow. I peeled my shirt off with my left hand. Every time something hit the bare nerves in the wound I went into a paroxysmic cascade of thrashing pain and had to force myself motionless until it subsided. I got the shirt free in a series of intervals, then drew it down my right arm and wrapped it around, then pulled it tight enough for pressure. That hurt even worse. The jolts of pain lanced through me in metallic lightning spikes.

The blood ran right through and kept dripping in slow, surreal trickle-drops.

I limped, wincing, through the corridor. The few people who saw me recoiled in horror. They didn't offer to help.

I managed to get phone signal once I was near a more habitable area. Silver answered at once.

"I'm cut. Need medical support fast. Moving along Passage Q, outbound."

"Okay," she said, apparently frightened. I wondered what my voice sounded like.

The fatigue, nausea, shock and some initial effects from blood loss were getting to me by then. My ears rang and I heard rushing waves. Eyes fuzzy. I couldn't Boost again. It wouldn't be safe. I just kept moving, every step causing burning sparks to shoot through my arm, from fingers to behind my eye.

Ahead, I heard warbling sirens, then I saw the cart, then I heard clattering feet as I collapsed and tried not to throw up.

An hour later, I was somewhat more intact, sitting in a bed, trying to recline it even more to ease my churning guts. My arm was now blissfully numb, and under the bandages was glued, stitched, grafted and taped back together.

"Ah, you're awake."

I hadn't noticed the nurse. She was probably pretty under all the protective clothing.

"I am. I got cut pretty badly."

"Yes, but you should recover completely. You're scheduled for nerve stimulators and regenerative medicine."

"How long?"

"A week or so, according to the surgeon."

"That's a long time."

"I'll let them know you're awake. I'll also call your wife."

"Please," I said. I should have remembered that as the first thing to ask for. I was not fully responsive.

The nurse left. I'd apparently woken as she checked the room, whether by design or accident.

I didn't wait long, but the woman who came in was obviously a cop, even in casual clothes and a doctor's coat.

"Mr. Ash," she started. "How are you doing?" She took a seat and leaned over me.

"I'm not in pain at the moment, but I cringe when I think about it. I hope they can finish fixing it soon."

"Very good. I need to find out how this happened."

"I don't know, really," I said. "I was in the passageway, minding—"

"—your own business," she finished for me. "IPMOB. We hear that all the time."

She continued, "Now, you're allegedly a tourist, you're smart enough, and yet you decided to visit an area of the station occupied by lowlifes and thugs. I'm happy to keep things secret. Nor are you in any trouble at this point—"

nice disclaimer, I thought "—but public safety means I have to find out. I don't have to say anything to your wife. So level with me. Drugs? Hooker? Trade deal?"

If she was going to give me easy outs, I'd take them.

"Yeah, I was meeting a girl, or I was supposed to. She didn't show. Instead, this guy cuts me and takes off with my pouch. Ellie's not sure what I was doing. I told her I went sightseeing and got lost."

"They got your pouch," she said, "but not your very expensive commlink."

"I had a pretty tight grip on it and I'd already called for help."

"No, you hadn't," she said. "Even if the call didn't connect, the attempt would be archived. It's not.

"So, what are you doing that you'd try not to report a fight like that the second it happened? Your first call was to your wife, who called medics only, not police."

"Alright, dammit," I said. I went for the embarrassed whisper. "I was meeting a man."

She snorted, leaned back and said, "Is it industrial or political spying?"

"What? I am not a spy!"

"Stow the fake outrage. I'm not impressed."

"I can tell," I said, giving in with a smile. "You're very sleek in that coat. What are you wearing underneath?"

She stood, restraining a disgusted look.

"This conversation is not over. You will not be leaving here without escort and interview," she said. I could feel the heat.

We'd see about that.

I felt my body from inside. I had legs and balance and

the pain was controlled with medication. I could walk. Sooner was better, so I gave her twenty minutes to clear the building. Then I eased myself out of bed, turned off the monitor so it read "Disconnected," not flatline. A nurse assistant arrived at once, but I said, "I need to walk. It helps me focus. Exercise."

"I need to check with the doctor before I allow that, sir," he said.

"Of course," I said. I extended my good arm, and he took it, so to assist me back to bed.

I dragged for just a moment so he thought I was a little weak. He leaned to lift me.

That's when I hit him, hard up into the solar plexus. He whuffed and curled up, unable to breathe, and I levered him into the bed. I pinned him with my weak hand and my weight on his throat, snagged a restraint, then another and pulled his limbs out like a starfish. It had to make his guts hurt even worse, but he seemed to understand he wasn't going to be hurt further, and stopped resisting.

His nose seemed clear enough, so I gagged him with a handful of gloves, then selected a mild tranquilizer that would keep his vitals near normal. I slapped it on his arm.

That left me free to walk out.

It hurt like hell, but I put on a calm face and walked out toward the monitor station.

Ideally, I'd walk past with a nod and they'd not question it. Though if they recognized me and connected that to the monitor I wasn't using, they might question me. Or if the investigator had said anything to them.

One of the monitors saw me and jumped up.

"Sir, you're not allowed to be out here," she said as

she came around the counter and through the ratchet turnstile.

"I'm much better and I will follow up with a private doctor at once," I said. "I have some important matters to attend to."

"You can't do that. You have to stay here."

"Says who? I have freedom of travel, don't I?"

She raised herself up and said, "Not under medical supervision, no."

Perfect.

It's a cultural thing on Earth. People don't talk back to authority figures. If you do, you're either a criminal, or powerful. I did not present as criminal.

The trick is not to threaten with an "attorney." No one ever believes that.

"Ma'am, I'm a close personal friend of Assemblywoman Vingai, of Quebec. You may recall her campaign has had considerable hassle from right wing corporatists. We're taking such attacks very seriously, and they will be addressed after the election. I promise you, if I am detained, it will make the news."

"Sir, I don't want any trouble, but the investigator said—"

"That 'investigator' is a plant by ADM to embarrass the assemblywoman. You call up the bureau and ask about her. They won't tell you anything because she's not on official business."

"Sir, you're hurt, and—"

"I'm only slightly hurt due to a private matter of mine. This has no bearing on the assemblywoman. I have a right to free association. Are you questioning our rights?"

I'd twisted the argument from me, to a politician, and implied the investigator was fake. I'd like to pull out an official looking ID in a moment and make them cringe. However, all my possessions were in their custody.

The icing on the cake was invoking Assemblywoman Vingai. She was one of the intellectual property movement, who'd trademarked her name. Just using it without her consent was an invitation to a lawsuit. If I mentioned her loudly and publicly, of course I had to be associated with her. No one wanted the attention arguing with me would bring. The cop might yell at them, or have someone come down and harass administration. The assemblywoman could have an entire agency come down on someone. Trump card. The irony, of course, is that such an act was as "right wing" as was possible.

It's amazing how definitions change over time and by location. The entire Earth system was "right wing corporatist." The only question was how much corporatism you wanted. The government controlled the corporations to ensure jobs for rabble and taxes. The consumers paid for both in the end price of goods and services, and paid taxes on top of it. Earth was the epitome of fascism, which they insisted was "democracy."

"Sir, of course you have the right to leave. If you'll sign here, and please come back at once if there's anything else we can do."

"If I need to, I will. Thank you."

I signed my print, and made a show of punching a code into her phone. I spoke to Silver, "Ma'am, I expect to be back on task shortly. The hospital did the right thing and released me."

"Understood. I will send a buggy."

Great NCO. She and I made a good team.

She met me outside and led me only a short distance as I struggled agonizingly into a fresh suit coat she'd stuffed into her pack. The low G was all that let me stay upright. In an access entrance that didn't appear to have any cameras, I changed to a vest. She ran the entrance lock with a coder, walked in with a notepad held up to block the camera inside, then we moved a few meters down the passage, out another door and into a maintenance area. She snagged two bump caps and stuck one on my head. With her leading, holding the notepad, and nodding preemptively, no one questioned us.

She spoke loudly enough for anyone to hear, "—inspections are quite good here, so it doesn't look like we'll need to do much crosschecking. The important thing is—"

We crossed, went down another corridor as she pointed along the ceiling, "—though I think we might have to have a leak test on that line—" with a finger out from her hand holding the pad to minimize camera view.

We slipped through another exit, took several turns in the corridors and disappeared into crowds, through them, changed outfits twice at stores, and I made a point not to favor the damaged arm by giving it light tasks so it looked busy. I did a couple of left-handed hairstyle changes, and put on some makeup. We split then, her going ahead, me leaving through a different store door. I wandered along window shopping for exotic games and gadgets, alert for any apprehension. I could fight with one arm if I had to; I was trained to. It wouldn't be anyone's definition of fun, though.

Silver paged me with an intersection location, and I showed up looking different enough it took her a few moments to recognize me. We made a show of discussing business matters and disappeared into a new hotel.

There was a man in the room. Tall, rangy, well-dressed and no-nonsense in demeanor.

"Private doc," she said. "He's good at the basics."

"I'm an EMT and former Special Unit medic," he said.

"What's a T Nine?" I asked. I slipped out of the coat, shaking and gasping as I did so, then peeled my shirt. He eased over to help me as he replied.

"A long range HAHO insertion canopy, fitted into a T Seven C or T Ten A container. Your associate already quizzed me."

"Well, good. Should I lie down?"

"Yes, this is going to hurt. He did a number on you."

"Yes he did. The ER took care of some of it." I started to lie down gingerly, then collapsed in a starburst of agony.

He said, "They did a decent job. There isn't much I can add. I have some neural rebuilding nanos, and a nonnarcotic analgesic that will take the edge off. Start doing gentle exercise for therapy and work your way up. Give it at least a week before you even consider pushups. Knuckles?"

I held out my hand. He frowned and considered, then pulled out some kind of combination. He used an old-style needle and shot me in each knuckle in turn as I sweated, gritted my teeth and grunted in pain. Yes, I knew I'd need several treatments for this, but damn, it hurt. It felt as if that needle was being inserted up to my elbow.

Then he pulled out a pressure injector and went to work around my arm. That was only mildly excruciating.

It was a good thing I was lying down. Pain washed through me in waves interspersed with cold sweats. Blotches and colors before my eyes melted with twangy waveforms in my ears.

I heard his tinny voice say, "She said something about your ribs."

"Previous attack."

"I hope you're dishing it out as well as taking it."

"I hope so, too."

"They're healing crooked. Want me to break them?"

"No. Will they hinder me before I'm done with my contract?"

"About five percent, but you're taking cumulative damage here. Those on one side, the arm on the other. You get degraded and lose capability."

"Can't be helped. Am I in danger of another pneumothorax?"

He had an ultrasonic scanner and looked. "No, it's going to hurt, though. I'll follow up on the tendons in a couple of days. That's all for now."

He stood, and Silver handed him a grand in cash. I presumed that was on top of any down payment. He nodded and left.

"I'm going to sleep now," I said, and passed out.

◎ CHAPTER 22 ◎

I SNAPPED AWAKE, an involuntary stretch of each leg raising my blood pressure and forcing alertness. The stretches were mostly internal; I didn't move more than a fraction. It hurt when I did. Something was bothering me.

Silver looked worried.

"You were talking in your sleep. Something about Pony Three."

"Ah," I said. "Fire support gone bad on Mtali. UN arty blew up a few of their own people and almost zeroed us, too."

"I heard stuff like that happened," she said.

"It did. Occasionally our people screwed up, too. The trauma must be acting as a trigger."

"How are you feeling?" she asked.

"Pained, but better. How long was I out?" I was too groggy to check the time myself.

"Most of a div. I let you sleep."

"Thanks. But we need to be back on the chase."

"You'll work better when rested."

"So will he."

"What, then?"

"I'm assuming he's headed for the surface, on that flight you mentioned. There are a few targets out this way, but most will be there, and anyone in a different jump point will be most easily reached through system, or out and around. Our best interception is from the surface in that case."

"Are you sure you want to do this?" she asked, and I could hear a tremor in her voice.

"No. I don't see much choice, though."

"Okay. I'll book travel."

"Book us completely separate for this leg. Different terminals. I'll do my own."

She nodded. "Got it."

We'd patterned as couple or companions. We needed to change that.

If she was scared, I was terrified. Logically, I should be safe enough, fifteen Earth years later, looking different, with different ID, some of it official and real and clean, with the common story that we'd all died in the war. Part of me still feared what would happen if I were IDed, and another part was on the precipice of flashbacks to the worst mayhem in human history. Mine.

Then, the local cops were already looking for me under other ID, with prints. We had a limited supply of imitation pads I could wear, but their efficacy was limited and of course, one time per ID, mostly Freehold. After that we'd have to fabricate back stories for new IDs, and try to fake a trail to explain how a person with those prints had gotten through port and bond without leaving them. This was the worst place in the universe for espionage. As I knew. I'd done it before.

That helped a little. Or I told myself it did. I knew it was all rationalization, but it was all I had.

With improved shuttles, the trip insystem would only be six days. I used my arm gently, stifling pain as needed, and tensed up as I reached security. I wasn't wearing the necklace chip. Silver had programmed a spoof one into my phone, but it wouldn't look quite right. Even in my chest pocket, it sent a signal, told them I was someone, and that matched the ID I used. It should; it was coded through my own phone using their protocols.

The process was similar to entry, and holding my arms up to be scanned hurt like hell even in low G, but I didn't dare admit it. Once again, they didn't recognize my face structure by scan. They were bored, busy and let me through, probably assuming tourists meant money.

Luckily, it's common for passengers to take tranks or sedatives to relax or sleep on the trip insystem. I mixed a cocktail that gave me long days, short, deep sleep periods with my senses semiaccessible while I slept behind a locked and barricaded stateroom door with a notepad in hand for use as a club, blissfully icy calm and wired sensitive all at once. In six days, I was three kilos lighter and rather nauseous, but I hadn't been apprehended.

We were a day from Earth when a news load reported that Ministry of State Undersecretary Boulain had been killed in front of her house, in front of her children. Someone had burned her down to a smoking greasy spot with a linear energy release gun. Nothing like a concentrated beam of superhot radiation to make a hit with the kids.

The gun had been recovered at scene. Investigators were working on it. That to me meant he'd left nothing they could trace and didn't care about the gun. I was curious as to how he'd gotten that on Earth. Those were largely in test phase and not available. Had he looted a lab?

So what next?

From Peace Station over the Americas I took another AtmoSurf down to North America, landing in Virginia. I was very glad for the trank. This is where it had all started ten years, sixteen Earth years before.

Silver had left a message for me. I got my bag, took a slideway to another to a train station, from the train to an autocar to one of the megascrapers they'd rebuilt, to a slideway, an elevator, a level. The light gravity was helpful, but the polluted, thick air was not. I managed on medication over the nausea, pain and quivering panic I felt.

At the level nineteen plaza, she met me. She didn't acknowledge, just paced me for a while, and moved in closer as I followed her directions. One hall contained a hotel, and the door ahead opened for her.

"Well, hi," she said, coming alongside.

"Hello," I returned smoothly. We assembled as a friendly pair, and proceeded to the room. She clicked the door, we went in, and I sat carefully on the bed. It was a smallish room, a bit stale, adequately clean and with sterile polymer furniture. It would do fine.

I was in pain from the exertion of walking, though somewhat improved. I wondered how his dislocated elbow felt. I'd hit it pretty hard. Still, he'd cut me thoroughly.

She said, "I got down about three hours ago. Are you okay?"

"Pain. Weakness. Nausea." The room spun, and the air didn't help. I appreciated the extra O_2 Earth has, but the pressure and humidity were thick and irritating. It reminded me of last time. I'd started in a cheaper, but similar room.

"Rest a bit. I'm running news searches, but there are so many people there are so many targets." She looked dejected.

"Just plan on tracking him when he does. It's harder to get resources here. We spent a year building and developing. He's got days and has only had hours."

"I remember the report, but I welcome any first-hand intel," she agreed.

The planet is different from the outer system. Space dwellers everywhere have a streak of independence and self-reliance. It comes with the nonnatural environment. Earth's isn't natural either, but is very carefully built to fit every human want.

So it felt different from the station. That had been bureaucratic and annoying. This was outright hostile. The propaganda machine of the news never stopped.

The word on Earth now was that the Freehold had collapsed, and was dependent on UN charity. So much for free markets, ha ha, look at the stupid peasants.

It pissed me off.

It wasn't that it was untrue. It was propaganda. By definition it was untrue. It's that they could have used that story from the word go, and we'd never have fought. It's not as if anyone on Grainne really gives a crap what Earth thinks; as far as the Halo, as long as the bank drafts clear, they don't care what anyone thinks. But ego and moral outrage on the part of Earth's overlords had dictated we be a scapegoat.

The other pisser was that it was dangerously close to, "Look what you made me do!" I've never liked that argument. It's a cop out. Earth's billions of casualties were because my commander and I had decided they were a target in total war. My government had eventually concurred, and I was told to be the most vicious bastard in history. I had done so. I had done so well. They didn't make us do it, we chose to do it as an object lesson, for right or wrong.

Nothing about this situation made me feel better.

Then it took a turn for the worse. My phone buzzed.

We both stared at it. I assumed a wrong code or a marketing call, and answered, audio only.

"Hello."

"Hello, Dan. I have your phone code."

Well, that was exciting. I pointed at Silver, pointed at the phone, and she went to work trying to get a trace. He was probably doing the same. Who had the better gear and training?

"You have one of my phone codes," I said laconically. "I'm very impressed. You shall get a first mark on Electronic Intel Basic."

"You seem to be popular on Earth now," he said.

"Yeah, I spent all day getting photographed and tagging people," I said. "I never really thought of myself as a war hero."

"Hero," he snorted. "You're the one who ran away before we got hit, remember?"

"I was busy doing something that was mission critical at the time."

"So, you left the three of them to die?"

"I'd hoped you'd take care of things in my absence. I wasn't able to find any evidence that you did. It seems you were busy running in fear."

He snapped back, "What do you care? You didn't even touch your daughter. You just left her."

He didn't know I recovered her. Well, good. That was one less threat to me, for now. I was greatly relieved, and needed to not draw attention to it. So I said, "You wouldn't understand the mission."

That definitely triggered him. "You and your fucking mission. You killed two billion innocent people to prove a point. For the same casualties, we could have wiped out their military and been done."

"They would have rebuilt."

He didn't like it when I stayed calm. Good.

He said, "Screw the politics. I only kill a few people, I charge enough to weed out vendettas, and I make sure they deserve to die."

"So, are you Allah or Jehovah? I've never met a god before. I expected a deity to have a bigger bank account, actually." I was conversational, cheerful, derisive. The more seriously someone takes themselves, the more mockery will anger them. Was that his only account, though? It hurt him regardless.

He fairly exploded. "Hey, fuck you, asshole." Clearly, this was not going the way he wanted.

"Me? I'm not deciding people's fates based on perceptions." I paced around the room, though there was nowhere to take more than a couple of steps.

"No, you just kill at random."

"Not anymore. I kill specifically. I'm here to kill you."

"You have to catch me first."

"I have caught you."

"Not enough. I beat you last time."

I snickered and shook my head. "You hurt me slightly last time. It's not the first time I've been cut." I wasn't going to admit to it. I'd used that in combat before I met him. Never let them see you bleed. Be dispassionate and unkillable. "How's your elbow?"

"Elbow's fine," he said, but didn't sound sure. "You were hurt enough. You're not so tough."

That was a handy opening. "So says the guy who never actually went through Operative training."

"I qualified for everything. You ran it yourself."

"Yeah, but it was rushed and second rate. You never had the stress the rest of us did."

"The mission was that."

"Just keep telling yourself that and maybe you'll believe it. I figured to lose all you accessories in the process. That's how I had you filed mentally. Accessories. You were brought along to die regardless. If it saved one real Operative, it was worth it."

"I think I proved my point. I survived."

"Not for much longer. I'm sure you can figure out the ending, if you think hard enough."

I wanted to probe him into thinking I had all the cards. Extreme paranoia leads to mistakes, which I'd exploit.

"Ending?"

"How you're going to die. You waste a lot of time on graphic finales. It's like you're some kind of artist who craves recognition. Whereas, I want your death to be silent and unnoticed. I'm sure you can figure it out."

I disconnected.

He didn't call back, though I'd hoped he would.

I'd hurt him. He'd brought up my daughter. I'd not taken the bait. He couldn't know if she was dead or raised somewhere on Earth. He'd been a good man, helping with delivery, paying attention to Chelsea, acting daddy-like in a lot of ways. He thought me utterly inhuman. Good. He didn't know she existed, so he couldn't rush in to save her, or use her against me. Good.

"Nothing concrete," Silver said. "The signal was broken and resent from several sources. But I'm pretty sure he's in this city."

"That's good. It narrows it down. He's scared and going to get clumsy. It's very important that we not."

"I understand," she said, with a firm nod. Then she trembled.

"I can't do that," she said.

"Do what?"

"I can't hack an unknown phone within divs, hours."

"He's had a lot of experience."

"He's better than me, and I don't know how to avoid it. He scrambled his own signal in a couple of hours."

"He's got resources already set. We're making it up as we go. I suspect he cultivated friends of Timurhin. In fact, Timurhin may not even know this is happening."

"I know, but—"

I cut her off. "Silver, I have every confidence in you." I didn't, actually. I'd rather have had Kimbo, but he was the target and the loon, she was all I had, and she was probably second best. And of course, this is what she needed to hear. "I'm not worried about what he comes up with. He's desperate. Just keep me going."

She nodded and got the quivers under control.

I said, "I trained him. I trained them all, with a lot of personal attention. I managed while we all shared knowledge. He needs to prove he's better than me. At the same time, he's scared of me. No one else could have stuck with him this long. We're going to keep dialing up the tension until he slips. There's no sportingship here. If I get a shot at his back, I'll take it. If you do, you take it. If we can mine something to blow him up, we do it, even if takes some collaterals. If we can get him beaten to death in custody, we do that, too, though it's not something to plan on because it's not effective. If they half beat him to death, I'll walk up and gap him as he's released in a powered chair. He knows this, too, and will try to flee if he can, kill us if he can't."

She nodded, looking young and scared and with the tremble again.

"Endgame," I said.

Then I pulled power and circuit from the phone.

"Scratch that one," I said. "Also, be ready to bolt in a hurry."

"I am," she said. "This place is creepy. It's like a prison."

"Very much, and worse since the War, it looks."

She suddenly turned back to her system. "Silly," she said.

"What?"

"The comm system and my sensors can't backtrack the phone, but the provider can."

"Careful," I advised.

"I've got a customer code, and now to request account . . . and slam it . . . and there. Request log, reverse for incoming, and I've got it. Disconnecting."

"You've got it?"

"He's two buildings over. Would he be doing something there?"

"Let's look, and let's get out of here. We'll find transient space. Pull all phones and comm unless we're using them."

She disabled the spares, but left the console unit up while we both went through news, event listings and schedules.

The problem with the megascrapers is they're huge. Four hundred meters square by five hundred tall huge, some to a thousand. Since we'd blown several tens of them into crematoria during the War, through sabotage, they had very, very tight security on the technical areas. They'd shoot kids and then claim terrorist intent. But that wouldn't stop us; the military attack included nukes, kinetic energy weapons and destructive star drive points detonated overhead, but they were terrified of, and played on, the threat of infiltrators.

She said, "Three conferences over there. One medical, one materials science, one software."

"What about the software?"

"Marketing."

"What's the medical?" I was wondering if someone had failed to save a life and relatives were petty or frazzled enough to want revenge, but that didn't sound like something he'd take. Materials science. Had a building collapsed? That would be possible. I said so.

"Looking," she said, "this is going to take time, though and he knows where we are."

"He's also got to make money. I'm secondary, and dangerous. I need to know where to get him."

"I can take one show, you the other, I call when I see anything?"

"Not enough response time."

I'd been down less than half a div, barely over an Earth hour, and we were this close that fast. Something would go wrong for him. Something had to.

She said, "I'm not finding any reason to kill a materials scientist or professor. It would have to be personal. No major deaths listed in medical attendee histories. Is it just a building resident?"

"Possible, but few very high-profile people live in these. Box Proles low down, Box Tops up high, middle-class managers, engineers, etc. The management are resident and similar to a city council."

"Guests?"

"No idea, and hard to tell. What's the marketing convention?"

"Node-based Broadcast Direct Marketing Strategies."

"There!" I almost shouted.

"Yeah, everyone hates those fuckers."

"Organizer? Lead speaker?"

"Organizer's been in the news a lot. He's milking the notoriety and getting more business from it. He's found loopholes in Earth's laws and several regions."

"Him."

I was up and moving.

"How are you getting in?"

"They're spammers. They won't exactly close off access to potential customers. You lead. I'll follow."

She grabbed a handful of things, stuffed them into pockets and tossed my chip and a new phone at me.

"Look the part," she said.

I remembered now, and it still applied. Earthies are in constant chat with friends and relatives. For a while they'd even kept video running, until it became both a security and a safety issue. Audio, though, ran pretty much nonstop except in government buildings and there were courtesy areas and terminals there as well. The entire planet was so urbanized that being held incommunicado was considered worse than actual violence, and considered "brutality."

As tourists, that wasn't as much of an issue, but we'd be noticeable if we didn't seem to be connected. With earbuds in and constantly chattering about stupid crap, no one would see us.

Just before we popped the door, she asked, "Could this be a setup?"

"Yes, but we have to try," I said. I was sure I could handle any public attack, and I'd try not to get private if it was avoidable.

I have no idea how people live in those boxes. We walked out of the hotel, stepped onto a slideway, and then followed it past several clubs, as it escalated down a level, around one side and past shops and a playground, then stepped off and took a lateral between blocks.

It was pretty much impossible to draw a mental map, but I snapped images with my phone at each change so I'd be able to retrace. I also tapped in exits and slides for getaway. I was likely to need them.

The convention was two hundred meters up, fifty levels approximately, though "level" varies greatly inside these rat mazes. It was in a hall taking up three verticals, spread along corridors and with other events in between. We got in a line meters long and waited for admission while scanning the area for threats. The registrars and desk rolled along past us, with program loads and passes.

The guy ahead of Silver joked, "What if I spoof the pass?"

The registrar was probably a hired model and stared as if the man were stupid. "We expect that in this crowd. There'll be enough compensation in downloads." I'm sure she'd heard the same joke ten times already.

Silver swiped a cash card for both of us, took two passes, and thanked her. She moved on.

Events were well under way, and there were a lot of people here. We walked down the corridor, into the main hall, and there were a hundred displays or more for various methods and approaches to massaging information from people, accessing their comms "with consent" to pimp stuff to them, or worse, use them as distribution nodes to promote to their friends. Everything here was technically legal even under the restrictive laws of Earth, and just proved that supply and demand will survive any idealistic attempt to manage people. Signs insisted that no illicit access would be tolerated, subject to removal of pass and ejection, legal action, etc. They were probably honest about that, for liability reasons, but I had no reason to believe the clients would abide by it more than they had to.

Silver had DNA gear out. We just might succeed in locating him in this crush, and if so, I was confident of my ability to get in close and go for a bare-handed kill.

She said, "Minor trace, all over."

"Schedule?" I asked.

"Principal is speaking in thirty minutes."

"IDs?"

"He's still in this area but not where a camera can monitor. They don't seem to have them in here."

Some guy overheard us, quiet as we were, and said, "Yeah, privacy. They don't allow cams in events. Just at the exits and entrances. You need to find someone? I can get a page in."

I said, "Thanks, but we don't need a page. We'll find him."

"Isn't his phone live?"

"Yeah, we got it. Thanks," I assured him, then turned my back and shut him physically out while we relocated. He took the hint.

I continued to Silver, "We watch, I get close to the stage, you stay near the access door. Best we can do."

"Okay," she agreed, sounding casual. Then she spoke into her dead mic, "Yeah, the event's great. All kinds of goober stuff for promo."

I followed her lead. "Nance has samples, you should try to make it for tomorrow at least."

We slid through the crowd like fish through weeds. It's a practiced skill, but more art than training. You just look for any opening and ease into it, and people move around you. For Earth, I do recommend keeping your phone in hand and any valuables in inside chest pockets. It hurt my arm with every jostle, but I was healing.

There were numerous exhibits and I would have appreciated checking them out as much as I hate these dogfuckers. There were parallels between our trades, much as I hated to admit it.

I wormed my way toward the front. It would be a bitch to get on stage from here, but I assumed I'd have to. The MC said, "—our generation's greatest market promoter, Jason 'The Hit Man' Groom."

There was light applause, Groom ran from the wings and stepped up on the riser.

Then he burst into flame.

I recognized the weapon at once. A hypergolic base with a flammable powder, sprayed right up from under the riser. Groom screamed and dove, creditably fast. He was cooked badly, though. I could smell the fried bologna stench from here.

Then a moment later, the screens switched to a pan of the audience, swept from back to front then back to me. My face popped up on the screens three meters high, holding my phone. It caught me by surprise and I twitched.

I stayed right where I was, staring at the stage and looking horrified with everyone else. There was nothing else I could do. Either some camera operator had chosen my expression for the news loads, or Randall had staged it to gain extra leverage.

It wasn't more than a second, and then a few brave

souls figured out the flaming man was real and rushed the stage, which triggered most of the rest to flee screaming for the exits. I chose the exit. There was nothing I could accomplish onstage; it had gone sour last time, and I might run into Randall. While I wanted to find him, it had to be on my terms. He'd won this round tactically.

I was scared, though. That was a clear shot of my face, and I might have been snapped several times on Earth during the attacks. I'd escaped then because most infrastructure was down, and because I'd left as soon as they put word out. They'd had no reason to look for me on the way in. If they did a search now, though, I was dead. Deliberate or not, that image of me was a problem, and I was sure it was going to come up.

I pinged Silver and said, "Three turns back," and headed for that location.

There was a press at the door, with several suited security guards reciting, "Remain calm, keep walking." They had no actual power, they were mostly for courtesy, which makes little sense, but it meant I could ignore them.

Once out the doors, the crowd thinned out, and kept moving quickly, but the flow slowed, much like a river delta, into the mass of people who hadn't seen anything and weren't aware of it. Rumors propagated out, and distorted into stories of cooking demos gone wrong, pyrotechnic failures, and the inevitable "Fake!" comments.

I walked slowly, and Silver was waiting at the marked spot. We linked back up in a general way, nearby but not with each other, so she could evade if I got snagged.

We took ramps, slides and escalators down fast, though

"fast" is relative when we're talking fifty to sixty levels. I did not want to be in an elevator. That would be too easy to stop or stall. I also wanted lots of witnesses and shields against apprehension or attack. I was worried more about cops than Randall on that.

The news caught up fairly quickly. Groom was critical but alive and being evacuated. Cops were arriving in swarms to secure the area, interview witnesses and look for evidence. Incendiary attacks were frightening to Earthies, especially after the War. I didn't blame them. We'd cooked millions.

I was glad, though. If I couldn't intercept, I appreciated the victim surviving, even if he was scum. In this case, the target survived because Randall was trying to be too cute and clever. He thought he could orchestrate my downfall with it. That just wasn't going to happen. I was going to vacate the area and start over, though.

It took most of an hour to get down to ground level in a hurry without looking like it. We found a way out to the street, though it's hard to tell they're streets with all the buildings around, the waste heat, and the crowds. The light's a bit different is all.

I needed to move farther out of town.

I snagged a cab, left the door open and Silver climbed in a few seconds later. I gave an address two squares away, swiped a card and off we went. This was standard urban evasion. There's not much can be done to stop it, and it just takes practice.

I tapped a message on screen, showed it to Silver well out of sight of the forward-mounted security camera. It gave a location well out of town I'd used during the War, a park. It was west and south. She reached over and deleted it.

At the stop, I climbed out; she went on. She would bail out herself within a few blocks. I grabbed another cab and went another three squares while changing my jacket down behind the seat, walked half a square, took another cab, walked some more, rode again.

It was almost eight hours of walking, riding, walking and occasionally sprinting and ducking before I reached the safe area.

◎ CHAPTER 23 ◎

IT WASN'T SAFE. Though I didn't find that out at first.

What had been a park was now a commercial complex. I couldn't loiter in a cab, it was late night, and most places were closed or quiet.

I got out and let the last cab run, and walked around the area. There were quite a few wholesalers and some mass retail outlets. I decided to go around back and pretend to be a laborer. I headed that way.

It was a big complex, and I should have had the cab drop me round back initially. Mistake on my part.

It all added up. I was a tourist by ID chip, walking through a closed area alone, heading for the back, and clearly out of place. A cop got me.

I heard the motion, pretended to ignore it at first while tracking it audibly, then turned and gave a slight wave and nod. It didn't work.

He hit the spotlight, revved up and braked in front of me.

This was not good. Detention would pretty much be the end for me. I had to be polite, though, if I wanted to get out of this.

He stepped out, armed and armored and polite but sturdy.

"Good evening. What are you doing here?"

I said, "Good evening, sir. I'm in wholesale back home and thought I'd take a look at some of the operations here." There was no point in lying about being an offworlder.

"You should probably do that in daylight," he said. "It's not something done in the dark on Earth."

"I apologize," I said.

"No harm done yet. I'll need to see your system ID and scan your chip. You are wearing it, yes?"

I had a fake one on the phone in my pocket. It did match my ID.

"I have it with me," I agreed, while looking for a way out of this. I was worried about that ID, because we had limited resources. I should have changed it in the escape, but didn't have a spare on hand.

He waved a scanner, I handed the card over carefully, and it pinged somehow. Likely, they'd tagged everyone leaving that convention.

"Were you at the Direct Marketing Strategies convention in Destiny Block earlier today?"

"I passed through there, yes. Professional interest. I didn't see much that would translate to what I do," I said.

"Did you hear about the incident?"

"I heard something. I was heading out as it happened, I think, and decided I was better off not being in the way."

I'd been as reasonable as possible, and so had he. However, there were too many flags for him to let me go.

He tried the standard routine. "I must detain you. Please stand in place, put your hands on your head, and don't move."

I complied. I needed him close. I was surprised he was alone; usually they're in at least pairs. It was probable his partner was in the area, too, and this was considered a nicer area. Safe. Family friendly. That's why I stood out.

He approached cautiously, and I remained relaxed inside, stiff and compliant outside.

Then he hooked my ankle to pull me off balance, and reached for my left hand with the binders.

I reversed that with a kick and twist. He was off balance. I had his arm, turned into a bar locking it back against his elbow armor. I had to wiggle a bit to get past his helmet and tap him in the throat, but that and a knee to the solar plexus, even through armor, slowed him down. It also made my knee hurt like hell. He had a plate in there. He grunted and slumped a bit.

Still, I had enough time to flip his stunner from the holster and away. I pulled his flex baton, passed it up to my right hand, poked it into his throat, and continued pulling stuff from him. I caught his phone and slung it, tossed his gas dispenser away, pulled out the stickyweb gun and the knife in his pocket. That last was illegal, for some unfathomable reason, but almost all cops carried one anyway. We spun around three times like some kind of bizarre dance.

I smashed the baton into his headset and it blinked a fault as I unsnapped his helmet and peeled it up. Then I bent him over my knee. I took a moment to clip the web gun to my belt.

"I need information. I require that you provide it. This is within the law, your oath and the practicalities of this situation."

He still tried to argue.

"Assaulting an officer is an—OWWW!"

I wasn't going to break his elbow. Not yet.

"I'm doing the fucking explaining. Give me the information, you'll be fine. Try to fight, you die. You are nothing in this fight. Nothing," I repeated. "You and a thousand like you can die and not matter. Now you can give it to me and live, or I can pluck your fucking eyes out and jam them against the scanner while they're still warm." I was nose to nose with him, intimately close and encroaching, and I had him pinned. It hit all the panic buttons of an Earthie. In his position, he expected to have physical and psychological superiority over a single detainee. I wasn't playing by the rules.

"Oh, god," he muttered. His struggles changed from aggressive to fearful, just like that. He wasn't prepared for that kind of emotional onslaught backed up by someone who actually knew how to fight.

I really had scared him to that level. He was completely limp and unresisting, without even a bluff of authority.

"I'm looking for the individual who orchestrated that attack. That's why I was there."

"Yes, sir."

"I need to find him, so this can stop. You may have heard of a pattern of killings in other systems."

I forced him down into his seat, with his own knife

against his throat and the free arm bent far back. He could still call for help, but I could kill him in a second. He'd never even have time to pop the safeties on the car's internal systems, much less trigger gas. He'd get one command out, but not two.

He did as I said, clearly believing I would kill him if I didn't like the answers. He scrolled through reports and brought up a fuzzy image of Randall. He'd beaten me out by less than an Earth minute.

"Is that him?" he asked as the image came up.

"Very good. What else do you have?"

"He's associated with another assassin who . . . oh, god."

Yes, that was my picture on screen.

"As I said, I am far more concerned with him than with you. Please copy a file of everything you have on him."

While he did so, I tried not to clench my ass too tight, or cut his throat in shiver reflex. Randall the idiot had escalated the stakes to an insane level. Well, that meant I had him scared. It also meant he was edging into unstable. Hell, he'd swan-dived into it.

I watched the monitor, confirmed the load, snagged the rom, leaned back and said, "I'm going to depart now, sir. If I were you, I'd let me. If you locate that individual, I recommend calling the military and not trying to apprehend him either. Have a good evening and a healthy life."

I skipped, flipped and ran. He didn't follow me, but I assumed he did make some kind of report. Half the fight would have been on camera.

I deemed it prudent to withdraw and wait for Randall. Earth was too hot. The outer planets and stations would care about a reward, but otherwise were only peripherally part of Earth. Suburbs, culturally. Subterrae. Exoterrae. I'd look for the event, have more intel to work with, and could even slip some to the UN Intelligence Directorate. It's not as if it mattered who took him down, as long as someone did.

My immediate need was to E&E the area. I coded a message to Silver to use that trace we'd set up and locate me. I dodged several times, pulled out a hat, flipped my jacket, and crossed a highway. The vehicles were autocontrolled, and civilians prohibited, but I found a hole in the fence used by others, went down, across each carriageway in shadows, and back up. That put me in a completely different zone for everything, and should hinder pursuit. Eventually, they'd have cameras everywhere, and I was sure the cop and video would be out there.

They'd marked Randall as a suspect. That was predictable, with the fear factor we'd instilled in them. They'd never gotten over it, and it was a point of contention for civil rights activists. Sadly, our presence was going to justify all the additional intrusion and fascism they'd piled on the already thick layer. He'd attempted assassination, which would just trigger demands for more intrusion.

I found an open food place, snagged a machine-built sandwich and settled in the corner, sat down. The store had its own security cameras, which the police could cut into with a warrant. They didn't have to present the warrant, though, and if they cut in illegally it wouldn't matter to me anyway.

A while later Silver came in, grabbed something and left. I waited a short time and followed her.

We took a manned cab to the travel station

I wish I could have enjoyed it more. The driver was cordial. "Is it warm enough?"

I realized it had been quite cool outside. Late fall.

"Yes, fine. Thanks."

"No problem. I come here from India. When I arrive, I get ride. I ask driver for more heat. He tell me it cost five marks. Illegal."

"Wow."

"I ask him about music. He says music is free, so I told him turn the music up and I stay warm listening. So now I drive cab. My business is Premier Shuttle. You know why it's 'Premier'?"

"No."

"The heat is free."

I had to laugh. "Excellent. I appreciate it."

Shortly, we were at the travel station, and Silver tipped him a little. It's not done much on Earth anymore, but he deserved it, and I did feel better with the warmth, and the story.

The bustrain rolled up, we boarded, and were on the controlled road in minutes. The seat requested my ticket, I fed it in, and nothing else happened. We made it back into the city in short order.

We took a cheaper hotel, to minimize risk. We did not look the part of high-end tourists, though, and the cheaper ones were at ground level, away from the entertainment and thrills, closer to the street and utilities.

Once in the door, Silver had enough exposure to me to read my expression.

"We're leaving?"

"Offplanet, right now. We need a flight, under plausible and completely deniable names. I want to be at a jump point and ready to take rapid transit on anything we can find."

"Working," she said, and pulled up a screen within a screen within a screen. I hoped that was secure enough. "May I ask?" she said.

"Check news."

She glanced at a side window which had my picture, and said, "Shit."

"Exactly. He's desperate, which means I am, too."

"They've got an excellent shot of your face from arrival. I can't do surgery here and they've got a very high probability of making you."

"We need to find a cover, then, with a backup."

"I'm busy. Can you do that?" She sounded concerned. Probably because I sounded stressed.

"Give me a moment," I said.

"Got tickets for eighteen hundred tomorrow, but it's going to be expensive and burn two IDs each. Our last ones."

"Can't be helped. I can't chase him and avoid twenty-eight billion enraged aardvarks at the same time."

"I understand," she said.

I kept thinking. What I wanted was something outré enough that it would be unseen, looked right past.

"We need to find a sex shop," I said.

"I'm not sure my contract goes quite that far," she said, with a nervous grin. "Unless you need advice on selection, in which case I can't offer much."

"Not quite. I want D/s culture gear."

"That's definitely not in my enlistment contract."

"Who said you're the bottom?"

She gaped.

"You've got it," I said. "Lead me through the port like a pet on a leash."

"It's ridiculous."

"It is. And a recognized social subculture that includes several assemblypersons and governors. No one will hinder us and they won't be looking for me in that context. Not even he's likely to. It also gives an excuse to wear partial masks that can't be called into question. They're cultural."

"Let me first say, 'wow.' Then let me say that, while I've had a sex life with some variation and experimentation, it's going to take serious work for me to lead you on a leash through a spaceport without flushing red or bursting into laughter."

"Our lives depend on it."

She closed her eyes and said, "That's sufficient motivation. I'll still have to work at it."

"You can do so while you shop."

"Um . . . yes." She flushed red at once. That was not a good sign.

"What do you need?" I asked.

"I suppose I need to open up," she said.

A part of my brain thought, *so to speak*.

"Yes?" I said. "Does it help if I admit to using node fora, anonymous friends and some really good sensual programs for most of the last decade? Except for a very sweet escort aboard the *Caroline* whom I hammered into submission while dosed on CNS?"

She smiled slightly. "Yeah, that helps." She leaned back, took a breath, and flushed. "Okay, I can do women but I like men. A little open-air teasing or foreplay or nudity I'm fine with. I've used the usual toys both ways, and I've even done some restraint. I've scened my share of things in private, including interrogator play with a manfriend from security branch. I'm passingly familiar with the toys used for D/s, but the thought of being a domme in public in costume, with a sub in tow, especially someone with your background, especially you, is an entirely new level." She took a breath. "And I guess I'm down to smiles from giggles."

"Hopefully you'll be over it by the time you're done shopping."

"Or much worse, but I'll see what I can do. Back soon," she said. She faced the screens, pulled an address, blocked a transit route, grabbed her coat and was out the door in under one hundred seconds.

I spent the time keeping alert for threats on our scanners, and looking for any further signs of Randall. He was good. I'd never admit it to his face, but he was good.

I twitched when she unlocked the door. I had the webgun out, and she stared at it, and me, then smiled.

She dumped the purchases out on the bed.

I had second thoughts about going through with this.

There was a head and eye mask in violet stretch vinyl with feathers, shorts built around a jockstrap with restraints built in and an attached ponytail, S-curved heeled boots, a half-shirt and a half-cape of black vinyl.

"That is utterly ridiculous."

My second thoughts were about me keeping a straight face, even if my life depended on it.

"I asked the clerk to keep the outfit consistent between culture fetishes. Said I was new at it. We also need to wear bandanas with specific colors and knots to indicate our availability and orientation."

"Doesn't anybody just do a nice double penetration with sheep anymore?" I asked.

We both convulsed in hysterics.

However, staying alive has always been a good motivation for me. I pulled on the briefs and half-shirt that hid my arm damage, wrapped the shoulder cloak around and fastened it, sat down and pulled on the boots, put on the hood and stood so she could fasten the collar around my neck.

"Well done on the boots," I said. "They're heeled enough to fit the outfit, low enough I can still run."

She burst into helpless peals of laughter.

"Running in that outfit. So very discreet," she said.

I choked for a moment myself, but got it under iron control. I tapped her cheek with fingertips to get her attention.

She snarled, "Show some respect, slave," and then lost it again.

Dammit, this was not going to be easy. I snickered myself.

She continued, "Perhaps you should sleep on the floor until you learn proper respect."

"Will that stop you laughing?" I asked.

That dropped her jaw again.

"Yes. It does. I think I'm just squicked enough at the

idea of treating someone like that, that it's no longer funny."

"Well, good as it goes," I said. "So let me change back for now and we can get a few hours sleep in shifts. I want one of us awake and both of us in work clothes for now in case we have to bail."

She'd also bought some contact paper, and printed out copies of various travel stickers, which we distressed against the carpet and our shoes. She had more throwaway accessories for costuming, and those went into the bag.

Four hours before departure time, we were ready, and gradually getting over the snickers. Something that helped me was that she looked spectacular in a high-hipped fake leather leotard. Too spectacular, even with the fitness fetish common in that community. Very few people on Earth have muscle tone like that, and certainly not in the urban supersprawls. I was a bit older, so I could mask it a bit better. But we did stand out. Hopefully, the disguise was so blatant no one would be able to mark the discrepancies.

Feeling ridiculous, and very nervous because I had no weapons or decent clothing, I opened the door and pre-ceded her into the hallway. She carried a doccase in one hand. I carried a rolling bag in my left. I let her take the lead and get a gentle tug on the leash.

That was strictly a costume piece. She'd stitched it with a breakaway fastener, because if it came to a fight, the last thing I needed was either a collar or a rein.

There are two ways to evade notice. Either be so drab you're invisible or so blatant no one notices anything except the distraction. This was that. At each turn or change or floor, Silver made a light tug on the leash, and said, "Come, boy," or, "Stand here, boy." It was way out of my character, of any military or police guideline, and our faces were masked enough we shouldn't show. We had fresh tourist ID. My concern was her accent. I was better, but an expert would know we were Freeholders. I was betting on both discomfort for the security; D/s is not uncommon, but public presentation is, and makes a lot of people squeamish. If they were fascinated, same deal. The ID had codes and stamps for previous visits, so we could present as ex-pats.

There was a train station in the sublevel. I paid us through with a cash card, made a point of handing it back to my "mistress." We boarded, I stood, she sat, and no one said a word for the duration of the trip. They even left room around me, though not her. She managed it well, but I could tell she wasn't thrilled with Earthies rubbing against her scanty outfit.

Her outfit was more elaborate than mine. The leotard had a built in corset with boning and cups, scintillating bars running up the outside, with bright metal highlights. As I was more visible than she, though we were presumably both wanted, she stood out more. I was merely a muscular sub in a mask, half-shirt and shorts. With glitter on my chest.

We debarked in a gaggle, both of us keeping tight hold of our luggage and personal pouches. Petty theft was so common on Earth it wasn't even reportable. No one carried enough to even bother with insurance claims.

It worked. We passed several cameras and walked right by a police stand. No one twigged, no one came for us. The male cops eyed her up and down and ignored me completely. The two female cops glanced at me, shrugged and grinned. One looked embarrassed, the other amused.

Port security was still a madhouse of silliness. There were cameras, sniffers, penetrating sonar, chemical sensors, the works. We passed through each stage, being eyeballed and scanned and directed around. It certainly felt as if they were thorough. They never once actually looked at our ID, though, or even asked about the masks. Social "culture" meant hands off. They even had a warning about a known enemy from a high-G planet, and chose to randomly harass an ancient lady in a powered chair in front of me instead. Utter waste of resources.

One of them asked Silver, "Where are you bound, ma'am?"

"A resort on Govannon. A gift from my uncle."

"Nice," he said, sounding impressed. He was discreetly ogling her cleavage as he interacted. Some fetish crowd appreciated being looked at, and her bandanna was apparently folded for that. She smiled and leaned slightly.

"How long is that?" he asked.

"Only a couple of weeks, then we move on."

"I've heard it's expensive."

"Ten thousand a day, and that's not one of the groulier places." She handled the slang well.

He recoiled a bit.

"Trif. Have a good trip." He handed our cards back.

"Thanks," she said, and then, "Forward, boy."

In the Freehold, someone might say, "Slave." Not here. It wasn't illegal per se, but it was certainly impolite. Not that this type of thing had a lot of market in the

Freehold, at least not in public. There was no shock factor
to be gained, and the public display was of little cultural
value.

Then we were through, into the port proper, and only
had a few thousand wandering goons to worry about—
facility security, line security, port police, local police,
regional police, UN police, drug inspectors, contraband
inspectors, information inspectors. Ordinarily, I'd have
one questionable item for them to seize as a precaution,
with a pro-forma objection. This time, we were the
questionable item and walked right past them all.

If we played this right, we could transit completely out
of the system without ever talking to another person.
We'd been inspected, detected, stamped and approved,
and no one cared anymore. There were cameras here, too,
but of much lower priority than at the gates. If someone
reviewing data made us in the outfits, I wanted to be
out of them and go to the other end of the spectrum:
completely mundane.

We found a family friendly restroom, which should
only have an emergency camera, and went in. Again, normal
for the subculture. The sub went with the domme. Some
even helped each other with toilet functions. I found that
disturbing in the context of pleasure. For a casualty, sure.
For fun? Yuck.

I was a bit concerned about someone seeing us come
out, but if we took a few minutes, it shouldn't be obvious.
Silver changed into a business suit in black, pulled her
hair back severely, oiled it down and put on dark lipstick
and broad eye shadow past the eyebrows. I threw on
slacks and a coat and iridescent shades of the newest type.

I slapped the well-distressed travel stickers over the bag, we swapped, and out we went.

However, bad security didn't mean no security.

We'd cleared train, station, a section cordon, and were approaching the controlled area for departures when some kind of message came down. Several extra personnel came out into the security lines, and started asking travelers for ID. Then I saw them make another offworlder pull out his chip and physically show it them, while they scanned it. They were on to us. We couldn't use the ones we'd come in with, and if I handed them a phone with a fake, that was it.

"Divert," I said softly, and Silver nodded.

We stopped and talked for a moment, about nothing. She pointed casually, I nodded, and we walked into a vid store. We perused, bought a vid that was in the popular rack, *Best of Sik Pranks*, and left. We walked back the way we'd come, took a turn, took a slide and headed for the exit. It was easy to get out toward the trains, and there was a substantial crowd. However, someone had seen us. There were cops coming into the area.

I had the doccase that was largely a prop, filled with meaningful-looking docs and notes that would yield nothing. There was text, pictures of various buildings, and contact numbers at semirandom. It would keep them busy and distracted for a bit while we tried to formulate other plans.

At this point, I simply wanted them to misinterpret our intent. Walking would indicate a local destination, so we walked.

The cops were on to us. They had a good cordon set up

and I could see them closing in. They weren't as good at stealth as they thought they were. However, they were close enough to negate any public transport. We'd have to E&E on foot, and meet up at our agreed point.

I gave Silver a brief nod, which she interpreted as a command of preparation to bail. We reached a corner, I found a likely person, meaning the first one who made eye contact with me, and I shoved the case into his hands. He looked surprised, and Silver and I pivoted, took two steps in different directions, then sprinted.

I didn't watch but could hear. A cluster of cops dogpiled the poor bastard, turning him into another innocent person abused by the system. It wasn't going to hurt the system. It probably hurt him. I wondered how long it would take for him to be released.

However, I had my own issues. Someone stepped up to me and took my injured arm. It was still weak, hurt after the fight with the cop, and caused me to be a little less than graceful. I kicked his knee sideways in a fashion designed to be effective even through flex-armor, disengaged and kept going.

It would have worked, except they'd correctly decided it was worth a large response to get me. A drone package whipped overhead and dropped a sticky net over the entire corner. In seconds, I was surrounded by more than a squad with heavy stunners and obviously twitchy trigger fingers.

I hoped Silver was free.

☯ CHAPTER 24 ☯

EARTH COPS KNOW how to arrest someone.

I was immobilized in a field, and when the effect went away, I was out of the web, shackled with hands to a belt, strapped to a dolly with a blindfold and mouth bit. "For the detainee's protection," they insist. They don't explain why.

The process actually was rather fast. They wheeled me into a vehicle, I was driven around somewhere with three other detainees; I could hear their breathing and smell them. We stopped, they undogged us, rolled us inside. When I didn't read on their implant scanner, someone pulled the gag and asked, "Passport."

"Left chest pocket," I said.

He replaced the gag, too. Bastard.

It probably wasn't over thirty minutes, but felt forever in those restraints. I was released under immobility, and when it stopped, I was in a cell. At least I was alone this time.

I had nothing, though. They'd stripped every item from every pocket. None of it would be suspicious, but a lot of it was useful.

As there was nothing else to do, I lay down and waited.

The clock/vid/scheduler on the wall kept time. I ignored the sports and shock shows. I just didn't feel like putting on any particular act. Nothing is harder to read than no act at all.

When they finally came for me, four hours later, there were no restraints. Two guards and I were locked through section by section, until I was left alone in an interview room. I took a seat. A few minutes later, with a camera indicating recording in progress, a man came in.

"Good day," he said. He didn't mean it. He wore a plain but expensive suit and obviously had money for biosculp.

"Hello," I agreed.

"From your DNA and image, you are a certain individual wanted for some activities fifteen years ago. Do you mind if I am not specific at this point in the conversation?" It was the voice of a viper.

"I don't mind." Oh, shit. I was going to die. Shock trickled through me, icy in my fingers and toes, and my balls shriveled up along with my ass.

He sat down and stared at me. "You are definitely confirmed as that individual. This is problematic from both a public relations and an international relations point of view."

"I understand," I said.

"Good. I must have positive confirmation of your intentions on Earth, or there will be problems."

"May I ask who you are?" I asked.

"Here," he said. He took out ID and laid it on the table, using his hand to shield it from the camera.

Deputy Director for Foreign Intelligence Vandler. I thought back to their hierarchy. This was the number four person in the UN intelligence apparatus.

"I see," I acknowledged.

"I don't have your name," he said. "I don't really need it. Who you are and what you did is on record. I really do need that information."

I appreciated that he was treating me as a fellow professional. What he was saying was, "Either you assure me you're not here on business, or you don't leave this room alive and the file gets scrubbed. Believe it."

"I am here on tangentially related business," I said. I might actually live through this. I'd need to talk carefully.

Oh, did that get his attention. He started sweating.

"I need you to elaborate," he said, fingering his phone.

Okay, he was who he said he was. No one could fake that reaction if they hadn't studied what I did.

"I am not here to cause trouble on Earth. That was a long time ago, and no good could come of revisiting it."

"Yes." He nodded. He still fingered the phone, ready to make that call . . .

"One of my former subordinates is here to cause trouble. He's why I was leaked. He did it. He implemented that incident yesterday. I'm here to stop him."

He clearly had someone feeding him audio. He paused, nodded and said, "We require that you move that activity out of Sol space. Immediately."

"That's up to him, and you," I said. "If you order me to leave, I will. I was trying to. He's killed two people, though, and probably plans to kill others. Likely people high enough to create a major incident. You are obviously aware that you can't stop him."

That got his teeth gritting.

I said, "Rothman, Lee, Janich, Lenz, Roberti, Rosencrans, Boulain, Groom. That's him."

"It could as well be you, trying to distract attention."

I shrugged. "I'll remain here until the next assassination if you like. I hope after that you'll give me all the intel you have to help chase him down."

That seemed to register.

"Will you come with me peacefully? Where we can discuss that in greater detail?"

"I would very much appreciate that," I agreed. "The information will be useful."

"This way, then," he said, and stood. He never took his eyes off me. He gestured for me to go first.

They didn't do badly. There were armed guards in enough angles to make any firefight lethal. I'd probably get most of them, but I'd be unlikely to get all. They had lethal and nonlethal weapons, and their armor was head-to-toe, so they could blaze away at a melee.

I preceded him into a limo and immobility kicked in again. I don't blame him, and didn't think it was rude. I was nervous myself. I couldn't do anything here. If I started a major fight, they'd certainly kill me. If they were smart, they'd just blow up a building with me under it, and blame me. That would leave me dead, my daughter distressed, and Randall on the loose.

We got out underground of some tower or other in the Washington area. It wasn't their actual HQ, but probably had a secure pipe to it. We went into a carpeted conference room that obviously had full shielding. He even left his phone outside.

They were professionally cordial. I accepted a sealed bottle of mineral water, though of course it could still have been doctored. We were going to feel each other out until we had some level of trust.

"There were four people in my section," I offered. "Apparently, two of us escaped."

"Where was this?" he asked.

"Minneapolis. Two zero nine five six East Trone Road, Executive Storage Solutions."

He nodded. "That checks."

"I wasn't there, and apparently he escaped."

"And he is . . . ?"

I wasn't going to give real names even after the fact. "It hardly matters. He never uses it, and never did. At the time, he was going by Doug Rognan."

"What name did he use to escape?"

"I would have no idea. We had multiple IDs cleared ahead of time, and none of us knew any of the others, nor even some of our own."

It was true. I wasn't going to tell him we had buried caches on Earth. They might still be here and I might still need some.

"You understand that you are . . . reviled here."

"I do," I said. "I'm not going to make excuses about the events during War. There's nothing I can do about that now."

I tried not to let that show. I didn't want to think about it, because I couldn't function if I did.

He said, "We didn't find you, of course. We didn't find him, either. We have nothing on him at all. I reviewed all the videos of those events today. Nothing."

That caused an acidic burn inside.

I said, "You viewed them today?"

"I did. Are they useful to you?"

"Yes, very."

"Then I want a name."

"I went by Marquette," I told him, deliberately misunderstanding the question. "He left Earth, I took over his persona. He didn't know what for and was resettled elsewhere. I think everyone who might know where he is now is dead. We were in Minneapolis."

It worked, though. He nodded and spoke to the desk.

"Play video, this archive, of Minneapolis assault."

I turned to the wall.

It was raw footage. They hadn't stabilized the bobbing of the helmet cameras, nor clarified anything. This was an intelligence file.

They were good, I had to admit. Their first assault tried hitting the building's roof from two adjoining ones. The mines, zap fields and other boobytraps we'd laid disabled several troopers, probably killed two who fell twenty meters. They stopped that as soon as the first wave hit it.

A ground team materialized from several directions, stacked and hit the door in under five seconds. They threw low-grade explosives, jammers and EMP ahead, to clear the entrance. They made it past the first few traps unhindered, before taking two casualties to nonlethal stuff we'd set against common gangers or thieves.

It was less than another ten seconds before they hit the stairs. I watched the multiple views along the sides as well as the photographer's view center screen.

And there was Deni, alone on the first landing of the stairs. It was just a glimpse, but even after fifteen Earth years her face was burned in my brain. Seeing her was gut wrenching.

The camera operator was back just far enough, or maybe she IDed him and didn't waste ammo on him. But in front of him, Uno government goons were dying, and I felt a flush of vengeful glee. I had to force myself not to cheer, because it was very satisfying to see them die, bullets ripping through heads, necks, torsos, accompanied by screams and wails. She was ten times the soldier the lot of them were, and a thousand times the human being. We'd targeted the infrastructure and innocent people had died. These were the scum who needed it. They'd been unreachable, though I had one across the table from me now . . .

Then the stunner bolt caught her and she went limp, eyes focused on some euphoric tickle that was actually within her brain. They had her. She'd taken twelve of them down at least, but they had her.

As they rushed past, two of them knelt to ID her or restrain her, and one of them just had time to say, "Look out! She—" and then the camera jolted, the image suddenly focusing on a wall as it tumbled back down stairs.

At least fourteen. She'd rigged a charge, and I was betting, because I didn't dare ask, that she'd worn it right over her belly.

That was why they didn't know to look for a child. A child she hadn't been holding. A child I'd found three days later, who had kept me just sane enough to not go on a killing spree of these . . . filth.

Then another camera took over, and I raised Deni's count to at least fifteen.

They regrouped and got reinforcements from another platoon, and advanced at once, shooting anything that looked like a mine or sensor, three of them wearing jammer packs. It was a professional assault, for its time.

Next was Tyler. She was in great concealment, near a water heater that was operating because the hot water was on throughout the building and drawing on it and the pipes from it. The combination of heat and noise had ruined any sensor image of her. Tyler was not carrying a baby. Tyler was carrying a UN-issue machine gun, and tore an entire squad apart. All they saw was a snarl and incoming tungsten.

She dropped the gun and went to pistol, and I counted her tally. She'd never been a lover, though she could have been. We'd been close enough, she was a buddy, a comrade and a friend, and I was proud to have known her. When the screams were done, at least nineteen more were dead, including one who got his larynx crushed when he tried to administer first aid. No, she wasn't going to be kept alive to be tortured or murdered later. The grimace on her face at that moment was frightening, even to me, even after all that had happened.

No baby.

I didn't pay much attention to the clearing of the rest of the building. Kimbo had escaped and they only had his most recent destroyed Earth ID to work from.

And it had to be him who'd hidden my sedated daughter up top.

It made sense. Deni *had* to be first and *had* to die in a fashion that made it impossible to tell she was a mother. Yes, there are ways to tell even from protoplasm, but they had no reason to look that closely.

It wasn't cowardice that he was last. He was a better medic than Tyler. She was better with weapons. It was utterly logical, had been a decision reached in seconds or less . . .

And it made my target, my arch-nemesis, the shame of our unit, into the man who had saved my daughter's life, and mine by extension.

I couldn't tell *anyone*.

With that one act, however, he'd redeemed himself.

And I was going to use that knowledge to shame and humiliate him with his "cowardice" until I could get him off guard and kill him.

There are days when I really want the entire race wiped out by alien invasion, or a brutal virus. Then there are days I want to do it myself.

I realized Vandler was staring at me.

"I presume he left through the top window, east side."

"How do you figure?"

"Because when I reconnoitered later, I left through the west in a hurry, past some of your police. I didn't see anything of him."

"What did you go back for?" he asked casually.

My neck hair turned into wire.

"Comm codes. No risk to us, but I needed them for exfiltrating."

"I understand," he said. "You were reported, and then we went through the building in detail for several days. It was hard to tell much of anything, really. There were only the four of you? Then, what can you tell me about this man, who's going by what name?"

He wanted intel. It couldn't hurt now, and gave me some goodwill to bargain with.

"Just the four there. At one time he was Kimbo Randall. I doubt that will lead to anything, though."

"Likely not. You have no comment on your two female compatriots killing thirty-eight of our best tactical troops?"

"Not really," I said. "About average, really, though at the time I'd have commended them as a matter of course. We were all decorated after the fact, as were your troops who dropped kinetic kills on our bases and nuked New Hilo, not to mention the bio weapons scientists. It's not relevant to what we're doing now, and I'd hope we can all put all of it behind us."

"You are very reasonable," he said. "That makes me personally hate you even more, that you're dispassionate over it."

What would he say to the inner me, screaming, weeping, shivering?

"I don't think there's any attitude I could have that would help," I said.

"Probably not," he said. He was as cold and dispassionate as I. Here we were, discussing the mass slaughter of billions, and the hand-to-hand slaughter of hundreds, with nary a raised eyebrow.

"So how dangerous is he, then?"

"If surprised, you'll lose tens, and he'll disappear. Try to trap him, he'll do what he did on Caledonia. You heard?" He nodded. "Chase him, you'll never find him."

He said, "I would accuse you of arrogance, but I have no reason to doubt your statements."

"Well, I went home, eventually, and into hiding. I wanted nothing to do with the military, or the people who sent me, after the fact. There's a line between infrastructure damage with collateral casualties and mass slaughter. I ran over it in a tank."

"It's a shame you didn't decide that beforehand. But go on."

I shrugged.

"He came home and went freelance. Eventually, our people figured that out. Later, they found me. I trained him, so I have a chance of bringing him in, or down."

I realized at once he hadn't known as much as he let on. He'd lulled me into talking.

"You were in charge of the entire operation?" He prickled as he asked it.

Liquid nitrogen chills, phosphorus burns, high-voltage jolts and earthquake tremors hit my nerves all at once. I wasn't worried about dying. I was worried how long it would take me to die.

Then part of me decided, if that would appease them, at least I could die with a clear conscience.

"I was. I was directed to plan, train, insert and await, and then after the attack and occupation of our system, I was ordered to implement."

"*This was done in anticipation?*" he fairly shouted.

"Wasn't your own attack? Four million on our planet, wasn't it? Does the number of zeroes matter?"

I realized that "zeroes" could refer not only to the hordes killed, but to the insignificant people making up those hordes. Except I knew that no one was insignificant to themselves and their friends.

This asshole felt some kind of moral superiority because "only" millions had died on his government's orders, and he hadn't done it personally. No one had. They'd pushed buttons. I'd been angry and belittling of them when I mentioned our bombardment controllers to Andre, but here was the other side, where that was considered perfectly acceptable. For me to engage personally was dirty.

Is there really much difference between shoveling shit and handling it?

I suddenly didn't know how I felt, or how I should feel. I wanted to feel justified, I wanted to feel remorse, and I wanted them to at least share some of that remorse. They did strike first, they did cause the deaths of near four million people, but they wanted to use me to let them claim the moral high ground.

I was not going to be anyone's poster child or talking point.

I stared back at him and waited for him to tell me I was going to die, or just have me coshed and hauled off to be tortured. I no longer cared at all, about anyone on any side. We were all murderous fucking criminals, we were all pawns, and I suddenly knew why Randall was doing what he did. It just didn't matter, and a few more dead assholes of the class of people who implemented this stuff was no loss to the human race at all. It might even be a benefit.

I wasn't, and never had been the person to do such things myself, but I had never pretended that I really cared about dead politicians and spammers, and in this case, I'd been correct. No one should care.

Then I remembered back to the surgery on my arm and the artificial opiates that had obliterated my memory for most of a day.

I understood why people would do that. One could be alive, and just not there. When life was too hard and death too easy, massive amounts of drugs could destroy you temporarily, so you could try it again later, reliving and escaping the world in turn.

He intruded into my philosophical musings with, "How do you rate your odds of stopping him?"

"Good," I said. "Better now. He saw fit to expose our past, which he had no need to do. It's a panic reaction because he believes my odds are good."

"Meaning you want me to let you out of here." He almost snarled.

I said, "That's entirely up to you, sir. If you don't, he keeps killing for quite some time. If you do, I can probably stop him." Maybe. Maybe I could stop him. Maybe they'd let me go.

"Will you?"

"I haven't chased him halfway across space to ask for a date."

"And after that?"

"I go home and tell the universe to go fuck itself again."

He stared at me, considering.

So I asked, "This seems to be a bit personal for you, too."

He continued to stare, then nodded, "I drew second camera duty for that team," he said. "I was backup medic, backup right, and backup camera. I had to do all three in a matter of two minutes. I know what kind of carnage is involved, because everyone I worked with died in those two minutes. My best friend had his throat ripped out."

"Two of mine got riddled with bullets, and I have to stalk the remaining one down personally," I said.

"Then I will release you to do so," he said. "I'm going to implant you with a tracer that is also an explosive. You may have it deactivated at any jump point station at our office. If you mess with it, it will blow a hole through your carotid artery. That won't bother me at all." His expression was completely dead.

A medic came in with an insertion gun, and we each nodded. He leaned over and shot me in the left side of the neck.

Son of a bitch, that hurt like a dogfucker.

The medic left while I watched blotches swim in front of my eyes and rubbed my neck in pain.

"What if I have to turn around?"

"You tell us, and we'll escort you. I prefer risking a death here to letting you remain."

"Tactically, I can't fault you," I said.

"You will also give us all the intel you have. Now," he said.

Blackmail and veiled threats of death. I probably didn't know anything critical to current ops, I'd die before I'd talk about mine, and what he asked was perfectly reasonable.

I said, "It mostly came from your files, but I'll turn over what I have. I can't do it here."

"Can she?" he asked, flashing an image of Silver.

"She can," I said. "She's also obviously younger, recent, and is not part of my outfit. She's support only. Is she in custody?"

"Yes, she is nearby. She said nothing."

Really? Good woman.

"She knows nothing about the past. She's my technical expert."

"As your 'technical expert' falsified chips that are supposed to be impossible to fake, hacked into our police nets, changed IDs and disabled two officers when apprehended, naturally I'm not going to trust that."

"I don't expect you will," I said. "Do you need anything else?"

Now that I was equipped with a bomb he controlled, he finally let his emotion show in a grimace of hate.

"No. I'll book you semi-official travel with codes that ensure you won't be harrassed. Get off my planet." He fairly spat it at me.

I said, "You've got the events on Caledonia, Mtali, Novaja Rossia, and here. You've got the fight I had with him at Station Starlight. You have all that video. You have the assets you confiscated, which are serious violations of our intel and I wouldn't let you have if I didn't have to. I really am serious about the threat he poses, and I suggest you take it as seriously as you did fifteen years ago."

"Very well," he said.

I eased back from the table and headed for the door. He didn't bow, rise to open it for me, or acknowledge me other than to follow me with his eyes. Another cop opened it for me, and there was still a whole squad of them.

"Mr. Vandler," I said as I reached the door. I turned to face him and met his eyes.

I said, "I am sorrier, and more ashamed of those events than you can imagine. I can't undo the past. I can only proceed with the future. That future requires that I kill a friend."

"I would like to feel sorry for you," he said. "If you die, I'll consider it a small balance of justice. If you live, I'll consider it fair that you feel that remorse, and know the hatred that exists here. I would strongly suggest you never return to Earth after this."

"Yes, sir," I said.

With that same blank expression he said, "I wish you luck killing your friend."

He meant that to be cruel, and I understood him.

"Thank you," I nodded, turned and left.

✷ CHAPTER 25 ✷

THEY TOOK US DIRECTLY to the spaceport, past all security, and delivered us, with only the clothes on our backs, to a flight bound for the Freehold. That wasn't where I wanted to go, but we didn't have much choice at this point.

Once in orbit, we were able to shop, with a very blatant escort loitering near us, and more obviously armed guards outside them. I made sure they could see my movements, so they didn't get happy with a trigger by accident. If they did so by intent . . .

We settled for basic clothes, a bag each and new phones. I hope they enjoyed the ones we'd left with them. Without a proper access code the first time, they should have completely slagged the memory cores. It was possible they disabled them, removed the cores and tried to crack them. If so, they'd have only the information we had on Randall. Everything related I'd pulled and scorched before we'd started our departure.

At the jump point, I warned Silver. "We need these things out of our necks. They may want to kill us, or just screw up and do so by accident, so sorry. I may need to intimidate someone into responding. I could need your help. That could be dangerous."

"I have your back," she said.

It was good to hear that, but I really didn't want to have her die over something silly.

We sought the UNBI office. Their receptionist was young, probably a college boy doing intern work. He recognized it as important, and relayed the information. They let me sit twenty minutes before coming out.

The woman who came out tried hard to put on the bureaucrat face, but it didn't work. She looked us over and hesitated.

"Mr. Destin, I have your file here. What do you want us to do?"

"I want you to disable this bomb in my throat," I said, pointing at the faint scar.

"I'm not sure what authority I have to remove devices implanted by a higher echelon."

"Because they said you should," I tried reasonably.

"Yes, I saw your load. I need to confirm that with them, though. This will take some time."

"Then I will sit in this chair until you have that information," I said. "I wouldn't want you to have any doubt of my whereabouts, being the dangerous man I am." I gave her a stare. Silver tapped her foot and managed to match the glower.

She disappeared into her office. Three minutes later, someone came out with medical gear, swabbed my neck, sprayed an anesthetic, slid in a probe and pulled out a capsule. They did the same for Silver. She winced. I hadn't.

"Thank you," I said, and stood and left, Silver at my heels.

She clung to me for a moment.

"I'm playing the girlfriend role for a moment. I was really worried about you there."

"So was I. Yes, it could have been ugly for both of us."

She said, "I don't want to be melodramatic. I nearly died."

"At least twice. We are really not welcome here."

"I know," she said, and was quiet.

After we vacated the government's office, though they permeate everything, like a bad smell, I said, "So now we can figure out which way to hop. I want to get aboard a non-UN ship fast."

We didn't have a choice. A ship's officer met us in the waiting room. They apparently paid fare for us on an Earth ship bound for the Freehold. It was a luxury commercial liner.

"Good day, Mr. Destin. I'm Third Officer Kwan. I'm directed to make sure you are very comfortable in your cabin for departure."

I could have taken him out, but I suspected there was a squad with weapons behind the door, and that they had orders not to worry about collateral casualties. We were leaving on this ship and heading in the direction of home, at least for now.

"I accept the situation, sir. Please show us to our stateroom."

He smiled as he said, "Please go ahead of me to your right. Dock Four."

We preceded him with enough distance to minimize advantages. I could have taken him, but unless I planned to start a battle in the station, or immobilize everyone aboard and fly it myself, no cards. Even then, the current route would definitely take us to a system where Earth had warships.

It was aggravating, but inevitable.

We got VIP passage through the gate, aboard ship, and into a stateroom. It was better than basic, but not first class. No complaints. Kwan sat with us until they undocked, then said, "Enjoy the trip," and left.

Silver and I gripped each other in comfort, release, aggravation, exhaustion. My own apprentice had run an end-around past me. I'd been IDed, my past dug up, and I hated the universe.

"I have to message the boss," I said.

"This is an Earth ship."

"Yeah, can't be helped. I'll be discreet."

I assumed they read the message, and I assumed they knew the background, but I kept it in phrased language. I wasn't going to compromise even an outdated code, and without context, it should be safe enough. I sent, "No luck. Intercepted. Regrouping."

Then all we could do was wait. There was nothing we could access on the nodes without compromising more, apart from watching the news.

I became more distraught as it went on. The combination of age, refreshed post-combat stress, distance from my daughter and the ongoing wear of the mission had gotten me. I couldn't do any more. I'd only succeeded in hurting Randall's arm, blowing his cover, killing his assets and destroying his main patron. Good stuff, all, but he was still alive and still operating. We are just that hard to take out. Naumann was going to have to bite the bullet, send an entire platoon, and accept the visibility.

Insystem in the Freehold, I felt a bit better. They were on my territory now, and I was pretty sure my word could hold this ship. Not that I needed that. The crew had been keeping an eye on us, but relaxed somewhat now.

We were off fast enough to satisfy them. I needed to get groundside fast, find better intel and decide if I was going to bother with continuing, take the kid and disappear again, or try to settle back down. None of it appealed

One thing bothered me. We presented immunization declaration, and it was accepted. No test was done. It used to be standard that everyone was tested for bloodborne pathogens before system entry, including diplomats. Inviolable law. Apparently, it had been reinterpreted so a doctor's declaration was sufficient, and they didn't check on the status of the doctor too much. I'd hoped we'd have a confirmable DNA trace on Randall. No such luck.

We boarded a Skywheel shuttle and headed for the surface and Jefferson Starport.

Quietly, but without worrying about mics, I told Silver, "First thing is a hotel. Discreet. I can't rush home and we can't rush on base."

"Understood," she said.

At least here it was easy. We were down without luggage to worry about; we'd pick it up later from claims.

We were outside in hot, bright summer Iolight within seconds after debarking. We took a cab to the Renaissance and checked in. All they cared about was the cash and our polite request for a third-floor room. That would slow any potential attackers, and I could jump it if I had to.

"I need to debrief before I go home," I said. I didn't want to go straight to my daughter. I wanted some distance for both moral safety, and in case anyone was tracking me. We'd have to do some sanitizing to make sure we were safe, and keep an eye on Earth. I wasn't overly worried about the government, but out of twenty-eight billion, some vengeful psycho was inevitable. If one decided to fund a trip out here . . .

"Good idea," she said. "I'm sorry the evasion on Earth didn't work."

"Not your fault. He obviously had some prep time and gear in place. We did not. Had we used embassy resources, it would only have made the leak bigger. You did well."

"It feels like failure," she said.

"It is failure, but that doesn't mean you did anything wrong. We did hurt him, a lot. He's also more visible, but that was probably unavoidable. That hinders his operations, though. He's made himself a pop star assassin. Not what it takes. He was always good at the short term, never a long-term thinker."

"Thanks," she said.

"You're welcome, and I'll be reporting it as such. Not to help your career, but because it's true."

She just nodded. We were both wrung out.

I sat down and sighed.

I was able to reach my own accounts, and went through the tedious process of deleting stuff that didn't apply, authorizing stuff that had enough interest I wanted to look at it, filing stuff to follow up later. I'd have to work on the business again, too; it had atrophied of course, with months of doing nothing. I still wasn't sure if a node was smart. I was known now. Not widely, and hopefully the story would be minor old news for most, but for Earth I was a monster, and for some reason here I was a hero. Neither appealed.

Then I saw a message entitled, "Trone Street."

I really wanted these tingles of impending doom to stop, but there were too many reasons for them. I opened the message, and yes, I was scared.

"Call me. Urgent," and a code.

I showed it to Silver, and asked, "Do we have a vacant phone?"

"I can get one from the hotel shop. There's a coded repeater close enough we can use it. He won't track us here."

I said, "Or if he can, we're pronged."

She brought up a phone, and I realized I could have run that errand myself. Then I realized I was beat and hurt. Did it show? It must.

I punched in the code and waited.

Randall answered. "I'm calling a truce," he said.

"No truce," I replied, and disconnected. I pulled Naumann's code and was about to call when Randall called back. Good. Psychology was working.

"They have your daughter," he said.

That brought everything to a complete stop.

"What?" I said.

"Timurhin has your daughter."

"How?"

"Apparently, the discussion I had with him about who was tracing me was after he hired you. By 'discussion' I mean he screamed, then threatened after I told him, and I should have killed him on the spot, regardless of outcome. I guess he was able to track you through the same methods we use, once he knew your current name. This is my mistake. I'm calling truce. We go get her."

"I can't do that." Oh, fuck me, this was bad. Nausea gripped me at once, worse than anything I'd ever felt. My daughter. My *raison d'etre*.

"Then you get to decide if you want me more than her, because I'm going to get her. You can run your own op, or team up, or kill me and lose her. Your call, tough man."

It took less than a second for me to agree, "Truce. Only until then."

"Good. You need to meet me."

"When do they tell me they have her?"

"They told me. I'm supposed to salvage my honor by bringing you in. They kill you and let her go."

"Do you believe them?"

"If I did we wouldn't be talking."

"Smart man. We could have avoided all this if you'd been silent."

"Yeah, well, I learn slow."

"You always did. We'll discuss that later. What do I need to know?"

"Yeah, as if I'll hang around for you to nail me. Meet me at the warehouse in Plainfield, corner of Wright and Industry."

"On my way," I said, but he'd already disconnected.

So this was the plan. They wanted us to face off and the best assassin win. Then they'd bribe or blackmail us into further missions, they thought.

Under other circumstances, it would be amusing to watch them try to manipulate us. They really thought they were clever. They really thought they had leverage. My only concern was that my daughter might be roughed up, frightened, or worse, raped in the meantime. Part of that concern was that if they did so, I'd kill them all. I'd hunt them down in detail and show them what painful death really was. It wouldn't bring her back, though. If they took her from me, I'd just start killing, and keep killing until someone stopped me . . .

Shit.

Under these circumstances, I had to be ice cold, try for subtlety. My goal was to get my daughter out as gently as possible.

Then I had to kill Kimbo before he disappeared.

Of course, he was planning to keep her alive, then disappear.

The meat puppets of Timurhin were just bugs to be stepped on in the process. They were already dead and probably didn't know it.

Dammit, I couldn't underestimate them. Some were probably former professionals. Ego had ruined me last time. I couldn't do it again.

And they really did have my daughter.

I double checked that. It was easy enough, but I'd take his word on nothing.

Her phone was shut off, out of the net. No answer at the house. Her school hadn't seen her.

Finally, "Andre, it's Dan."

"Dan! Are you back groundside?"

I paused a long, aching second to simulate a call from space. "Shortly. Have you seen Chelsea?"

"Not today. There's been an older guy around her. I assume he's one of the guards?"

Pause. "Ah, yes." Dammit, no. They wouldn't interact with her, and she shouldn't know they were there. They also couldn't do around the clock. They were facilities monitors and checked her whereabouts periodically. So this guy was a plant.

"Okay, I should be back in a few days, then," I said.

I disconnected and slumped, shivering and twitching.

Silver said, "What can I do to help?"

I said nothing, but faced the wall and wondered how this had come about.

"Is it a trap?" she asked. "Would he go after her?"

"No. Nothing in his background for that, nothing I can imagine. Nor was he anything but gentle and fatherly around her."

Kimbo was right. This was his fault. He'd blown my cover, and knowing he was indiscreet, Timurhin's people would be afraid of me doing the same. Then, they knew I was a double agent. They had no reason to trust me. That, and my pursuit had definitely antagonized Randall into some of the stunts. They didn't really want her. She was a hook to get me. I hadn't caused the leak, but people with that kind of money and that level of risk didn't care about why, just what. They wanted out of the game before it got worse. They'd want me and Randall both.

In that context, it didn't make sense for us to show up together.

If he had set this up, I shouldn't go.

But they had my daughter, and I was incapable of being rational about her.

The problem from my end is that they'd crossed a personal line, and a professional one. I could not assume any intent not to harm my daughter. I had to break her loose, and then try for Randall.

I said, "I need armored clothing and the most discreet tracers and phone you can give me so you can track me as closely as you can. While I know our people are professionals, I'm not being rational, and I don't want them interfering. She's my daughter, I have to do this."

"I understand," she said. "I need a div." She squeezed my shoulder and strode to the door.

I spent a div, 2.7 Earth hours, fretting and running scenarios, and packing away room service food I didn't taste, but needed.

When she came back, I swallowed enough stims to keep me going for a full day, grabbed the phone, swallowed the transponder, and changed quickly into the clothes. They were neutral tan and gray military style with lots of room to move, and she handed me a day pack.

She said, "Knife, pistol, two flashbangs, spectral glasses, high-strength two-millimeter cord with loops and hook, pick tools, door coder, climbing gloves and foot spikes.

Naumann is standing by, and says he understands your request for him to hold off."

"Understands, dogshit, did he agree?"

"Yes. 'Tell him I understand and will be nearby waiting.'"

"Good." Good.

First, meet Randall and determine bona fides. Second, kill everyone between me and my daughter. Third . . . we'd see.

We rented a car for cash, and I let her drive. I was trembling from stress, fatigue and stims when we started. The impending fight calmed me down by the time we drove the twenty segs to the warehouse. Yes, pending life and death warfare calm me down. I am just too fucked up for words.

"There," I said. It was not a well-populated part of town. They were small and rich, and new construction was cheaper than reusing old stuff. This building had probably been abandoned since the War.

She drove past, I got out a block away, and walked back through the long, Ioset shadows. I trusted her to track and pursue. I hoped she wouldn't wind up in the fight. Everyone had underestimated Randall and me.

◉ CHAPTER 26 ◉

THE WAREHOUSE was structurally sound, and the windows were hazed but intact. It looked well-boarded, but there was a possible entrance on the side, where there had once been a delivery alley. The buildings on either side might have been occupied since the War, but were also vacant now.

Yes, that door was functional. I found a piece of splintered wood and placed a spare tracer under it. Then I secured my pistol, took a deep breath, and pulled the door. It opened. Nothing obvious jumped at me. I paused, scanned for wires, beams, anything. It was dark and my glasses showed little.

With a bit of distance, his voice said, "It's safe. Come in and we'll talk."

I dove in and tingled and rolled for cover. Whatever field I'd come through—

"That's to make sure you're clean," he said, and stepped out ahead of me. He was far enough away I couldn't have taken him if I'd wanted to.

Yup. Massive gauss and EM field. Some devices might survive it, but the basic tracker I had, and my phone, were fried.

I said, "I'm a man of my word. First we get my daughter. Then we can discuss the rest." I could shoot him here, but I didn't know where to go, and I needed the backup.

He approached, trying to look unworried. Good. This was going to take work, and wasn't going to be neat, and I was going to let him use himself up.

The universe had no place for heroes or villains.

He said, "So, you really did care about the baby."

"Yes," I said.

"Odd way of showing it you had."

"You have intel?" I asked. This would stay professional, with me playing the sociopath.

It bothered me at last, how easy it was for me to play that.

"Some," he admitted. "I did a remote recon by eye and drone. I managed to locate the builder's drawings, too. Here's how it's looked for three nights."

I moved in closer, but sat far enough away to move on him. I trusted him to help Chel; he'd done so before and had a bit of attachment to her back then. It seemed he still did. I wasn't putting it past him to take me out and then save her, though. In fact, it seemed to me he was considering that.

He'd done a three-D, time-tracked animation of movement. The patterns weren't perfect, but people do tend to repeat familiar actions on a predictable basis. We ran it several times fast, then slowed to close in on specifics.

"Alright," I said, "we're going in silently. We kill anyone we have to, and proceed. We need to get inside with her, and take down whoever is there. We need her behind hard cover or armor. At that point it doesn't matter what they send."

"It does. They don't have that much to send, though."

"Mass matters. If I could get backup faster . . . "

"Yeah, an entire squad is what I want around me right now, of course," he said.

I didn't blame him for being sarcastic about it.

"How do we proceed?"

"You get in the car and drive. I tell you where to go. The car is mined and I keep a gun on you."

"Smart."

"I plan to live."

I didn't have a chance to grab the tracer I'd left outside. I just hoped Silver had a good OP and was watching.

It hurt me to get into the vehicle. I knew I was safe. I knew he really cared about my daughter. He could have killed me, or tried to, already. So he really planned to help rescue her. In the few weeks he'd been associated with the little grub, he'd acted more like a father than I had at the time, and he had no stake in the matter. In fact, he'd been very angry about the issue, and concerned about my failure in being involved with a subordinate. It had risked the mission and he'd been livid.

In some ways, he was a very good man. Those were the ways I was going to exploit to kill him.

I drove as he directed, out toward the mountains, and I hoped Silver was following. She could have drones, or visual on the ground, or might already have a unit keyed and ready. I didn't know, and it was better that I didn't.

I still had a paranoid fear that Timurhin had some kind of inside source. Massaging intel wasn't hard. I've given most of the basics in here. Find people out eating or drinking, ask what they saw going on at the base. Were a bunch of vertols lifting? Lots of guys with gear? Which way? Maybe an exercise in the mountains, or was it possibly a fire?

How fast could Naumann mobilize a unit, get them into civvies and vehicles and dispersed? Probably fast enough.

Did I want him to?

It took awhile to reach our destination, and it was a very deserted road. More than a couple of vehicles would be obvious, and there were no air approaches. This was scrubby, rain shadow foothill.

"Timurhin has a house here, I take it," I asked.

"Yes. He comes here in spring and fall. It's where I met him eight years ago."

"You started here?"

"I've never taken a job here and won't, but yes."

I pondered killing him right now. I could . . .

"You seem to have healed well," he said.

I said nothing. No small talk.

Eventually he said, "I'd pull into one of these clearings and hide the car. We're within a few Ks."

I found one and did so. Shadows moved eerily in the headlights.

He made me get out first, lay the pack on the hood, and he went through it.

"Fair enough," he said. "We go that way about three Ks. We can meet on the southeast corner, about two hundred meters out."

He grabbed his own bag. He had another chameleon suit, and an attachable pistol and knife.

"I only have the one suit," he said.

"I'm fine," I said. "I have something better."

"Oh? What?"

"Me."

I dodged and slipped into the shadows and left him to wonder.

Three Ks doesn't take long, but I had to shift about and change movement so I wouldn't sound like a person on any monitors. I kept an eye out for wires, cameras, other sensors in any frequency I could find. I also relied on my senses. Gadgets are tools. People are weapons.

They did have a few cams set up, in game runs. I wondered if those were for hunting or security, or both. I kept an eye out for spookable game. Earth deer had been introduced here, and there were local forms that filled the same niche. There were also local predators. There was nothing I could do if I met a ripper, but they tended to stick farther north and inland. This was the edge of their range.

I reached the point he'd designated, and found a spot to wait, and listen. That gave me time to doubt him all over again. Was this a setup? No reason for it. He could have killed me in the car. Still.

I heard a faint rustle, and placed it to the east. I'd deduced it was him when I heard a whistle. It was a pattern we'd used in training. I raised my hand and waved.

I heard delicate rustling, saw a faint shimmer, then I felt him move in. He had the chameleon open just enough to vent heat without breaking visual camo.

From the distortion in the air, his voice said, "You move well."

I said nothing. I wasn't going to make noise I didn't have to, nor explain that I was old and out of practice, but had been in better practice for years before he joined for that one mission.

He said, "If we move in we'll see the perimeter. It's about a hundred meters out from the house. They've got guards up."

"Noted. What do you suggest?"

"We take them out when we get a chance. Inside, I know the general layout. They'll want her as a hostage. They won't kill her until after you're dead."

I said, "I'm not taking that bet."

The shimmer in front of me said, "Neither am I. I'll take the other corner. They're expecting me to call before the third div shuttle."

"So we've got a div to penetrate."

"I think so," he said.

"Okay. I'll move on your sign as soon as we have an opening. You lead inside. I'll be right behind."

"Sounds simple."

"It always does."

He said nothing else, but slipped away. He was quieter than I expected.

I slunk in slower and lower one limb at a time until I was on hands and knees, delicately placed. Once I saw the clearing, I went prone and shimmied slowly, resembling a snake. It shouldn't sound like a person, and I moved slow enough there shouldn't be any disruptive noise. I got right to the edge, then pulled some leaves over my head to kill my outline and reflection.

There were two guards at the front door. I faced them from the side. Beyond them was a long driveway, bricked and paved and with beautiful borders. Timurhin liked his style. Shame he didn't have the culture to go with it. I assumed there were more guards at the gate, but maybe not.

Just in from me was a sensor wire, and I could see beams faintly in the dust. Had they been thinking better, this place would be a walled prison. They apparently had little enough respect for Randall they thought he'd bring me in, and that I'd go along. Either that or they figured I'd have killed him and then they'd contact me for further deals. Staying alive might be as easy as me proving he was dead and bowing out. But, as I said, the problem was I had no way to trust them.

The guards checked in periodically, and they had an officer of the watch as well. What I wanted to do was catch the officer with these two, and dispose of all three at once. If he was late elsewhere, they'd be suspicious, but it would take time for worry to propagate. If he found someone down or missing, it would be an instant alarm. I needed him gone.

I settled down to wait. It would be a little while longer. At least they didn't have any visible IR or thermal filters. They relied on the lights around the property, and presumably the sensors in the woods I'd carefully passed by.

The good came with the bad. The watch officer arrived with their shift replacement. There were now five of them. After that, it would be some time before he returned.

It wasn't ideal, but it did offer the chance to take out five hostiles at once.

There were two main strategies I could use. Either wander up, looking helpless, or full frontal charge. The first wouldn't work. Out here, they'd assume something was wrong and alert on a stranger. Then they'd probably recognize me.

So I Boosted. As soon as I felt the ripple, I dropped into a sprint. I leapt clean and high over the perimeter sensors.

I came in on a long curve. Eventually they saw the movement, looked confused at the speed and my odd silhouette, IDed me as human and an attacker, and by then I was within ten meters. I dodged twice. They fired and missed, though not by much, then I was on them.

I hit the first one in the throat with my thumb, turning up under the jaw with a hand heel strike. His head snapped back and he dropped. I caught the second with a V of my thumb and fingers into his throat. He turned horizontal and fell, and I stomped on his face as I dove at the third. En route I snagged the gun from the one I'd just smeared.

I caught the third, the watch officer, shoulder first in the chest, throwing his arms back, then driving my knee so his balls reached his stomach. I shoved the pistol muzzle in his kidney and shot, the report damped to a wet thump, like it would in mud.

I stood up with his rapidly dying body in front of me, casually pointed at the fourth and shot him in the face. The other turned to run but hadn't moved a step—I was that fast—and I shot him in the base of the spine, then in the base of the skull. I dropped the meat shield and scanned for incoming. Safe for the moment.

In two more seconds, I had another pistol, a knife and a shotgun—an Alesis. I scanned again, rummaged and found a wrist phone and a key coder on the shift leader. I decided the shotgun was too bulky, and tossed it into the brush. Two pistols would do me.

A shuffling shadow was Randall. Barely visible, and went past me, snagging the coder as he went.

Beyond the recovery breathing from the exertion, I had to avoid hyperventilating in panic. Logic and tactics said they'd use my daughter against me. However, there was a slim but real chance they'd just kill her.

My bet was they wouldn't consider that until they knew other options were exhausted. The noise outside was disturbing, but not overly loud. They had modern, quiet guns.

So I had to clear this building fast, while my temporary ally was ahead.

I heard a crackle and smiled. They had the same cracker he'd used on me, and his chameleon was defunct. Of course, that meant he had to undress from it.

He'd closed the door behind him, but I heard some action. I pulled it open, slipped inside, closed it and sought a cubby. I found one, but it had a tabled vase in it. Across from that was a recess for shoes and coats. I slid into that. The house had tile everywhere, nice wood, granite edging.

This was a very nice place, and why shouldn't a major underworld figure have a nice cottage on Grainne, where no one would actively bother with him, and he had ready access to banks and travel?

Randall had dumped the chameleon in a heap in the parlor to the left. I heard combat in the back and headed that way, nerves naked for threats, pistol in each hand.

I passed one corpse and one almost. He'd smashed them, not shot them. I didn't think it made much difference now. I saw movement, and a head protruded from a doorway.

"Don't sh—" he said as I shot him. It looked as if he'd already been wounded. My shot ended his pain forever.

It was anticlimactic for now. Five down outside, four down inside, and a boobytrap on the wall near the kitchen shot to hell. Randall was good, no doubt about it.

Then there was a rush as four more goons poured through a door with subguns. They shouted and screamed, both to distract me and in fear. They weren't sure of their odds.

I Boosted, dropped, rolled, shot, rolled again, sprung hard enough I broke the leg on a table as I went through it, got one guy in the shin and he tumbled screaming, his buddies piling on top of him. The CNS on top of the stims and fatigue just burned me into a nauseated frenzy. I paused in my accelerated race enough to pick my targets. Two shots, two heads erupted spattering mist, and I bounced behind a chair that didn't stop the bullets the two tangled survivors fired at me, but I wasn't there when they did. I caught one obliquely in his gun arm, realized it was the same one I'd legshot earlier. They tried to aim, tangled in each other and I shot again, then twice more.

My ribs hurt like hell where I'd gone through the table, but I was intact otherwise.

Then I heard a muffled noise.

It was very faint, but after a decade of exposure, I knew that was my daughter. Tiny hints of noise in familiar patterns were a clear ID, better than any image.

I kicked Boost again, and wondered how long I could do this. I was eating up my own adrenaline, cortisol and glycogen, in addition to the bonus levels the bioplant provided.

Still, I'd IDed the sound and location. I had one full pistol and one with two shots I decided to stuff into a pocket. I didn't have time to disarm the corpses, but I wasn't leaving this one around.

I estimated the room size below based on echoes and reflections, liked what I came up with, and went in full bore.

I ripped down the stairs in two jumps, into the room and saw bodies. Most were down. Two were up. It was evenly lit by long light tubes. There was a couch, a vid and a small fridge. Clearly, this was set up as a prison, with this as the guard room.

Randall had reached Chel first. She'd been locked in a bare bathroom in the corner I could see through a heavy reinforced door. She had some bruising. He'd stunned her and dragged her out.

He was behind her, had her in a hard arch that immobilized her, and I could just see his eyes over her. I could make that shot, maybe, but it probably wouldn't kill him fast enough.

My heart turned to a lump of cold stone.

"Thank you, Kimbo." I met his eyes. I deliberately did not meet hers. I tried to send a psychic message as I faced him. *No, girl, this does not involve you. This is between him and me. And please, please don't try to help. Please.*

His voice was muffled around her. He said, "You're welcome. Now please ensure the vehicle is handy. I parked it a hundred meters south of the drive." Right. They thought they could trust him. I thought I could. He'd driven that three kilometers and waited, hoping I'd either kill the goons for him or die in the process.

He said, "Your daughter and I have a trip to make. I'll release her once I'm at the jump point unharmed."

"I can't do that."

His eyes crinkled in a smile I couldn't see. It was creepy. "Yet you must. I have life and death control here. I have a deadman switch on me and a small charge against her shoulder." He raised his gun but didn't shoot.

I forced my voice to be steady as I said, "That means I kill you." Would he really? I thought kids were off limits. They had been so far. But this case was special . . .

"If you kill me, you have to jump on her to save her life, with her left torso pulverized. She's my insurance. The best insurance possible." Then he did shoot twice, and I cartwheeled for cover, but there was no cover. I made it behind the couch, it was concealment at least. I kept the stairs guarded. He wasn't leaving if I had anything to say about it.

Even without looking at her, I could tell she was trembling in utter fear. I was scared too. I was also pissed off. This was so crude, so inelegant. He really had nothing left besides kidnapping.

I needed to piss him off in return, enrage him to illogic, and then move before he did try to harm her. I hit Boost again. I paused for a moment as my vision blurred and steadied, the rush tingling, burning hotly through me.

Then I said, "So, is that what happened with Deni and Tyler? You left them to cover for you?"

Oh, that hit him. And he wasn't about to say Deni had . . . killed herself while he hung back. I had him pegged. Brave, but very bothered about perceptions. Nothing wrong with that, but it was a slight, very slight emotional weakness and I was going for it. He shook in rage. Emotional response. I was winning.

He didn't shout, but his voice did quaver. "I fought, goddam you. I didn't leave until I had your daughter hid. You owe me."

"Thanks for that. Now you rig her as a shield. I think we're even." I stood slowly, tossed in a twitch of the corner of my mouth. I couldn't manage a real smile.

He said, "Pity she didn't mean more to you earlier." It was an attempt to probe me.

I said nothing, just made a sniff of disdain. He lightened his grip slightly, but I had to believe him about that charge. I could see the tape on her shoulder. I mentally begged for her not to mess with it. If Silver could catch up, I'd have more room. She might disarm it.

He kept talking. Good. "I could have let everyone die. Deni was first. Don't you care? Even about her? She caught them on the stairs and made a mess."

I nodded marginally. "I saw the mess. Not bad, really."

He continued. "I was up top by then, hid the baby and

went down the wall. I figured I was dead. Earth screwed us big time, I have no problem making them pay."

"So what do you want?"

"To be left alone. I'm not taking missions here, no threat to anyone." He said it in a reasonable, bargaining tone.

"I can't do that."

He shrugged, trying to look dispassionate and failing. "Then you die. Or she does, which is worse. You'll never know when I'm coming for her. Want to pit your demolitions skill against mine?"

I laughed loudly. "Anytime, asshole." Confidence is a weapon. And I knew I was better.

"Yeah? But I know where you are."

"You didn't for ten years. You only do now because it fit my plans."

I felt the tingle fading, and I needed everything I could get, so I Boosted again.

He grinned. "That's why you're sweating and shaking, old man. Too much for you?"

Of course I was sweating. I . . .

And it hit me.

He didn't know I had a CNS bioplant. It was never mentioned to the newcomers. It was an open secret now, but mostly mentioned in context of Blazer Assault or Combat Rescue. We were never mentioned because we didn't exist, and as infiltrators, it was less obviously needed. That's why I'd not had everyone implanted. In retrospect, I used mine twice on Earth and should have had it for everyone. But now . . .

I had him. It was an even better ace when he didn't

know it was coming. Except the Boost was killing me. I'd taken four shots in a row and one earlier. Two was the maximum safe. Three in succession was a battlefield override for escape, and as far as I knew had never been done. Four. I could feel a burn in my muscles and tingle in my nerve endings. I was effectively oxidizing my tissues, my metabolism almost double the max I'd get in a hard workout, and I wasn't moving at all to burn it off.

I felt another shiver of weakness. I couldn't have that. I was at the point where doing nothing was worse than full power. Each hit weakened my wrecked metabolism.

Five.

I heard a whine in my ears. Very odd. I wondered when my heart would explode.

As long as I killed him first, or kept him from my daughter, that would be fine.

I said, "So this is all you have left? Really? A bomb and a hostage? I'm ashamed. I trained you, I expected a better class of tactics. Are you admitting that deprived of one account, cut off from your boss, faced with arrest on every civilized planet and sought by a few intel agencies, you can't figure an intellectual escape? This is all it took to stop you?" I made a disdainful snort with slight toss of my head. That whine sounded again. It seemed familiar now.

He tried gamely to play. "How many injuries have you taken doing this? How much money? It seems you used an awful lot of resources for one man. I'm thinking I probably should have killed your girlfriend. She is, isn't she? An unrequited passion? You had Deni. I know you had a sweat for Tyler. Attractive female troops are a weakness for you, Ken."

It was a pretty good attempt, and it did hurt, but he was in part correct, I was highly pissed, and more worried about my daughter, so it didn't have the effect he wanted. Still, if he wanted to talk about that, fine. I just needed an opening before I died from toxicity and overload. Just one moment.

In my ears I heard *whhiinnnne,* "testing" clearly this time, and I got it.

Implant transceiver. Silver had hacked into it. I didn't twitch, but went ahead with my response.

"Yeah, steamy chicks make great cover. You ever figure out I'm a voyeur? Watching guys twitch at the thought of me with hot young stuff they can't touch is rather sweet. She's also a volunteer and really into the role, so I got to prong her and call it business. You really got the short end of the stick, so to speak. It's a perk we don't talk about much in the teams, but an awesome one." I wasn't worried about how Silver would take that; it was psyops. I did want her to figure out why I was doing it.

He believed me, and he looked pissed. I'd broken his brain and his psyche, and we were almost there. But I was dying. My brain raced, my heart galloped in syncopation, my breathing and temperature were elevated. I had a high-grade fever, oxygen toxicity in my muscles, near drunkenness from O_2 and sugar levels in the brain. I shivered and felt my extremities numbing. I had no other options myself, but he hadn't figured that out yet.

Six.

He trembled a bit. I had him emotionally bent. He'd thrown everything he had, and I was laughing at him. He should have known me well enough to catch the act, but we were both wrung out. His gun hand started twitching in tiny, tense tremors.

A moment. I only needed a moment . . .

Silver's voice said, "Stand by, keep stalling," in my head. Then there was a disruption crack and things went quiet. Had she done it? I heard distant, muffled shots and a bang up above.

Silver's voice said, "Go."

She'd hacked it.

"I've had enough of this," Chel said and stepped just barely to the side, perhaps two centimeters.

He put a hand on her shoulder. It was a mistake borne of familiarity.

My daughter, the person I love more than life itself, for whom I'd go to any lengths and have, did exactly the right thing. Her arm came up almost casually, slapped over his wrist and she gripped and twisted, one foot forward and one back for balance, dropping down and aside my shooting plane.

In that moment, he was off balance, eyes wide in surprise and mouth making that shape that presages a yelp as the nerves in the wrist are pinched.

His eyes met mine, and he tried to maneuver his pistol around between the two of us. It was perfect. He had just long enough, perhaps one tenth of a second, to know he was dead. In that frozen moment, he dropped the gun.

I shot him before it hit the floor. The first round went through his left eye, as Chelsea dropped and rolled clear. Second round was center of mass. Third was the right eye. Then I poured out the magazine into torso and head, because I was not taking any chances on him getting up again. His body thrashed and convulsed and bent in angles impossible for a living being, then thrummed and twitched and stopped.

There was no explosion.

I let my awareness check around for threats, and then ran forward to hug Chelsea, because she was such a good girl, a perfect daughter, who'd done just what she should have done, and I was crying.

I made it two steps and staggered down toward the floor.

⚙ CHAPTER 27 ⚙

I WOKE IN A HOSPITAL. My entire body ached, even my eyelashes. I was stiff, as if I'd overdone it with every fiber in my body. *Yes, Ken, you did,* I thought. *You're an old man by military standards.*

"Dad!"

It was Chelsea, with huge bags under her red eyes from drugs, fatigue hormones and worry. But her grin was all I needed. She leapt from the chair to hug me, and I tensed. That made me convulse in agony. She got the hint and stopped, settling for laying a hand on mine. I now knew what too much CNS felt like, though. It felt as if someone had beaten every muscle in my body with a gravel-covered bat. I wouldn't be moving for days.

"I'm alive," I said. "So are you. It's all good."

I passed out again, but I've never felt so warm and happy about it.

I wasn't happy when I woke up. Chel wasn't there. Naumann was. His goon stood in the corner.

"Hello," he said.

"Yes," I said simply.

"You did well. I'm sorry the circumstances were so tough."

"No, you're not, and I wish you wouldn't say so."

He looked a little perturbed. Only a little.

He said, "While I am less emotional than many, I don't lack an understanding of it."

"No, it's just an intellectual exercise for you. One more skill you've cultivated to bend people to your will."

"That's true enough."

"I'm done."

"Absolutely. I do need a summary, though, for follow up."

Yeah, the debriefing and after-action was the part I always hated. Not enough to have adminwork before the mission, there had to be more afterward, while reviewing every splash of blood and spatter of guts.

He said, "You may want to know that Timurhin has decided this is not a system he cares to operate from."

"Good, I suppose. None of his targets mattered to us either way, and most had illicit connections. I can't say it was a bad thing overall."

"It's bad that we can take the blame from several directions. A crime figure living here. A rogue operator using our training."

"So it's done."

"Yes. What do you plan to do after you heal?"

The conversational inquiry, so casual, seeking intel, really pissed me off.

"Naumann, I don't like you."

"There is no reason you should," he said. "I am not very likeable."

"You owe me."

"Within reason, yes," he agreed.

I snarled, "'Within reason' dogshit. You fucking owe me." He actually twitched. And I was in a hospital bed. Damn. I thought for a moment and realized, yes, I really was that angry.

"As I know you don't want money, what is it to be?"

The bastard. Actually, I did plan to ask about my back pay. I also knew families who deserved some help. But that was for later.

"Kimbo Randall. Mark him killed in action on Earth. Add him to the list. And apart from that Citizens' Medal we all have, you will award the Valorous Service Medal I'm going to write up."

"I believe I understand," he said. Yeah, he probably did.

It was ten of our years later, but that battle on Earth had killed him as surely as it had killed the rest of us. I could despise what he'd done since then, but he'd done all his nation asked of him and more. For all of that, he was a hero. His illness was not a crime.

I hated his actions. I respected, and loved, the man.

Then I came out of self-absorption again.

"Oh, yes. Silver gets a Meritorious Action Medal. She went far beyond material support, to intel and operations. And she did it while dealing with me."

He nodded.

"I can see how that would be tough."

I wasn't sure if the bastard was joking. I was too tired to care.

I drifted back out, and woke muzzily awhile later. Naumann was gone. He didn't come back.

Chel was there, and looked much more relaxed and rested. That made me feel better.

"Hi, Dad," she said, once she was sure I was awake.

"Chelsea, I can't do anything except talk. But I need to tell you a few things now. You're old enough. We'll go into my background later."

She nodded. "There's a lot of that on the hypernodes. No names, but it has events and activities." She looked a bit distant. Yes, one more person who had to personally wonder what kind of man I was. My daughter.

I nodded, then stopped when pain shot through me. Then I sighed. "I need to tell you what it felt like. I don't know that I can, and you shouldn't have to know. But you need some small measure of it to understand me."

"I don't need to understand you," she said, gripping my hand until it hurt. "You're the best father I could ever have and I know how much you love me." She was crying now. No one could go through what we'd just gone through the day before and not feel something.

"I love you, kid," I said. "We'll talk about that later. I will also tell you everything about your mother, as I promised you five years ago. For now . . . I need to tell you about your godfather."

◎ EPILOGUE ◎

SILVER CAME BACK IN. She was recovering well. She'd certainly gone beyond Projects and fought respectably, and in envelope-pushing circumstances. Naumann had been correct in his assessment, as much as I hated to admit it. I hoped she managed to avoid further interaction with him. She deserved better.

"You're too stubborn to die," she said. "Was that training? Or you?" She looked raggedly tired.

"The one reinforces the other," I said.

"Yeah. Well, they're releasing you in a couple of days."

"Oh. Good," I said. I hadn't heard. The patient never does.

"I was late," she said. "I coordinated for the others, Naumann and I snuck up on the house, and we waited for the shooting. When you and Randall opened fire, we came down, but he was dead and we thought you were. We had to peel your daughter off and sedate her. I didn't tell you that last," she said.

"He didn't shoot," I said. Yes, I believed Chel would do that. I'd not mention it if she didn't.

Silver said, "Yes, he did. You took two in the guts."

I wondered on that. Was I that stoned on CNS I didn't notice the wounds? Apparently. Or else it was anger.

"You came in?" I asked. "And Naumann? I know you got my implant transceiver working and jammed Randall's device."

"Yes. His prerogative as commander in chief, mine as your teammate. I'm sorry we weren't sooner. We were busy silencing three more thugs up top and then securing other traps." She held up her hand, which I now noticed was splinted.

"Did I really miss that many threats?"

"You did."

"Thank you," I said.

She said, "His bomb was a fake, though."

What?

"It was?"

"Yes. I was terrified of detonating it, and had to analyze the arm code. There was nothing there. It wasn't a constant circuit. I said 'Go,' we jammed the entire spectrum, and Naumann flashed Chelsea from the corner of the stairs. Then you shot him. Naumann went in first, I followed. He didn't have a detonator at all."

That put it in a new perspective. He really couldn't hurt her. It was all bluff. In the end, he'd known how it had to balance, and had thrown what he had left into saving my daughter again.

He really was a hero, and I'd killed him twice.

She interrupted my musing with, "As soon as we get home, we're taking a shower."

"I'm pretty much sterilized here. Wait . . . 'Home?' 'We?' Let me switch gears here."

"You idiot," she said with a scowl. "You weren't the only one frustrated aboard ship. I spent weeks being felt and kissed in public, and had nothing beyond the tease. I lay there faking sleep most nights. Why do you think I spent half a div taking a shower?"

I actually chuckled. "You put on a great act. I never twigged."

"Of course not. You were thinking of yourself, and your daughter. It's all that keeps you alive."

"I believe so," I said. Or else I was that narcissistic.

"You pissed me off," she said. "I was frustrated too, and you didn't catch it at all."

"Sorry," I said.

"You owe me." She smiled faintly then.

"We'll just have to see. It's been awhile. Er, Chelsea's going to be home."

"No she's not. I already spoke to her about that. Promised to skin her if she was home before midnight."

"Oh? How did she respond to that?"

"Said she'd do anything to help a potential stepmother, and didn't need a threat."

"Stepmother . . . this is moving way too fast."

"So deal with it."

She delivered that with a predatory grin.

I have no idea where this will go. There was nothing in my training to cover this, and it's all up to me.

JOHN RINGO

Master of Military SF
The Posleen War Saga

A Hymn Before Battle
(pb) 0-6713-1841-1 • $7.99

Gust Front
(pb) 0-7434-3525-7 • $7.99

When the Devil Dances
(pb) 0-7434-3602-4 • $7.99

Hell's Faire
(pb) 0-7434-8842-3 • $7.99

Eye of the Storm
(hc) 978-1-4391-3273-9 • $26.00
(pb) 978-1-4391-3362-0 • $7.99

Cally's War with Julie Cochrane
(pb) 1-4165-2052-X • $7.99

Sister Time with Julie Cochrane
(hc) 1-4165-4232-9 • $26.00
(pb) 1-4165-5590-0 • $7.99

Honor of the Clan with Julie Cochrane
(pb) 978-1439133354 • $7.99·

Watch on the Rhine with Tom Kratman
(pb) 1-4165-2120-8 • $7.99

Yellow Eyes with Tom Kratman
(pb) 1-4165-5571-4 • $7.99

The Tuloriad with Tom Kratman
(hc) 978-1-4391-3304-0 • $26.00
(pb) 978-1-4391-3409-2 • $7.99

The Hero with Michael Z. Williamson
(pb) 1-4165-0914-3 • $7.99

■ ■ ■

Citizens ed. by John Ringo & Brian M. Thomsen
(trade pb) 978-1-4391-3347-7 • $16.00
(pb) 978-1-4391-3460-3 • $7.99

Master of Epic SF
The Council War Series
There Will Be Dragons
(pb) 0-7434-8859-8 • $7.99

Emerald Sea
(pb) 1-4165-0920-8 • $7.99

Against the Tide
(pb) 1-4165-2057-0 • $7.99

East of the Sun, West of the Moon
(pb) 1-4165-5518-87 • $7.99

Master of Real SF
The Troy Rising Series
Live Free or Die
(hc) 1-4391-3332-8 • $26.00
(pb) 978-1-4391-3397-2 • $7.99

Citadel
(hc) 978-1-4391-3400-9 • $26.00
(pb) 978-1-4516-3757-1 • $7.99

The Hot Gate
(hc) 978-1-4391-3432-0 • $26.00

■ ■ ■

Von Neumann's War with Travis S. Taylor
(pb) 1-4165-5530-8 • $7.99

The Looking Glass Series
Into the Looking Glass
(pb) 1-4165-2105-4 • $7.99

Vorpal Blade with Travis S. Taylor
(hc) 1-4165-2129-1 • $25.00
(pb) 1-4165-5586-2 • $7.99

Manxome Foe with Travis S. Taylor
(pb) 1-4165-9165-6 • $7.99

Claws That Catch with Travis S. Taylor
(hc) 1-4165-5587-0 • $25.00
(pb) 978-1-4391-3313-2 • $7.99

Master of Hard-Core Thrillers
The Last Centurion
(hc) 1-4165-5553-6 • $25.00
(pb) 978-1-4391-3291-3 • $7.99

■ ■ ■

The Kildar Saga
Ghost
(pb) 1-4165-2087-2 • $7.99

Kildar
(pb) 1-4165-2133-X • $7.99

Choosers of the Slain
(hc) 1-4165-2070-8 • $25.00
(pb) 1-4165-7384-4 • $7.99

Unto the Breach
(hc) 1-4165-0940-2 • $26.00
(pb) 1-4165-5535-8 • $7.99

A Deeper Blue
(hc) 1-4165-2128-3 • $26.00

(pb) 1-4165-5550-1 • $7.99

Master of Dark Fantasy
Princess of Wands
(hc) 1-4165-0923-2 • $25.00
(pb) 1-4165-7386-0 • $7.99

Master of Bolos
The Road to Damascus with Linda Evans
(pb) 0-7434-9916-6 • $7.99

And don't miss Ringo's NY Times bestselling epic adventures written with David Weber:
March Upcountry
(pb) 0-7434-3538-9 • $7.99

March to the Sea
(pb) 0-7434-3580-X • $7.99

March to the Stars
(pb) 0-7434-8818-0 • $7.99

We Few
(pb) 1-4165-2084-8 • $7.99

Available in bookstores everywhere.
Or order online at our secure, easy to use website:
www.baen.com

For fans of David Drake and John Ringo,
military SF adventures set in the
Freehold Universe of

MICHAEL Z. WILLIAMSON

"This fast-paced, compulsive read, with its military action
and alien cultures, will appeal to fans of John Ringo, David
Drake, Lois McMaster Bujold, and David Weber."—*Kliatt*

Freehold
(PB) 0-7434-7179-2 • $7.99
The Freehold of Grainne is the last bastion of freedom in
the galaxy. But things are about to go royally to hell . . .

The Weapon
(PB) 1-4165-2118-6 • $7.99
Kenneth Chinran infiltrated a fascistic, militaristic planet:
Earth. He lived in deep cover for years, until Earth forces
attacked his home system. Now Earth will pay the price.

Better to Beg Forgiveness
(PB) 1-4165-9151-6 • $7.99
The deadliest mercenaries in the galaxy have suddenly
become free agents, on a world that's ripe for the picking . . .

Contact with Chaos
(HC) 1-4165-9154-0 • $24.00
(PB) 978-1-4391-3373-6 • $7.99
Caution: Contact with intelligent aliens can be hazardous
to your health.

Do Unto Others
(HC) 978-1-4391-3383-5 • $22.00
When your enormous wealth makes you a target, it's time
to do unto others *before* they do unto you!

Available in bookstores everywhere.
Or order online at our secure, easy to use website:
www.baen.com